SHERLOCK HOLMES
AND THE SECRET ALLIANCE

Other Minnesota Mysteries by Larry Millett
Published by the University of Minnesota Press

The Disappearance of Sherlock Holmes
The Magic Bullet
Sherlock Holmes and the Ice Palace Murders
Sherlock Holmes and the Red Demon
Sherlock Holmes and the Rune Stone Mystery

SHERLOCK HOLMES

AND THE

SECRET ALLIANCE

Larry Millett

A Minnesota Mystery Featuring Shadwell Rafferty

University of Minnesota Press

Minneapolis

London

The Fesler–Lampert Minnesota Heritage Book Series

This series is published with the generous assistance of the John K. and Elsie Lampert Fesler Fund and David R. and Elizabeth P. Fesler. Its mission is to republish significant out-of-print books that contribute to our understanding and appreciation of Minnesota and the Upper Midwest.

Originally published in 2001 by Viking Penguin

First University of Minnesota Press edition, 2012

Published by the University of Minnesota Press
111 Third Avenue South, Suite 290
Minneapolis, MN 55401-2520
http://www.upress.umn.edu

Library of Congress Cataloging-in-Publication Data

Millett, Larry, 1947–
  Sherlock Holmes and the secret alliance / Larry Millett. — 1st University of
  Minnesota Press ed.
  ISBN 978-0-8166-7705-4 (pb : alk. paper)
  1. Holmes, Sherlock (Fictitious character) — Fiction. 2. Private investigators —
  Minnesota — Minneapolis — Fiction. 3. British — Minnesota — Fiction.
  4. Minneapolis (Minn.) — Fiction. I. Title.
  PS3563.I42193S54 2012
  813'.54 — dc23
                                          2011051279

Printed on acid-free paper

The University of Minnesota is an equal-opportunity educator and employer.

CONTENTS

Railroad Tracks ▪▪▪▪▪▪▪▪▪▪▪

Streetcar Lines ▪▪▪▪▪▪▪▪▪▪▪

Sherlock Holmes and the Secret Alliance

PROLOGUE

Minneapolis, September 28, 1899

As he wandered down Tenth Street at two in the morning, stoppig now and then to consult the flask of whisky tucked in his hip pocket, Sid the Ratman did his best to look inconspicuous. Discretion, he had learned through hard experience, was everything, especially when it came to dealing with the police of Minneapolis. He knew only too well that the coppers viewed him as a nuisance — and a smelly, crazy one at that — despite the signal service he had done in fighting the malignant army of rats that constantly threatened to overrun the city. Someday, when the dirty little creatures gained complete control, springing upon people in their beds and consuming their flesh, the police would be sorry they had not listened to him. Oh yes, they would be very sorry indeed. But until that moment of retribution arrived, the Ratman would lay low, which explained his presence along Tenth, a drowsy street generally ignored by the forces of law and order.

It was, the Ratman thought, a fine night to be roaming the city, the air fresh with the moist scents of a late-season thunderstorm. Although the rain had long since stopped, wisps of white fog lingered in the dampness, moving in ghostly procession past the gas lamps posted at regular intervals along the street. At this hour the Ratman felt confident he would have Tenth to himself, for Minneapolis was a God-fearing, Mammon-loving, early-to-bed midwestern city, which meant that even its strong-armed robbers, shoulder pushers, and other species of low life preferred to retire before midnight, unless some irresistible opportunity for plunder dictated otherwise.

It was not only the quiet of Tenth Street that appealed to the Ratman. Truth was, he also liked its aura of genteel decay. Tenth had once been the heart of the city's finest residential district, home to row upon row of towered mansions dolled up like plump Parisian tarts in the ornate manner of the French Second Empire. These enormous, awkward piles had been built in the 1860s and 1870s by the city's first generation of merchant princes, hard-driven men who took great pleasure in flaunting their newfound wealth with all the parvenu grandeur money could buy.

But Minneapolis had always been impatient with its own history (which went back only to 1855), and so a goodly number of the old mansions were already gone, swept away by the powerful tides of progress that regularly rearranged the city's downtown like so much sand on a beach. Stores, offices, institutional buildings, and even several of those disreputable apartment dwellings known as French flats had by the early 1890s replaced many of the houses on Tenth. The new public library, at the corner of Hennepin Avenue, was one especially notable addition, and the Ratman—an obsessive student of the city's brief but colorful past—would often spend his afternoons there paging through dusty archives of municipal history in the cool, inviting quiet of the reading room.[1]

Yet even as the new century drew near, the transformation of Tenth was far from complete, and close to a dozen old mansions still stood along the street as evidence of the city's hurried past. Set well back from the street in leafy yards guarded by tall iron fences and unruly hedges, the houses seemed to occupy their own private world in the midst of the bustling, anxious city. A few had found useful second lives as rooming houses for the army of poor but respectable clerks who toiled in the office buildings several blocks to the north. But most were empty hulks, somber and shuttered, waiting in patient decay for the wreckers to arrive. The Ratman, who had been a respected building contractor until the evil rodents set out to destroy his life, loved the old houses and felt a bond with them. Like him, or so he thought, they were shamefully neglected old-timers, proud citizens of the city who, through no fault of their own, had fallen on hard times.

Near the intersection of First Avenue South was a house he particularly admired, and he paused to inspect it in the soft glow of a corner gas lamp. Built of blood-red brick, the house sported a massive central tower, gaunt windows hooded with stone, porches trimmed with an extravagance of gingerbread, and the usual mansarded roof of dark slate topped with a spiky forest of iron cresting. A tall spreading hedge, unattended for years, surrounded the property, which occupied a full quarter of a block.

Although the house was now a gloomy ruin—its stained glass lost to thieves, its brick chimneys crumbling, its porches drooping like wilted flowers—it had once been the showpiece of the rambunctious young city. Known locally as the Adams house, it had in fact been built in 1870 by Charles Frederick Wellington, founder of the famed Wellington Flour Mills at the Falls of St. Anthony. But after the stupendous tragedy at his mighty A Mill in 1878, Wellington had moved away, and the house was bought by Arthur Alonzo Adams, a legendary five-time mayor of the city. Triple A, as Adams was called, had not stayed long in the house either, for he soon died in a carriage accident on his way, so it was said, to his mistress's apartment. The house then reverted to his oldest son, who despite becoming mayor of Minneapolis in his own right had little use for such an ungainly antique. Some speculated that Arthur Adams Jr., known to his friends as A.A., left the old family manse standing out of sentiment. Others, never having detected evidence of a heart beating within the mayor's broad chest, said he was simply holding out for a better price as development continued spreading south, block by block.[2]

Among many other things, the Ratman fancied himself as the street's unofficial historian, and as he ambled along he conducted his own private tour, lecturing the appreciative air. "Now then, the house before us was constructed in 1870—though some records suggest 1869—by Mr. Charles Frederick Wellington, one of the pioneers of Minneapolis. Mr. Wellington—"

The Ratman's monologue was brought to a sudden halt when three figures unexpectedly emerged from the house's front door and onto the porch. They all appeared to be wearing dark hoods. They were also carrying a long piece of rolled-up carpet. Instinctively, the Ratman slipped through an opening into the thick hedge and took cover, crouching as low as he could. This was a matter of self-preservation, since for all he knew the three figures might be ruffians of the sort who would find cruel amusement in taunting a solitary old man in the wee hours of the morning.

"Move it, Earl," he heard one of the figures growl in a daunting basso as the trio descended the steps from the porch and moved toward a century-old oak that spread majestically in the front yard.

"I'm doing the best I can," came the reply. "Jesus, but he's heavy."

"Jesus doesn't have a thing to do with it," said the first man. "Now then, let's be done with this as quickly as we can. Anybody coming our way, Jack?"

"All clear," said the third member of the trio, who apparently had gone out to the sidewalk to inspect the street. "Not a soul stirring."

This, of course, was not true, since the Ratman was no more than twenty yards away, yet so well concealed that he was just another shadow in the dim light. Once he had dropped behind the hedge, the Ratman could no longer see the figures who had disturbed his peace and perhaps even threatened his well-being. But he could hear them, talking and grunting, and he could not help wondering what had brought them out at so late an hour in such an unlikely place.

"Roll him out," he heard the first man say, the man whose name he still had not heard. The voice was brisk, powerful, commanding. It reminded the Ratman of the way his first sergeant had barked out orders back in the days when he was a private in the Second Minnesota Regiment, helping William Tecumseh Sherman lay waste to Georgia.[3]

Jack, who had a boyish voice, said, "He's ready."

"All right, help me up." It was the "sergeant" talking now. "Hurry."

The Ratman heard more sounds—grunting again, the rustle of leaves, the creaking of tree limbs.

"Throw me the rope," the sergeant ordered.

There was brief silence, then the hard clump of boots hitting the ground.

"Ready?" the sergeant asked.

"Yeah, we got him," said Earl.

"Up he goes then," the sergeant said. "Pull! Pull!"

The Ratman heard more grunting, more creaking. He couldn't imagine what the men might be doing.

"All right," the sergeant announced. "That should do the trick. He's not going anywhere. You might say he's a monument to Wellington now."

The other two figures found this cryptic remark amusing, and the one called Earl laughed so hard that the sergeant had to tell him to "pipe down."

Then the sergeant said: "You know the plan. I'll call the newspapers. Remember, if you see anybody, just cross the street and keep your head down. We can't afford to be spotted."

Without another word the trio left the yard, their footsteps muffled in the damp night air. The Ratman almost panicked when he realized that one set of footsteps was coming his way down the sidewalk. But he was too frozen with fear to move, and all he could do was pray that the darkness and thick hedge would protect him. They did. As the man went past, he whistled like a happy workman. Then, chancing a peek, the Ratman saw the man from behind as he reached up to remove the hood from his head. What could have been so secret that a man would wear a hood in the dead of night?

Thoroughly frightened, the Ratman waited in his hiding place several minutes, as still and silent as the old house that loomed across the yard. When he was satisfied that he had the yard to himself, the Ratman looked out along the sidewalk. He saw no one for blocks in either direction, so he inched his way back through the hedge and into the yard. His hands, he noticed, were shaking. What he saw next made them shake even more. Hanging by his neck from a low branch of the oak tree, his body slowly turning, was a naked man. The Ratman was no stranger to the spectacle of violent death—Uncle Billy Sherman had seen to that—but this was different. A lynching was not something he ever expected to see in the middle of modern Minneapolis.

The Ratman's first instinct was to flee the horrible scene, but he found that he could not. The force of curiosity was simply too strong. Pausing to collect his senses and calm his nerves, the Ratman got out his flask, downed a slug of whisky, and walked slowly toward the body, which faced away from him. The light from the corner gas lamp was dim at best, but the Ratman had no trouble seeing that the back of the victim's head had been demolished by something large and heavy, the skull caved in like a broken piece of pottery. There were also bruises on the back, arms, and legs, suggesting that the man had been brutally beaten. As the body swung around, the Ratman—his curiosity having advanced to the morbid stage—lit a match to get a better look at the man's features. Sighing, he estimated that the victim was probably not much more than thirty. The dead man had a broad face, sandy hair combed to one side, and large eyes caught startled in the moment of death. But what really sent chills down the Ratman's spine was something else—a piece of board that hung from the man's neck. Scrawled across it in large letters was a message: THE SECRET ALLIANCE HAS SPOKEN.

"Oh, bad news, very bad news," the Ratman muttered, for he had no doubt as to the identity of the alliance, nor would anybody else in Minneapolis when the news got out. The alliance was a dark and violent organization, the Ratman knew, well funded by the power brokers of the city and subject to no law save its own.

Feeling in need of a smoke, the Ratman fumbled for the briar pipe, to-bacco pouch, and matches he kept in one of the deep front pockets of his ragged jacket. Though his hands were shaking badly, he managed to fill the pipe bowl and light it. Once he had felt the first soothing rush of nicotine, the Ratman's mind seemed to clear and he knew what he had to do. He reached into his other coat pocket and removed a steel-hinged rat trap—he always traveled with at least two of the kind guaranteed by Sears Roebuck to "kill instantly without drawing blood"—and baited it with a small piece of hard cheese. After making sure the spring was set, he carefully placed the trap on the ground beneath the dangling body.

"All right then, rest easy, young fellow," he said when he was finished. "At least the rats won't get you now." Then the Ratman went back across the yard, slipped through the hedge, and headed down Tenth as fast as his legs would carry him.

BOOK ONE

The Mystery of
Michael O'Donnell

Chapter One

ʒʟ

"They Strung Up Michael"

FROM THE JOURNALS OF DR. JOHN WATSON:[1]

WED., SEPT. 27, 1899, WALDORF-ASTORIA HOTEL, N.Y., 10:30 P.M.: Arrived here at 4:30 P.M. after smooth passage from Southampton aboard *Campania.* Hotel as advertised — posh as any in London or Paris, perhaps more so — & J[ohn] J[acob] Astor IV spared no expense in providing finest rooms in the house. Told us our suite "fit for kings," to which H[olmes] responded with usual wit: "Then we shall try to behave regally."[2]

Timing could not be better in some ways, as city in state of high excitement over naval parade planned in honor of Comm. [George] Dewey, hero of Manila Bay & other battles with Spanish. Hundreds of vessels, led by Dewey's flagship, *Olympia,* to take part in parade Friday & it will doubtless be grand spectacle of triumphant American navy. Was surprised to read in *N.Y. Times,* however, that Pres. [William] McKinley would not be on hand for event because he was leaving that day for trip to Midwest (St. Paul & Mpls. — cities with which H & I quite familiar — among his destinations). Told H he should use influence to secure place for us with British delegation at parade but he showed little interest in idea, saying he would be too busy "attending to the matter which brought us here."[3]

. . . Have first meeting with Astor tomorrow but H not looking forward to it. Reason no doubt stems from nature of case, which involves long-standing feud within Astor family. Cases of this nature always "irksome & dreary" (to use H's phrase), tho H's fee, I believe, will be largest of career. Indeed, this may be source of H's unhappiness, as he has always contended detective should work for truth first & money second. Would note that truth, while admirable, does not pay rent.[4]

Best news of day was letter we found waiting for us from dear friend S[hadwell]R[afferty] of St. Paul. H read it aloud & we took enjoyment from SR's highly adorned tale of "monster pike" that got away at Lake Osakis. Letter full of SR's usual good cheer & humor & reminded us again of how much we miss him. Seems only yesterday that three of us were tramping thru fields & woods of western Minnesota in search of rune stone, tho when we parted in April hardly thought H & I would return to America so soon. But when an Astor pleads for help & opens his ample checkbook, even the great SH must respond![5]

SR reported life in St. Paul "intolerably dull" & wrote he is waiting for "a fine murder or other act of mayhem to shake the town up and give a poor detective such as myself some useful work." Remarkable how much he & H are alike—both can tolerate anything save boredom.

H: "Mr. Rafferty is sounding desperate for adventure. Perhaps we should go to Minnesota & stir up some mischief on his behalf."

W[ATSON]: "I have seen all the mischief in Minnesota that I care to see. Besides, I do not think Mr. Astor would be pleased to hear of our departure."

H, SMILING: "You are right, my dear Watson. Well then, Mr. Rafferty will simply have to find trouble on his own."

Which he is certainly capable of doing . . .

Shadwell Rafferty was by long habit a late riser, and so it was nearly ten o'clock by the time he climbed out of bed on the morning of September 28, 1899, and went into the bathroom to wash up and shave. Because he had no reason to think it would be a remarkable day, he was in no hurry as he went about his morning ritual. Rubbing sleep from his eyes, he stared into the bathroom mirror and saw a big round face as creased and wrinkled as an old work shirt, pierced by deep-set blue eyes and crowned by a curling extravagance of reddish-gray hair. It was, Rafferty liked to say, a "historic sort of face," marked not merely by the usual weathering of time but also by the violent work of living, most notably in the form of a slashing scar over his left eye. The scar, from a long-ago knife fight in the Nevada silver fields, always reminded Rafferty of just how lucky he was to be alive, considering the life he had led.

After splashing water on his face, he stirred up a handful of lather in his shaving mug and set to work with a straight edge on the night's growth of stubble. Shaving was a duty Rafferty had only recently resumed. For most of his adult life he had sported a luxuriously unruly beard—a growth so long and snowy that Dr. Watson had once likened Rafferty to old St. Nick himself. Rafferty couldn't say exactly why he had decided to shed his beard, but he found that he somehow felt lighter, and even younger, without it.

Once finished shaving, he went into a large dressing room—part of a five-room suite he had maintained at the Ryan Hotel for almost ten years—and selected his clothes. A decidedly eccentric dresser, Rafferty's taste ran toward bright reds and even brighter oranges—and the more plaid the better. But as he intended to spend the entire day at his saloon, he saw no reason to be overly fancy. He therefore settled on a maroon jacket, dark-striped pants, a white shirt with small silver studs and cufflinks, and a tie whose color and pattern were unknown in the better circles of haberdashery.

Satisfied with his garb, Rafferty returned to his bedroom, where he was greeted by the excited barking of a small brown bulldog. "Hey, big boy, how are you?" Rafferty said, bending down to rub the dog's ears. "'Tis a treat you're lookin' for, Sherlock, if I'm not mistaken. Am I right?"

The dog, for whom the word "treat" was like a matador's red cape, began a whirling dance as Rafferty took out a piece of dried beef from a large jar. "All right now, don't hurt yourself," he said before handing over the precious morsel, which was consumed in an instant.

Besides being a loyal companion, the dog—a gift from Holmes—served as a living reminder of what had happened three years earlier, in the midst of the ice palace case. Rafferty always felt an acute sense of embarrassment as he recalled the scene where he had violated his own credo and gotten horribly drunk. Since then, he had hardly touched a drop of liquor.[6]

With Sherlock in tow Rafferty left his apartment and walked down three flights of stairs to the lobby of the Ryan Hotel. At one end of the heavily marbled, skylit lobby, he went through another door and into the saloon that was his pride and livelihood. There, as usual, his friend and business partner, George Washington Thomas, was already hard at work.[7]

Thomas—the dark dome of his forehead matching the color of the long mahogany bar—had nearly completed his preparations for the noon rush, laying up piles of fixings and making sure the beer kegs were in order. The rush would start around half past eleven, when hungry men from the factories in Lowertown and the tall office buildings that clustered along Robert Street would come racing in for free sandwiches and plenty of beer to wash them down.

Known simply as Shad's, the saloon was the largest and most popular watering hole in St. Paul, and it had made Rafferty, at age fifty-six, comfortable if not quite rich by the standards of the time. In an era when most saloons were tawdry establishments held in disrepute by "respectable" people, Shad's offered a place to drink in comfort, safety, and style. There was heavy oak paneling imported from an old Irish manor house, a forty-foot-long bar carved from fine mahogany, and quiet booths where a gentleman might even dare to entertain a lady over drinks. The saloon's popularity was due in large measure to Rafferty's gregarious temperament and his uncanny ability to remember a patron's name no matter how long it had been since his last visit. But Thomas's skill as a businessman—he was "a genius with the greenbacks," as Rafferty liked to say—was equally important to the establishment's success.

A man of many talents, Thomas had once made his living as a cook, and Rafferty stood in stark admiration before his partner's skill at the griddle. In days gone by Rafferty would have fully availed himself of Thomas's culinary talent by packing in a trencherman's breakfast— three eggs over hard, a nice cut of steak, a rasher of bacon fired to a crisp, steaming hash brown potatoes, maybe a pile of well-buttered flapjacks, and plenty of toast.

But in recent months Rafferty had done the unthinkable and gone on a diet. He had taken this extreme and painful step one day in July after looking at himself in a full-length mirror. He saw to his chagrin that his girth, never modest, had begun to widen alarmingly, though at six feet four inches tall Rafferty could, as he put it, "afford to spread a bit without lookin' entirely lopsided." Still, it was apparent that something had to be done. Otherwise, he told Thomas, "you will soon have to lead me off to the stockyards with the other fatted creatures."

Rafferty had then adopted a new morning regimen—cutting back from three of his beloved eggs to one, skipping the hash browns and steak, and beginning each day (when he didn't oversleep) with a long walk through downtown St. Paul. He'd already lost thirty pounds, and while he would never be accused of being svelte, Rafferty thought he looked more than respectable for a man of his age.

Thomas had already been through all three of St. Paul's morning papers—the *Globe,* the *News,* and the *Pioneer Press*—before Rafferty came in to join him.

"Anything interestin' from the gentlemen of the Fourth Estate?" Rafferty asked as he slid onto one of the heavy plush stools at the bar to begin working on the breakfast Thomas had prepared. Sherlock, meanwhile, took up his customary position beneath the stool, waiting impatiently for the pieces of bacon Rafferty always managed to drop from his plate.

"Just the usual," Thomas said. "They can't seem to get enough of the Philippines."

Rafferty nodded and gazed down at the front page of the *Pioneer Press,* which offered yet another breathless account of the goings on in the Philippines, where American troops were busy fighting what Rafferty was pleased to call "Bill McKinley's silly little war." Today's bulletin, however, was more interesting than most, for the *Pioneer Press* reported that plans had now been confirmed for a presidential visit to the Twin Cities on October 8—just ten days away. McKinley, the newspaper said, would welcome home the Thirteenth Minnesota Regiment, which had been among those doing his dirty work in the Philippines.[8]

Rafferty was about to deliver his standard speech on the folly of McKinley's military conduct when the telephone rang. Thomas went over to answer. After a moment he put down the receiver and said, "It's for you, Shad. Maj Burke. Sounds like she's mighty upset about something."

Majesty Burke was the owner of a stand-up saloon in Minneapolis. Rafferty had known—and admired—her for years. He picked up the phone and said, "Good mornin' to you, Maj. How are you this fine bright day?"

The abrupt response came in the form of another question: "Have you heard the awful news?"

"You must be referrin' to the president's visit," Rafferty joked. "I'm no enthusiast for Bill McKinley either, and I care nothin' at all for his little war. By the way, did I ever tell you I met him once, at Antietam?"[9]

"You have told me several times," said Burke, exasperation evident in her smoky contralto. "I don't care about McKinley, Shad. I'm talking about the lynching over here last night."

"Lynchin'?" Rafferty repeated, not quite believing what he had just heard. Lynching was virtually unknown in Minnesota, though Rafferty recalled that some poor fellow had been jerked to Jesus by a mob in Minneapolis back in the early 1880s. He said, "This is all news to me, Maj. Tell me what happened."

"It was Michael," she said, fighting back sobs. "For God's sake, Shad, they strung up Michael last night. And they left him there naked, the dirty bastards."

Rafferty paused to retrieve the name from the vast filing system in his head. Who was Michael? Then it came to him. "You mean Michael O'Donnell, your barman?"

"Yes. I'm telling you, Shad, it's all wrong. He was no child molester like they're saying."

"Who is sayin' that?"

"The police. It's all a lie. Michael would never do a thing like that."

"Of course not," said Rafferty, trying to picture the young man. He finally caught him in his mind's eye. Sandy hair, blue eyes, a broad face, pleasant manners. They had met some months earlier when Rafferty had helped Burke with a matter involving a troublesome city inspector who threatened to shut down her saloon unless he received certain sexual favors. Rafferty had found a way to take care of the greedy inspector, thereby earning Maj Burke's eternal gratitude in the process. As Rafferty recalled, Michael O'Donnell had been ready to take on the obnoxious inspector with his fists. Rafferty had calmed the young man and then silenced the inspector by threatening to expose his fondness for certain unnatural acts at a notorious downtown bordello.

Rafferty said, "Now, take a deep breath, Maj, and fill me in on what happened to poor Michael."

"It's just too upsetting on the phone," she said, her voice still choking with tears. "I can tell you the whole story if you'll come over here. I need your help, Shad. I loved Michael like my own son. It just wasn't right, and the police will do nothing." She paused for a moment, then added, almost in a whisper, "Shad, you must understand something. It was the alliance that killed Michael."

"Jesus," Rafferty murmured, for he had little doubt which "alliance"

Burke was referring to. Although its official name was the Citizens Alliance for the Maintenance of Order and the Freedom of Labor, it was better known simply as the Secret Alliance. The organization had earned this title because of its penchant for undercover antiunion activities and because no one was certain exactly which of the city's business leaders financed its often brutal conduct. "And how do you know that the alliance was behind the crime?" Rafferty asked.

"A copper friend told me on the Q.T. He said there was a placard hung around Michael's neck with the message, 'The Secret Alliance Has Spoken.' Can you imagine such a sick thing, Shad? Those bastards wanted everybody to know what they'd done. And the coppers will sweep it under the rug, you just wait and see. Or they'll say it was a trick or something. Nobody in this town dares go against Randolph Hadley."

Like everyone in the Twin Cities, Rafferty had heard many stories about the Secret Alliance and its chief enforcer. On paper, the alliance was simply a trade group designed to advance the interests of business while promoting the so-called right to work. In reality, the organization was a paramilitary posse devoted to union busting and strikebreaking by means fair or foul. Its special deputies, as they were called, came mostly from the ranks of ex–military men. They engaged in spying, intimidation, and various degrees of out-and-out thuggery to achieve the ends of their employers. Hadley, a former army colonel and U.S. marshal, ran the alliance with an iron hand and was said to have once personally administered a savage beating to a union organizer who dared cross him. Still, Rafferty had never heard of the alliance resorting to murder.

He looked at the clock behind the bar and saw that it was going on eleven o'clock — opening time. "Listen, Maj, we'll talk more later," he promised. "I'll come over right after the noon rush. Will you be all right until then?"

"I don't know if I'll ever be all right after this," she said, "but I know I'll be better when I see you."

After he'd rung off Rafferty told Thomas about the lynching, but didn't go into all the details. There would be time for that later. Besides, he wanted to see first what the newspapers would have to say about Michael O'Donnell's death. The first run of St. Paul's best afternoon paper, the *Dispatch*, would be out in about an hour. Rafferty went back into the hotel lobby and found a bellboy, who promised to bring over a copy of the newspaper as soon as it hit the streets.

The bellboy was as good as his word, delivering the *Dispatch* just before noon. Rafferty slid out from behind the noisy bar and went into his office to read the paper. He found the story he was looking for on the bottom of page one, beneath a deck of the usual lurid headlines:

HANGING ON 10TH ST.—GRISLY SCENE AT MAYOR'S OLD HOUSE LAST NIGHT—VICTIM MICHAEL O'DONNELL, MILL WORKER—BODY LEFT NAKED—HUNG FROM TREE LIMB IN YARD—POLICE SEEK CLUES

Although the article beneath included several surprising details, it was also notable for a significant omission:

> The police were called early today to the scene of a most shocking incident at the old home of Mayor Adams's father at Tenth Street and First Avenue South in downtown Minneapolis. A young Minneapolis man by the name of Michael O'Donnell, believed to be about 30 years of age, was found hanging by the neck from an oak tree in front of the house, his body left naked. The gruesome scene was discovered by a cartman collecting night soil in the area.
>
> Dr. Smythe, the county coroner, stated upon examination of the corpse that the victim had been killed by means of a blow to the head before being hung. There was also evidence that the victim had been beaten badly before the death blow was delivered. Because of the cause of death, the case is not being treated as a lynching, the last and only of which occurred in Minneapolis in 1882.[10]
>
> Police Chief Thomas Childress, who was called to the scene at once, said no effort will be spared in finding those responsible for O'Donnell's death. However, the chief said certain "anonymous communications" received by his department claimed that O'Donnell had been killed because he was caught "taking liberties" with a young girl who lives in the area. The chief noted that regardless of what offenses the victim may have committed, "vigilante justice will not be tolerated in the city of Minneapolis."
>
> For his part, Mayor Adams said he knew of no reason why the young man would have been strung up at his old family home. "I do not know Mr. O'Donnell and do not believe I have ever met him," the mayor said. "The house has been boarded up for many years and is surrounded by a tall hedge, so I can only suppose that the men who committed this terrible deed simply chose it for the privacy it offered."

O'Donnell had recently gone to work at the Wellington Flour Mills as a bagger and was said to be well liked by his fellow employees. Ironically, the house where O'Donnell's body was discovered was built in about 1870 by Charles Wellington, who later sold the property to the mayor's father.

Before his employment at the mill, O'Donnell worked as a barman at the tavern operated by Mrs. Burke on Washington Avenue North. That lady told the *Dispatch* that O'Donnell had been in her employ for about a year and was a "very reliable and conscientious young man." O'Donnell was recently married and had come to this area from Chicago, according to Mrs. Burke. The dead man's widow is said to be disconsolate.

Rafferty thought it most interesting that the *Dispatch*'s account mentioned not one word about the placard implicating the alliance. He wondered what else had been omitted from the story and made a note to pay a visit to Joseph Pyle, his friend at the *St. Paul Globe*. Then Rafferty went back into the saloon to help with the noon rush. As they worked the bar he told Thomas what he had learned from the story in the *Dispatch*.

"Well, it's a mighty strange business, if you ask me," Thomas said, "but at least it wasn't a black man they strung up. Still, any time there's a lynching, it gives certain people ideas."

Thomas, who had been with Rafferty since shortly after the Civil War, was chairman of the state chapter of the Anti-Lynching League, a group devoted to lobbying for strict laws that would put an end to the continuing epidemic of lynchings in the South and parts of the Midwest.

"'Tis a good fight you're fightin', Wash," Rafferty said, "but this case doesn't seem to qualify as a lynchin', despite what Maj Burke seems to think. From the looks of it, O'Donnell was dead before bein' dangled from that tree."

"But why would anybody strip a dead man naked and then hang him?"

"Ah, that's the very question I've been askin' myself, Wash, and I can think of only one answer, and not a pleasant one. I'm sure Maj Burke will be able to tell me more."

Two hundred miles to the north, in Minnesota's remote Arrowhead region, two men sat talking that same morning in a plain but well-equipped office that served as headquarters of the Soudan Iron Mine. One of the men was small, neatly dressed, and wore wire-rimmed glasses with thick lenses. The other man was much larger and had a wide fleshy face and suspicious black eyes.

The smaller man worked as a supply clerk for the Soudan—the largest mine on the Vermilion Range—where iron ore had first been discovered in Minnesota. Unlike the open-pit mines only recently established on the incomparably rich Mesabi Range to the south, the Soudan was an underground mine, with a maze of shafts blasted a thousand feet or more into the depths of the earth. Such work required dynamite, fuse cords, drills, bits, axes, picks, lamps, oil, and plenty of miscellaneous equipment; and the clerk's job was to make sure that adequate supplies of such essentials were always kept on hand. About the middle of every month he inventoried the mine's stores, and that was how in July he had discovered, to his great distress, a brazen act of thievery.[11]

The large man, who was a Pinkerton agent based in Duluth, had come out to the mine that same day to investigate, quickly concluding that the crime was an "inside job." This sterling deduction had failed to impress the clerk, who knew the theft could hardly have been otherwise given the remoteness of the mine and the careful steps taken to guard its supplies.

The clerk didn't much care for the Pinkerton man, who had never even bothered to give his name. Instead, back in July, he had simply introduced himself as "Operative No. 6" and announced, with a self-important air, that he was to have "full cooperation." The clerk had heard all about the Pinkertons and knew they were roundly hated by miners as traitors and spies of the worst kind. But the mighty Minnesota Iron Company, which operated the Soudan, thought very highly of the Pinkertons, and so the clerk knew he had no choice but to do as he was told.

Now the Pinkerton man was back for the third time with questions about a miner—long since gone—who remained the prime suspect in the case. The miner had left the area, without bothering to collect his pay, a few days before the theft was discovered. Suspicion therefore fell on him immediately. At first, Operative No. 6 had thought that tracking down the miner would be easy, but both he and the stolen goods had abruptly dropped from sight after being traced as far as Minneapolis. There was some evidence to suggest he had gone on to Chicago, though the trail beyond Minneapolis was indistinct at best.

"I am looking for any small detail you can remember that might help us find this Smith fellow," the agent said.

"So you are still certain he is your man?"

"Yes."

"Well, I have told you everything I know," the clerk said. "I do not see how I can be of further help."

"Go over his description again, if you would."

The clerk sighed and said, "Very well. His name, as you know, was Earl Smith, and his stated age was forty-one. He was of average height and weight—about five feet ten, I should guess, and perhaps 160 pounds. He had a broad face, curly black hair cut quite short, brown eyes, a bushy beard streaked with gray, and a mustache. There was nothing especially remarkable about his appearance, in other words."

"And he was a good worker?"

"Yes, excellent. It was obvious he had experience as a miner."

"I believe you also stated earlier that he showed no favoritism toward unions or any radical tendencies. Is that correct?"

"Yes. Mr. Smith was very quiet and went about his work without complaint or question. I take it, however, that you believe he might in fact have been a radical or anarchist of some kind."

"It is very likely," said the Pinkerton man.

"I see. Then you must be very worried about what he intends to do next."

"That would be an understatement," said Operative No. 6.

CHAPTER TWO

∂ℓ℘

"Do You Know Who This Man Is?"

FROM THE JOURNALS OF DR. JOHN WATSON:

THURS., SEPT. 28, 1899, DELMONICO'S RESTAURANT, N.Y., 2 P.M.: Astor asked us to join him at this celebrated establishment for lunch. Over excellent dish called lobster thermidor—specialty of the house, I am told—he talked for hour re troubles & what he expects of H. Talk centered on cousin William, with whom Astor embroiled in bitter dispute, exact nature of which I cannot yet commit to paper. Astor demanded William be stopped "at once" from carrying out insidious plans, etc., etc. H finally cut him short with assurances everything would be taken care of "expeditiously." After Astor left, H in sour mood.[1]

H: "Mr. Astor belongs to that breed of men made thoroughly impossible by an excess of money & a want of judgment."

Clearly, H still having second thoughts re Astor matter, which likely to prove arduous in particulars but unlikely to offer adventure he craves. Also, family feuds always unpleasant, especially when great wealth involved. Do not doubt H would be far happier working on another case with SR, even if it meant going to Minnesota again. As I write, H already returned to hotel to "think in misery," as he put it. . . .

Majesty Burke's establishment was in the Minneapolis warehouse and sawmill district just north of downtown. Rafferty took the University Avenue streetcar for the hour-long trip to Minneapolis, alighted at the intersection of Washington and Hennepin Avenues, and then walked up to the saloon.

Washington itself was lined with new brick warehouses, but the area to the north and east, along the low, clotted banks of the Mississippi, belonged to the sawmillers. Powered by sawdust-burning steam engines that sent out unremitting clouds of acrid smoke, the mills worked day and night to process logs sent down river from the last virgin white pine forest on the continent, in far northern Minnesota.[2]

It was quarter past three when Rafferty reached the saloon, housed in an old two-story building with red clapboard siding and faded green shutters adorning the upstairs windows. The day shift at the sawmills had just ended, and the place was packed with a raucous crowd of men dressed in dungarees and checkered shirts. All of them appeared to be striving mightily to drink as much beer as they could before heading home or moving on to the next watering hole. Rafferty made his way through the crowd to Burke's small office, knocked, and was told at once to come in.

Majesty Burke, looking elegant as always in a pleated brown skirt beneath a bright silk shirtwaist with puffed sleeves and a choker collar, sat at an old rolltop desk, a ledger book spread before her. When she looked up at Rafferty, he could see the tracks of tears streaking down her proud face. "My God, Shad," she said, rushing over and kissing him on the cheek, "I cannot tell you how good it is to see you. But what have you done to yourself? Have you quit eating, dear man? And what happened to that fine beard of yours?"

"Ah, I have adopted a new look in hopes of impressin' beautiful ladies such as yourself," Rafferty said, wrapping her in his arms with a bear hug before standing back to look at her. "Now then, Maj, how long has it been? Six months?"

"Almost a year. I last saw you at Bobby's wedding."

"And how is that strappin' lad of yours? I trust marriage suits him well."

"He's fine," she said, motioning Rafferty to take a seat by the desk. "Better than I am, Shad, I'll tell you that."

"Well, you look grand as always, Maj," Rafferty said, and he meant it, for at age forty-five Majesty Burke was still the sort of woman who drew admiring looks from men young and old. Tall and striking, she had a fine-boned oval face, sensuous lips, large green eyes, luxuriant brown hair barely tinged with gray, and a full, but by no means matronly, figure. Her real first name was Madge, but over the years this had evolved, by barroom consensus, into Majesty—an appellation that reflected both her regal bearing and her queenly ability to command the respect of rough men not generally accustomed to taking orders from a woman.

She had married John Burke, then a handsome young rake with ambitions in saloon keeping, when she was twenty. Many unhappy suitors had been left behind in Chicago, where both hailed from, and opinion was unanimous among them that she could have done infinitely better in her choice of mate.

But she loved Johnny and soon moved with him to Minneapolis, where he fulfilled his life's dream by buying a saloon of his own. Their life together ended on a December day in 1890 when Johnny was crushed while trying to stop a runaway wagon. He died a week later in what the newspapers described as "unspeakable agony." Majesty Burke, with two children to support, then saw no choice but to take over the business, becoming the first female saloonkeeper (at least the first who was not also a madam) in the city's history.

Saloon keeping was a rough enough business for a man—Rafferty had been shot at three times during his career behind the bar—and certainly no job for a woman, or so it was thought. But Burke had defied the popular wisdom, and under her steady hand the saloon flourished. She had once joked to Rafferty that her success stemmed from the fact that half of her customers thought they were in love with her and the other half thought she was in love with them. It was her business acumen, above all else, that had already earned her enough money to retire whenever she wished. And she had been thinking recently that she knew just the man she'd like to retire with, if he was willing.

For the moment, however, she could think of little except Michael O'Donnell's brutal death. She also knew that Rafferty was the one man who just might be able to get to the bottom of the crime.

"I am sick at heart about Michael's murder," she told him. "No one should have to do die like that."

"The two of you were close, I gather."

"He was like another son, especially after Bobby moved away to Milwaukee with his wife. Michael was very reliable and no drinker either. It's hard to find young men like that in this business, as you well know."

"Well, I'm truly sorry for your loss, Maj," Rafferty said as she daubed a new tear from her cheek. "May I ask when you last saw him?"

"About two weeks ago. He stopped by one evening. He was working by then down at the Wellington A Mill."

"Ah, I read that in the papers."

She nodded sadly. "I did my best to talk him out of it, of course, but he said he wanted to try his hand at something else. I told him the mills were no place for a smart fellow such as himself, but he had his mind made up, and his wife was all for him doing it. She's a pretty young woman, Shad. You can imagine what she's going through now."

"They were married just recently, I understand."

"In July. Jacqueline is her name."

"I'll talk to her," Rafferty said. "Now tell me this, Maj, and be honest with me. Did Michael have any peculiarities that you know of when it came to children, especially young girls?"

She gave a derisive laugh. "Do not believe any of that for a minute, Shad. It's just a dirty lie told by the police. They were over here this morning asking me all sorts of questions. I gave them a piece of my mind."

"I imagine you did. What did the coppers have to say?"

"Very little. But I did find out that they don't seem to know a thing about the girl Michael supposedly molested. They couldn't tell me her name, her age, where she lived, or anything else. Don't you see, Shad? It's all a big cover-up. The Secret Alliance, and nobody else, murdered Michael. Here, let me show you something the coppers don't know about."

She reached into one of the cubbyholes in her desk and removed a small box made of inlaid wood. "Michael kept a duffel bag here in the office with a change of clothes, since he was always getting splashed with beer or worse by those madmen out there. Anyway, he forgot to take the bag with him when he left to work at the mill. Well, I forgot about it, too, until this morning, after the police had left. So I went through the bag and found this Chinese puzzle box."

"And bein' the curious woman you are, you had to open it, I imagine."

"I did, though it took me a while to figure out the trick. Wait until you see what I found inside. You're the first person I'm showing this to, Shad, so you need to keep it under your hat."

She now opened another desk drawer, took out a photograph, and handed it to Rafferty. "Do you know who that is?" she asked.

Rafferty looked at the picture and let out a soft whistle. The face of a man he didn't recognize was clearly visible in the picture, but so was a great deal else. The man was stark naked, as was the woman—her face hidden from view—lying beneath him. They were on a bed and there could be no doubt what they were doing. Rafferty was a good amateur photographer, and he could tell by the quality of the image that it had been taken with an expensive camera and not one of the cheap Kodaks everyone was buying. The detail was such that through an open window behind the amatory couple, Rafferty could make out the cornice of a nearby building. As for the photographer, he must have been stationed in front of the bed, though Rafferty wondered whether the busy couple knew their moment of passion was being recorded for posterity.

"'Tis quite a picture," Rafferty said. "And just who are the lady and gentleman caught in such an indelicate pose?"

Majesty Burke smiled and said, "I don't know about the lady, if you could call her that. But the gentleman would be none other than Randolph Hadley himself, in the flesh as it were."

Rafferty understood at once that the photograph was as explosively dangerous as a vial of nitroglycerin. "Ah, Maj," he said softly, "this is trouble you've handed me. I hope you know that."

"I do. I also know that there's no one better than you to handle it. Will you help me, Shad? Will you prove that Hadley and his men murdered Michael? There is no one else I can turn to."

Rafferty leaned back in his chair and scratched the back of his head. Finally, he said, "Why not? I'm not plannin' to live forever anyway."

That afternoon Randolph Hadley also had photographs on his mind when he met with Mayor Arthur Adams.

"We've got a problem," he told Adams bluntly. "We went through O'Donnell's house, checked his locker down at the mill, and looked everywhere else we could think of. No pictures."

They were sitting in the mayor's musty office in the old city hall at Bridge Square, just a few blocks from Burke's saloon. The office was surprisingly small for so important a public official, but Arthur Adams liked it that way, since it gave the impression of modesty—an important virtue to cultivate among the city's Scandinavian electorate. Adams also liked the view, for out his big window he could look down to the new Hennepin Avenue bridge and the Mississippi River, gathering speed for its plunge over the Falls of St. Anthony. Minneapolis had started right along the river, between the bridge and the falls, and had gone in half a century from wild Indian territory to a booming city of two hundred thousand people. And now, Adams liked to think, it was his city—every lucrative inch of it.[3]

Adams and Hadley met in the mayor's office almost every afternoon to talk. The two men worked well together, even though they were different in nearly every aspect. Arthur Adams was large, broad shouldered, and handsome, a cheerfully amoral man who possessed a nimble intellect, a golden tongue, and a fine talent for boodle in all of its infinite varieties. He also had a taste for the finer things in life, including Cuban cigars and single malt Scotch whisky—Glenlivet in particular when he could get it. Randolph Hadley, by contrast, was tall and gaunt, with a parched Puritan's face dominated by heavily lidded gray eyes. He did not smoke, abhorred alcohol, served as a deacon at the First Baptist Church downtown, and was, as far as the public knew, a faithful husband and father. He was also ferociously strong willed, fearless, and extremely handy with weaponry.

Despite their differences, the two men understood each other perfectly. The mayor's job was to make sure that the police of Minneapolis would do nothing to interfere with the extralegal and often violent measures by which Hadley's crew of thugs kept the working classes in line. For their part, Hadley and the businessmen behind the alliance turned a blind eye to the mayor's systematic pilfering of the municipal treasury.

"How about a camera, Dolph?" the mayor now asked, unwrapping a cigar and showing no sign of being perturbed by Hadley's gloomy report. "Did you find one? It could tell us a lot."

"No, we drew a complete blank. No camera, no negatives, no prints—not a thing. Of course, it's possible the little weasel squirreled all the stuff away in a place nobody will ever find."

"I do not feel that lucky," the mayor said. "No, I'm betting somebody out there has the goods. The question is who. His grieving widow perchance?"

"I had the police talk to her, but they didn't get anything. Maybe she knows something, maybe she doesn't. It's always hard to tell with women. I've heard, though, that she thinks her husband was a saint."

"Then perhaps it's best he did not live to disappoint her. If not the widow, who then might be our best suspect?" Adams asked, finally lighting his cigar. "A friend? A lover? Someone else in the family?"

"Could be anybody. But if you want my guess, it's that sister of his."

"Ah yes, Miss Addie O'Donnell, the outspoken friend of the working-man. Have you gone through her place yet with your usual destructive thoroughness?"

"No. We do that and she'll raise a big stink in the newspapers."

"True. The First Amendment is a constant bother, isn't it, Dolph? If the Founding Fathers had only started with the Second, our lives would be immeasurably easier. Well, I think you'll have to search her place anyway. Or maybe our friend, Mr. McParland, can send in one of his innumerable operatives. God knows, he owes us a favor."

"That's not a bad idea. Why don't you press him on it, A.A."

"I will," Arthur Adams said, studying the smoke that curled up from his cigar. "I don't need to tell you how important this is. If any of the pictures get out, there'll be hell to pay for all of us."

"Don't worry, we'll find them — one way or the other."

"You do that, Dolph," the mayor said. "And the sooner the better."

❦

On his way back to St. Paul in the early evening, Shadwell Rafferty smoked a cigar on the streetcar's rear platform and thought about what lay ahead. As a rule, Rafferty — who liked to say he was "happier digestin' food than thoughts" — was not given to prolonged bouts of passive contemplation. He much preferred to think on his feet, to let his mind move with the flow of events and improvise as needed. And the more dangerous and demanding the circumstances, the clearer Rafferty's mind seemed to become.

During his Civil War days, in the ranks of the First Minnesota Regiment, Rafferty had exhibited the quality that soldiers admire more than any other — coolness under fire. This quality was often taken to mean indifference to danger, but it was not that at all. From First Bull Run, where his regiment suffered more casualties than any other Union outfit on the field, all the way through the crucible at Gettysburg, Rafferty had never been indifferent to danger. He had no more desire than the next man to die a glorious death, if there was such a thing, for his country. No, coolness under fire was the ability — God-given, Rafferty was convinced — to think clearly and quickly in the midst of chaos. He had known many brave and good men, from privates to generals, who simply could not think at all once the minié balls started flying and the twelve-pounders sent their lethal cargo screaming through the air. Yet it was in just such situations that Rafferty was at his best, and he could no more explain why this was so than he could account for the fact that he liked peas but detested carrots.[4]

But as his trolley sped through the open country between Minneapolis and St. Paul, Rafferty realized he could not rely solely on improvisation if he hoped to solve the ugly business of Michael O'Donnell's death. The murder had obviously been carefully planned—how else to explain the placard left on the body?—and Rafferty knew that he would have to be equally deliberate in his investigation. He also understood that once he stepped into the affair he would be walking into the middle of something akin to war.

Randolph Hadley's presence at the center of the case was particularly worrisome, for war seemed to be Hadley's chief occupation. Although Rafferty had never met the man, he had read a good many newspaper accounts of the Secret Alliance and its brutal suppression of unions, beginning in 1889 when streetcar workers in both cities had gone out on strike. There were pitched battles in the street—and men shot dead—during that grim affair. Hadley had been in the middle of it, earning a reputation for cunning and ruthlessness that made him a hated man among the working classes.

Despite Hadley's influence and power, Rafferty had promised Majesty Burke that he would investigate the death of her former barman. It wasn't really a reasonable decision, as Rafferty would have been the first to acknowledge. Minneapolis was foreign ground to him, and the case did not promise to be quick or easy. The truth was, however, that Rafferty liked nothing better than a good fight, and his appetite for detective work was as strong as ever. There was also the fact that the O'Donnell case promised to offer far more than run-of-the-mill intrigue, not only because of Hadley's involvement but also because of what Rafferty had learned about the young man himself.

Michael O'Donnell, it seemed, had an interesting political history—a fact Majesty Burke had acknowledged only after some forceful prodding by Rafferty. There was, to begin with, a connection with Mayor Arthur Adams, for whose machine O'Donnell had once worked as an assistant precinct captain before graduating to the position of "small-time bagman," as Burke had put it. Then something strange had happened: O'Donnell suddenly renounced his affiliation with the mayor and began to associate with a far different crowd—union radicals and even a few "crazy anarchists," according to Burke. As for what had caused this sudden change of heart, she had no idea, for Michael O'Donnell simply would not talk about it.

Rafferty had also questioned Burke about the placard supposedly found on O'Donnell's body, hoping she'd tell him where she got the information. But she had steadfastly refused to identify her source in the police department, saying she couldn't betray a confidence. All of which meant Rafferty would be wiser to postpone approaching the police for answers. And he knew another source of information that was just as good, and maybe better.

The offices of the *Daily Globe* occupied an ornate ten-story pile of brick and stone at a prominent corner in downtown St. Paul. For a brief period, the building had been the city's tallest, but the newspaper's hated rival, the *Pioneer Press*, had shortly thereafter built a new twelve-story home of its own—an act of dominion that extended into other areas as well. The *Globe* was, in fact, falling behind in the newspaper wars that seemed to rage without end in the last months of the century, and within a few years its owner, James J. Hill, would close it for good. Until that unhappy day, Joseph G. Pyle remained editor in chief, and he ran the paper, as all good editors do, on the assumption that each day's diet of news, however paltry and insubstantial, was the food of kings. The *Globe* also published a Minneapolis edition and therefore planned to devote considerable space in the next morning's paper to Michael O'Donnell's hanging.

Although Rafferty had known Pyle for years in a casual sort of way, their friendship had not become fully cemented until the perilous days of the ice palace case in 1896. More than once in the course of that affair, Pyle had proved his mettle, not only as a wise factotum to the imperial Hill, but also as the sort of man who could handle himself in a tight spot. He was, in addition, an excellent journalist—a rarity at a time when the press often functioned as little more than a yipping lap dog for the rich and powerful.[5]

Rafferty had arrived back in St. Paul at about six o'clock, and he went at once to Pyle's office. There, behind a massive rolltop desk that seemed to act as a magnet for loose papers of every kind, sat the editor—a compact man in his midforties with unremarkable features except for a pugnacious chin and slate-blue eyes that when irritated, as they often were, could stare down a locomotive.

"Shad, how are you?" Pyle said, rising to greet Rafferty. "My God, I don't think I've seen you since Holmes and Dr. Watson left for England."

Rafferty smiled and said, "'Tis because you have been derelict, Joseph, in practicin' the first duty of every newspaperman, which is to patronize all saloons within walkin' distance of his office. I trust you have not allied yourself with the dry faction or I'll have no choice but to disown you."

"Not on my deathbed," Pyle promised, motioning Rafferty to a chair beside his desk. "Now, to what do I owe the pleasure of your distinguished company?"

Rafferty inserted his considerable bulk into the chair, removed the bowler hat he sometimes wore, and reached into his vest pocket for a cigar. Clipping off one end, he lit the cigar and said, "'Tis this awful business of the hangin' in Minneapolis, Joseph. I'm curious what your man on the scene has heard about the case."

Pyle greeted the question with a quizzical look of his own, then said, "I can see by the look on that big Irish mug of yours that you're up to something, Shad. Care to tell me about it?"

"Not at the moment. But if you're kind to me, Joseph, I just may be able to give you a genuine, bona fide scoop."

"Fair enough. What I know about the case is, to be honest, not much more than what you have already read in the afternoon newspapers. Nelson Griggs, our man in Minneapolis, is a decent enough reporter, though there are better. I had to get after him this morning to do more legwork on identifying the child who supposedly was assaulted by O'Donnell. The police were not talking much about the child."

"Is that customary in your experience?"

"No."

"Nor was it the way business was done during my days as a patrolman in St. Paul," Rafferty noted. "When we caught a molester, 'twas big news and you could count on seein' the poor child's parents in the papers tellin' all the world how grateful they were that the fine officers of the St. Paul Police Department had captured the despicable miscreant. Coppers love to see their names in print, but in this matter the police in Minneapolis seem uncommonly shy."

"It's unusual," Pyle agreed. "Of course, it's not every day that the suspected molester gets beaten to death and strung up, either. Maybe that's why the police are being so cautious."

"Maybe, though I'm not so sure. In any case, would you give me a call if your man Griggs comes up with the name of the alleged victim?"

"Of course. I expect to hear from him shortly. It will be interesting to see what he's found out today. But may I ask, Shad, what you're driving at?"

"I'll get to that. First, I'd like to ask if Mr. Griggs made any mention to you of somethin' found on Michael O'Donnell's body?"

"What do you mean?"

"I mean anything—anything at all out of the ordinary—that might have been discovered on the body."

"No, I have heard of no such thing. But the man was found naked, Shad, so I don't see—"

"Humor me, Joseph, humor me. Now tell me this: Did Griggs actually see the body as it was hangin' naked from the tree?"

"No, Griggs didn't and neither did any of the other local newsies, as far as I know. The body, as I understand it, was cut down immediately by the police, for reasons of decency if no other, I should imagine."

"Ah, I doubt that decency had much to do with it. All right then, what about the cartman who discovered the body? Did Mr. Griggs by chance talk with the gentleman or get his name?"

"Funny you should ask that, Shad. I instructed Griggs this very morning to search out the fellow, since it's obvious he could provide details that the police appear to be holding back."

"Good work, Joseph. I would like to talk to this cartman myself. 'Tis likely he's the only person who saw the body before the coppers got their hands on it."

Pyle had been listening with growing impatience to Rafferty's questions and finally burst out, "Very well, Shad, it's your turn now. What do you know about this matter? You promised a scoop and I would like to hear it this instant."

"And you shall," said Rafferty, crushing out his cigar in an ashtray on Pyle's desk. "What I know, Joseph, is that the Secret Alliance is involved in this."

Pyle gave his friend a curious stare and said, "Don't tell me they called you, too?"

"Joseph, you've lost me. Who are you talkin' about?"

"Well, when you mentioned the alliance, I figured you must have gotten one of those anonymous telephone calls."

"What sort of call?"

"Every paper in the Twin Cities got a call early this morning from a fellow offering some cock-and-bull story about the alliance murdering O'Donnell. The caller had no proof, mind you, nor even any details about the crime, and he wouldn't identify himself. Of course, we couldn't print such a thing. We did check with our police sources, and they all said there was nothing to it—just some agitator trying to stir up trouble. Happens all the time."

Rafferty could only shake his head in disbelief. "Ah, Joseph, you of all people should know that the coppers can shade the truth as well as anyone."

"What are you saying?"

"I'm sayin' you would be wise to check into what the caller told you. Fact is, I've got firsthand information that the alliance left its calling card at the scene of the crime." Rafferty then told Pyle about his conversation with Majesty Burke. He did not, however, mention the compromising photograph of Randolph Hadley.

Pyle said, "My God, Shad, are you saying someone from the alliance actually committed the murder?"

"I'm sayin' only that it's possible. What's certain is that the coppers did some cleanin' up at the scene, hopin' nobody would find out about the placard. But it's obvious from your anonymous caller that word leaked out anyway."

"Well, if the alliance was involved, for whatever reason, then you're playing with fire, Shad. I trust you know that."

"Oh, I do, Joseph, I do. Still, it's an odd business all the way around if you think about it. If I were a member of the alliance and felt the urge to eliminate somebody, I'd broadcast the fact only if I thought it could strike terror into the hearts of my enemies. But in this case the coppers did everything they could to cover up what the alliance had done, even though it's common knowledge that the leaders of the police department and the alliance always work hand in glove. So I must ask myself, what was that placard doin' on the body in the first place? I must also ask myself who made those anonymous calls to all the newspapers."

"And do you have any answers?" Pyle asked.

Rafferty lifted himself out of the chair and walked toward the door. "Not yet, Joseph. But when I do, then I imagine I'll also know why Michael O'Donnell was murdered and who did the murderin'. In the meantime, I've got a telegram to send that just might help me answer some questions."

"Who's it going to?" Pyle asked.

"A fellow named Sherlock Holmes," Rafferty said with a mischievous grin. "Ever hear of him?"

ℰ𝓎𝓅

Another man, from a very different station in life, was also considering the matter of who murdered Michael O'Donnell. But unlike Rafferty — or the police, for that matter — Joe Shelton, the cartman who had discovered O'Donnell's body, thought he had an inside track when it came to knowing who was behind the awful deed. And this knowledge, he believed, could prove highly lucrative if he played his cards right.

Shelton occupied a peculiar position in the hierarchy of life in Minneapolis. People did not like to see him coming, but they could not do without him, either. For twenty years he had worked in the dead of night, emptying the privy vaults of rich and poor alike. The only lesson he had drawn from his unpleasant line of work was a democratic one, for as he liked to put it, "Everybody's s—t looks the same." He shoveled out this night soil, as it was euphemistically called, and then hauled it away in a covered cart and dumped it into the river.

Although his work was essential, it was not well paid, and it was becoming more competitive all the time because of the growing popularity of indoor plumbing as the city's sewer system expanded. With more and more houses connecting to sewers, the number of vaults available for emptying decreased every year. Still, Shelton managed to eke out a living, working only at night in accord with city ordinances that limited the hours his smelly cart could be on the street.

It was because of these late hours that he had stumbled upon O'Donnell's body. He had stopped his cart by the Adams house, as he had many nights before, and gone into the big yard for a quiet smoke. Finding the man hanging there had given him the scare of his life, and he was also none too happy with the way the coppers had treated him, making it seem at first as though he had done something wrong.

After answering many questions, Shelton had then been instructed to keep quiet about the sign on the body, or else. Well, he would see about that. Maybe, just maybe, the newspapers might pay for such a piece of information. Judging by their stories they didn't seem to know a thing about it. Yes, sir, he might just have to go over to the *Tribune* tomorrow and have a little chat with a reporter there he knew. A scoop had to be worth something.

But the real money, the cartman believed, would come from another source — the fellow he had seen on Tenth Street just minutes before he stumbled on the dead man. The man had crossed the street when he saw

Shelton's cart and then disappeared into the night. Shelton hadn't seen the man's face but he had noticed his peculiar walk—the long loping stride, the head craning forward, the distinctive way the shoulders hunched. Unless Shelton was mistaken, he had seen that walk before.

Shelton hadn't mentioned this little incident to the coppers, since he didn't trust them as far as he could spit, but he had made a couple of inquiries on his own. The results were very interesting. Knowledge was money, the way Shelton looked at it, and he figured it just might be worth some cold hard cash if he presented the situation to the man in question. After all, times were hard and a man had to look out for himself as best he could.

CHAPTER THREE

I Want a Man Who Thirsts for Justice

FROM THE JOURNALS OF DR. JOHN WATSON:

THURS., SEPT. 28, 1899, WALDORF-ASTORIA HOTEL, N.Y., 9:30 P.M.: Telegram from SR arrived within hour & H seized upon it like starving dog. H desperately wishes to take mind off case here, which is becoming nightmare for reasons I will spell out later. SR's message thus most welcome, if for no other reason than that, in H's words, "it deals with a crime as opposed to a quarrel, & the former are invariably easier to resolve than the latter."

Telegram as follows: CURIOUS MURDER IN MPLS. MAN HANGED FROM TREE DOWNTOWN. KILLED FIRST. FOUND NAKED. WAS UNION MAN. SECRET ANTILABOR ALLIANCE PRIME SUSPECT. DETAILS WILL INTEREST YOU. LETTER TO FOLLOW. RAFFERTY.

H: "Mr. Rafferty has given us something to chew on, Watson, even if it lacks meaty detail. There are, however, some reasonable inferences which might be drawn from what little information we possess. To begin with, I would note that a hanging generally requires the action of several men to accomplish. It tends to be a mob activity, as the many terrible lynchings in America demonstrate. But to hang a man who is already dead, & to leave him naked—that, Watson, is a peculiar act. I can think of a number of reasons why such a thing might be done. One, however, stands out above all others."

W: "Humiliation perhaps?"

H, SHRUGGING: "That is certainly a good possibility. Let us see, however, what Mr. Rafferty says in his letter. He may well have the same idea."

H offered several other observations—none startling, to my mind—after which he called bellboy & wrote out telegram to SR acknowledging receipt of his, wishing him "a good hunt," etc. . . .

The next morning, a chilly Friday, Rafferty arose just before eight o'clock—an ungodly hour by his standards—and wrote a letter to Holmes in which he thanked him for his encouraging telegram and then described the burgeoning mystery of the O'Donnell case. Rafferty also enclosed a selection of newspaper clippings that he thought Holmes would find helpful.

It was Holmes's presence in New York—a piece of intelligence Rafferty had gleaned from James J. Hill, the railroad tycoon who always seemed to know everything—that led Rafferty to write. Had Holmes been in London as usual, a letter would have taken far too long to do any good, and telegrams or long-distance telephone calls were too expensive—and too public—to convey detailed information. But with Manhattan only thirty-six hours by train from St. Paul, a letter could get there in two days via special delivery.[1]

In composing his letter, Rafferty made a frank plea for assistance. Holmes was brilliant when it came to perceiving what he liked to call the essential lines of a case, and that was where Rafferty needed help, since the O'Donnell investigation looked as if it could go off in any number of promising directions. Rafferty also knew that the hanging, with its many unusual elements, was just the sort of crime that would appeal to Holmes's insatiable intellect.

After posting the letter, Rafferty boarded a streetcar for Minneapolis. His destination was a place known as Hell's Half Acre, where he hoped to find out more about Michael O'Donnell. He had brought along his copies of all three St. Paul morning newspapers, and he carefully reread the stories about Michael O'Donnell's murder. By far the best story was in Pyle's *Globe*, which had the scoop of the day thanks to Rafferty's tip about the placard left dangling around Michael O'Donnell's neck. Although the newspaper dutifully printed statements from Minneapolis authorities dismissing the placard as a red herring, the revelation nonetheless created a sensation among the working classes, who required little persuading to believe that the alliance was capable of murder.

From Rafferty's point of view, however, the most intriguing part of the *Globe*'s story was the response it elicited from Randolph Hadley. Not surprisingly, Hadley denied that the alliance had anything to do with O'Donnell's demise. But he took his defense a step further, stating that "certain evidence discovered at the scene suggests Mr. O'Donnell, a well-known union agitator, was in fact murdered by his own kind." Both Hadley and the police, however, refused to say exactly what sort of "evidence" supported this controversial claim.

The *Globe*'s story went on to note with an undercurrent of malicious glee that the official version of events had changed within a mere twenty-four hours:

> Just yesterday the police were circulating a story that Mr. O'Donnell had been murdered by a vengeful mob after supposedly assaulting a young girl in the vicinity of Tenth Street. These vigilantes, however, now appear to have been a chimera, as, it seems, was the "victim" herself, since no woman or child has come forward with a claim of being violated. Asked to explain the department's sudden about-face, Chief Childress stated that "we received some false information which we believe was intended to mislead us in our investigation. The real criminals will find that the police of this city cannot be put off so easily."

Rafferty chuckled as he read the chief's last comment, since it was well known that the police of Minneapolis were in fact easily "put off" — if the size of the bribe was sufficient. There was, however, nothing amusing about the latest developments as reported by the *Globe*. To Rafferty's practiced eye, the official investigation into Michael O'Donnell's murder had the flimsy look of a hastily conceived cover-up, just as Majesty Burke had suggested. But Rafferty was less certain as to the reason for the cover-up. Minneapolis, he knew, was an utterly corrupt city, a place where men at every level of authority were bought and paid for by the mayor's mighty machine. In such a place there would be all too many people — including many in positions of power — with something to hide.

As his streetcar entered southeast Minneapolis and approached the campus of the University of Minnesota, Rafferty tried to recall the last time he had been to the Mill City twice in one week, let alone on successive days, but he drew a blank. The truth was that Rafferty, like many St. Paulites, had only rarely seen fit to cross the Mississippi into the terra incognita of that "damned Swede town," as he called Minneapolis.

He couldn't say exactly why he disliked the Mill City. Part of it was simple hometown boosterism. Yet there was also something about the layout of Minneapolis that made Rafferty ill at ease. He had been raised in the crabbed confines of Boston and thus found himself strangely uncomfortable with Minneapolis's flat, seemingly endless gridiron of broad streets and avenues, most of which were carefully alphabetized or numbered, suggesting that the founders of the city—transplanted New Englanders for the most part—valued order above all else. Rafferty much preferred the lunatic inconsistencies of St. Paul, where every street was a crooked adventure, for he believed that good cities should be mysteries at heart, like the people who built them.

Yet Minneapolis's devotion to order and reason seemed to be paying off, and as the new century approached it was rapidly pulling away from its older twin to become the dominant city of the Northwest. Back in 1890 St. Paul's census takers had tried to combat this insidious trend by conjuring up all manner of phantom citizens, including two dozen men who were officially listed as residing in a basement barbershop, where they presumably led crowded but neatly trimmed lives. The gambit hadn't worked, however, and by 1900 Minneapolis would have 200,000 people, while St. Paul would lag far behind with 130,000. Yet even in 1899 Minneapolis remained rawboned, having shot up so fast that it seemed barely able to accommodate its own exuberant energies, or to fully comprehend its spectacular vices. It was a city, Rafferty knew, where almost anything could happen, even under the color of law.[2]

Hell's Half Acre, where Rafferty found himself at about ten o'clock after a short walk from his streetcar stop, was one of the city's most unruly precincts, though its reputation for crime and debauchery had been enhanced by the usual journalistic hyperbole. In reality, the place was not so much hellish as it was simply run-down, a small-scale slum no different from others in the city except for its unusual location. Occupying two blocks along Eighth Street behind the towering stone Church of the Redeemer, the half acre of shacks and shanties was improbably sandwiched between tall office buildings to the north and the fading mansions of Tenth Street to the south. How it had managed to resist the city's infatuation with progress for so long was something of a mystery. Rumor had it, however, that Mayor Adams himself controlled the property through a series of dummy corporations, and intended to sell it all off as soon as the stubborn depression of the 1890s finally came to an end.[3]

Rafferty had gotten O'Donnell's address from Majesty Burke, and he had no trouble finding the wooden shack where the young man had lived. Like all of its immediate neighbors, the shack was a tumbledown affair, with a sagging roof and tilted side walls that were losing their contest with gravity. The small yard—enclosed by an unpainted picket fence—was neatly kept, however, and was even adorned with an apple tree. The day was bright and warm for so late in September, and Rafferty noted that occupants from nearby cabins were out working in their yards.

Passing through the gate, Rafferty went up to the front door and delivered a pair of firm knocks. When the door swung open, he found himself looking into the piercing gray eyes of a woman who said sharply, "Go away. There is nothing more for you here."

Rafferty removed his bowler and said, "My apologies for botherin' you, Mrs. O'Donnell, but—"

"I am not Mrs. O'Donnell," said the woman, whose attire—a simple white blouse over a black serge skirt—was as plain and direct as her speech, "and I care nothing for your apologies, sir." She tried to shut the door but Rafferty pushed it open with his shoulder.

"Then just who might you be?" he inquired, looking inside over her shoulder. He was surprised by what he saw. The shack—which had but one room that appeared to function as kitchen, parlor, and sleeping quarters all in one—was in complete disarray. A bed in one corner had been overturned, as had a nearby dresser, its drawers emptied of their contents. Clothes were strewn on the floor, along with sheets and pillows, books, papers, plates and cups, and stray pieces of silverware. Rafferty also noticed that floorboards had been pulled up in several places and that pine planking had been ripped from the walls, exposing old newspapers used for insulation.

"Haven't you done enough damage already?" the woman replied, answering Rafferty's question with one of her own while maintaining a defiant stare. She looked to be around thirty and was quite attractive in an angular sort of way. Tall and sturdily built—Irish through and through, Rafferty thought—she had straight brown hair cut square at her shoulders and a long, narrow face dominated by high cheekbones and a determined chin. Her eyes, small and close set, bored in on Rafferty like concentrated beams of light.

"Please go away," she now repeated.

"I will when you tell me who you are," Rafferty promised.

The woman let out a sigh and said: "Very well, since you are being so troublesome. I am Addie O'Donnell, and I am trying to sort what remains of my brother's belongings. As you can see, the cretinous thugs who call themselves police in this city have already done a thorough job of destruction. So if you are with the police, there is nothing for you to do here except leave."

Rafferty tipped his hat and said, "'Tis a pleasure to meet you, Miss O'Donnell. Please accept my condolences on your brother's death. My name is Shadwell Rafferty and I am not from the police."

"Then what are you doing here?" she asked.

"I am trying to find out why the Citizens Alliance may have killed your brother."

Rafferty had her attention now. She gave him another long stare and said, "Exactly who are you?"

"'Tis a question not easy to answer, Miss O'Donnell. I own a saloon in St. Paul, but I also have been known to work as a private investigator. Your brother's former employer, Mrs. Burke, asked me to look into the matter of his death, and that's why I've come here. You may talk to Mrs. Burke at any time and she will vouch for me. Now, ma'am, may I come in?"

"All right," she said. "I guess there is no harm to be done."

She directed Rafferty to a large rocking chair, while she took a seat at a table in the center of the room, where she had begun to pile up some of her brother's belongings.

"The police and some of the alliance's henchmen were here all day yesterday," she said, surveying the devastated room. "They were perfect brutes, of course."

"I'm sorry to hear that, but I can't say I'm surprised," Rafferty said. "By the way, may I ask where Mrs. O'Donnell is? This terrible turn of events must be as hard on her as it is on you."

"She left last night. Packed her bags and went out the door. Said she would come back to clean up when she could, but I wouldn't count on it."

"If you'll pardon me for sayin' it, Miss O'Donnell, you don't seem very sympathetic toward the grievin' widow."

"Sympathy is an overrated virtue, Mr. Rafferty. It is of no help to the dead and of very little use to the living, in my estimation. What is wanted in this world is action. Warm sentiments are no match for the guns and clubs of oppressors."

"Ah, so I imagine you have shed no tears for your murdered brother, then," Rafferty remarked. "After all, they would not be useful, would they?"

"No," she said slowly, suddenly blinking her eyes, "no, they would not." Then after a pause, she changed the subject: "You were inquiring about Jacqueline. I will tell you honestly that she and I were not on the best of terms. Beyond that I will let you draw your own conclusions. As to where she is now, my guess is that she has taken refuge with the nuns."

"The nuns?"

"At Immaculate Conception Convent. Jacqueline has no family here, but she is a devout Catholic. There's a nun at Immaculate Conception — Sister Perpetua is her name, I believe — with whom she's very close. They are probably praying as we speak, for all the good it will do."

"Thank you," said Rafferty. "I will pay the widow a call."

"Do that. Now, sir, if you are who you claim to be, tell me how I can be of help to you. As you can see, there is little to be done here. The police have all but destroyed the house."

"Do you know what they might have been looking for?" Rafferty asked.

"No, but I can only presume they wanted to make sure there was no evidence here which might undermine their cover-up of the truth. Even before I learned of the placard left on Michael's body, I knew in my heart that he had been killed for his beliefs."

"I would like to ask you about those beliefs, Miss O'Donnell, but first I'm curious as to how you found out about the placard, which is not a matter generally known to the public."

"I am afraid I cannot tell you that."

"May I ask why?"

"You may ask, but you will receive no answer."

"All right," Rafferty said with a sigh, "I can see when I'm buttin' into a wall. Tell me, then, about your brother's beliefs and why you think they got him killed."

"Michael was a union man," she said in a manner suggesting this was as great an honor as being declared a saint by the Vatican. "He fought for the oppressed masses. He was not the first to pay with his life in this great struggle, and he will not be the last."

"I see. And what exactly did Michael do as a union man?" Rafferty asked.

"He was most recently working to organize the flour packers and nailers at the Wellington Mills. Those poor men do terribly hard work for ten hours a day, six days a week, and yet they are lucky to earn sixty dollar a month for their labor. As you may remember, some of the packers and nailers tried to organize in 1894 and even went out on strike briefly. But times were hard and they were crushed by the millers, who since then have done everything in their power to destroy the union movement. The alliance has been their chief tool of oppression in this regard. I know for a fact that men have been threatened—and even beaten—for daring to speak up on behalf of the laboring class."[4]

Rafferty did not doubt what he had just heard—employers and their workers had been in violent conflict all through the 1890s—but he also knew that the partisan rhetoric on both sides could be extreme. He asked, "Was Michael himself threatened by the alliance or anyone else?"

"Many times, I'm sure," Addie O'Donnell said, "though Michael did not like to talk about such things, as he feared I might become unduly worried. But there can be no doubt that his work on behalf of the cause was dangerous and required much discretion. To this day, mere mention of the word 'union' will get a man fired in the packing room at the Wellington Mills, or any other in Minneapolis for that matter."

"You seem unusually well informed on labor matters, Miss O'Donnell."

"I believe in the cause of the working man and woman, Mr. Rafferty, and I make it a point to know as much about the union movement as I can. There is also the fact that, until yesterday, I myself worked in the office of the Wellington Mills as a typist. Before that I worked at the North Star Woolen Mill, which is close by. I am therefore well informed as to how the businesses of this city treat their workers."

"Ah, I see. And you quit because of what happened to your brother?"

"That—and other reasons. I had no desire to spend the rest of my days typing invoices to further the profits of a class of men who are already obscenely rich. I have plans for my life, Mr. Rafferty."

"What sort, if I may ask?"

"Let us just say, sir, that I plan to raise a ruckus, and this city will never be the same afterward."

She delivered this promise—or was it a threat?—with the passionate serenity of a true believer. Rafferty asked, "Am I safe in assumin', Miss O'Donnell, that like your brother you are a union organizer?"

"Let us just say that I am in the fight and that I do what I can," she replied. "I am not at liberty to discuss specifics, as I'm sure you understand."

"'Tis a hard fight, I imagine, what with the alliance and so many other forces opposin' you," Rafferty noted.

"Easy jobs do not interest me," she said.

"Somehow I'm not surprised to hear that, ma'am. Speakin' of jobs, how long did you work in the mills?"

"About five months. I have only been in Minneapolis since April, when I came up from Chicago."

"I see. I presume your brother invited you to join him here."

"Actually, I met Michael here quite by accident. He'd left home when he was eighteen, and I had not see him for years until I stumbled into him at a protest meeting in July outside the Shevlin-Carpenter Sawmill. It was one of the happiest days of my life, and also one of the most surprising."

"In what way?"

"Before that meeting I had never known Michael to be interested in the cause of labor. Even now I cannot be sure what brought about his change of heart, but I will always be proud of him for doing what he did, even if it cost him his life."

"So you are certain he was killed because of his union activities?"

"Absolutely."

"And yet he'd worked on behalf of the laborin' man for only a few months before he was murdered. What do you suppose he might have done in so short a time to make him a target of the alliance?"

"I do not know."

"You mean you don't know, or you won't say?"

She stared hard at Rafferty and said, "I am in the habit, sir, of saying what I mean and meaning what I say. You have heard my answer."

"So I have," said Rafferty. "Still, it is one thing to say that your brother was murdered by the Secret Alliance and quite another to prove it. May I ask what proof you have to offer, other than the placard, which — as you surely must be aware — could have been planted by anybody?"

"I offer the proof of the world," she replied, making a sweeping gesture with her arms. "Look around you, Mr. Rafferty. The rich and the poor of this country are at war, and in wars people are killed. That is what happened to Michael. I need no other proof."

"'Tis well and good for you to say that, ma'am, but a court of law is bound to view the matter differently, as do I. Proof of the most substantial and convincin' sort will be needed if those who murdered your brother are to pay for their crime. That's why I'd like to talk with some of Michael's union friends. They might be able to tell me if your brother had any run-ins with the alliance while he was about his union business. If you could give me a few names—"

Addie O'Donnell shook her head and told Rafferty, "No, I cannot do that. I have only your word, sir, that you are who you claim to be. There are informants everywhere these days. The alliance sees to that. Therefore, I shall have to keep any such names to myself for the moment."

"I can't help you, ma'am, if you're not willin' to help me," Rafferty said.

"And I cannot trust you, sir, until you have earned my trust."

"Very well then, I guess we must declare an impasse," Rafferty said, wondering if he should ask her about the incriminating photograph of Randolph Hadley. If her brother was a blackmailer, he could well have been working at the behest of one of the unions Miss O'Donnell so ardently defended. For that matter, she herself could be part of the tawdry business. Rafferty decided to keep the photograph to himself until he had a better grip on the situation.

He said, "I have but one more question, ma'am. When did you last see your brother and how did he appear at the time?"

"I believe it was a week ago, right here. We talked about his progress at the mill and other things. He seemed his usual self in every way. I had no sense that anything was wrong. Now, is there any other way I can be of help to you?"

Rafferty took a last look at the disheveled room, which he calculated would take hours to search thoroughly, and even then he doubted he would find anything the police had missed. Turning back to Miss O'Donnell, he said, "I have found you, ma'am, and that is certainly more than I hoped for."

For the first time, she offered a smile that suggested some measure of warmth and said, "You are a man of the charming sort, I see. Such men are common in this world, but I do not find them very useful."

"And just what is it you find 'useful' in a man?" Rafferty asked, adding, "I know it isn't sympathy, or tears."

She looked at him with her hard, steady eyes and said, "I want a man who is fearless in the face of danger, who will not bow down before the wealthy and powerful. More than anything else I want a man who thirsts for justice, Mr. Rafferty, and who will not stop until he has found it. That is my idea of a useful man. Are you by chance such a man?"

"Yes," said Shadwell Rafferty without hesitation, "I am."

S̸R

James McParland, one of the most famous Pinkerton men in America, also thought of himself as an agent of justice, though not of the sort Addie O'Donnell had in mind. To McParland's way of thinking, justice was not some vague, noble ideal. No, justice was law and order — nothing more and nothing less — and he had spent a lucrative lifetime working to ensure that justice was delivered on behalf of the men who paid for it.[5]

But as he sped north that morning by train toward Minneapolis, McParland was worried that law and order might soon give way to chaos unless something could be done to quell the uproar sure to build around Michael O'Donnell's death. It was, he knew, a rum business all the way around, a situation so complex and volatile that it would test even his legendary cunning. Indeed, O'Donnell's death had already produced "unexpected complications," as Mayor Arthur Adams had so delicately phrased it, and now McParland was needed in Minneapolis for an "urgent consultation."

McParland had been at the Palmer House in Chicago, enjoying the company of an attractive young woman to whom he was not married, when the mayor rang him up at six in the morning, just hours after the discovery of O'Donnell's body. Adams had sounded calm, even insouciant, though it was clear by a certain faint stammer in his voice that he was deeply concerned about the events unfolding in Minneapolis. The mayor wanted to meet, the sooner the better. McParland knew there was no talking Arthur Adams out of anything, and so he had made arrangements to come up to Minneapolis the next day.[6]

As always, he made the trip in style, for whenever McParland traveled outside of Chicago he always had a private railcar at his disposal, courtesy of the Pullman Palace Car Company. No one seemed to know exactly why McParland, alone among all the operatives of the Pinkerton National Detective Agency, merited such lavish treatment, though there were rumors he had performed some especially valuable service for the car company's founder, George Pullman, during the regrettable labor unrest of 1894. As Pullman himself was dead — sent to his grave, some thought, by the violent strike that had torn apart his supposedly ideal company town near Chicago — the exact nature of McParland's service remained unknown. Even so, certain prying newspaper reporters, always an ill-mannered and suspicious breed, believed the favor had been of a personal nature and had saved the reclusive Pullman from some great public humiliation.[7]

Like the Buddha that he was, McParland never deigned to comment on the circumstances that had brought about his good fortune when it came to rail travel, and he always enjoyed the ride. Yet even his luxurious accommodations had failed to put McParland in a good frame of mind. Instead, he found himself hopelessly preoccupied with the "Minneapolis problem," as it was politely known in the agency.

McParland had been roped into the affair by an accident of geography. He managed operations for the Pinkertons west of the Mississippi. Minneapolis, or at least most of it, was west of the river. Therefore, when the problem reared its ugly head, Robert Pinkerton himself had assigned McParland the unenviable task of making it go away.[8]

He had already been in Minneapolis earlier to meet the mayor and Randolph Hadley. Arthur Adams was as slippery a snake as McParland had ever run across, though the mayor was refreshingly candid about his devotion to large-scale dishonesty. Hadley, on the other hand, seemed to care little for politics but clearly enjoyed his rough work as an enforcer for the city's propertied interests. Both men were used to having their own way and had little patience.

Now they were breathing down McParland's neck, demanding an instant fix to a problem that grew uglier and more menacing by the moment. Worst of all, it was a problem that could easily spread like a contagion, destroying everyone it touched, including McParland himself. Unfortunately, McParland knew there was no quick fix, especially in light of Michael O'Donnell's death.

Still, McParland thought that, with a little luck, there might be a way clear of the whole mess. It would require all of his considerable skills to pull it off, for he would have to screw down the lid on Michael O'Donnell's death so tightly that there was no possibility for even the faintest breath of truth to escape. The mayor and Hadley had already set the cover-up in motion, but McParland knew it wouldn't be complete until he could find and destroy the incriminating photographs. McParland also knew just how difficult his task would be. One nosy person—a cop, a newspaper reporter, a private detective—could destroy his plans in an instant and set off an unstoppable avalanche of scandal. McParland would do everything in his power to keep that from happening.

ꝏ

After leaving Addie O'Donnell, Rafferty decided to look at the scene of her brother's murder—only three blocks from Hell's Half Acre. As Rafferty strolled toward Tenth Street, he found it hard to get Addie

O'Donnell out of his mind. She had certainly made quite an impression, burning with the sort of white-hot idealism that only the young can manage gracefully. That alone made her worthy of Rafferty's regard, for he had been the same way once, eager to turn the bitter seed of the world into fresh, bright fruit. It couldn't be done, of course, but there was poetry in the attempt, and Rafferty liked that as well as her passion for justice—the most necessary and elusive of human ideals.

It was an ideal, as Rafferty had made clear to her, that he shared. Yet he had also found her very intensity—the liquid fire in her eye—made him uncomfortable. Rafferty instinctively distrusted zealots of any kind, from religious revivalists to municipal reformers to Bryan's free-silver fanatics. He reserved his deepest abhorrence for the temperance movement, whose supporters he viewed as noxious enemies of humanity, especially that portion of which who owned saloons. In Addie O'Donnell's case, it was too early to tell if she was a true believer of the dangerous sort. But Rafferty wanted to find out more about her—and about the union activities to which she and her late brother were so devoted—because it was already clear to him that a great passion of some kind lay behind Michael O'Donnell's murder.

Rafferty based this conclusion on the manner in which the young man had been killed. He had not merely been murdered, which could have been efficiently accomplished in any number of straightforward ways. Instead, O'Donnell had been humiliated in death—brutally beaten, hung, and then left naked to the world. Only a murderer driven by seething rage could commit such a crime. Yet blind rage was not all that motivated the killer, for O'Donnell's carefully staged death was also clearly intended as a public statement, much as the English used to hang the severed heads of highwaymen from posts as a warning to would-be robbers. The fact that the newspapers had been anonymously notified of the murder served to confirm that O'Donnell's death was indeed meant to serve as a moral of some kind, however twisted.

When Rafferty reached the old Adams House, he found it to be a gloomy and rotting pile afflicted with that peculiar sense of loss that lingers around the abandoned haunts of the rich. And in Minneapolis, where a decade ago was ancient history, the house seemed especially pathetic. It was what the city had left behind on its way to somewhere else, like an old piece of luggage tossed away on the side of the road.

A goodly number of curiosity seekers were gathered around the house, drawn by the irresistible prospect of contemplating someone else's misfortune. Rafferty joined the crowd, peering through the tall iron gate at the front porch, where a copper stood guard in case anyone tried to jump the fence in search of a grisly souvenir.

"Quite something, isn't it, isn't it?" said a small, bent man who had sidled up beside Rafferty. "Death and destruction, sin and suffering, it is all here, don't you think, sir, don't you think?"

"'Tis one way of lookin' at it," Rafferty agreed, struck by the man's glittering ferret eyes, long beard, and peculiar way of speaking.

"One piece of advice, sir, if you please," the man said, staring up at Rafferty. "Watch for rats. They will eat the flesh of the living and dead, the living and the dead. Rats, sir, you must always look out for them. Always!"

"I thank you for that sound counsel," Rafferty said as the strange little man scurried away, apparently intent on issuing his rodent alert to others nearby.

Rafferty realized at once who the man must have been. Sid the Ratman was a legendary figure in Minneapolis. King of the city's considerable population of impoverished flaneurs, the Ratman was known not only for his aversion to rodents but for his entertaining, impromptu sidewalk speeches that often drew large and enthusiastic crowds. But until this moment Rafferty had never encountered the Ratman in person.[9]

Rafferty now turned his attention once again to the house. He very much wanted to get inside because he suspected Michael O'Donnell had been beaten to death there before being strung up out in the yard. If so, Rafferty hoped he might find some useful evidence, assuming the police hadn't already torn the place to shreds. Rafferty lit a cigar and made a leisurely tour around the edge of the grounds. At the back of the house, sheltered by a row of whispering poplars, he saw a storm door that looked as though it would offer the easiest way to enter the house without being spotted. Come one night soon, guard or no guard, Rafferty planned to have a go at that door.

CHAPTER FOUR

ᴥ

"God Cuts Many Paths"

FROM THE JOURNALS OF DR. JOHN WATSON:

FRI., SEPT. 29, 1899, WALDORF-ASTORIA HOTEL, N.Y., 5 P.M.:
... Watched naval parade in Dewey's honor this A.M. & effect
was splendid, tho crowds at Battery so huge had difficulty seeing as
ships steamed thru harbor & up Hudson toward Grant's Tomb. H,
however, in foul mood & stayed behind at hotel, saying he found little
to admire in "pointless display of patriotism." Too bad, for he missed
truly magnificent display of might of this new continent. . . .[1]

After returning to the hotel, found letter from C[lifton] Wooldridge, of Chicago Police Dept. First met him in 1896 while investigating matter for P[otter] Palmer in Chicago. Wool[dridge] took us
on memorable tour of Levee & Holmes's other house of horror. Still
shudder to think of that gruesome scene. . . .[2]

Wondered how Wool knew we were in N.Y., but could only assume he had been in contact with our acquaintance, [Wilson] Hargreave, of N.Y. police. Had visited with Hargreave shortly after our
arrival to thank him personally for his help in strange case of "Dancing Men" a year ago.[3]

Tho we are fully occupied here, Wool invited us to Chicago,
where he is, according to letter, "hot on the trail of the last of the
Lauer gang." These German-born anarchists who last year tried to
dynamite Chicago's old water tower. The Lauers—Adolph & son,

Willy, as I recall — were executed following trial that received much press coverage, in England as well as America. At least one other conspirator (a woman!) thought to have escaped, possibly with man, tho identities never firmly established, Wool reported. Now says he has leads re escaped criminals but as yet unable to track them down. Wool concluded, "Any help from Sherlock Holmes would be deeply appreciated."[4]

H pronounced letter "of some interest" but instructed me to decline Wool's request for assistance.

H: "I have great regard for the Chicago detective, but my regard for Mr. Rafferty is even greater, & his is the only other case I shall concern myself with at the moment."

Speaking of which, no additional news from SR today, tho expect we will hear from him shortly. . . .

✍

Satisfied that he had seen everything he needed to at the Adams house, Rafferty walked back to Nicollet Avenue, where he turned north toward the heart of downtown. The city's department stores — E. E. Atkinson's, Donaldson's, S. E. Olson's — formed a grand row on Nicollet between Seventh and Fifth Streets, and the sidewalks were dense with crowds of high-hatted women hunting for bargains. Policemen directed traffic at every intersection, struggling to maintain order amid the roaring tide of carriages, drays, wagons, and other vehicles that washed over the street.[5]

As he watched one of the coppers at work, Rafferty was reminded of his own days wearing a badge — he had spent five years as a patrolman and, briefly, a detective in St. Paul. As a result, he knew the police force there inside and out and had plenty of sources he could tap for information. Minneapolis was a different story. Rafferty had no contacts of note in the Minneapolis department, which in turn meant he had no back channels where he could comfortably troll for information. This was a significant handicap, since the Minneapolis coppers had already lied about a key piece of evidence in the case and presumably would keep on prevaricating if it suited their purpose. More than ever, Rafferty thought, he would have to rely on his friends in the Fourth Estate if he hoped to learn what the police really knew, as opposed to what they were telling the public.

Rafferty continued down Nicollet to Third, then turned west toward the Church of the Immaculate Conception, where he hoped to talk with Michael O'Donnell's widow. The church, he soon discovered, was a precarious house of God wedged amid massive temples to Mammon. It had been built in the early 1870s, its stone spire towering over what was then a modest residential neighborhood. But in the 1880s, as the city exploded with growth, huge brick warehouses—each one seemingly bigger than the next—began to creep toward the church like an army of infidels. By the turn of the century, the once impressive church looked old and shrunken, overwhelmed by its brawny mercantile competition. Even so, the parish, which supported a well-attended school next to the church, continued to hang on, though there was already talk of relocating to a more suitable part of the city.[6]

When Rafferty reached the church, he spotted a small brick building around the corner that had the unmistakably prim look of a convent. A small plaque mounted next to the front door confirmed his guess. Rafferty rang the bell. An elderly nun dressed head to toe in black, except for a starched white wimple, answered the door.

"Yes, what is it?" she asked, giving Rafferty the look he remembered all too well from his days as a schoolboy in Boston. It was an expression that said, "I know you're up to something, young man, and there is not a chance you will get away with it."

Rafferty removed his hat and said, "Good afternoon, Sister. My name is Shadwell Rafferty, and I wish to speak at once with Mrs. Jacqueline O'Donnell on a matter of the greatest urgency."

"She is not receiving visitors at the moment," the nun replied, "but if you would care to leave your card, I will let her know you called."

"I think she'll want to see me today," said Rafferty, removing a business card from his wallet and scribbling a few words on the back. "Would you give this to her at once?" Normally, Rafferty would have followed such a request with a small gratuity, but he didn't know how to bribe a woman of God, so all he could offer the old nun was his most winning smile.

The nun looked at the card and said, "Wait here." Then she closed the door.

She was back shortly. "Come in. Mrs. O'Donnell will see you now."

The nun led Rafferty down a narrow hall and into a small parlor furnished with a settee, a couple of upholstered arm chairs, and a small table. Religious paintings—a glowing Jesus, Gabriel and the Virgin Mary at the Annunciation, a print of Millet's ever popular *Angelus*—adorned the walls along with a large silver crucifix. The room also had that distinctive musty odor, a mix of dust and holy water, perhaps, that Rafferty always associated with the inner sanctums of the Catholic Church.

When Jacqueline O'Donnell appeared, Rafferty could not help but notice that she was a most striking woman, though her beauty was not of the voluptuary kind. Instead, she conveyed a sense of the ethereal. She was slender and very small, hardly over five feet, with doelike brown eyes, china-white skin, delicate features, and curly light brown hair, cut very short. And even though she was dressed in a black mourning outfit that made her resemble one of the nuns, she had a glow to her that Rafferty had seldom seen among the good sisters. Rafferty guessed her age at twenty-five, though it was hard to tell in view of her youthful features. She might have been ten years older for all he could tell.

As she entered the room, she looked at Rafferty with a gaze that seemed to peel away all pretense. It was the sort of look, Rafferty imagined, that St. Peter directed at aspirants to heaven, and it suggested that no matter how pure you might be, you would never be pure enough to join the kingdom of the Lord.

"Good afternoon, ma'am," said Rafferty as she sat down on the settee and adjusted her skirt. "I hope I'm not inconveniencin' you in any way."

"No, not at all, though you have the advantage over me, sir, since you know me, but I do not know you. However, if you have any information about what happened to Michael, I am anxious to hear it. Have you truly identified his murderer?"

What Rafferty had scrawled on his business card was: "I know who murdered your husband." This wasn't entirely true, of course, but Rafferty had feared that Jacqueline O'Donnell would not agree to see him unless he somehow commanded her attention.

He now introduced himself, offered the usual condolences, explained how he had been engaged by Majesty Burke, and then said, "I cannot name the man who murdered your husband, Mrs. O'Donnell, but I believe I know the elements who were behind the crime. As I'm sure you're aware, there's evidence to suggest that your husband was murdered on account of his union activities, quite possibly by individuals connected with the Secret Alliance."

"Yes, I am aware of that," she said. "Addie told me what was left on his body. I never wanted Michael to become involved with the unions, but he would not listen, and there was always Addie to egg him on. If only I had put my foot down, as a good wife should, he would still be alive today, I am sure."

"You must not blame yourself," Rafferty said. "There is nothing you could have done to stop what happened."

"It is kind of you to say that," she said, using a handkerchief to daub a tear from her eye. "I so wish he were here with me now, but I am confident that God, into whose just and glorious hands Michael has now been delivered, will see fit to right the wrongs that have been done."

"I'm sure He will," said Rafferty, who in fact was sure of no such thing. "Now, would you mind if I asked a few questions?"

"Not in the least. I wish to see justice done."

"As do I," Rafferty assured her. "I'm particularly interested in Michael's activities at the Wellington Mills. Do you know when your husband became so passionate about union causes?"

"I'm afraid I don't understand what you mean. Michael has been passionate in that way as long as I have known him."

"I see. And when did the two of you meet, if I may ask?"

"It was in July, at a picnic. We were married two weeks later by a judge."

"'Twas quite a whirlwind courtship," Rafferty observed.

She blushed slightly. "Yes, he stole my heart. It truly was love at first sight. I never believed in such a thing until it happened to me."

"Ah, I know exactly what you mean," said Rafferty, thinking back to the first time he had seen Mary Rutherford, the woman he was to marry, on a wintry day long ago in St. Paul. With great effort, he banished the thought and moved on. "Did Michael ever talk to you about how he came upon his particular views? I've been led to believe that he had a sudden conversion to unionism not long before he met you."

"No, he did not talk about that, I'm afraid. The truth is, I do not know much about Michael's life before we met. I was so happy with our present that I had no interest in the past. It was foolish of me, I suppose, but don't they say love will do that to a person? Make them foolish, I mean."

"They do," Rafferty replied with a smile. "Now, can you tell me what Michael did in the week or so before he died? Did anything at all unusual happen at his job or with his union activities, for instance?"

"There was one thing," she said after a moment's thought. "On Monday—or perhaps it was Tuesday—Michael received a letter in the mail. He opened it after supper and I remember a cloud seemed to pass across his face. I asked what was wrong and he said it was nothing, just a threatening letter from an old creditor. He said I should not worry about it."

"Did he show you the letter?"

"No. He crumpled it up and threw it in the fire. But I could see he was upset, so I asked him about it again. And now that I think about it, I can recall exactly what he said, because it seemed rather odd. He said: 'I will give them a taste of their own medicine if they try anything. They do not frighten me.'"

"Did he indicate who 'they' were?"

"No. Michael was like most men in that he did not readily share his heart, even with me. I wonder now if the letter might have been a threat of some kind from the alliance."

"Well, I guess we will never know for sure. Did he receive any other threats that you're aware of?"

"I'm afraid not. If he did, he must have hidden them from me."

Rafferty said, "I know it must be painful for you, but can you tell me about the day he died? When did you last see him?"

"In the morning, before we went to work."

"Ah, so you work outside the house, is that right?"

"Yes, at the North Star Woolen Mill, which is only a block from the Wellington Mills, where Michael was working when he . . . well, when it happened. Of course, I was not really supposed to be working at the woolen mill once we were married—the owners prefer single girls—but we needed the money and Michael thought it would be all right until we had a family. He very much wanted a son and we—"[7]

She suddenly stopped and began to sob. When she had composed herself, Rafferty said, "You told me you last saw Michael in the morning. He did not come home that night after work, I take it. Were you worried when he didn't show up as usual?"

"Oh no. Michael had told me in the morning he would be very late and that I shouldn't wait up for him. He said he had to meet with a couple of fellows after work on important business."

"Do you know who these fellows were?"

"Michael didn't say. I really didn't know his union friends, if that is what you would call them. I didn't even like Michael to discuss union matters in the house. You see, I wanted our home to be quiet and peaceful. Was I wrong, Mr. Rafferty, in wanting that?"

"No, you weren't wrong," Rafferty said gently. "Now, let me ask you this. When Michael told you not to wait up for him, did you follow that advice?"

Mrs. O'Donnell smiled. "A woman must always wait for her man," she said. "But I was very tired myself that night and I must have fallen asleep about midnight. The next thing I remember is the police knocking at my door and telling me the terrible news."

"I see. And did the police at that time mention any suspicions that your husband had somehow been involved with molesting a young girl?"

For the first time, anger broke through Jacqueline O'Donnell's mournful presence. "That is the most ridiculous thing I have ever heard," she said. "I will never forgive the police for spreading such a vicious lie. I cannot believe they could be so cruel."

"You're right, ma'am. 'Twas a terrible thing to do. By the way, do you know if Michael was acquainted at all with Randolph Hadley, who heads the Secret Alliance?"

"Not that I know of."

"And are you aware of any specific disagreement he might have had with Hadley or anyone else in the alliance?"

"No, but I am certain he was hated for his union views."

"I'm sure he was," Rafferty agreed as he rose to his feet. "Well then, I will trouble you no more. 'Twas a privilege to meet you, ma'am. I promise you I will do everything in my power to bring your husband's murderers to justice."

"I pray you will be successful, sir, and I also pray you will keep me informed of your work. I am sure God has sent you to me for a reason."

"I wouldn't go that far, ma'am," Rafferty said, donning his hat. "I have been accused of many things but never of being an agent of the Lord."

"But that is a thing you can never know," she said, her eyes locking onto Rafferty. "God cuts many paths through the thickets of the world and sometimes we can follow one unawares, until we arrive quite suddenly at wisdom and peace, don't you think?"

"Perhaps," Rafferty acknowledged with a smile, "though I'm inclined to think the best paths are the ones we make ourselves. In any case, I'll let you know what I find out about your husband's death. And if you remember anything else about his last days, please get in touch. I'm an easy man to find."

"I will do that."

"Oh, before I forget, there is one more thing. Did Michael by chance happen to own a camera of any kind?"

"Why, yes."

"Can you tell me what kind?"

"I'm sorry, but I don't really know. It was just a plain camera. I can show it to you if you wish."

"That would be helpful."

She got up and led Rafferty down the hall to the small room where she was staying. Its furnishings were sparse — a rocking chair and bed, a wardrobe, a small bookcase with a pair of blackened stone bookends, and a few family portraits hanging on the wall.

"I have not had the heart to take most of the furnishings from our —" she began as she opened the wardrobe. She paused to fight back tears before resuming, "I was going to say, 'from our house,' but now it is no one's house as far as I am concerned. And the horrible police have made a mess of it anyway."

"So I have seen," Rafferty said gently. "I stopped by the house earlier and met your sister-in-law."

"Did you?" she said, bending down to look for the camera in the bottom of the wardrobe. "Isn't Addie wonderful? She is very strong. I wish I could be more that way. Ah, here it is." She pulled out a Kodak box camera, stood up, and handed it to Rafferty. "Is this what you're looking for?"[8]

"I'm afraid not," said Rafferty, inspecting the camera. The photograph of Hadley, he knew, could not have been taken with such a small, unsophisticated camera. He returned the Kodak to her and said, "Gettin' back to the police for a minute, did they ever say what they were lookin' for at your house?"

"No."

"So they never mentioned a camera, photographs, negatives, or anything like that?"

"I don't believe so. Is there a reason why you ask?"

"Simple curiosity," said Rafferty. "Speakin' of which, may I ask what you intend to do now, ma'am?"

"I guess I'll stay here in the city for a while. But once I've saved up enough money, I intend to leave Minneapolis. I do not like this city anymore, Mr. Rafferty. There are no good memories for me here."

"I can understand that. Well, I wish you Godspeed, ma'am. I know what it's like to lose a loved one. All I can tell you is that time will make the wound more bearable."

"But it will never heal completely, will it?"

"No," Rafferty said, bending over and kissing her hand. "I fear not."

Shadwell Rafferty's saloon was unique among the drinking establishments of St. Paul by virtue of its diverse clientele. Although the lunch crowd tended to be from the working classes, at night a visitor to the saloon might find a ditch digger at one end of the bar and a judge, or perhaps a doctor, at the other — all drawn by Thomas's excellent food as well as Raf-

ferty's magnetic personality and magnificent stock of stories, which ranged
in height from modest to exceedingly tall. Even James J. Hill himself had
been known to stop in on occasion to chat with Rafferty, who was "all
around the best talker in St. Paul," as one city guidebook described him.

Rafferty also ran a notably "clean" place, and it was known far and
wide that he would consent to having his heart plucked beating from his
chest before he would stoop to the unforgivable sin of watering a drink.
Equally important was his unquestioned ability to enforce the long-
standing rules of the house — no loud cussing, no gambling, no drunken-
ness, and above all else, no fighting.

"'Tis a civilized bar I run here," Rafferty would tell any customer who
became obstreperous, "and if it's some civilizin' you're in need of, I'm
just the man to do it." But few men were brave, or foolish, enough to
challenge Rafferty, who enjoyed a reputation, fully earned, as the one
man in St. Paul you did not wish, under any circumstances, to enrage.

On Friday night, after his return from Minneapolis, Rafferty was at
his usual station behind the bar, dispensing liquor and opinions with
equal facility, when he saw a familiar face come through the door.

"Ah, the apostate returns," he said in a booming voice as Joseph Pyle
made his way through the saloon. "'Tis good to see you again, Joseph.
I'm hopin' you have some news for me."

"Indeed I do," said Pyle, climbing aboard one of the bar's high stools.

"Ah, I take it your enterprisin' fellow Mr. Griggs has come across
something," said Rafferty as he poured a shot of good Tennessee whisky
for the newspaper editor.

Pyle downed the shot in one gulp and said, "You're right, though part
of what Griggs has learned falls in the category of incomplete information, which is not the kind I like to have. You see, Griggs has found out
from a source that the cops over in Minneapolis are apparently sitting
on another clue found at the scene of O'Donnell's death."

"What sort of clue?"

"That's just it. Grigg's source won't say. It's all very hush-hush over
there. Nobody's talking to the press, but I've got Griggs and another fellow
digging as hard as they can. Something's bound to break soon enough."

Rafferty nodded and said, "Well, let's hope they dig up some treasure.
Now, what else has Mr. Griggs unearthed?"

"Well, he did manage to find out quite a bit more about the cartman
who discovered the body. His name is Joe Shelton. He's apparently
pretty well known in Minneapolis. Won a big lawsuit a few years back
over something or other. He's been a night soil collector for years."

"Never heard of him," said Rafferty, pouring Pyle another drink, "but I intend to make his acquaintance soon."

At one o'clock the next morning, just as Rafferty was closing his saloon for the night, Joe Shelton was on his way to the Mississippi River with a load of waste collected from a dozen privy vaults in south Minneapolis. He was not feeling especially good, for his hopes of realizing some profit from Michael O'Donnell's death had been dashed on all fronts. The *Globe* had stolen his thunder by reporting on the placard found around the dead man's neck. Worse yet, the man Shelton had seen walking away from the Adams house had flatly denied being in the area the night of the murder. As a consequence, he had refused even to consider the idea of paying hush money, despite Shelton's threat of going to the police. Shelton now had to decide if he should carry out his threat, since he wasn't sure what sort of reaction he would receive from the coppers.

He mulled over the possibilities as he approached the wide set of railroad tracks that paralleled the river along Second Street South, not far from the flour-milling district. Shelton kept a sharp eye out for trains. Goldie, his horse, was skittish around them, and he had to maintain a strong grip on the reins so she wouldn't get too excited. Shelton was almost at the tracks when he saw a man coming out of an alley by an old brick building that was home to a notorious tippling house. The man was weaving and bobbing, and as he approached Shelton, he said in a slurred voice, "Hey fella, how about a ride, what'd you say?"

This was rich, Shelton thought. The man wanted to ride on a cart plumb full of human excrement.

"Sure," Shelton said, waiting for the inevitable reaction when the man got closer. "You just come on up."

Surprisingly, the man, who wore a long dark raincoat and had a broad face pocked with old acne scars, seemed indifferent to the odor. He climbed up next to Shelton and said, "Thanks, buddy, I couldn't have walked another foot. A little too much to drink, you know. Uh-oh, is that a train over there?" The man looked suddenly to his right.

Shelton turned as well, and he never saw the heavy metal pipe that cracked the back of his skull. Nor did he have a chance to hear, a mile uptown on Tenth Street, the tremendous explosion that blew apart the old Adams house and awoke half the city.

CHAPTER FIVE

"Spite, You See,
Can Be a Form of Idealism"

FROM THE JOURNALS OF DR. JOHN WATSON:

S AT., SEPT. 30, 1899, WALDORF-ASTORIA HOTEL, N.Y., 4:30 P.M.:
H uncommonly restless & went out for long walk in A.M. despite huge crowds gathering for Dewey's "land parade," as newspapers called it, at Madison Square, not far from our hotel. Crowds too much for me & I stayed in lobby, reading newspapers until H returned. . . .[1]

Astor matter weighing him down more than ever, as more complications became apparent today. . . . H reluctant to talk about problems except to describe Astor as "a perfect ass." Forced to agree. Man proving insufferable & I do not know how long it will be before everything blows up.

Had hoped SR's letter might arrive today, as news from our friend would cheer up H. But no doubt unrealistic to expect a letter to reach here from St. Paul in just two days.

Rafferty first read about the explosion in the early Saturday edition of the *St. Paul Dispatch,* which said the blast was "so powerful that it shattered windows six blocks away." As for the Adams house, it was described as "little more than scattered debris, with perhaps enough wood left as kindling to make a decent bonfire." The article, which Rafferty pored over as he enjoyed a cup of coffee with Wash Thomas in the saloon before opening time, went on to report that "investigators have already discovered evidence that old gas valves in the basement of the long-vacant house were forced open, after which a fire was set some distance away. This act of arson triggered the devastating explosion which tore the house apart." The *Dispatch*'s correspondent concluded by noting that "there is much speculation that the fire and explosion must somehow be related to the bizarre murder recently committed at the house."

Now there's a dazzling deduction, Rafferty thought as he went back over the story, which included comments from Mayor Arthur Adams — "a very sad day for our family"—and even a statement from Charles Wellington. The flour-milling magnate, who had built the house almost thirty years earlier and who was still going strong at age seventy-five, did not seem overwhelmed by sentiment. "The house meant nothing to me," he told the *Dispatch*. "I am only happy that no one was injured by this act of madness."

Rafferty was disturbed by the house's destruction because of the sheer excess of the act. Even if the intention had merely been to destroy evidence, which Rafferty doubted, there would have been no need to open the gas valves, since a simple fire would have done the job nicely. As Rafferty saw it, the chilling hatred that seemed to be behind the murder of Michael O'Donnell was also evident in this latest crime.

Unfortunately, it was far less evident who might be behind this latest crime. One possibility, of course, was that the fire and explosion were part of a continuing cover-up, an effort to link the murder to wild-eyed labor agitators—the universal bogeyman of the moment. Explosions were especially associated in the public mind with anarchists, assassins, and other revolutionaries. But would the alliance and its friends at city hall actually go so far as to blow up the old family home of the mayor? Rafferty had his doubts.

"Well, Shad, how do you account for this latest business?" Thomas asked after Rafferty put down the newspaper. "I am thinking somebody has an awful grudge."

"You're right, Wash. This is all very personal in some nasty way. Trouble is, I'm long on possibilities and short on facts at the moment. I'm nibblin' on peas when what I really need is some good red meat."

Thomas nodded and said, "Seems to me you've got one piece of meat already—that photograph of Randolph Hadley. Maybe you ought to start grinding at it to see if you can draw out any blood."

It was, Rafferty had to admit, sound advice, but then he had always found Wash Thomas to be a man with a rare knack for getting to the heart of a matter. Thomas wasn't much of a talker, but he was a quiet, steady thinker, which meant that when he did speak, it always counted for something—as Rafferty knew better than anyone else.

George Washington Thomas had been with Rafferty for more than thirty years, since a chance meeting in Virginia City, Nevada, in the years after the Civil War, when silver flowed like sweet spring water from the great mines on Mount Davidson. As with many another veteran of the war, Rafferty had drifted west to seek his fortune but had found instead only dust, hard labor, and new opportunities for violent death in the mining country. But then, as he liked to say, he found the one good thing that Virginia City had to offer—Wash Thomas.[2]

Thomas's life, like Rafferty's, was a spectacular essay in survival. Born to slavery on a Virginia plantation in the 1840s, Thomas escaped to the North when he was sixteen and lived for a time with a kindly Pennsylvania Quaker family, who taught him to read and write. A few years later he satisfied his thirst for adventure by going to sea, and spent a brutal but undeniably adventurous year about a China clipper. He moved on to New York City, where he found work as a teamster and waiter. All the while he carefully saved his money, intent on going west when the opportunity arose.

Not believing northern whites were on the whole any better disposed toward blacks than those in the South, Thomas saw no reason to become involved in the great war supposedly being fought to free his race. Then, in July of 1863, he became caught in the middle of the New York draft riots, barely surviving a pitched battle with a marauding band of Irishmen at Crook's Restaurant on Chatham Street. Sometimes in his dreams he still saw the mob approaching, shouting, "Kill the niggers," their wide eyes mad with hate. Two days after five Union regiments fresh from Gettysburg finally subdued the rioters with rifle and bayonet, Thomas packed his belongings in a duffel bag and boarded a ship for California.[3]

He worked at odd jobs in San Francisco and then found his way to the Nevada mines, finally settling in Virginia City. It was a wide-open town, rough and unforgiving, but he found that while skin color still mattered, it didn't matter quite as much there as in other places. If a man could pull his fair share of the load, people would mostly leave him alone, and that was all Thomas asked.

Then, on a hot summer evening in 1868, a young teamster from one of the mining camps got dead drunk and thought it would be amusing to fire off his pistol as he rode out of town. One of the rounds, after passing through the wall of a house, ended up in the brain of a two-year-old boy asleep in his bed. This ugly and wasteful homicide so enraged the people of Virginia City that a lynch mob laid siege to the county jail shortly after the teamster, by then sober and terrified, was taken into custody.

It was at the jail that Thomas first met Rafferty, who had come to Virginia City some months earlier to work as a miner. Both were known in town for their strong antilynching sentiments and had therefore been called in by the sheriff to act as special deputies. They stood guard through the night until reinforcements arrived and the teamster was taken to a more secure jail in Carson City by a group of heavily armed lawmen.

As Rafferty would later tell the story, in versions that seemed to grow more filigreed by the year, he had on at least one occasion during that memorable night saved Thomas's life by coldcocking a member of the mob who was about to draw his pistol and use it to no good purpose. Thomas's standard response to this tale was a loud snort, which was his general way of indicating skepticism. Thomas himself was not much for telling stories, but he did once observe, "Shad was the first Irishman I met who did not seem interested in killing me, so I thought it would be wise to make his acquaintance."

The truth was, after a span of so many years, neither man could say exactly what had happened on that long-ago night at a Nevada jail. But they had been together ever since then, and they now shared a fifty-fifty stake in the saloon, which Rafferty with his geniality and Thomas with his head for figures had quickly turned into a great success. Their relationship was based on absolute trust and mutual regard. During his investigations, Rafferty always shared his thoughts with Thomas, who in turn felt free to offer ideas of his own.

Such was the case now, for Thomas said after a long silence, "It would be nice to know, I think, where that picture of Mr. Hadley was taken."

"'Twould be," Rafferty agreed. "And another question is how. Any thoughts, Wash?"

"Maybe," said Thomas. "Let me look at it again when I have the chance."

"Be my guest. God knows I've stared at it enough already," said Rafferty, who had persuaded Majesty Burke to lend him the photograph capturing Hadley in what must have been a moment of illicit lovemaking. The photograph, Rafferty knew, presented a series of tantalizing questions: How had Michael O'Donnell obtained it in the first place, and what did he intend to do with it? Where and when was it taken? Did Hadley know he was being photographed, or was the picture taken secretly? Who was the woman enjoying Hadley's manly attentions?

When these questions began to pile up like snow drifts in the back of Rafferty's head, he knew it was time to turn to more productive lines of inquiry. He said, "I'm wonderin' about something, Wash. You've been involved from time to time with the local laborin' community. If I was lookin' for someone who might know all the ins and outs of organized labor in Minneapolis, who might I see? Mind you, I'd prefer not to go to somebody in the unions—or with business, for that matter. I'm lookin' for a man who could tell me what Michael O'Donnell was doin' and what he was runnin' up against. Any suggestions?"

Said Thomas, "I would judge that J. Winston Phelps is your man, Shad, if you can stand the sight of him. You know his reputation."

"I know," said Rafferty, "but I'll chance it. In fact, I'll call the infamous barrister today and see if he'll talk with me."

Feeling as though he was making progress at last, Rafferty returned to his perusal of the *Dispatch*. He soon felt much worse again, however, for buried at the bottom of an inside page, next to an advertisement touting the latest miracle cure for neuralgia, was a brief story that read as follows:

> Joseph Shelton, a night soil collector in Minneapolis, was found dead early this morning on the Northern Pacific tracks along Second Street South near the milling district. As the body was terribly mangled, it is supposed he was struck by a train while attempting to cross the tracks in his cart.

♦♭

J. Winston Phelps was the kind of lawyer who gave rich men a bad name, at least in the eyes of the rich men who despised him. He was the grandson of one of the founders of the village of St. Anthony, a small community on the east side of the Mississippi that had been settled several years earlier than Minneapolis, only to be swallowed up twenty years later by its dynamic young competitor on the opposite shore. The grandfather had made a tidy sum in saw milling, an inheritance that

Phelps's father then parlayed into an even tidier sum through shrewd dealing in real estate and commodities. When the father dropped dead at age forty-five, the family fortune fell conveniently into the lap of his only son, who thereafter devoted himself to spending it as unwisely—and even scandalously—as possible.

He had begun his career as a criminal lawyer and quickly rose to the highest ranks of that dubious profession. His elegant manner and dress belied the fact that, once let loose in a courtroom, he was a legal carnivore who liked nothing better than dining on witnesses for lunch. Feared for his tart tongue and his command of case law, he was the attorney every criminal in Minneapolis dreamed of hiring, but he was affordable only to those of considerable means. Indeed, he had sprung so many felons over the years that it was commonly said the only way to be really certain of a man's guilt was if Phelps had gotten him off.

But it was Phelps's unlikely commitment to radical causes, more than his libertine habits or his fondness for freeing criminals, that had earned him the undying enmity of Minneapolis's business elite. No one seemed to know why he had "turned on his own kind," as one newspaper article put it, although there were plenty of theories. Some said that as a youngster, while at his grandfather's sawmill, he had witnessed a gruesome accident in which a worker was decapitated. Others suggested that Phelps had come under the sway of anarchists and their ilk at Harvard, where he had been a brilliant if unruly student. Still others were inclined to think he was simply a contrarian who took delight doing—and saying—the unexpected.

He had first made a name for himself in the streetcar workers strike of 1889. During a series of cases spawned by the strike, he had proved to be a brilliant defender of labor's rights and an incomparable cross-examiner whose courtroom theatrics invariably drew a packed house. Rafferty had seen Phelps in action only once, when he had gotten one of the alliance's henchmen on the witness stand and quickly reduced the poor man to blithering idiocy.

"'Twas like watching a tiger play with a fly," Rafferty later told Thomas. "Why, had the poor man tried to testify that the sky was blue, I've no doubt Mr. Phelps would soon have gotten him to admit that, no, it was pink, or maybe orange, with a touch of green for good measure."

Phelps's manner of living was as unorthodox as his politics, for it was widely known in Minneapolis that the famed lawyer much preferred the companionship of young men to that of women. Rafferty himself had never been bothered by such things. He had seen enough over the years to know that sex was the great wild card in human life, and that accounting for its infinite variations was as impossible as trying to figure out the weather or the next dip in the stock market. Still, Rafferty had known few if any men who dared to be as open about their predilections as Phelps apparently was.

Rafferty had telephoned Phelps shortly after talking with Thomas, and the lawyer—who seemed very much interested in Rafferty's inquiries—had agreed to a meeting that evening at his apartment. Rafferty took the Marshall-Lake streetcar to south Minneapolis, then transferred on Nicollet to LaVeta Terrace, the large brick-and-stone row house where Phelps lived. He was greeted at the door by the great defender himself.[4]

Phelps's apartment occupied the corner unit of the row house and was therefore the largest in the building. Rafferty was led to a spacious parlor decorated with salmon-pink wallpaper and a plush rug of the same color. Several paintings, including a male nude that left nothing to the imagination, hung from the walls, and the furnishings throughout were of the best kind.

Phelps himself wore a velvet-lined silk smoking jacket, dark slacks, and oriental slippers that lent an exotic touch to his appearance. He was a tall, almost gaunt man, with a languorous face marked by a narrow nose, a tight mouth beneath the dark slash of a pencil mustache, hazel eyes with an odd yellowish cast to them, and thin black hair slicked back from his high forehead. He was perhaps forty-five, though he was one of those men whose age is never easy to guess.

"Ah, Mr. Rafferty, it is a pleasure to meet you," he said in a surprisingly deep and strong voice. "Care for a whisky?"

"No, thank you. I have made it a rule for many years not to drink before midnight."

"What a pity," said Phelps, taking a seat on a long divan facing a marbled fireplace and motioning Rafferty toward a thickly stuffed chair to one side. "I have found that life without alcohol is like life without sex—it can be done, but not at all well. Don't you agree?"

Well, thought Rafferty, this is going to be an interesting conversation. "'Tis not wise to disagree with you, sir, or so I have heard."

Phelps arched an eyebrow and said, "It depends on the nature of the disagreement. I am actually a most agreeable fellow once you get to know me, but I do not suppose you came all the way over here for idle chitchat, did you, Mr. Rafferty? You are interested in Michael O'Donnell, as I understand it."

"Yes, I'm investigatin' his death on behalf of a friend."

"That would be Majesty Burke, I should imagine."

"I will not deny it."

Phelps took a cigarette from a small gold case and lit it. Then, leaning back on the divan, he eyed Rafferty as though he were a connoisseur considering a rather dubious work of art. Finally, he said, "If you are a clever man, Mr. Rafferty, and I have it on good information that you are, then you must believe that there is more to Mr. O'Donnell's murder than has thus far appeared in the accounts furnished by our local press."

"I do."

"Good for you. Tell me then, if you would, what your theory is. Who do you think murdered Mr. O'Donnell and why did they do it?"

"Ah, I was hopin' to ask those very same questions of you, Mr. Phelps."

"Really? I'm flattered by your attention, but I must wonder why you have come to me. I would think Randolph Hadley is the man you should be talking to."

"I will get to him soon enough, Mr. Phelps, but before I do, I need to know as much as possible about Michael O'Donnell's work for organized labor, since that is what appears to have gotten him killed."

Phelps nodded and took another long drag on his cigarette. "Very well, I see no reason why I can't share certain facts with you — on the understanding, of course, that my comments will be treated as strictly confidential."

"Of course."

"Here, then, is what I can tell you: Young Michael, as I suspect you already know, actually started out on the opposite side of the fence, working for our beloved mayor and his merry band of crooks."

"Do you know if he was close to the mayor?"

"I doubt it. He was on the lower rungs of the ladder and may never even have met the mayor, for all I know. In any case, he saw enough graft and boodle to give him the radical religion. He could not stomach all the thievery he saw and so decided to devote his life to helping working people. It was a genuine conversion, rather like Paul on the road to Damascus."

"And what exactly did he do once he'd seen the light?"

"He looked for ways to help the cause. As you presumably know, he recently took a job at the Wellington Mills in hopes of convincing the lower-paid men there to join a union. The nailers and packers first tried to organize back in 1894, but Mr. Wellington and the other mill owners beat them down in the end. The poor fellows never did manage to form a union. It was therefore a difficult job that Michael took on, given the industry's rabid opposition to organized labor."

"Why did he pick the Wellington Mills? Was it his sister's idea?"

"Ah, so you have met the fiery Miss O'Donnell. What did you think?"

"I liked her."

"Good for you, sir. Most men are put off by her—how shall I put it?—bluntness. Yes, I think she had a positive influence on her brother. She can be a most persuasive woman."

"So I've learned," Rafferty said. "By the way, was Mr. O'Donnell working for an existin' union in his effort to organize the mill workers?"

"No. The Northwestern Flour Mill Employees Union, the only one that now represents any mill workers, is strictly craft oriented. Michael and his sister wanted to help out the ordinary laborers at the bottom of the ladder."

Rafferty had been harboring an idea and he now floated it before Phelps: "Do you think it possible that Mr. O'Donnell had become involved with the most radical elements of the labor movement, as it were?"

Phelps seemed amused by the question. "Do you mean, was he an anarchist or, God forbid, a socialist?"

"Something like that," Rafferty said.

"I rather doubt it. Besides, the anarchist underground that the newspapers cite so often is a figment of the public imagination, though I suppose the explosion last night will cause all God-fearing citizens of the city to be on the lookout for bearded madmen carrying sticks of dynamite in one hand and copies of the *Communist Manifesto* in the other. If you ask me, it was probably some henchman for the alliance who blew up the house."

"Why would the alliance do such a thing?"

"Two reasons. First, to eliminate any incriminating evidence in the event Michael's death is ever properly investigated. Second, to convince the gullible public that Minneapolis is a hotbed of anarchism, thereby increasing support for the alliance's campaign of terror against the working people of this city. Of course, the truth is far more prosaic. Minneapolis is not full of desperate men in dingy basements assembling bombs and plotting to overthrow the capitalists, though I must say that that is an excellent idea whose time may one day come."

Rafferty looked around at the opulent parlor and its expensive furniture and artwork. He said, "'Twould appear you have done well with the fruits of capitalism, Mr. Phelps. I'm surprised to hear you wish to cut down the tree."

"Ah, so you think me a hypocrite?"

"No, I am merely tryin' to gain an understandin' of your point of view."

"My point of view is that I am, despite my wealth, an outcast from polite society, Mr. Rafferty, for reasons which I am sure you are aware of. There is also the unpleasant fact that my family's fortune was ill-gotten, as was most of the 'old' money here. My grandfather raped the North Woods to make his pile, while my father had to content himself with manipulating the commodity markets. He was, in other words, a bunco artist. So you see, I am living—comfortably, God knows—on the sins of the past."

Phelps seemed to be enjoying himself—this was obviously a speech the lawyer had delivered many times before—so Rafferty made no effort to interrupt. "Therefore," Phelps continued, "since wealthy and respectable people will have no truck me with, and since I do not, in any case, deserve the fortune I am too spoiled to give up, I have decided to use my legal skills to help the poor and the innocent. And if one day the impoverished masses rise up into a great mob and ransack the mansions on Lowry Hill, well sir, I shall greatly enjoy the spectacle."[5]

Then, like the master litigator he was, Phelps paused for dramatic effect before concluding, "Spite, you see, can be a form of idealism."

"'Tis an interestin' way of putting it," said Rafferty, "though I hope that when the mobs come, they don't find this apartment. Was Mr. O'Donnell of a similar viewpoint regardin' our society?"

"Michael was not a deep thinker, Mr. Rafferty, but he certainly believed he was working for the cause of justice. Still, I tried to warn him that he must be careful about his activities because the Secret Alliance has spies everywhere."

"So you knew him personally?"

"I did. He was a very handsome and appealing young man, if a trifle naive. I was very fond of him."

Rafferty wondered just what form that fondness had taken but decided to leave the question for another time. Instead, he asked, "Do you know of anybody Mr. O'Donnell worked with at the mills who might be able to tell me more about his union activities?"

"I'm afraid not, but as I indicated before, you should talk with Randolph Hadley. After all, the alliance seems to have known Michael well enough to kill him. Perhaps Mr. Hadley will share his investigative files with you."

"I'm not countin' on that," Rafferty said. "But I would be interested in anything you could tell me about Mr. Hadley and his organization."

"Hadley and his men are the Cossacks of Minneapolis, Mr. Rafferty. Their mission is to terrorize the working men of the city and thereby keep them in line. That is all you need to know."

"And what of Mr. Hadley himself? Is there anything about him I should know? Is he, for example, a man with secrets?"

"All men have secrets," Phelps said "Hadley, I'm sure, is no exception. Do you have something specific in mind?"

Rafferty weighed his response carefully. "As a matter of fact, I do. You see, I think Mr. O'Donnell might have found out something about Hadley. Do you know if Mr. O'Donnell was by any chance a photographer?"

"What an odd question, Mr. Rafferty," Phelps said, staring at Rafferty with a kind of skeptical curiosity. "Now you have whetted my interest. What do you suppose Michael 'found out,' as you put it?"

"I don't know," Rafferty lied. "I'm merely tossin' out ideas here."

"And these ideas apparently involve the thought that Michael may have been taking some—how shall I put it—unauthorized photographs? Is that what you're suggesting, Mr. Rafferty?"

"If you don't mind, I'd like to get back to my question," Rafferty said, aware that he would be in for a long cross-examination if he didn't watch himself. "Was Mr. O'Donnell a photographer?"

"I have no idea," Phelps said, "but it's clear that you do. Why don't you tell me more, Mr. Rafferty? You're beginning to intrigue me."

Rafferty could see that the conversation had turned down a street that offered nothing but the opportunity for a bad accident. Phelps was simply too clever to fence with, and Rafferty decided his best move would be to leave.

"Well, I'll be troublin' you no more, Mr. Phelps," he said, standing up. "I have other business this evenin'. You've been most helpful."

"As have you, Mr. Rafferty," Phelps said with a crooked smile. "Have a nice evening, and if you wish to talk again, you know where to find me."

Dusk was settling in as Rafferty left LaVeta Terrace. He caught a streetcar almost at once and rode the mile or so down Nicollet to Lake Street, where he transferred to a St. Paul–bound car. The car wasn't crowded and, as always, Rafferty carefully observed his surroundings.

He therefore could not help but notice that one of his fellow passengers, sitting in the rear, was a short, swarthy man with a broad, acne-scarred face. As it happened, Rafferty had noticed the very same man aboard the streetcars he had taken earlier from St. Paul. Now, it appeared, the man was going to accompany Rafferty back home as well.

It was dark by the time Rafferty got off the trolley at Fourth and Robert Streets in downtown St. Paul. His shadow, however, stayed aboard. Normally, Rafferty would have walked up Robert two blocks to his saloon at Sixth, but his curiosity was aroused, so he crossed over to the Pioneer Press Building and peered around the corner down Fourth to see if his tail would get off at the next stop. The man did and then began double-timing back toward Robert.[6]

There was a large arched vestibule in the newspaper building, and Rafferty stepped inside to wait. Before long, the man with the scarred face came rushing past, no doubt looking for Rafferty somewhere up ahead on Robert. Rafferty fell in behind him. There was a sudden flurry of traffic on Fifth, and the man had to wait to cross. He was about to step into the street when Rafferty tapped him on the shoulder.

The man turned around, saw at once that he had been found out, and tried to make a run for it. Rafferty got one hand on the man's left wrist and yanked it back as easily as if he were pulling in a walleye from his beloved Lake Osakis.

"Not so fast, my friend," Rafferty said, swinging the man around and backing him against the brick wall of a building. "We've got some talkin' to do."

"Hey, let me go," the man said. "I ain't done nothin'."

The man was about forty years old and wore heavy brown trousers and a brown coat over a plain white shirt. His pock-marked face and long, curly black hair were his most distinctive features.

"You've been followin' me," Rafferty said, keeping the man pinned against the building. "Why would you be doin' a thing like that?"

"I don't know what you're talkin' about. I was just out for a walk. Now get your hands off of me."

"I'll keep my hands on you as long as I please, my friend, and it would serve you well to be polite when talkin' to a gentleman. Now then, who're you working for? Mr. Hadley perhaps?"

"I don't know what you're talkin' about," the man repeated.

"'Tis woeful to find so ignorant a fellow in this day and age," Rafferty said. "What's your name?"

"None of your business."

"Ah, but I'm makin' it my business," Rafferty said, reaching around to pull the wallet from the man's back pocket. As he did so, however, his left shoulder—which had the man pinned—pulled back slightly. That was all the room the man needed. With a quick and skillful move, he slid out from under Rafferty and took off down Fifth at full speed.

Rafferty was surprisingly fast on his feet for a big man, but he knew there was no chance he could outrun a fellow twenty years younger and a hundred pounds lighter. As the man disappeared into the night, Rafferty took a moment to curse his own ineptitude. Then, after an impromptu stop at a nearby Western Union office, he headed up Robert to his saloon, where he was sure the mood of the patrons would be far jollier than his own.

Chapter Six

❦

"We've Met"

FROM THE JOURNALS OF DR. JOHN WATSON:

SAT., SEPT. 30, 1899, WALDORF-ASTORIA HOTEL, N.Y., 8 P.M.: Another telegram from SR! Tonic H very much needed. Message as follows: PLOT THICKENS. CARTMAN WHO FOUND HANGING VICTIM KILLED BY TRAIN. NO ACCIDENT I'M SURE. ALSO HOUSE AT CRIME SCENE BLOWN UP. WHY? AM BEING FOLLOWED BY UNKNOWN PARTY. HAVE IDEA THAT NOTHING IN CASE AS IT SEEMS. HOPE YOU WILL RESPOND TO MY LETTER ASAP. RAFFERTY.

H: "It sounds as though our friend has gotten himself into a most interesting situation. I only wish I had Mr. Rafferty's letter in hand."

W: "By the sound of it, his case is far more interesting than our own."

H: "Do not remind me of that, Watson. I am prepared to curse the day that I agreed to take on this matter."

W: "You could always cite the press of other business & resign."

H: "I do not leave an investigation until the problem at hand has been solved. That has always been my professional policy, as you well know."

W: "Yes, but what would you do if Mr. Rafferty, say, called at this moment & asked for your help in Minnesota?"

H, SMILING: "I imagine I would begin looking for a warmer coat."

9 P.M.: H sent off telegram to SR, saying he was "giving much thought" to Mpls. murders & posing several interesting questions. . . .

The Cathedral of St. Paul, which dated back to 1858, was ancient by the city's standards, although old age did not confer upon it any grandeur. Situated on an ordinary downtown corner, it lacked a tower, stained glass, sculpture, or other flourishes common to the mighty cathedrals of Europe. Built for a mere thirty-three thousand dollars, with walls quarried from the rugged blue-gray limestone that underlay the city, the church was very much a provincial building, as raw and unadorned as St. Paul itself had been in its pioneer days. Still, Shadwell Rafferty loved the old church and was sorry to hear that Archbishop John Ireland, the ambitious and dynamic leader of St. Paul's large Catholic population, intended to replace it with a far more imposing edifice as soon as he could raise the money to do so.[1]

Rafferty had been married in the cathedral, in 1875, to the beautiful Mary Rutherford, she of the silky auburn hair and flashing blue eyes. She was long gone now—dead with their son in childbirth—and he came to the church on Sunday morning to light a candle in her memory and to think, until he could not stand it any more, of the happy family that might have been. This was a private and painful rite he performed every day that he was in St. Paul, no matter how busy he might otherwise be. As he knelt before the candles, worshippers began filing into the cavernous church, which could hold a thousand people. Rafferty decided to stay for mass, even though he was not on the whole a religious man.

During his youth in Boston, Rafferty had been tutored by the Jesuits, and only later did he come to realize what a mad lot of Christians they were, afire with God and logic in nearly equal proportions. They had taught him well, but in the end he had shed their religion, not in any rebellious way but more in the manner of tossing out a coat that no longer fit. He was not proud of his apostasy, but it did not haunt him either, for he had long ago abandoned any search for the meaning of the world— that, he knew, was work best left to idle young men.

After he had found a seat in one of the transepts, Rafferty gave himself over to the sensual pleasures of the mass—the sacred chants he knew by heart, the familiar aroma of incense, the old Latin hymns with their rich and mysterious cadences—and let his mind wander. Such easy and casual thinking was Rafferty's way. He had found that by freeing his mind to roam—"like a horse grazin' in a fine pasture," as he once put it—he was sometimes able to make fantastic leaps of insight that came from a place far beyond the rigorous realm of logic. Wash Thomas, who had seen more of Rafferty in action than any other man, called these moments of insight startlements—a coinage that Rafferty immediately adopted as his own.

Rafferty, of course, could never tell when a startlement might arrive, for by its very nature it was unpredictable. But now, as he listened to the choir launch into the familiar strains of the *Tantum Ergo*, filling the church with echoing voices, Rafferty's mind suddenly received one of those famous jolts from the blue. It was just the bare outline of an idea, a rough map leading to an unexpected place. Yet if there was even a kernel of truth in it, then Rafferty knew he might soon find himself in the middle of events far more sinister than he had ever anticipated.

The germ of the idea had actually been planted in the telegram he'd received the night before from Holmes. Rafferty took the telegram from his shirt pocket and read it again. The message was at once cryptic and suggestive—standard Holmes, in other words. It read: YOUR CASE INTRIGUING. QUESTIONS: HOW LONG AFTER HANGING CARTMAN'S DEATH? WHERE VICTIM'S CLOTHES? WAS VICTIM CRIMINAL? LETTER TO FOLLOW. SH. Rafferty knew the answer to the first question and couldn't for the life of him see why Holmes had asked the second. The third question, however, had resonated in Rafferty's mind and led to the idea that he now found so intriguing.

⌀ℓℓ

Later that morning, over breakfast with Thomas at the saloon, Rafferty came to an important decision.

"I'm doin' the unthinkable for a loyal citizen of St. Paul," he said. "I'm goin' over to stay in Minneapolis. It won't be for long—a few nights, I'm thinkin', at most. This O'Donnell business has got so many angles to it, Wash, that I need to be on the scene for a while if I'm to make any sense of it. As it is, I'm runnin' over there every day, so I might as well save the car fare. Just tell the customers I've taken a couple of days off. I'll stay at the West Hotel, so you won't have any trouble findin' me if you need to."

Thomas was hardly surprised by this plan, for he could tell that the O'Donnell case had "gotten Shad's attention," as he liked to put it. And once Rafferty got deep into an investigation—well, he had at least one thing in common with the great Sherlock Holmes himself. Thomas had watched the two of them at work during the ice palace affair, and at first they seemed different in almost every way. Holmes was gaunt, reserved, rational to a fault; Rafferty was heavyset, outgoing, intensely intuitive. Yet Thomas soon came to realize that these two otherwise disparate men shared one dominating trait—an irresistible love for the hunt.

"Well, after being followed by that fellow last night and everything else that has happened, I trust you know what you're doing," Thomas said, adding dryly, "not that it would make any difference if you don't, since I can see you are determined to see this business through to the end."

"I am," Rafferty acknowledged.

"Then I have something for you," Thomas said, taking a large manila envelope from a shelf behind the bar and handing it to Rafferty. "Just developed it this morning."

Rafferty opened the envelope and found an eight-by-ten-inch photograph. At first Rafferty was puzzled by the grainy picture, but as he looked at it more closely, he soon realized that it was an enlargement made from a small section of the incriminating photograph of Randolph Hadley. The enlargement focused on a cornice visible through the window in the room where Hadley and his lady friend were cavorting. Rafferty had wondered about that cornice, thinking it might be a way to track down where the mysterious photograph had been taken, but he hadn't gotten around to doing anything about it. Now Thomas had saved him the trouble. Like Rafferty, Thomas was a skilled photographer who often developed pictures in the well-equipped darkroom they shared in the basement of the Ryan.

"Well, Wash, I see that you have been readin' my mind again," Rafferty said. "This will be very helpful."

"Could be," Thomas agreed, "if the photograph was taken in Minneapolis, like you think."

"Well, let's just hope it was," Rafferty said as he studied the enlargement. The cornice appeared to be of light-colored material, probably stone, and consisted of several layers, including a row of heavy brackets and, below, a much thinner line of small projecting blocks that resembled a set of teeth. If the cornice did indeed cap a building in Minneapolis, Rafferty figured there must be somebody—an architect, a builder, a city official—who would recognize it. The trick would be finding that person, as quickly as possible, and Rafferty knew just where to start his search.

A few minutes later he was talking over the telephone with Joseph Pyle, who had numerous contacts in every profession, including architecture. After the usual pleasantries, Rafferty explained what he was looking for. He did not, however, explain why he hoped to find the cornice in question.

"I must say that of all the strange things you have asked me over the years, Shad, this may be the strangest," Pyle observed.

"Trust me, Joseph, I have good reasons. Now, who would most likely know such a thing off the top of his head? I don't wish to spend days searchin' for this cornice if I can help it. Would there be a fellow from the city building inspector's office, say, who would be the expert in such matters?"

"Perhaps," said Pyle, "but there is one man who reputedly knows the buildings of Minneapolis, brick by brick and stone by stone, better than anyone else. Have you ever heard of a character named Sid the Ratman?"

Фω

By three o'clock that afternoon, after taking a train from St. Paul with his luggage, Rafferty was ensconced in a comfortable suite at the West Hotel in Minneapolis. On the brief train ride, he had let his mind roam through the O'Donnell case, toting up all the possibilities that presented themselves. It was a daunting list, and now as he sat by the big corner window in his room, idly gazing out at the traffic on Hennepin Avenue, he felt like a hunter who had startled such a huge flock of ducks that he didn't know which one to shoot at. Rafferty considered the problem in his rather disorganized way, lighting a particularly aromatic panatela to help ignite the process, and concluded that his only hope was to decide, for better or worse, which duck to go after first.[2]

One would certainly have to be Sid the Ratman, but before he tracked down the Ratman, Rafferty wanted to have another talk with Majesty Burke. He rang the hotel switchboard and asked the operator to call Burke's apartment, which was above her saloon. She answered almost immediately and sounded pleased that Rafferty wished to pay her a call. Although Rafferty would never have admitted it, he too was pleased with the thought of spending time with the beautiful widow, even if the visit was intended to be all business.

Rafferty planned to question Burke in greater detail about the troubling matter of Michael O'Donnell's sudden conversion to the cause of organized labor. For reasons that Rafferty could not fully explain, he believed that O'Donnell's change of heart might well be the hinge upon which the entire case turned. J. Winston Phelps had suggested that O'Donnell's exposure to municipal corruption had spurred this transformation, but Rafferty wasn't so sure. Unless O'Donnell had been a downy-cheeked innocent—and that seemed unlikely given that he hailed from Chicago—then it was hard to see why he would have been appalled by the workings of Mayor Adams's political machine. No, something else must have caused the young man to become a sworn enemy of the system.

Before heading out for the short walk to Burke's saloon, Rafferty double-checked the derringer he always carried under his sleeve and found it to be in perfect working order. Then he left his suite and let the door shut behind him, after which he took a small piece of thread, wet it, and carefully placed it across the crack between the jamb and the door. It was an old detective's trick, a way for Rafferty to determine whether anyone had entered his room while he was gone. In a case where powerful and dangerous men might be involved, Rafferty believed, it paid to take every possible precaution.

"Come in, come in," Majesty Burke said when she greeted Rafferty at the door of her apartment. "I have been thinking about you."

"'Twould make any man proud to know he is in your thoughts," Rafferty replied, though he couldn't resist adding, "of course, that is assumin' the thoughts are favorable."

She smiled and said, "With you, Shad, they must always be favorable. Now sit down"—she directed him to a plush upholstered chair in front of the parlor's fireplace—"and I'll get some tea."

While she went into the kitchen, Rafferty surveyed the parlor. The room was small, but his hostess had made it seem spacious by avoiding the darkly patterned excesses of wallpaper, furniture, and carpeting still common in "better" households. Instead, the parlor felt bright and clean—a sensation Rafferty enjoyed given the state of disarray that usually prevailed in his own living quarters.

When Maj Burke returned with the tea, he noted that her clothes reflected the same simple good taste of her living quarters. She wore a crisply tailored skirt and jacket of black cheviot, lightly trimmed with velvet but otherwise unornamented. All in all, Rafferty thought, it was unlikely there was a handsomer women of her age to be found anywhere in the Twin Cities. Indeed, he wondered—as must have many other men—why she had never remarried. Then again, he supposed, the same question might have been asked of him.

After she had poured tea and taken a seat across from Rafferty, she leaned forward, put a hand on his knee, and said, "Now, Shad, what is it you want to talk about? You know I will help you in any way I can."

Rafferty took a sip of tea—he hated the stuff, no matter what variety, but still made a show of savoring it—then said, "What I'm hopin' is that you might be able to tell me a bit more about Michael. I'm still puzzled by how he came to be a union man so fast after workin' for the mayor."

"I really can't say," she said, though Rafferty didn't think she sounded very convincing.

"Or is it that you really don't want to say, Maj?"

"You read me too well, Shad," she said, giving a slight shake to her head. "Very well, I will tell you what I think, but you must not repeat what I'm about to say to anyone. Will you promise me that?"

"Of course."

"Then I will tell you that I blame Michael's sister for turning him into an agitator. She is a dangerous woman, and I think poor Michael fell under her spell."

"That is not her version of events, Maj. She says Michael's conversion was a mystery to her and everyone else."

"And you believe that?"

Rafferty shrugged and said, "I'm more interested in what I know than what I believe. Do you know for a fact that she lied to me? Did you, for example, ever overhear Miss O'Donnell hectorin' her brother to join the labor cause?"

"No," Burke admitted. "But it is exactly what she would do. I heard her speak at a union picnic this summer at North Commons and she was practically inviting everyone there to arm themselves for insurrection."[3]

There was a distinct note of anger in Burke's voice as she spoke. Rafferty said, "'Tis plain you dislike the woman. Is it because of her views or is there something else, Maj?"

"Yes, I dislike her and her kind, and I will tell you why. I am tired of all the talk of strikes and protests and bringing down the system, whatever that is. No good will ever come from any of it, as far as I'm concerned."

"I'm not so sure of that," Rafferty said gently. "The union movement has done much to ease the lot of the workin' man."

"Oh, I saw all I ever wanted to see of the 'movement' years ago in Chicago. Do you remember the summer of 1877 and the troubles then?"

"Yes."

"Well, we were still living in Chicago at that time, and early that year Johnny lost his job—he was a laborer at the McCormick works—on account of the depression. This was not long after Bobby was born. We were destitute and we finally went to live with my parents until we could get back on our feet. Of course, we didn't know what was about to happen with the 'Great Uprising,' as the newspapers called it."[4]

"You are talkin' about the railroad strike, I presume."

"Yes, only it seemed to me then that the whole city had gone mad, like Paris in the French Revolution. Papa was an engineer for the Chicago, Burlington & Quincy, and at first he thought the strike was a good thing. But before long, as the mobs took to the streets, we all began to fear for our lives. My parents lived in a house on Halsted, and I will never forget the day the mobs stormed the roundhouse at West Sixteenth and destroyed several locomotives. We heard the strikers roaring and screaming, and then the police started shooting and before long all the men came running back past our house. One of them, a young man with the most startling blue eyes I had ever seen, and beautiful blond hair, collapsed by our front gate. We tried to help but the bullet had gone through his stomach, and he screamed in agony for half an hour until death finally took him. So I guess that is what I see when I think of the labor movement, and I want no part of it."

"And you think Addie O'Donnell is intent on stirrin' up the same kind of trouble here?"

"If she can. I fear Michael will not be the only victim. The alliance and its secret army have tasted blood, and they will want more, I am sure. That is always the way it is with men, isn't it."

Rafferty, who had been through the most sanguinary battle in the history of the continent, at Gettysburg, could hardly dispute her observation. Even so, he said, perhaps foolishly, "There won't be any more bloodshed here if I have anything to say about it, Maj."

"I hope you're right, Shad. Now, is there anything else you wish to know?"

"There are a couple of things. When exactly did Michael become an ardent union man, as best you can remember?"

"It was in May or maybe even April, not long after his sister showed up here. It happened very suddenly, I can tell you that."

"I see. Now, besides Addie, what other union people did Michael become involved with? Any names would be very helpful."

Burke said, "Jack Pruitt would be one man you'd want to talk to. He works at the Shevlin-Carpenter Sawmill not far from here."

"Is this Pruitt fellow a union organizer of some kind?"

"I don't think so, but he and Michael used to be pretty good friends. Sometimes when business was slow, they'd sit at the bar and talk for hours."

"Do you know what they talked about?"

"Union things. Michael was forever asking Jack questions about this or that union. It was like he could never know enough once he decided to commit himself to the cause."

"I'll have to have a talk with Mr. Pruitt," Rafferty said. "Now, did Michael have any other union friends you can think of?"

"I know there was one fellow from the Wellington Mills that he hooked up with. I can't remember his name, though. I think it might have been Eddie or Earl or something like that. He was in the saloon a few times with Michael. He was a tough-looking character, that I can tell you."

"Can you describe him?"

"Well, Prince Charming he wasn't," she said with a smile. "I remember that his face was so full of holes it looked like he'd been shot with a BB gun at close range."

"You don't say. And was he short, with a dark complexion and curly hair?"

"That's him. Do you know him, Shad?"

"We've met," said Rafferty.

That same evening Mayor Arthur Adams went out for a ride in the handsome coach the city provided to him under a grossly inflated contract with a liveryman who paid a tidy 15 percent kickback for the honor of serving His Honor. The coach was well known around the city, and at almost every intersection, as the driver slowed, Adams would lean out the window and wave at one of his "subjects," as he was wont to call the citizens of Minneapolis.

Like many accomplished swindlers, Arthur Adams was a conspicuously handsome man. He had silvery-blue eyes that twinkled like Christmas lights, a noble brow, a thick and curly head of red hair hardly touched by gray, and full lips sheltered by a fine flowing mustache that curled down in a broad arch to the edges of his wide, fleshy chin. He was a dazzling talker, a magnificent dresser, the best dancer in the city, the life of every party he attended. As the proud possessor of so many manly virtues, he was the city's most prized, if elusive, bachelor. He was rumored to have enjoyed a succession of affairs with prominent ladies, several of whom suffered from the inconvenience of having husbands. Had it not been for Adams's regrettable fondness for thievery on a grand scale, he might even have been a great man, or so some people thought.

Since taking office in 1896, Adams had created a system of organized plunder that went far beyond anything the city had ever seen before. Much of the boodle that flowed into the hands of the mayor and his minions was the product of time-honored forms of graft and corruption. The biggest stream of revenue came in from gambling dens, brothels, tippling houses, and other illegal businesses that were permitted to operate in exchange for payments to the police. Such old standbys as kickbacks on city contracts and payoffs for various political favors were also part of the business mix. By 1899 Adams's well-greased political machine was so entrenched and so well protected by men of power and influence, who liked the way he cracked down on organized labor, that it seemed utterly beyond the reach of the law.

Adams came by his political instincts naturally, for his father had served five terms as mayor of Minneapolis. Unlike his father, who was regarded as an amiable politician of no more than normal dishonesty, Arthur Jr. from the very start was a perverse visionary. He knew exactly what he wanted in life, and it was not the university education his father had insisted upon. After spending a miserable year at Harvard, young Arthur left in 1870 to obtain a real education in urban politics from the master himself—William "Boss" Tweed of New York City.

Tweed was the Mozart of municipal corruption, a genius who had managed to make plunder a kind of dark art. No one was ever quite sure how much he and his gang ultimately fleeced from the city treasury, but some thought the total might have reached $300 million. To learn how Tweed had done it, Adams went to work for the master's organization. Although he was only twenty years old, Adams was quick-witted and possessed a sharp eye for numbers, and in the fall of 1870 he talked his way into a job as an assistant ward heeler for Tammany Hall in Yorkville, a neighborhood on Manhattan's Upper East Side. There he learned firsthand how a political machine operated and, as he would never tire of telling later, once met the Boss himself at a Christmas party. "You will go far young man," Tweed had allegedly told young Adams, though even some of the mayor's most ardent supporters were inclined to think these remarks were apocryphal.[5]

Adams had stayed in New York City just long enough to see Tweed brought down in 1872 by the revelations of a jealous subordinate, some hard-nosed investigating on the part of the *New York Times*, and Thomas Nast's brutally effective cartoons in *Harper's Weekly*. Ultimately, Tweed died behind bars, a broken man. All of this was not lost on Adams, who thought Tweed's biggest mistake was that he had come to believe in his own invincibility and was therefore convinced he could get away with anything.

The mayor of Minneapolis did not intend to make the same mistake, for he understood that if municipal corruption became too blatant, even the most docile and lethargic electorate would begin to take offense at the sight and smell of it. He also knew that a single untoward incident, especially if it involved conspicuously immoral private conduct, could easily ignite the flame of public indignation, which once burning was almost impossible to extinguish. "The good citizens of Minneapolis do not mind a little jobbery," Adams once remarked to a crony, "but God help you if you get caught with your hands under the wrong petticoat." He had therefore been extremely discreet in conducting his affairs, despite the rumors that inevitably arose.

Adams was beginning to worry, however, that the death of Michael O'Donnell could be the kind of incident that might easily spiral out of control despite all efforts to make it go away. The fact that some Irishman from St. Paul was nosing around, asking impertinent questions, didn't help matters. And if those damn pictures ever saw the light of day—well, Adams would have to be on the first fast train out of town or face the consequences.

Now, as he rode down Hennepin Avenue in the cool September twilight, past the gaudy lights of legitimate theaters and the more discreetly illuminated entrances to illegitimate gambling dens, Adams had a decision to make. It hinged on a deceptively simple question: How far should he go to keep his lovely system of corruption from breaking down, as it inevitably would if the truth about Michael O'Donnell ever became public? The mayor did not consider himself a violent man — he preferred to rule by indirection rather than force — but when so much was at stake, could he say no to those counseling the most direct action of all? Or, for that matter, dare he say no?

Randolph Hadley had been among those championing a possible resort to force, but the alliance's director always favored guns and clubs over more subtle means of persuasion. There was also the fact that Hadley didn't quite know the complete story, and thus might become a problem in his own right if the whole truth somehow came out. A very big problem indeed, Adams thought. Then there was that damned snake McParland, who had also suggested that "extreme measures," as he called them, might be required.

As the coach neared Tenth Street, Adams directed the driver to go past the old family home, or what little was left of it. Looking upon the scene of the blast, he wondered once again who had destroyed the house, and why. Adams liked to think he knew everything — and when it came to the financial intricacies of his system of corruption, he did — but the O'Donnell case had proved to be disturbingly opaque. There were aspects of it that even the mayor did not understand, and he was beginning to think that he never would. These are strange days, he thought to himself, strange days.

The coach now approached a large red brick row house with frontages extending along two streets. A carved stone sign at the corner of the building identified it as Zier Row. Adams's driver knew the routine. He swung the coach into an alley, came to a stop in a small courtyard at the rear of the row house, and let Adams out.

"Pick me up at the usual time," Adams instructed the driver, who nodded and gave a shake to the reins, setting his team back in motion. The mayor watched the coach go off down the alley and then walked toward the back door of one of the houses, where he planned to meet a friend for perhaps the last time.

ᚠᚤᚱ

The Minneapolis office of the Pinkerton Agency was located in the Boston Block, a faded old office building just two blocks down Hennepin Avenue from Rafferty's hotel. In charge of the office was a thin, bilious little man named William Borden, who had spent the past three years trying, without success, to escape to warmer and more profitable climes.[6]

As Borden knew better than anyone else, his office had been in recent years a major disappointment to the agency. The problem was that in Minneapolis the agency's most profitable line of business—infiltrating radical organizations—had been all but eliminated by the work of the Secret Alliance. Deprived of the rich array of fees and expenses that infiltrations provided, Borden and his operatives had had to make do with far less lucrative tasks, such as investigating occasional cases of employee theft. As a result, the Minneapolis office had earned a reputation as a kind of Pinkerton Siberia, to the point that even Duluth—where an operative could always find undercover work on one of the iron ranges—was considered a choicer assignment.

As if he didn't have enough trouble already, Borden had been called into the office on Sunday evening to meet with none other than James McParland, who was not known within the agency for his gentle hand with subordinates. Borden knew nothing officially about the "Minneapolis problem," though if what he'd heard through back channels was true—well, a good many Pinkertons would soon be looking for some other form of employment.

When he arrived at the office, Borden found McParland waiting with his two bodyguards—one a big chunk of a man, the other a slender cowboy who enjoyed playing with a gaudy pair of pearl-handled revolvers. McParland introduced himself and instructed Borden to take a seat, while the bodyguards hovered to one side like suspicious angels.

"I have an assignment for you, Mr. Borden," McParland said without preamble. "It is an operation of the utmost importance to the Pinkerton Agency. I have heard good things about you, and therefore I am confident you will complete the operation successfully."

"I will certainly do my best," Borden said.

"Just make sure your best is good enough," McParland replied, staring a hole through Borden's forehead, "or you will not enjoy the consequences." He then handed Borden a loose-leaf notebook containing a brief dossier prepared in record time by the agency's St. Paul office.

"We will begin at the beginning," he said as Borden glanced down at the document. "Have you ever heard of a man by the name of Shadwell Rafferty?"

CHAPTER SEVEN

✦

"Go Back to St. Paul"

FROM THE JOURNALS OF DR. JOHN WATSON:

MON., OCT. 2, 1899, WALDORF-ASTORIA HOTEL, N.Y., 9:30 P.M.: SR's letter at last! It arrived late afternoon just before dinner with Astor in hotel dining room. Escargot excellent. H listened with ill humor to Astor's continuing complaints, ate no food, & excused self at 7 P.M., stating he needed to "consider new developments." I was left to entertain Astor but escaped after hour of idle talk . . .

Went back to room & found H anxious to discuss SR's letter, which included clippings from St. Paul & Mpls. papers re murder case. H much stimulated by SR's missive & again bemoaned fact that our case "as impenetrable a bog as the Grimpen Mire."[1]

Will copy more info later but "most intriguing details" in SR's mailing, according to H, are these: 1) police tried to hide fact that placard found around neck of victim—man called Michael O'Donnell—with warning from antiunion group known as Secret Alliance; 2) "blackmail-type photo" (SR's term) depicting chief of alliance, ex-army officer called Randolph Hadley, discovered in victim's belongings; 3) O'Donnell once worked for mayor of Mpls., man known to be "a midwestern Tweed" (another of SR's phrases), but then converted to cause of labor; & finally 4) SR believes O'Donnell left naked "to further humiliate him"—just as I, & H, suspected.

SR concluded by stating, "What a farrago this business is, Mr. Holmes, but I cannot deny I'm enjoying myself as I try to sort it all out. For you, I imagine, it would be a great feast—the kind of case any detective worth his salt would want to sink his teeth into. A pity you can't join me, but even at a distance of a thousand miles, your advice is the best I could possibly have, & I will look forward to hearing from you as soon as possible."

H: PACING ROOM IN USUAL FASHION: "It sounds as if Mr. Rafferty has gotten himself involved in a capital affair, Watson. The photograph is particularly interesting, & opens up many potential lines of inquiry."

For next half hour, H entertained me with analysis of SR's case, identifying key questions & concerns. Found H's insights to be quite remarkable in view of how few details provided. H promised to send letter to SR at once offering ideas & suggestions.

H ended remarks, however, with disturbing prediction, saying he feared case would prove to be "great trouble" for SR.

W: "Why do you say that?"

H: "Two reasons, Watson. First, there is the hanging itself, which has an unusually sinister aspect. Some powerful passion is behind the killing, for the dark perfume of vengeance scents the air all around it. I can smell it even from a thousand miles away! Second, there is the fact that this singularly ugly crime has occurred in a city where, if Mr. Rafferty is be believed, all the usual institutions of law & order have been thoroughly subverted. In a world in which order has become disorder, & justice an orphan, anything can happen. I only hope that Mr. Rafferty will be extremely careful."

W: "Caution is not his strong suit, from what I have seen."

H, SMILING: "Thankfully so. Were it otherwise, neither of us would be alive at the moment."

How true, I thought, recalling foggy January night in 1896, during ice palace affair, when SR rescued us from frozen waters of

Mississippi in St. Paul. Few other men would have had the courage—let along physical strength—to have accomplished that deed under such trying conditions.

One day, I hope, we shall have chance to repay our debt. . . .

Early on Monday, which dawned cold and dreary, Rafferty downed a breakfast of eggs, pancakes, and bacon in the West Hotel's sumptuous Moorish-style dining room. He read all the newspapers he could lay his hands on, but found no revelations regarding the O'Donnell case. As he pored over the newspapers, Rafferty laid out his plans for the day. First he intended to talk to Jack Pruitt at the Shevlin-Carpenter Sawmill. After that he hoped to track down Sid the Ratman to see if he could identify the cornice visible in the incriminating photograph of Randolph Hadley. And after that—well, Rafferty would figure things out as he went along, as he usually did.

Before leaving his room, Rafferty had again affixed a small thread to the door so he would know if anyone had "visited" in his absence. The fact that he had been followed at least once by the man with the pockmarked face left no doubt that someone was interested in Rafferty's progress. Although his shadow was probably a mere foot soldier, Rafferty hoped to see him again. If that happened, there was no chance the man would escape a second time.

The Shevlin-Carpenter Mill was less than a mile from the hotel, so Rafferty decided to walk in spite of the weather. As he strolled down Hennepin and then north on Washington, past the twin-towered Bijou Opera House, Rafferty kept a sharp eye out for any uninvited company. He saw no one following him, which either meant his tail had given up or was too clever to be spotted.

At Fourth Avenue North, Rafferty turned east toward the Mississippi and entered a bleak landscape of railroad tracks, lumber yards, and sawmills. The slate-gray sky, soiled by locomotive soot and acrid wood smoke, only intensified the harsh, sullen look of the place. Rafferty crossed the Northern Pacific Railroad yards, dodging a couple of slow-moving switch engines as he went. Then he walked past the long brick freight house of another railroad before he finally came upon the Shevlin-Carpenter Sawmill. It was not an impressive sight.

The flour millers of Minneapolis had built for the ages, erecting massive stone structures designed to withstand the assault of time. The city's sawmillers had no such illusions. They knew all too well that the magnificent pineries that formed a crescent across northern Minnesota were a finite resource whose plunder would be the quick work of a generation. In Minneapolis alone, sawmills were churning out lumber at a phenomenal rate. It was claimed that if all the boards produced on an average day in the city were piled on top of one another, they would reach twenty-six thousand feet high, or nearly the equivalent of Mount Everest. Such a pace could not be maintained for long. And so the Shevlin-Carpenter Sawmill, like all the others in Minneapolis, seemed to flaunt its impermanence, for it was nothing more than a collection of oversized wooden sheds attached to a big steam engine and a towering steel smokestack.[2]

Rafferty found his way to the mill's office, where a clerk told him that Jack Pruitt worked in the lumber stacks outside. Like all sawmills, the Shevlin-Carpenter was surrounded by huge piles of green lumber — boards and planks of every dimension that had to be dried out before being sold. These piles, some as high as thirty feet, were one of the distinctive features of the city, for Minneapolis in 1899 was the biggest sawmilling center on earth, cutting half a billion board feet of lumber annually.

The odor of fresh wood and sawdust, which the mills used to power their steam engines, hung thick as fog in the air as Rafferty went back outside to look for Pruitt. Majesty Burke had already provided Rafferty with a description of the mill worker — he was tall and rangy, with red hair and blue eyes. Rafferty saw only a few men at work amid the long rows of lumber that occupied several square blocks around the mill. After a brief search, Rafferty spotted his man walking down one of the deep, narrow aisles that separated the lumber piles.

"Mr. Pruitt," he called out, "could I have a word with you?"

Looking irritated, the man came out to the sidewalk where Rafferty stood. He was just as described, one of those lean and sinewy men who might have made a good cavalryman or gymnast. Though he was quite young — no more than thirty, Rafferty thought — Pruitt already had the furrowed, leathery face of a man who had spent years outdoors. Rafferty guessed that he worked as a lumberjack during the winter months, for he wore the classic outfit of the trade — heavy boots, thick wool pants known as malones, red suspenders, and a checkered wool shirt buttoned up tightly at the neck.

Pruitt's pale blue eyes took in Rafferty with no sign of recognition. "Do I know you?" he asked. It was not a friendly question.

"You do not, sir," Rafferty replied, "but you will soon enough, I trust.

The name is Rafferty, and I have been retained by someone with an interest in justice to investigate the death of Michael O'Donnell." Rafferty then handed Pruitt one of his cards, which read SHADWELL RAFFERTY, BARTENDING AND DISCREET INVESTIGATIONS, RYAN HOTEL, ST. PAUL.

Pruitt glanced down at the card and said, "I wouldn't know anything about the matter, except that what the papers say is mostly a lie. But then I guess you would know that, wouldn't you?"

"What do you mean?"

"Do I look stupid?" Pruitt snapped. "What are you—a Pinkerton man or just one of Hadley's spies?"

"Neither," said Rafferty calmly. "I'm simply tryin' to get to the truth of this business. I owe no allegiance to Randolph Hadley or anyone else. If you wish to talk to Majesty Burke, who I understand is a mutual acquaintance, she will vouch for me."

Pruitt stared at Rafferty for a moment and said, "All right, let's just say you are who you claim to be. What is it you want from me?"

"I want to know what Michael O'Donnell may have been doin' that got him murdered. I've heard that you were a friend of his and shared his views regardin' the unions and other matters."

"And what if I did?"

"Then I have come to see the right man," Rafferty said amiably. "If the two of you were involved in radical activities of one kind or another, I need to know what you might have done to draw the wrath of the Secret Alliance. 'Tis as simple as that."

"So you say."

Rafferty said, "I understand your reluctance, Mr. Pruitt, but the fact is, unless you and others like you help me, I'll never be able to prove that the alliance was behind Michael's murder."

Pruitt let out a brief, bitter laugh. "Why, everybody in this city knows who really killed Michael. The proof was left right on his body, no matter how many denials the newspapers print."

"'Tis not, I fear, the kind of proof that would hold up in a court of law," Rafferty noted. "Much more is needed. Now, can you tell me anything at all about the kinds of activities he was involved in?"

"I don't think so," Pruitt said. "Answering questions like that can be unhealthy for a man."

"It could be even more unhealthy if you don't answer them. Look what happened to Michael."

"I'll take my chances."

"All right, let me ask you something else. I understand there was a fellow named Earl, or maybe Eddie, from the Wellington Mills that Michael got to know pretty well. Could you tell me how to get in touch with him?"

Pruitt laughed again and said, "You're behind the times, Mr. Rafferty. Haven't you heard?"

"Heard what?"

"Earl Smith, for that was the name he went by, is long gone. Left the mill the day Michael was killed and hasn't been seen since. Had a paycheck coming and never picked it up. Some folks think he might have been murdered, too."

"I wouldn't count on that," said Rafferty, "but you can count on the fact that you will not hurt yourself by helpin' me. I'm the only person investigatin' Michael O'Donnell's death who won't whitewash the whole thing. Maj Burke will tell you that. Will you at least talk to her and listen to what she says?"

Pruitt said, "Where can I reach you?"

"At the West Hotel."

"I will get in touch with you there if I find you are on the up and up."

"When will that be?"

"When I'm ready, Mr. Rafferty, and not one second before."

Without another word, Pruitt turned around and went back into the stacks of wood, where he soon vanished from view.

✑

Rafferty returned to his hotel room to pick up a pack of the cheap panatelas he favored. At the door he paused to look for the thread. It was just where he had left it, so Rafferty got out his key, turned the lock, and went in.

"You must be Mr. Rafferty," said a man sitting in a side chair near the window. "A comfortable place you have here. It looks as though you plan to stay awhile."

The man spoke in a nasal voice with a mild drawl to it. Indiana, Rafferty thought, or maybe Kentucky. Rafferty had seen the man before, though not in clothes.

"Mr. Randolph Hadley," said Rafferty, pausing to shut the door.

"I will not deny it," said Hadley, who sat with his back ramrod straight, as though settling into the chair would have been a violation of martial discipline. Rafferty judged Hadley to be well into his fifties, yet he retained the look of a sleek hunting animal, long and slender, with no visible fat. His fine-featured face was long as well, although he kept his graying blond hair cropped short. He wore an impeccably tailored gray suit, along with an ornate silver belt buckle and beautifully tooled black boots, and he looked up at Rafferty with heavy-lidded gray eyes that had the hard glitter of ice.

Rafferty recalled hearing that Hadley had been a military man, and he knew the type all too well. During the war Rafferty had seen plenty of Hadley's kind, brash young officers born to combat as surely as other men might be cut out for business or science. Unlike most men, the Hadleys of the world did not have to be taught to kill—it was in their blood, a trait passed down like any other. Such men were fearless and therefore doubly dangerous, for Rafferty knew that courage to excess was a dangerous sickness.

"As you can see, I let myself in," said Hadley. "You don't mind, do you, Mr. Rafferty?" It was more of a challenge than a question.

Rafferty decided not to accept the challenge—yet. "No, but I plan to count the silverware after you leave. Did you turn up anything in my absence?"

Although the room looked neat, Rafferty could tell by the location of certain objects and by a closet door left slightly ajar that the room had been searched.

Hadley said, "Not really, though I would note that your taste in suits is—how shall I put it?—extremely colorful. By the way, the little thread you left on the door is a trick that has grown hoary over the years. One of my men replaced it after I came in."

"To make a point, no doubt."

"Precisely. You are, I have been told, a most clever man, Mr. Rafferty. Yet I have found that no matter how clever a man is, there is always someone else who is even more clever."

"Well, you have my congratulations, Mr. Hadley. 'Tis clear you are a master when it comes to spottin' thread on a door."

Hadley ignored this backhanded compliment and continued to stare at Rafferty as though he were studying a curio at one of the downtown dime museums. Then he said, "I've been checking up on you, Mr. Rafferty, and I'm told that you are always armed. Would you happen to be carrying a pistol or other weapon at the moment?"

"'Tis possible," Rafferty acknowledged.

Hadley nodded slowly and said, "I'm not sure how things are done in St. Paul, which is known to be a rather backward place, but here in Minneapolis the authorities do not tolerate people carrying concealed weapons. Therefore, I suggest that you hand over your pistol, just so there are no misunderstandings."

"Not a chance," said Rafferty, moving toward Hadley and watching his hands. "Not a chance in hell."

Rafferty's sudden movement caught Hadley off guard, but he quickly recovered his poise and said, "You realize, of course, that by now there could be twenty policemen outside the door."

"Of course," said Rafferty. "In case there's any trouble, the two of us will be well protected, won't we? Still, I've always found that the coppers are never there when you need them most—always a step behind the bullet, as it were."

Hadley emitted a faint smile, like rusty water dribbling from a tap, and said, "I can see you are a direct man, Mr. Rafferty. I like that. Sit down and we'll talk."

"All right," said Rafferty, taking a chair by the other side of the window. "Speak your piece, Mr. Hadley."

Hadley nodded and said, "I will be as direct with you as you have been with me, Mr. Rafferty, by telling you that you are making a very big mistake."

"Really? What sort of mistake?"

"Simply this: You seem to believe, based on the message attached to Mr. O'Donnell's body, that the alliance played some role in his death."

"What makes you think I believe that? Or is mind readin' one of your skills, along with breakin' and enterin'?"

"Do not push your luck, Mr. Rafferty," Hadley said, a distinct edge in his voice. "Smart talk will get you nowhere. I know what sorts of questions you've been asking since coming over from St. Paul, and I'm here to tell you that the alliance played no role whatsoever in Mr. O'Donnell's death."

"'Tis good to hear you say that, Mr. Hadley, but I'm wonderin' why I should believe you."

"Because you have my word on it."

"Ah, I see. Well now, the fact is, I can't know the value of a man's word until I know the man, and I don't know you at all, Mr. Hadley"—here Rafferty paused before adding—"except by reputation."

"All right, Mr. Rafferty, since you appear to enjoy being difficult, I will try to appeal to your sense of logic. Let us begin by supposing for a moment that I decided, for whatever reason, to eliminate Mr. O'Donnell. I would never do such a thing, of course, because I am a law-abiding man."

"Some would say otherwise," Rafferty noted.

"And they would be wrong," Hadley said with conviction. "I am the law in this city and I take that responsibility seriously, despite whatever nonsense you may believe. Now, had I decided to kill Mr. O'Donnell, do you really think I would have staged the murder at the mayor's childhood home and then compounded my lunacy by advertising the deed?"

"I'm in no position to know what you might do, Mr. Hadley, but I take it you are sayin' it was merely an unlucky coincidence that the murder occurred at the mayor's old house?"

"It was no coincidence, I assure you."

"Explain yourself."

"I would like nothing better, but there are certain aspects of the official investigation which must, for the moment, remain confidential."

"I see. And the fire and explosion? What do the police make of that?" Rafferty asked.

"They have not yet identified the individuals responsible, but there is good reason to believe it was the work of the revolutionaries engaged in a conspiracy."

"Well now, there is nothin' like a good conspiracy to get a man's blood flowin'," Rafferty said. "But why do you suppose these conspirators would blow up an empty house? It doesn't make much sense to me, but then I'm not as experienced in these matters as you are."

"I am beginning to find you tiresome, Mr. Rafferty, very tiresome," Hadley said. "If you do not wish to cooperate—"

"Why, I'm always happy to cooperate," Rafferty cut in, "especially when the talk turns to conspiracy. Since we're on that subject, do you suppose it's possible that 'revolutionaries,' as you call them, might also have arranged the unfortunate 'accident' in which the night soil man— Shelton was his name, as I recall—got himself mangled by a train? The timin' of the mishap was quite a coincidence, don't you think?"

Hadley leaned back, rubbed his hands together and said, "I have found, Mr. Rafferty, that conspiratorial theories are like children at a lawn party—play with them too long and they get completely out of hand. There is not one shred of evidence to suggest Mr. Shelton's death was anything other than accidental."

"I see. Well then, I do have a theory about this business, Mr. Hadley, if you'd care to hear it."

"I probably will whether I want to or not. All right, go ahead."

Looking directly into Hadley's eyes, Rafferty said, "I'm thinkin' this case is full of secrets—the kinds of secrets that could embarrass a man and maybe even drive him to murder. I'm thinking maybe Michael O'Donnell knew too much about certain powerful people and died because of it. What do you think?"

If Rafferty's veiled reference to the photograph surprised Hadley, he gave no indication of it. He said, "I think secrets can indeed be dangerous in the hands of the wrong people, Mr. Rafferty, and you would do well to remember that. However, the sorts of secrets you seem to have in mind were not responsible for Mr. O'Donnell's death."

"Even if revealin' those secrets could have proved very damagin' to the alliance or Mayor Adams, or perhaps to other influential men?"

"You seem obsessed with secrets, Mr. Rafferty," Hadley replied coldly, "and that is not a healthy thing for a man. As I stated earlier, it is absurd to think that I, or anyone in the alliance, would be involved in Michael O'Donnell's death. Had I been behind it, you may be certain that the killing would have been accomplished quickly and quietly, with not one jot of evidence to connect the alliance to the crime. You see, Mr. Rafferty, I am not a careless man."

"So I have heard," said Rafferty. "Still, a person with a suspicious mind might look at the matter differently. Such a person might find it doubly clever for the alliance to kill Mr. O'Donnell, leave its calling card behind, and then argue to the world that it would never be so stupid as to incriminate itself in such a blatant way. 'Twould enable the alliance to deny the obvious and at the same time throw the fear of God into the workin' men of this city, who would not doubt for a minute who had done the dirty deed. As for committin' the crime at the mayor's old house, that would add a final brazen touch to the whole business, wouldn't it?"

Hadley shook his head in disbelief and said, "If I were that clever, Mr. Rafferty, I should be in the stock market and not the business I'm in."

"And just what is that business, I wonder?" Rafferty asked. "From my vantage point, it looks like you and the police are in the cover-up game. Why else would the police try to keep the public from learnin' about the message left hangin' around Mr. O'Donnell's neck? The coppers even circulated a phony story that the victim was killed for molestin' a young girl. Now, why would the police go to all that trouble if the alliance had no hand in Mr. O'Donnell's murder? 'Tis a regular conundrum, the way I see it."

"There has been no cover-up," Hadley insisted, his baleful eyes boring in on Rafferty. "The police did not promulgate the message because they knew that it was a ruse intended to divert suspicion from the real murderers. As for the charges of molestation, the police were only responding to an anonymous claim. It is unfortunate that the newspapers have made so much of the allegation, but that is not the fault of the police."

Rafferty said, "Well, perhaps I've been mistaken all along, and I must tell you I'm mightily intrigued by your mention of the 'real murderers.' In the newspapers, if I remember right, you speculated that Mr. O'Donnell might have been killed by 'his own kind.' Do you know who that might be?"

"Not yet," said Hadley, "but I am confident that the criminals will be brought to justice very soon. And that, Mr. Rafferty, brings me back to you. It is well known that you have been making inquiries into this matter on behalf of Mrs. Majesty Burke. I have no idea why you feel compelled to insinuate yourself into the investigation and I don't really care, but you would be well advised to cease and desist. Go back to St. Paul, Mr. Rafferty, and tend to your saloon. Otherwise, I cannot be responsible for what may happen."

"'Twould not be wise to threaten me," Rafferty said.

Hadley met Rafferty's eyes and said, "I am not foolish enough to believe that you would respond to threats, Mr. Rafferty. I have heard of your gallantry at Gettysburg. I myself was with the Twenty-seventh Indiana during that fateful battle. You are a fighting man at heart, as am I, and I must respect you for that. But be aware, sir, that if you persist in your investigation, you will find yourself in very deep and dangerous waters."[3]

"Then I shall be fine," said Rafferty with a smile, "for who floats better than a fat man?"

"We will see about that," said Hadley, abruptly rising from his chair and going over to the door. "You have been fairly warned."

Rafferty followed Hadley to the door and said, "By the way, I seem to recall hearing that you knew Michael O'Donnell quite well. Is that true?"

"You have been misinformed," Hadley said curtly. "I never met the man."

After Hadley left, Rafferty went back to his chair by the window, lit a cigar, and looked out toward the new city hall and county courthouse a few blocks away. The building's massive stone clock tower, the highest structure in Minneapolis, rose over three hundred feet into the gray autumn sky, dominating everything around it in a way that Rafferty could only envy.[4]

Rafferty wished that he had just such a tower, a place from which he could see every feature of the case before him. The truth was, he had no such prospect. Instead, he found himself in a fog of questions and conjectures. Still, he was sure of one thing — Randolph Hadley had lied about not knowing Michael O'Donnell. The tone of Hadley's denial simply didn't ring true, and of course there was also the provocative evidence of the photograph found in O'Donnell's possession. There had to be a connection between the two men, Rafferty thought, and as he gazed out the window, he grew more determined than ever to unlock the picture's naked secret.

❧

William Borden of the Pinkertons was not a heavy-drinking man, but as he sat in his office late that afternoon he felt the need for alcoholic solace. He kept a bottle of good Tennessee whisky in the bottom drawer of his desk for just such occasions, and he poured himself a generous shot while he considered how difficult his life had suddenly become, courtesy of James McParland.

From the moment of McParland's arrival in Minneapolis, Borden had known he was in for a time of it. McParland was not just another high pooh-bah within the Pinkerton Agency. Borden had seen his share of those—officious bastards all—and he could deal with them. McParland was a different matter entirely, for he was a legend, the most famous and most feared Pinkerton of all.

A quarter of a century earlier McParland had gone deep undercover into the violent world of the Molly Maguires in the Pennsylvania coalfields. It was a long walk on a thin tightrope, with death the penalty for the smallest slip, but McParland had somehow defied the odds for well over two years. By the time he was finished, he had provided enough evidence to destroy the Mollies and send a dozen men to the gallows. After this feat, he became the star of the Pinkerton Agency and eventually was tapped to lead its western district office in Denver. There he once again did battle with organized labor, especially the militant Western Federation of Miners.[5]

Now the great infiltrator had come to Minneapolis with orders for Borden to drop everything else so that he could serve at McParland's beck and call. Following McParland's instructions at their Sunday night meeting, Borden had already assigned three men to shadow Rafferty in shifts around the clock. This should have been a job for the St. Paul office, of course, but McParland thought Rafferty might well know some of that city's operatives, so Borden and his men had drawn the task, which was not proving easy. What few men Borden had left were also pulled off their existing assignments and ordered to take undercover jobs in the Wellington Mills in hopes of finding "troublemakers" there.

All of this would have been more palatable from Borden's point of view if he had known why his men were being rushed into these new assignments. McParland, however, had explained nothing. Instead, he contented himself with issuing gnomic pronouncements about "matters of the utmost urgency" and "sensitive issues requiring the greatest discretion." What the hell that meant Borden didn't know. At the same time, McParland insisted on detailed daily reports from the operatives, and Borden was left to understand that heads would roll like bowling balls if McParland found any of these reports to be inadequate.

It was all crazy as far as Borden was concerned—a waste of time and money. There was also the fact that one of the investigations his office had been forced to put on hold was extremely significant. It involved a large and troubling theft of dynamite from the Soudan Iron Mine north of the Twin Cities. Borden's men, with help from Operative No. 6 in Duluth, were still trying to draw a bead on the suspect—an ugly character named Earl Smith, who had disturbing connections to the Western Federation of Miners—when McParland blew into town and brought the investigation to a standstill.

But there wasn't a thing Borden could do about it. McParland gave orders, not suggestions, and it was clear he wasn't the least bit interested in anything Borden had to offer. So be it, thought Borden, as he treated himself to another shot. If trouble comes, let McParland take the blame.

Chapter Eight

సిప

"I Met a Man
Much Troubled by Rats"

From the journals of Dr. John Watson:

Mon., Oct. 2, 1899, Waldorf-Astoria Hotel, N.Y., 11:30 P.M.:
Before retiring, I feel compelled to copy down H's letter to
SR, which he completed only minutes ago & will send out by earliest post. Have a sense that one way or another we shall become
more deeply involved in murders in Mpls. & so wish to keep the
record current. H's letter:

My dear Rafferty:
In receipt of yours of Sept. 29, as well as telegrams, & trust you
are well despite the difficulties of your current case. Dr. Watson
offers his salutations & wonders if that dog of yours is as pugnacious & well fed as ever. As Mr. Hill informed you, we arrived in
New York on Sept. 27 on a matter of some urgency. I am not at
liberty to discuss the details at present, other than to note that
the Astor family is certainly among the most quarrelsome I have
ever encountered.

Our latest call to the New World came at an opportune
time, since in the previous months I had begun to feel like a clipper ship caught in the wide Sargasso Sea, with nary a breath of
wind to stir my sails. When Dr. Watson & I returned to London
in April after our singular adventure with you & the rune stone,

several cases of exceptional interest awaited us. By August, however, dead calm prevailed, & before long the good doctor was quite prepared to throw me out of our flat on the grounds that I was driving him mad! The Astor family provided the breath of air I needed, tho the case here has turned out to be more troublesome than I anticipated.

You, on the other hand, appear to be truly "on the hunt," & I can tell by your letter how highly pleased you are to be in that most stimulating of circumstances. I wish Dr. Watson & I could join you, but of course it is impossible at the moment, & so I can only offer you advice from afar which I nonetheless hope will prove helpful. Now, as to the particulars of your investigation, I offer the following observations:

First, you are quite right, I think, in your assessment of why young Mr. O'Donnell was hanged in the manner that he was. This was almost certainly a vengeance killing, although the identity of the aggrieved party, as you have stated, is by no means clear.

Second, the photograph is indeed a most intriguing feature of the case, & it raises all manner of questions about Mr. O'Donnell. Was he a blackmailer? A procurer? A sexual adventurer? Was he a secret associate of Mr. Hadley's or a sworn enemy out to embarrass him? If a blackmailer, was he working alone or was he someone's paid employee? Did he take the picture himself or acquire it from someone else? Your next step must be to find out where, by whom, & under what circumstances the photograph was taken. You must also find the woman in the picture. Her identity may be extremely important, or it may mean nothing. In any event, you need to talk with her if at all possible.

Third, the demise of the cartman bears close study. Something—or someone—he saw at the crime scene obviously led to his death. Yet he was not murdered until two days later, which suggests that a) the killers did not know at first that he had seen something, or b) that he tried to extort money from them in exchange for his silence & was permanently silenced as a result. In either case, it would be useful to know much more about him.

Fourth, I am struck by a sense that something which happened long ago may be driving all that is happening now. The destruction of the house, as well as the manner of Mr. O'Donnell's death, suggest that deep hatreds are at work in this affair,

Mr. Rafferty, & in my experience such profound & vicious ani-
mosity is usually the devil's own work of time. Indeed, I can feel
the weight of the past hanging over your case like heavy old
drapes. Open them, & the light of the truth will shine in.

I hope these observations will be of some benefit, & I shall
expect to hear from you shortly as to how matters are proceed-
ing. In the meantime, I urge you to be careful. I also entreat you
not to become discouraged. To be lost in mystery is the detective's burden; to find his way out is his triumph. Good luck &
Godspeed.

Your friend,
Sherlock Holmes

ϑℓ℗

"My dear father used to say that the St. Paul Irish are all alike,"
Arthur Adams remarked as he sipped a glass of port in the comfortable
library of his stately new house on Lowry Hill. "Tough, stubborn, and
with rocks for brains."

It was late afternoon and slanting sunlight cast a soft glow over the
downtown skyline, which was perfectly framed through the library's two
large windows. Adams took in the view with a look of satisfaction and then
said, "But this Rafferty fellow, I gather, has more than rocks in his head."

"He does," agreed Randolph Hadley, who had come over after dinner
to report on his encounter with Rafferty that afternoon. James McParland had also joined the company and was not thrilled by the mayor's
comments regarding the Irish, whether from St. Paul or anywhere else.
But the Pinkerton man said nothing as Hadley continued, "This Rafferty struck me as a very sharp fellow and not the kind of man who can
be bullied or bought off. He is trouble, A.A. I can feel it in my bones."

"I was afraid you were going to say that," Adams replied. "Mr. Mc-
Parland, what are your thoughts in this regard?"

"I have none at the moment, Your Honor," McParland answered,
putting a strange and by no means respectful emphasis on the last two
words. "I am under the impression you perform all of the thinking
chores around here."

"God knows someone has to," Adams shot back, a scowl darkening
his elegant features.

"Dolph, what else can you tell me about Rafferty?" the mayor asked.

"Any chance there's a skeleton or two in his closet we might exploit? An inordinate fondness for underage virgins or some such thing?"

"I'm looking into the possibilities," Hadley said, "but I'm not optimistic. There's also the problem that he has heavyweight connections, from what I understand."

"What sort of connections?"

"I'm told he's tight with James J. Hill and some of the other big businessmen in St. Paul. He's also close to some of the newspaper people over there. He won't be easy to push around."

"I see. How much do you think he knows?"

Hadley said, "It's hard to tell, A.A. What happens, for example, if he finds out about Zier Row?"

"That would be most inconvenient, but how would he find out?"

"Your guess is as good as mine. We do know, though, from the tail Mr. McParland put on him yesterday, that Rafferty was over at the Shevlin-Carpenter Mill. He talked to one of the workers there — Pruitt's his name. This Pruitt is a radical we've had our eye on for some time."

"Do you know what they talked about?" Adams asked, directing his question to McParland.

"My man could not get close enough to hear. But we will find out more about this Rafferty character soon enough."

"Do that, gentlemen," said Adams. "We must keep a lid on this business. I don't need to tell you what's at stake."

"I understand," said Hadley. "Maybe it's time for the police to haul Rafferty in and work him over."

Adams shook his head. "No, if the police bring him in, then he'll be certain that we're desperate to hide something. The offer of a bribe would undoubtedly have the same effect. That is why I think it best to watch and wait for the time being. If the situation becomes critical, we may have to consider some form of more direct action when it comes to Mr. Rafferty."

"That would be my pleasure," said Hadley.

After Randolph Hadley's departure, Rafferty remained in his hotel room for the better part of an hour, debating what to do next. One thing was immediately clear. Someone had tipped off Hadley, and presumably the police as well, about Rafferty's mission in Minneapolis. He wondered who that person might be. He also wondered if he was still being tailed, and although he had seen nothing suspicious on his walk up to the sawmill, he knew that he would have to take extra precautions in the future.

He was still mulling over his course of action when the telephone in his room — one of only a few in the hotel so equipped — rang with a noise sufficient to wake the dead. Rafferty answered and waited while the call was put through by the hotel operator. To his surprise, the caller was Addie O'Donnell.

"I am glad I found you," she said without preamble. "Mrs. Burke said you were at the West."

"Ah, so you talked to Maj. Did she vouch for me?"

"She did, and that is why I now wish to tell you something. It is about Michael. I did not tell you the complete truth when we talked."

There was a pause and Rafferty said, "Go on."

"Not over the telephone," she said. "You never know who might be listening."

"All right. Should I meet you at Michael's house?"

"No," she said, "I do not think that would be a good idea. I fear I am being watched, Mr. Rafferty."

"By whom?"

"Agents of the alliance, I should imagine. Do you remember a place I mentioned when we talked at the house. A place where Jacqueline had gone?"

She could only be referring to the Church of the Immaculate Conception. "Yes, I remember the place," Rafferty said.

"Then meet me there tomorrow night at ten o'clock, and take care that you are not followed."

"Why not sooner?"

"No, it must be tomorrow. There are things I must do today. You will not fail me, will you, Mr. Rafferty?" There was an almost plaintiff note in her usually firm voice.

"No, I won't fail you."

"Then we will talk tomorrow," she said and hung up.

It was well after noon by the time Rafferty set out to find Sid the Ratman. He did not have to go far for information, for one of the front desk clerks at the hotel was very familiar with the Ratman's "schedule."

"Basically, he don't come out until it's dark, or close to it," the clerk said. "God only knows where he's to be found during daylight hours. Probably in a deep hole somewhere, with all the other creatures of the night. Along about dusk, though, he likes to hang around Fourth Street near Newspaper Row. That would be your best chance to spot him."

The clerk, a slender young fellow with bushy eyebrows and a long, sharp nose, also provided a brief and, Rafferty thought, poignant history of the strange little man who had become something of a municipal institution. He said the Ratman's real name was Thomas Goodale, and in the 1880s he had been a highly respected contractor whose firm helped construct some of the city's most notable buildings.

One day in early 1889 he and his twenty-year-old son were at work on the roof of the new Minneapolis Globe Building, which at eight stories was one of the city's taller structures. Accounts vary as to what exactly happened, but one witness claimed that the younger Goodale was startled by a rat that suddenly crossed his path. In an instant he lost his footing and fell a hundred feet to an alley below. His father, who was on another part of the roof, heard his son's horrible scream as he plummeted to his death. The young man was killed instantly, his head split open in a wound so terrible to behold that even hardened policemen became sick at the sight of it.

After Goodale buried his son, he slowly slipped into madness, wandering the streets at all hours and buttonholing passersby with fantastic stories of rats and other noxious creatures. Yet like many a lunatic, Goodale was also touched with a peculiar kind of genius. His wanderings had led him to almost every corner of the city, and his builder's eye for detail had not vanished with his sanity. The clerk told Rafferty that Goodale would sometimes assemble a crowd on the street and delivery surprisingly learned lectures on local architecture, invariably ending with a chant that went: "I believe, I do, and you must, too, that the Globe is better than the Guaranty Loan, the Globe is better than the Guaranty Loan." So familiar had this chant become that the Ratman's audiences would invariably join along as he got to the name of the Guaranty Loan, a large downtown office block that had been completed not long after the Globe Building.[1]

Rafferty gave the clerk a dollar for his trouble and then went back up to his room. He read the newspapers—President McKinley's impending visit was still big news—then decided to take a nap. First, however, he pushed a heavy dresser in front of the door, just in case someone from the alliance, or the police, decided to pay an unannounced visit. Rafferty awoke at half past four, wrote out a brief letter to Holmes, then went down to the hotel dining room for dinner. After his meal he went into the men's washroom, which he knew from previous use had a large window overlooking an alley. He opened the window, stepped outside, and walked to Fourth Street, a half block away. No one followed, and Rafferty was confident that if he did indeed have a tail, he was now rid of him.

Newspaper Row was the name given to a stretch of Fourth, barely a block from the hotel, which was home to the *Globe*, the *Journal*, the *Tribune*, and Minneapolis's other dailies. Although it was not yet completely dark, Rafferty intended to hang around in hopes the Ratman would put in an appearance. No sooner had he turned down Fourth, however, than he saw, lecturing to a small crowd on the sidewalk, the Ratman in the flesh.[2]

"'Tis nice of you to arrive early this evenin', Mr. Ratman," Rafferty said to himself as he walked toward the crowd. But as he got closer, Rafferty saw that the "crowd" was actually a gang of young toughs—a half dozen or so—who were mercilessly taunting the Ratman. One of the toughs, who appeared to be the leader, was trying to grab a rodent trap that the Ratman wore like an amulet on a heavy chain around his neck.

"C'mon, Sid, let's see if we can catch you," the tough said, trying to pull the trap off its chain.

"Go away, go away," the Ratman shouted in a high, piercing voice.

Rafferty came up behind the ringleader, put a hand on his collar, and flung him like a doll out into the street, where he landed in a freshly deposited pile of horse manure.

Another of the toughs, more foolish than brave, made a run at Rafferty, but was stopped cold by the seemingly magical appearance of a pistol pressed to forehead. "I have no time for shenanigans at the moment," Rafferty said as he used his free hand to remove a small knife from the front pocket of the young man's trousers.

"'Tis not wise to carry a knife, my boy, when there are men about with guns," Rafferty told the young thug. After briefly examining the knife, which had a finely honed blade, Rafferty tossed it into a sewer grate, surveyed his opposition, and said, "Now, then, what's it to be, lads? 'Twould seem you're in the mood for trouble this evenin', and if that be the case, I'm the man to see. Who will be the first?"

The ringleader, whose shirt and trousers were smeared with manure, had by this time gotten back to his feet and began shouting obscenities at Rafferty while vowing revenge. However, he did not seem especially eager to wreak this terrible vengeance immediately, for he made sure to keep his distance from Rafferty. The threatening talk was a good sign from Rafferty's point of view. He knew from long experience that there were talkers and there were fighters, and that the former were seldom the latter.

Even so, Rafferty was surprised when, moments later, the whole gang suddenly took off down the street toward Nicollet Avenue. Rafferty turned around and saw the reason for their flight. A pair of coppers were coming up from Hennepin, no doubt having seen the trouble. Rafferty slipped his pistol back in his coat and greeted the officers genially when they arrived on the scene.

"'Twas a bunch of criminals botherin' poor Sid here," Rafferty told them, "but everything is fine now. The miscreants, it appears, did not wish to tangle with the strong arm of the law."

After Rafferty had provided a description of the toughs—who were identified at once as members of the well-known Charpentier gang—the two officers went on their way, assuring Rafferty that when they found the gang members they would mete out rough justice with their nightsticks.

Rafferty was now free to devote his full attention to the Ratman, who presented a remarkable spectacle. He was a small man, probably close to Rafferty's age, with a large round head marked by a long thin nose and close-set black eyes that lay within unusually deep sockets. His head was stubbled with hair, suggesting that he shaved it periodically, but the rest of his face had not been visited by a razor in years, as evidenced by the luxuriant brown and gray beard that dropped down to his breastbone. He wore a long, tattered, and very heavy wool overcoat, along with a pair of galoshes, even though the day was hardly wintry. The coat was open at the top to reveal the rat trap dangling around his neck. He also carried what appeared to be a ledger book with an elaborately tooled leather cover.

"I trust you are all right," Rafferty said. "I saw those men botherin' you and thought I might be of some help."

The Ratman looked up at Rafferty and in his high-pitched, rapid-fire voice said, "Did I tell you, sir, that when I worked out East—in Brooklyn it was, if you want to know—I met a man much troubled by rats. Now a rat is a clever creature, sir, clever as Old Nick himself, and dirty as well. Oh yes, there is nothing filthier than a rat, for think, sir, of where a rat goes, and what it eats! Well now, this man I knew who was troubled by rats, he came to me, he did, and he asked me—in a very friendly way, I might add—what shall I do about these rats? What shall I do? And do you know what I told him? Do you know, sir?"

"Please tell me," said Rafferty, "for I myself have been troubled by rats now and then."

"Ah, so then you understand. Well, I told him exactly what he should do, exactly! Set a trap, I told him, and catch one of those rats. Just one, mind you. And he did, and then do you know what I told him?"

"I do not," Rafferty admitted.

"Of course you don't, sir, because I have not told you yet, have I? Well now, I said to this man, I said, douse that rat, that filthy creature, in kerosene! Pour it on, I said, pour on like water, and then light it. Light it so that it blazes forth like the burning bush before Moses. So he did it, oh yes, he did it. He burned that rat, burned it alive, right there where all the other rats, hiding in their dirty secret places, could see and smell the fire. Oh yes, they watched that rat go up in flames. Purifying flames. Ha! And do you know what, sir? Do you know that this fellow has not been troubled by rats since!"

"A fascinatin' story," said Rafferty, who quickly added, "Did I tell you that a friend of mine, a very good friend, has had just the sort of trouble you speak of, at his very own home right here in this city?"

The Ratman nodded sagaciously and said, "It does not surprise me. No sir, it does not surprise me at all. Minneapolis is famous for its rats, if you must know. Famous. You have heard of the Norway rat, have you not?" he asked, dropping his voice and looking furtively up an down the street, as though fearful of eavesdroppers.

"I have," Rafferty acknowledged in an equally soft voice.

"Well then, you know the problem, don't you?"

"I'm not sure I understand," Rafferty admitted.

The Ratman, after again inspecting the street for any sign of interlopers, whispered, "Norwegians. They're everywhere in this city. Everywhere. They brought the rats, don't you see? The Swedes helped them, I'm sure."

"Ah, of course. And now that you mention it, I think my friend lives near a Norwegian, which must explain all of those rats. Here, let me show you something."

Rafferty got out his photograph of the cornice and showed it to the Ratman, who squinted at it in the dying light. "This is where the rats are hiding, my friend tells me. Right behind this cornice."

"Behind the cornice, you say? Well, sir, those dirty little devils can hide almost anywhere."

"A terrible thing," Rafferty agreed. "I also must tell you that I have a little problem, and you strike me as just the man who could help, since I have been told you are not only an expert on rats but also on the buildings of this city. You see, I am—"

"That is true," the Ratman broke in eagerly, handing Rafferty the leatherbound volume he was carrying. "It is all here, in the book of buildings. Yes, sir, it's all right here. Take a look for yourself."

Feeling as though he had stumbled upon the Mad Hatter's tea party, Rafferty opened the book, which was indeed a ledger. But instead of figures, the wide pages were filled with the Ratman's crabbed, virtually illegible handwriting, which went this way and that like the trail of a roaming animal. Here and there, however, Rafferty could make out a word—invariably the name of some building—along with an address and what appeared to be some sort of commentary.

"It is an account of every building within the fire limits of the city of Minneapolis," the Ratman said proudly. "Every building! I have missed nothing. It will shock the world when I publish it, sir, shock the world."

"I am sure it will," Rafferty said, finding himself at a loss for words.

"Shoddy construction, sir, shoddy construction. It is everywhere. The contractors of this city are little better than thieves and whores, and the architects their pimps. They will not be so happy when I expose them, will they? They are just like the rats, sir, just like the rats. They are dirty to the core and they respect nothing."

The Ratman took a moment to catch his breath, and Rafferty quickly weighed in with a question. His original idea had been to pretend that he had lost the address of his friend's rat-infested building and ask the Ratman's help. Now he saw an easier way to reach his goal. He asked, "Would I be right in supposin' that the building of the structure I have shown you is just such a thief and whore?"

"Of course he is!" replied the Ratman. "George Peterson is among the worst. He did many of those buildings in the vicinity of Fourth Avenue South. Horrible work. Weak foundations, leaky roofs, vermin everywhere. Oh yes, he will be exposed in the book of buildings like all the others. His day of judgment will come. You may count on that, sir."

Rafferty gave a sympathetic nod and said, "I am pleased to hear that." Then once again drawing the Ratman's attention to the photograph, he said, "Now that you mention it, this building is familiar. It's the one at Fourth Avenue South and Twelfth Street, as I recall."

"Ninth Street," the Ratman shot back without a moment's hesitation. "Across from Zier Row. The Bellingham Apartments. Built in 1895. A very shoddy piece of work, very shoddy. And now I am told it has rats in the cornice. Not a pretty picture, sir, not a pretty picture."

"Most unfortunate," Rafferty agreed with a shake of the head, adding, "I am much obliged for your help."

"Of course you are. Now, if you find those rats, skulking with their dirty little bodies up in the cornice, I trust you know what to do, sir."

"Burn them," said Rafferty with a smile as he turned to go, but not before slipping a five-dollar gold piece into the Ratman's coat pocket.

"Exactly," the Ratman said. "Exactly."

Although it was growing dark, Rafferty went at once toward the intersection of Ninth Street and Fourth Avenue South. He found it odd that he was going yet another time to the part of the city where Michael O'Donnell had lived and died. It was as though all the energies of the strange affair had concentrated themselves, like poison settling to the bottom of a bottle. Of course, Rafferty could not be sure that the Ratman's information was correct, but there was something about the man's crazed confidence that led him to believe he would finally find what he was looking for.

He walked east on Fourth Street until he reached the rather glum granite mass of the new city hall and courthouse. Then he turned south down Fourth Avenue, passing through what was still a largely residential area, although the inevitable commercial encroachment was already well underway. A couple of streetcars passed him, but otherwise traffic was light. Even though few other pedestrians were about, Rafferty kept a sharp eye out to see if he had any shadows. He saw nothing suspicious.

As he approached Ninth Street, the rugged outlines of a large brick row house came into view. Rafferty soon spotted a sign identifying it as Zier Row. When he got to the corner, he saw, directly across from one side of the row house, a narrow brick apartment building, three stories high. In the deepening dusk, he could just make out a familiar-looking cornice. "God bless the Ratman," Rafferty said softly to himself as he walked down to inspect the building, which bore the name BELLINGHAM over the entrance.[3]

He got out the photograph and studied it for a moment under the light of a street lamp. The Bellingham was directly across the street from the two end units of Zier Row, and Rafferty saw at once that it must have been in one of those apartments that the photograph of Randolph Hadley and his consort had been taken. Rafferty went across the street to inspect the two apartments, which were reached by common steps leading up to a stoop with adjacent doorways. After glancing around one last time, he walked up to the stoop.

Above the bell to the left door, in a small brass holder, was a card identifying the occupant as William Carter. The name was unfamiliar, so Rafferty moved over to the right-hand door, where to his immense surprise he found the name of Charles Wellington, the "flour king" of Minneapolis and the original owner of the house where Michael O'Donnell had died. Too bad Sid wasn't around, Rafferty thought, for he was definitely beginning to smell a rat.

CHAPTER NINE

&

"Rafferty Won't Be a Threat"

FROM THE JOURNALS OF DR. JOHN WATSON:

TUES., OCT 3, 1899, WALDORF-ASTORIA HOTEL, N.Y., 4:30 A.M.: H awoke me to report "most astonishing dream" regarding SR's case.

H: "It featured Jefferson Hope, the avenger you well remember from *A Study in Scarlet*. He was in a city I did not recognize but which looked very American. More to the point, he was in the process of hanging a man, pulling with all his strength on a rope dangling over the limb of a large tree."[1]

W: "You have been thinking about Mr. Rafferty's case, I see."

H: "Yes. But it is curious, is it not, Watson, that I should dream of a lone avenger in a case that supposedly involves organized murder."

W: "In my experience, Holmes, dreams are always curious."

H: "Yes, & that is why they must be respected. You see, there was one other aspect of my dream I have not mentioned. The man being hanged was Mr. Rafferty."

This was very strange & disturbing indeed.

W: "My God, do you see this as a portent?"

H: "I believe in reason, Watson, not portents. Nonetheless, I do not like the fact that I had such a dream. I do not like it at all."

H left without another word. Tried to get back to sleep but found it impossible. . . .

As he stared at the door of Wellington's townhouse, Rafferty toyed with the idea of knocking but decided to reconnoiter first. He went back down the steps and crossed the street, trying to look inconspicuous—no easy thing for a 250-pound man wearing a shovel hat and a bright red sport coat over a checkered shirt.

Once on the sidewalk, Rafferty paused to take out a cigar, deliberately fumbling for a few seconds as though trying to find his matches. As he did so, he glanced up at the townhouse. Next to the front door was a picture window with a stained-glass transom above. Lacy white curtains hung in the window and Rafferty caught a quick glimpse of a figure moving past them. The figure was small and appeared to have long hair. A woman was clearly at home in Wellington's townhouse.

After lighting his cigar, Rafferty decided to take a chance and knock on the door. The risk, as he saw it, was that no one would answer but that whoever was inside would be able to identify him through the window. He would then lose whatever advantage of surprise he might have later in the case. Still, he thought it likely that the woman inside was alone, reasoning that if the house was being used for assignations, the gentlemen who came calling would probably do so well after dark. Then again, for all Rafferty knew, old Charles Wellington himself might answer the door.

Tossing away his cigar, Rafferty recrossed the street, went up the steps, and rang the doorbell. No answer. He rang again. Still no answer. Thinking the bell might not be working, Rafferty used the door's brass knocker. But despite several minutes of knocking, the woman inside refused to come to the door. Perhaps she had indeed seen him through the window. It was even possible she knew him by sight.

Rafferty stood on the stoop considering his options, then turned around and left. As he walked down the steps, he consulted his watch and saw that it was half past six. Although it was now dark, Rafferty did not want to risk suspicion by hanging around in front of the townhouse, so he went up to the streetcar stop on Fourth Avenue South. Waiting there, he figured, would not attract much notice from occupants of any of the nearby apartments. He went through four more cigars and waved eight streetcars past him, all the while keeping an eye on Wellington's townhouse down the block. No one arrived for a visit with the woman inside.

Rafferty didn't plan to wait around forever, since the odds of seeing someone entering or leaving the house were hardly in his favor. By ten o'clock the scene was still quiet, and Rafferty decided to call it a night. As he took one last look down Ninth Street, however, he saw a coach come out from the alley behind Zier Row. This struck him as odd, for everyone who could afford the expense of such a large vehicle was not the sort of person who would normally come and go by the back door. The coach, pulled by a well-matched team and driven by a large man in a long black coat, came up under the street lamp at Fourth, then turned south, passing directly in front of Rafferty. There was no way to tell if anyone was inside because the curtains were drawn. But as the big coach rumbled past, Rafferty noted with considerable interest that its carefully polished doors bore the insignia of the city of Minneapolis.

Rafferty boarded the next streetcar that arrived, still keeping a watchful eye out for unwanted company. As he rode back to his hotel, he mulled over what he had just seen. Was it possible that Charles Wellington, in addition to his other achievements, had late in life managed to acquire a mistress — one whom he shared unwittingly with Hadley and perhaps the mayor of Minneapolis as well? Rafferty wasn't sure, but he did come to one conclusion: He needed to know much more about what was going on behind the lacy curtains at Zier Row.

Early the next morning Rafferty took the interurban streetcar back to St. Paul. He wanted to check in at the saloon and pick up some fresh clothes. Then he planned to return to Minneapolis and make a few more inquiries before his meeting with Addie O'Donnell. Aboard the streetcar he kept a careful watch to see if he was being followed, but he wasn't able to spot a shadow, if there was one, among the two dozen people in the car.

Along the way, he read the *Globe*, the *Tribune*, and the *Times*, hoping that one of the Minneapolis dailies would offer at least a few nuggets of wisdom about the O'Donnell case. But the dead man had already been relegated to the back pages or entirely forgotten. Instead, the press was already in a frenzy over William McKinley's visit, only six days away. Rafferty, however, had given the presidential appearance little thought— he had too much else to worry about.

Wash Thomas was waiting for him when he came into the saloon, as was Sherlock, who took a running leap into his master's arms. Rafferty spent half an hour playing with the bulldog, which had been "mopey" in his absence, according to Thomas. Then Thomas cooked up breakfast at the bar while Rafferty brought him up to date on developments in Minneapolis.

Thomas listened to Rafferty's report with his usual gravity and said, "There was a fellow here last night asking for you."

"What sort of a fellow?"

"Oh, a Pinkerton man, I expect."

His partner's calm, deadpan manner was, for Rafferty, a constant source of bemusement and wonder. Thomas could be discussing the most dreadful events imaginable, or the most richly comic, yet his demeanor never seemed to change. He was, Rafferty thought, that rarest and most valuable of allies—one who always knew more than most people believed possible.

"What makes you think he was a Pinkerton?"

"Everything. If you pay attention to people, you find that certain types tend to act in certain ways. I have dealt with Pinkertons before. This fellow was a Pinkerton."

Rafferty wasn't sure that Thomas's logic held up, but he didn't doubt his conclusion. If Wash Thomas thought the man was a Pinkerton, then he almost certainly was.

"What did he want?"

"Said he was collecting information for a book—you know, one of those kinds all the rich men pay to have their pictures in."

"A subscription book."

"Right. Anyway, this fellow said he wanted to know all about you— where you came from, who you knew, what you had done before becoming a saloonkeeper—that sort of thing. Of course, I told him he'd have to talk to you after you got back into town from your fishing trip."

"Did he seem agreeable to that?"

"No, he just kept asking more questions. Said he had a deadline to meet and needed to gather information as quickly as possible. I did finally answer one of his questions, though."

"What was that?"

"He wanted to know how you had become so successful in the saloon business."

"Ah, did he now? And what did you tell him?"

Thomas allowed himself the merest hint of a grin and said, "I told him you had a very smart partner."

Rafferty couldn't help letting out a big whoop of a laugh. "By God, Wash, you're turnin' into a regular comedian in your old age, though I can't deny the truth of it. If it was me watchin' the till, we'd be broke for sure. Now then, just what did this fellow look like?"

Thomas gave a meticulous description of the man—the upshot of which was that he was very average looking in every respect. He certainly wasn't the man with the pock-marked face who had followed Rafferty to and from J. Winston Phelps's house.

"Anything else about this fellow that struck you?" Rafferty asked.

"Just that he was wearing a pistol under his left armpit. A big one, judging by the bulge."

Rafferty nodded and said, "In my experience Pinkertons goin' about their normal detective work don't carry guns."

"No," said Wash Thomas, "they usually don't. If I were you, Shad, that's something I'd worry about."

"Your concern's duly noted," said Rafferty.

After breakfast Rafferty went to his office. There he carefully put away the photograph of the cornice he had been carrying around with him, seeing no further use for it at the moment. He hung on to the photograph of Hadley and his lover, thinking he might need it very soon. A copy had already been stored away where no searcher would ever find it.

Just before eleven o'clock, as Rafferty was helping Thomas prepare for the noon rush, Joseph Pyle telephoned to report that he had some "extremely interesting news."

"Spill it," said Rafferty.

"Not so fast. I'll need some refreshment first. What say I stop by in ten minutes?"

"You've got a deal."

When Pyle arrived, Rafferty drew a tall mug of Yeorg's best cave-aged lager, put it in front of the editor, and said, "All right, Joseph, here is your thirst quencher. Now then, what have you got for me?"

Pyle said, "Mr. Griggs has finally learned what the Minneapolis cops are hiding. You'll be surprised, Shad, by what they found beneath O'Donnell's body. Care to guess?"

"No."

"Are you sure?"

"Positive. Now, out with it, Joseph, before I'm forced to take that mug of beer away and give it to a more deservin' soul than yourself."

Pyle grinned and said, "All right, I won't keep you in suspense any longer. The coppers found, believe it or not, a baited rat trap. You'll read all about it in our story tomorrow."

"A rat trap. Now that is strange," said Rafferty. "And it was on the ground below where the young man was danglin'?"

"Exactly."

Rafferty thought for a minute and said, "This puts a new slant on things, wouldn't you say, Joseph?"

"It does. Makes you wonder if maybe O'Donnell was murdered by his own people and not the alliance after all. Randolph Hadley has been saying that all along. As you know, Shad, nobody likes an informant, and heaven knows there are plenty of those around these days, what with all the labor unrest."

"True enough," Rafferty said. "Of course, since this case is beginnin' to look more and more like a hall of mirrors, could be the trap is just another reverse image designed to lead us all astray."

"A false clue, you mean?"

"Maybe, but if that's the case—the alliance puttin' up a sign identifyin' its lethal deed, then sayin' the sign is a obviously fake and then plantin' a rat trap to suggest O'Donnell was murdered because he betrayed the unions—well, Joseph, we are enterin' a world of such murderous subtlety that 'twould be a wonder if anyone, least of all the coppers, could ever hope to appreciate it. 'Tis all too much, if you ask me. Tell me this: Just what sort of trap was it?"

"I thought you might ask," Pyle said, "so I got all the details from Griggs. According to a confidential police report he obtained, the trap was of the common spring type, made by the Erie Company, out of Cleveland. You can buy them at any hardware store or through the Sears catalog."[2]

"I have a few myself in the storeroom," Rafferty said. "Now, did I hear you right when you said the trap was baited?"

"With a moldy piece of hard cheese."

Rafferty scratched at his chin and said, "Ah, that is mighty curious, Joseph, mighty curious."

"Do you mean the cheese, or the trap, or both?"

"All of the above, but especially the cheese. By the way, do you know why the coppers tried to keep the trap a secret?"

"No. But it seems strange, doesn't it? You'd think the trap would make Hadley's point—you know, about O'Donnell being killed by his own kind."

"You would, unless—" Rafferty never finished the sentence, his voice trailing off as he considered a new possibility.

"Unless what?" Pyle finally asked.

"Unless the trap is not what we think it is. And if the murderers are startin' to think in the same way, then there's a certain fellow in Minneapolis who might be the next victim of an 'accident,' just like that poor cartman."

"Shad, I have no idea what you're talking about," said Pyle.

Rafferty smiled and drew another mug of lager for Pyle. "Ah, 'tis nothin' but a wild idea that crossed my mind, that's all. Well, drink up, Joseph, drink up, for I'm thinkin' it may be a while before we see each other again."

"I still think it dangerous to meet here," said J. Winston Phelps to the woman with whom he was having lunch that afternoon at Leonardo's, the most celebrated restaurant in Minneapolis. Located on the top floor of the Northwestern Guaranty Loan Building, the tallest office block in the city, Leonardo's was hardly the place for a discreet meal. Indeed, it was in many ways the city's most visible dining emporium, where the leading businessmen of Minneapolis gathered to eat thick steaks, drink fine wine, and make deals invariably designed to take advantage of the other fellow. In this clubby atmosphere of money and carefully calibrated chicanery, J. Winston Phelps was hardly a welcome figure, given his record as a champion of labor. But the lady, for reasons of her own, had insisted on Leonardo's, and could not be talked out of the idea.[3]

Not surprisingly, they had received more than a few stares from the assembled plutocrats when they were escorted to their table. Phelps was used to such treatment and gave it no concern other than to wonder whether the stares were directed at him because of his radicalism or because he was dining with an attractive woman. And she *was* attractive—no doubt about that—though even Phelps had to admit her disguise was extremely effective. The wig, the false eyelashes, the rouge, the oversized bustle—all had combined to make of her a much different woman from the one he had been used to seeing.

She loved disguises, and Phelps wondered whether the rootlessness of her life—the parents lost at such an early age, the orphanage, the terrible experiences in Chicago—had caused her to invent other selves as a way of rewriting her own bitter history. Now that she was home at last, Phelps knew there was only one history that really mattered to her.

They had been seated at a table by one of the restaurant's big windows that offered a stunning view of the city—a sepia-toned panorama of brick, stone, steel, and wood under a soot-stained sky. Their window faced east, as the woman had specified, which meant that the flour-milling district around St. Anthony Falls lay almost at their feet. The stone and brick mills combined to form a great wall along the west bank of the Mississippi, although one milling complex—Charles Wellington's—clearly dominated the scene.

"I like it here because you can see all the mills," the woman said, ignoring the cautionary statement with which Phelps had opened the conversation. "They're like pigs at a trough, lined up to drink from the river."

"Too bad there isn't enough water to go around this year," Phelps noted. "The river's very low, as you know. The mill owners are already in court fighting over who gets what."

"And Wellington will win that fight, won't he?"

"He usually does," Phelps acknowledged.

"How much do you suppose he'll spend to steal the water he needs?"

"A lot. Men like Charles Wellington do not hire inexpensive lawyers."

The woman laughed bitterly. "I imagine it will be far, far more than he spent on the monument at Lakewood, but then the monument never really mattered to him, did it? Only money matters to his kind of man."

She paused a moment, then said, "Think of all the poor men inside those mills and all the money they produce for a few rich men like Wellington. That is what the mills are, you know, just big machines for satisfying the obscene appetites of the wealthy."

"I have heard this speech before," Phelps said, hoping to stave off a lecture.

"And you can never hear it enough!" the woman replied angrily. "It is the only truth worth knowing about this city. The only truth!"

"I don't dispute that, but there are other matters we need to discuss at the moment. I hope you realize just how tight a situation we're in. If we're not careful, everything could fall apart in an instant."

"You're exaggerating again, Win. I don't see that anything has gone terribly wrong."

"Really?" he asked in disbelief. "Well, from where I sit everything is not exactly going like goddamn clockwork. In case you haven't noticed, the police force is on high alert, Hadley and that little weasel McParland have spies everywhere, your old nemesis Wooldridge is still sniffing around in Chicago, and Earl has a bad case of the shakes. And then, of course, there's the biggest problem of all—that fellow Rafferty. He's getting too close for comfort. Remember, he's already got at least one photograph, and if he's as sharp as he's reputed to be, he'll figure out what Michael was up to. And if that happens—"

"It won't happen," the woman said, "because we can't let it happen. Too much is at stake. All we need is another few days, and it will all be over, and the whole world will learn a lesson about justice. The Irishman won't stop us. I will see to that."

"How?"

"I have a plan," she said. "Rafferty won't be a threat, I assure you."

"I see, Mr. Borden, that your men managed to lose Rafferty last night," said James McParland as he reviewed the daily logs kept by the three Pinkerton agents who were supposed to be Rafferty's shadows. McParland had marched into Borden's shabby office early in the afternoon to examine the logs and, Borden knew, remove a piece of his hide. So far, however, McParland had been remarkably calm, though Borden knew it couldn't last.

McParland put down the last page of the logs and said, "It seems your ace agents didn't see Rafferty leave the West Hotel but, lo and behold, they did see him return at 10:35 P.M. Now, where do you suppose he went?"

William Borden shook his head slowly and said, "Obviously, sir, I do not know, but I have already expressed to the agents involved my extreme dissatisfaction with their performance. They must do a better job in the future."

"You're goddamned right they must!" McParland yelled, pounding his fist with such force on Borden's desk that a small paperweight tumbled to the floor. "These men are not paid to be idiots. Nor are you, I might add. Why wasn't one of them in the alley?"

"I don't know, sir," Borden admitted. "Standard procedure—"

"Standard procedure states that you don't lose your man," McParland cut in. Then he paused, obviously prepared to savor the next moment, and said, "It's a good thing I was on the scene last night, isn't it?"

"I don't understand—"

McParland again interrupted, "You seem to have trouble understanding much of anything today, Borden, so I will spell it out for you. I took the liberty of watching Rafferty myself last night. I saw him as he went into the washroom by the hotel restaurant. I waited a few moments before going in myself, as one of your men should have done. He had already gone out the window by that time. I was able to pick him up moments later outside the hotel and followed him."

"That was very good work, sir," Borden offered.

"How nice of you to say so," said McParland sarcastically. "Perhaps in the future, as you say, your men might also try doing good work. I will have your head, and theirs, on a platter if they lose Rafferty again. Is that clear?"

"Very clear," said Borden. "I assure you they will not let you down. By the way, if I may ask, sir, where did Rafferty go?"

"Where he shouldn't have," said McParland, rising from his chair and putting on his bowler hat, "and it will cost him dearly if he is not careful."

⁂

Before returning to Minneapolis that same afternoon, Rafferty stopped at the Western Union office a block from his saloon and sent off another telegram to Holmes. The message was brief: HAVE LEARNED BAITED RAT TRAP FOUND BENEATH O'DONNELL'S BODY. IDEAS WELCOME. RAFFERTY.

It was well after two by the time Rafferty checked back in at the West Hotel, where he had another talk with the desk clerk who seemed so well-informed about Sid the Ratman. The clerk provided Rafferty with a list of the half dozen or so downtown intersections the Ratman was known to favor, along with the best times of "Sid sightings," as the clerk called them. Rafferty also asked the clerk whether the Ratman was known to hang out along Tenth Street.

"Can't really say," the clerk replied, "but I know I've seen him once or twice at the library, which is up at Tenth and Hennepin, so I guess I wouldn't be surprised if he spends some time in that part of town."

Rafferty thanked the clerk, tipped him again, and said, "One more thing. I'd like a different room—one up toward the front of the hotel."

"Certainly. Is there a problem with the room you have now, sir?"

"No problem," said Rafferty, who had decided that changing rooms might be a wise precaution, since he had been away for much of the day. "I just like bein' closer to where there are plenty of people around."

After an early dinner Rafferty went out to look for the Ratman, and over the next several hours covered much of downtown Minneapolis on foot. The Ratman proved to be elusive. He didn't show up by Newspaper Row or near Donaldson's Glass Block, the city's largest department store, or along Tenth Street. Nor could Rafferty find anyone who had seen the Ratman that evening. At nine o'clock, he abandoned his search for the night and went back to the hotel, where he hoped there might be a telegram waiting from Holmes. Nothing had come in, so Rafferty went to his new room, put on a heavier coat to ward off the increasing chill of the night, and then went to meet Addie O'Donnell at the Church of the Immaculate Conception.

He found her standing by the front door of the church, which was locked and dark, as were the big brick warehouses that loomed nearby. Rafferty had taken a circuitous route from the hotel, hoping to shake off any tails, but in the darkness it was hard to tell if anyone was following.

"Good evenin', Miss O'Donnell," he said as she stepped out from beneath the deep archway that led into the church. "I trust you have come alone."

"I was not followed, if that is what you mean," she said. "Can the same be said of you?"

"I hope so, but I must be honest about it. When it's as black out as it is tonight, 'tis no easy thing to spot a tail, especially if he's a clever one."

"Well, I guess there is no harm even if we are seen together. The important thing is that no one else must hear what I am about to tell you."

She took a long look around, grabbed Rafferty by the arm, and pulled him back under the archway, which was dark as a cave.

"There now, I doubt we can be seen at all," she said, "and I know we can't be heard. I would begin, Mr. Rafferty, by telling you that I have talked to Majesty Burke and several other trustworthy people, and they have all vouched for your integrity. Therefore, I am willing to rely upon your discretion and good judgment in this terrible matter of my brother's murder. Now, can you tell me what you have learned thus far?"

"Ah, I'm afraid that's confidential, Miss O'Donnell. I like to play my cards close to the vest while I'm in the middle of things. Otherwise, you never know who might find out somethin' they shouldn't."

"So you do not trust me," she replied. "I am disappointed to hear that."

"'Tis not that I distrust you, Miss O'Donnell. I merely prefer to keep my own counsel. I will tell you, however, that I'm makin' progress in my investigation, though much remains to be learned. Therefore, I'd be mighty grateful for any new information you might be able to share with me."

"All right, I will have to trust you even if you do not return the sentiment," she said, removing a folded piece of paper from her handbag and pressing it into Rafferty's hands. "I think you will find this interesting. It's a clipping from the *Tribune* that you can read later. It has to do with the Tunnel Boys. I believe Michael may have been involved with them. I assume you've heard of the Tunnel Boys."

"Of course," said Rafferty, "though I'm not sure I believe most of what I've read."

The Tunnel Boys were, according to the newspapers, a gang of ruffians—many of them supposedly lads of twelve or younger—said to populate the maze of tailrace tunnels, sewers, and other passages that honeycombed the soft sandstone beneath the St. Anthony Falls milling district. The gang had first come to public attention a year or so earlier when an enterprising reporter for the *Minneapolis Tribune* claimed to have been led blindfolded into the tunnels for an interview with the gang's leader, a masked man who improbably identified himself as Robin Hood (which, by a convenient coincidence, also happened to be the name of a brand of flour made at the falls).[4]

In gilded prose not notable for its restraint, the *Tribune* article depicted the gang in a light at once romantic and lurid, describing its members "as the homeless human refuse of the city, including a large number of street urchins and other wayward boys who have banded together to fight for economic justice in a society that has spurned them." The gang, it was reported, was "by conservative estimate responsible for half the robberies in Minneapolis," but took money only from the rich so that it could be redistributed to the needy.

The story, as its clever writer intended, created a sensation, and by the next day every newspaper in the Twin Cities offered its own account of the doings of Robin Hood and his presumably merry men. Most of these articles, however, were so bereft of hard facts that Rafferty wrote them off as nothing more than spirited works of reportorial imagination. The police quickly reached the same conclusion, stating that the mysterious Robin Hood—or "Fagin," as some less charitable members of the Fourth Estate dubbed him—was nowhere to be found. In fact, a police sweep of the tunnels one day turned up only a couple of boys playing hooky and one adult who turned out to be none other than Sid the Rat-man (a fact Rafferty had long since forgotten).

Yet the legend of the Tunnel Boys proved impossible to kill and even became a self-fulfilling prophecy, for after the newspaper stories appeared many youngsters tried to make their way into the tunnels. For a time the mill owners were forced to hire special guards to keep the curious away, and even though the story soon disappeared from the newspapers, rumors continued to persist of a group of desperate men who prowled the tunnels, waylaying any strangers unfortunate enough to cross their path.

"As I recall, the Tunnel Boys made for an interestin' story," Rafferty now said, "but what leads you to believe, Miss O'Donnell, that your brother was runnin' around with a gang in the tunnels?"

"To begin with, there's the clipping I just gave you. I found it in a dresser drawer at Michael's house. The police must have seen it but apparently thought it was of no significance—their mistake. More important is the fact that two nights before his death, Michael told me he had been in the mill tunnels."

"But I thought—" Rafferty began before he was cut off.

"Yes, I lied to you," she said in a matter-of-fact way that suggested her deception had caused no pangs of remorse. "I could not be sure of your intentions the first time we talked, so I did not tell you everything, but I did talk to Michael on Tuesday night before he died. He stopped by my apartment—something he had never done before—and we talked about our childhood and such things. It seemed almost as if he wanted to say goodbye."

"And did he?"

"No. Michael was always a hard one to figure, if you want to know the truth. He was sly and secretive and I do not believe he every really opened his heart to anyone." She let out a small sigh and for an instant Rafferty thought she might break down into sobs.

Addie O'Donnell was made of stern stuff, however, and she said calmly, "There is no point discussing such matters now. In any case, Michael also mentioned that he had gone into the tunnels the night before and that—and these were his exact words—'you won't believe what is going on down there.'"

"Now that's a tantalizin' piece of information," Rafferty said. "What else did he tell you?"

"Nothing. I asked what he meant, of course, but he said his lips were sealed. However, he did tell me to watch the newspapers because 'something big' was going to happen."

"And I suppose he wasn't more specific than that?"

"No. That was all he said. He was very mysterious about it all, but then that was Michael's way. I must admit I found it all rather disturbing. I do not know exactly what Michael was doing, but I believe he became mixed up with very bad people."

"Do you have any idea who these people were?"

"No, not at all," she said, a little too quickly, as Rafferty saw it. "But I am hoping you will find out, Mr. Rafferty. Majesty Burke says you are the best detective there is. I am therefore hoping that you will go into the tunnels to see what you can find there. I would be happy to go with you, I might add."

"I'm sure you would be," Rafferty said, "but I don't think that will be necessary. However, I will certainly take a look at the tunnels."

"When?"

"As soon as I can."

"All right," she said. "But do not forget that I am still counting on your thirst for justice."

"I will try not to disappoint you," said Rafferty.

"Good. I do not like to be disappointed. Now, is there anything I can tell you, even if you do not trust me?"

Rafferty debated with himself for a moment before asking, "Do you happen to know a fellow by the name of Jack Pruitt, who works at the Shevlin-Carpenter Mill?"

There was a long pause before Addie O'Donnell said, "Yes, I know Jack."

"What can you tell me about him?"

"Only that he is a good union man who supports the cause."

"And if I wanted to talk to him about Michael's death, would you recommend me to him so that he would feel free to tell me what he knows?"

"Yes, I would do that."

"Would you do that for me tomorrow?"

"Yes," said Addie O'Donnell. "I will speak with Jack in the morning."

CHAPTER TEN

&

"Come Alone"

FROM THE JOURNALS OF DR. JOHN WATSON:

TUES., OCT. 3, 1899, WALDORF-ASTORIA HOTEL, N.Y., 7 P.M.: Arrived late back at hotel to find new telegram from SR. Reports strange news that rat trap baited with cheese found beneath body of man hanged in Mpls. H called this a "novel touch" & took some time to ponder implications before speaking up.

H: "What do you make of this latest news from our friend Rafferty?"

W: "I can only assume that the trap was meant to suggest that the victim was a traitor of some kind. If that is the case, then it certainly raises new questions about who actually killed the fellow."

H: "I will grant you that it does indeed seem to put a different complexion on the murder. However, I would also call your attention to one peculiar detail: the cheese."

W: "What is so peculiar about the cheese?"

H: "Nothing, I suppose, if you are trying to catch a rat. But if you are trying to make a statement, as you have suggested—a statement intended to show that the man you have just murdered is a 'rat' in the common meaning of that term—then what, pray tell, is the purpose of the bait?"

W: "Perhaps the murderers hoped a rat would be caught in the trap, thereby underscoring their point about the victim."

H: "That is possible, tho I am not inclined to think most murderers would be quite so thorough in their symbolism. There is another possibility, Watson, which is that the rat trap was put in place sometime after the murder occurred."

W: "But who would do such a strange thing?"

H: "I am sure Mr. Rafferty is already asking himself that very same question."

✎

Rafferty was indeed asking himself who might have put a rat trap by Michael O'Donnell's body. The answer seemed obvious, which is why he spent the next day—a cold, sodden Wednesday—scouring downtown Minneapolis to locate the Ratman, but his quarry proved frustratingly hard to find. It seemed that half the populace of the city knew where the Ratman *might* be found at any given time, but no one could say where he *would* be found. After traipsing from one end of downtown to another in a steady rain, Rafferty finally gave up the hunt late in the afternoon and went back to the hotel to dry out and consider how better to spend his time. The only solace he took from his wasted day was that if somebody was indeed following him, he would be just as wet and miserable as he was.

A telegram from Holmes was waiting for Rafferty at the front desk, and he smiled as he read the terse message: I SMELL A RAT. WHY BAIT? SH. It was obvious that he and Holmes, despite being a thousand miles apart, were thinking along identical lines. There was comfort in that knowledge.

✎

"It's an interesting theory you have, Dolph," said Arthur Adams over lunch at Leonardo's. "I can't imagine why it didn't occur to us sooner."

Randolph Hadley said, "Maybe it was just too obvious, A.A. In any case, we're looking for the Ratman."

Adams, who was working on some fresh pheasant and garlic potatoes, nodded and said, "I should think he'd be easy to find. He doesn't exactly blend in with the crowd."

"True, but he also doesn't have any known address. The Ratman is nothing if not mobile. I've got three men out looking for him and the coppers have half a dozen more, but they got nowhere this morning. He's probably holed up somewhere, waiting out the rain."

"Do you think he saw something?"

Hadley shrugged and said, "Who knows? We'll find him soon enough and then see if we can get an answer that makes any sense."

"Good. Now, let's consider our much bigger problem — Mr. Rafferty. How do you suppose he found out about Zier Row?"

"I have no idea, A.A."

"We are just damned fortunate that the lady of the house" — the mayor smirked as he uttered these words — "didn't open the door. Did Rafferty get a look at her?"

"McParland doesn't think so."

"And what else does the great Pinkerton think?"

"The Buddha isn't thinking," Hadley said contemptuously, "but as far as I'm concerned, it's time to deal with Rafferty once and for all."

"You mean kill him?"

"I see no other choice. He will be back at Zier Row, and he will find out what went on there unless we stop him."

"Perhaps there are other ways," Adams suggested. "Perhaps Mr. Rafferty could be bought off, or scared off."

"I wouldn't count on that. He is not known to be a venal man, and I can tell you from firsthand experience that he doesn't scare easily. No, he will keep on pushing, A.A. That is the kind of man he is."

"I see. Is McParland still shadowing him?"

"Yes. He left the West early this morning. The last I heard he was roaming around downtown."

"All right, let's just make sure we know where he is at all times. I don't want to do anything drastic quite yet. Killing Rafferty would create a huge furor, as you must be aware, Dolph. I believe it would also be considered immoral."

"And how would you know?" Hadley said, understanding as well as anyone that Arthur Adams considered morality to be nothing more than a stiff and uncomfortable suit to be worn on public occasions but otherwise kept in the closet. "As for Rafferty, remember that accidents happen."

"Well, if one happens to him, it had better be a damned convincing accident, Dolph. He is not some cartman hauling s——t. Let's see where Rafferty goes in the next day or two. Then we can decide what to do next."

"All right, A.A., I hope you know what you're doing. By the way, I've got another piece of news you won't like. I received a telegram today from Wooldridge, that police detective down in Chicago. He says he's been told by a confidential source that one or more members of the old Lauer gang, including a woman, may be in Minneapolis."

"That all sounds rather vague to me."

"It is. Wooldridge can't even provide a description of the woman other than that she's probably about thirty years old, but with McKinley coming to town we can't be too careful. I've alerted McParland, who knows all about the Lauer gang. From what I understand, the Pinkertons were involved in foiling the gang when they tried to blow up the Chicago water tower."

"Well, keep me posted, Dolph. I do not want anything interfering with the president's visit. That is going to be my day in the sun and I intend to bask in it. Now, do you have any more unpleasant news for me?"

"No."

"Good, then let us try to enjoy our meal. Incidentally, I heard an intriguing bit of gossip from Leonardo when I came in earlier. You'll never guess who was sitting over there"—Adams pointed to a nearby table—"for lunch yesterday."

"I'm not good at guessing games," said Hadley.

"That's your trouble, Dolph. You get no fun out of life. Well, for your information, Mr. J. Winston Phelps himself was sitting at that table, and he was with an attractive lady."

"That *is* curious. Was the woman anybody we know?"

"Not from what Leonardo tells me. At least we can be certain that her honor, assuming she has any, remains perfectly intact, since it can't have been a romantic lunch. Still, I've never heard of Phelps coming here before. This delightful establishment represents everything he detests."

"Well, I wouldn't worry about it, A.A. It seems to me you've got more important matters to keep you occupied."

"Sad but true," Adams sighed as he forked up another slice of pheasant, "but a man still has to eat and worry is bad for the appetite, or so they say. Now then, Dolph, how's that steak of yours?"

Rafferty went out again after dark to look for the Ratman, but the streets would not yield up the legendary wanderer and raconteur. The Ratman, it appeared, had gone to ground somewhere, and Rafferty wondered whether the strange little man had begun to sense that the wrong people might be looking for him. By ten o'clock Rafferty decided further searching would be futile and returned to the West.

As he entered the lobby, he noticed an ordinary-looking man in a pin-striped suit who was sitting in an armchair near the front desk. The man looked vaguely familiar, and Rafferty thought he might have seen him on one of his downtown walks. He was tempted to go over and shake the fellow down for the sheer satisfaction it would provide, but the man would undoubtedly deny that he had followed Rafferty. In any case, the lobby was no place to make a scene, so Rafferty went up to his room and retired for the night.

When he awoke at eight o'clock, he saw through the window that the rain had finally cleared away and bright sunshine prevailed. Rafferty couldn't say why, but he had the sense that something important was going to happen before the day was done. As if to confirm his prescience, the telephone rang and he soon found himself talking to Majesty Burke. She wanted him to come up to her apartment right away.

"There's something I must show you," she said.

"Ah, Maj, and what might that be?"

"You'll see when you get here. Oh, and Jacqueline O'Donnell will be here, too. See you soon."

She hung up before Rafferty could get out another question, so he saw no choice but to do as he had been asked. He didn't bother to look for tails on his way over to her apartment above the saloon. It was, after all, hardly a secret that Majesty Burke was his client. She was waiting for him at the door of her apartment and ushered him inside. Jacqueline O'Donnell was already seated in the parlor, sipping a cup of tea.

"I am pleased to see you again," she said as Rafferty took a seat across from her while Burke went to the kitchen for more tea.

Rafferty responded, "I didn't know you and Maj were friends."

"We have become so, since Michael's—well, since Michael died. Maj has been very kind to me."

"Well, you have picked a fine woman to be your friend," said Rafferty.

"I heard that," said Burke, coming in from the kitchen with a pot of that damned herb tea Rafferty hated. He smiled, took the proffered cup, and faked a sip of the awful substance before letting the cup rest in his lap.

"'Tis true, Maj," Rafferty said. "You are a fine woman, and that is a universal sentiment from what I hear."

"Well, it is nice of you to say that, Shad," she said, taking a chair next to Rafferty, "though some of my patrons think I can be a regular amazon when I'm crossed, which I might add, is all too often these days."

"Ah, you're seeing a rough crowd downstairs, I take it."

"Never rougher," she said. "The mills are running full blast like there's no tomorrow and the men are flush with money. Good for business but hard on the fixtures."

"I know exactly what you mean," said Rafferty, recalling the first saloon he and Wash Thomas had owned in St. Paul. It was a stand-up joint near Seven Corners and there were plenty of wild men among the customers.

Rafferty performed another tea-drinking charade and said, "Now then, Maj, what is it you wanted to show me?"

"I've got them right here," she said, going over to a small desk and taking two pieces of yellow paper from the top drawer. She handed the papers to Rafferty, who recognized them at once as Western Union telegrams. The messages, sent from Chicago in the previous June, were pure gibberish—words put together in no apparent order. Rafferty noticed, however, that many of the words were names of animals.

Burke said, "I found them just this morning when I went down to the basement to get the furnace going. They were in the pocket of an old shirt Michael used to put on when he shoveled out the coal bin, because he didn't like getting all the dust on his regular shirts. Anyway, I thought I might as well use the shirt for rags, but then I found the telegrams. Do you have any idea what they mean?"

"No," Rafferty said, "but the messages obviously are in commercial code. 'Tis commonly used when parties want to make sure pryin' eyes can't read their communications." He turned to Jacqueline O'Donnell and asked, "Did Michael ever speak of such things to you?"[1]

"Never. When Maj found the telegrams this morning, she called me and I came over to look at them, but I couldn't make any sense of them either."

"So you don't know if Michael had friends, say, or business acquaintances in Chicago that he regularly communicated with?"

"I'm sorry, Mr. Rafferty, but Michael never talked of such things. These messages are a great surprise to me."

"There's no need to apologize, Miss O'Donnell. I'm beginnin' to think Michael had a more interestin' and complicated life than even those close to him knew about. I'll do some checkin' to see what I can find out about these telegrams. May I keep them, Maj?"

"Certainly."

"One more question, Maj: Has Jack Pruitt talked with you at all this week?"

"Why do you ask?"

"I talked to him on Monday and he wasn't very helpful. 'Twas obvious he didn't trust me. I told him you could vouch for me."

"Well, he hasn't talked to me yet, Shad. But if I see him, I'll tell him you're as fine a man as God ever made," she said with a smile.

"I'd appreciate that, Maj, even if it's a slight stretch of the truth. Since we're talkin' about Mr. Pruitt, can you tell me anything else about him? I may be talkin' to him again soon and I'm just wonderin' what sort of fellow he is."

"I've already told you most of what I know," Burke said. "He works at the Shevlin-Carpenter mill and used to come into the saloon once a week or so, though I haven't seen much of him lately. He and Michael liked to talk about unions and such things, but Jack never talked much about himself. He struck me as a secretive sort of man, if you want to know the truth. I can't say if he and Michael were close friends. Maybe Jacqueline knows."

"I wish I could help you," Jacqueline O'Donnell said in response to Rafferty's questioning glance, "but I really don't know Mr. Pruitt very well. As I recall, Michael introduced him to me at a picnic once this past summer, but he was never at our house. As far as I know, he's just another union man that Michael met through his work. Do you think he knows something?"

"Possibly," said Rafferty as he stood up. "Well, ladies, thank you for your time and your information. I must be movin' along before the day gets away from me."

Jacqueline O'Donnell rose from her chair and put a hand on Rafferty's wrist, "Before you go, sir, I must know if you have found out anything more about Michael's death. Was it the Secret Alliance after all?"

Rafferty grasped her hand and said, "I have no answers yet, Mrs. O'Donnell, but I am getting closer by the day."

"Well, God be with you," she said, "for it is surely the Lord's work you are doing."

"Thank you," said Rafferty. "I will probably need the Lord's help before this business is done."

⊖φ

Once he'd returned to his hotel, Rafferty called Wash Thomas and read him the two coded telegrams found in Michael O'Donnell's shirt. Thomas had done a brief stint as a telegrapher in his Nevada days, and Rafferty hoped his partner might be able to make some sense of the messages.

"Read them again, more slowly," Thomas said.

Rafferty complied. After a pause, Thomas said, "I can't tell you what the messages say, Shad, but I do know of a company that liked to use animal names in its codes."

"And that company would be?"

"The Pinkerton Detective Agency. Of course, that was years ago. Maybe things have changed by now."

"Maybe," said Rafferty. "Could you do some checkin' about that for me?"

"Sure. I know a fellow at the Pinkerton office here I could run it by."

"No, that might not be a good idea, Wash. Don't talk to any Pinkertons—at least, not yet. Find out some other way if you can."

"All right, I'll ask around."

"Thanks. How's my favorite bull dog?"

"Lonely. Just how long are you planning to be in Minneapolis anyway?"

"I wish I knew," said Rafferty. "Call me here if you find out anything about those telegrams."

After lunch Rafferty decided to make one last effort to track down Sid the Ratman. The day had turned unexpectedly mild, courtesy of a fugitive warm front that had somehow made it all the way north from the Gulf of Mexico. A hint of summer humidity—surely the last of the season—still lingered in the air. Rafferty spent five hours searching every corner of downtown Minneapolis for the Ratman but again came up without a single clue. The Ratman, it seemed, had vanished off the face of the earth—not permanently, Rafferty hoped.

By the time Rafferty got back to the West, he was sweating profusely. He changed into fresh clothes, took a brief nap, and then came down for dinner. A message was waiting for him at the front desk. Rafferty sat down in the nearest chair, got out his spectacles, opened the envelope and read the following, printed in blocky letters: MEET ME AT 1 A.M. TONIGHT IN FRONT OF SHEVLIN-CARPENTER MILL OFFICE. COME ALONE. J. PRUITT.

This was a surprise, since Rafferty had not really expected to talk with Pruitt again, but he figured the reluctant sawyer must have talked with Maj Burke and learned from her that Rafferty could be relied upon. Curious about how Pruitt had delivered this message, Rafferty returned to the front desk and questioned the clerk, who said the note had been brought in by "a boy of twelve or so." This struck Rafferty as odd—unless Pruitt himself felt in some danger and did not wish to be seen in the hotel lobby.

Rafferty tucked the message into his jacket pocket and used a telephone in the lobby to call Wash Thomas, making very certain that he could not be overheard by any tails who might be hovering around the lobby. Then Rafferty went into the dining room to eat his supper.

Shadwell Rafferty had not survived Bull Run, Antietam, and Gettysburg, as well as several close brushes with death in the Wild West, by being stupid. It was therefore well before midnight when he reached the vicinity of the Shevlin-Carpenter Sawmill to scout out the territory, just in case somebody was planning trouble. He had taken a roundabout route to the mill and was confident that no one was following him. Wash Thomas, he knew, would be arriving soon as backup, and Rafferty felt confident that he was well prepared for any eventuality.

The night was unpleasantly humid, and Rafferty felt beads of perspiration tickling the back of his neck. Off to the south, strokes of lightning flickered ominously from roiling thunderheads, accompanied by the faint, eerie rumble of thunder. A night fit for witches, Rafferty thought, and no good likely to come from it. Workers from the second and last shift of the day were just leaving as Rafferty took up a position in the same lumberyard where he had talked with Pruitt a few days earlier. The stacks of lumber, separated by narrow aisles, provided excellent cover. Rafferty slipped into an aisle that allowed a clear view of the front of the mill's main building, and then began to watch and wait.

By half past twelve the mill was dark and silent, the last of its maintenance workers having left, and only a single weak light visible over the entrance to the office. The lumberyard itself was illuminated by a pair of electric arc lamps mounted on poles, but even their strong white glow could do no more than produce a kind of shadowy twilight at the bottom of the deep aisles that threaded through the tall stacks of wood. Behind the mill lay the dark, debris-laden waters of the Mississippi, and Rafferty could hear the river's distant murmur as it gathered itself for its tumble over the Falls of St. Anthony.

Rafferty had expected to see Thomas by now and could only assume that he had somehow been delayed on his way over from St. Paul. Still, Rafferty felt calm as he awaited Pruitt's arrival. Danger had always been in Rafferty's blood, and he knew that one reason he had taken on the case of Michael O'Donnell's murder was the simple thrill of testing himself again on one of life's killing grounds. As he waited, Rafferty lost track of time — it was too dark to read his watch and he didn't want to give away his position by lighting a match. He thought it was probably close to one o'clock when he at last saw a figure come into view, walking quickly toward the mill.

The figure, whose face Rafferty could not make out at first, slowed down and then stopped beneath the light in front of the mill's office. Pulling out his pistol — a Smith & Wesson double-action .44 caliber revolver that offered plenty of firepower — Rafferty squinted into the dim pool of light until he was certain that the figure was indeed Jack Pruitt.[2]

"Over here, Mr. Pruitt," Rafferty shouted, still making certain to stay out of sight. "Come slowly now and keep your hands in view."

Pruitt began moving toward the sound of Rafferty's voice, then stopped, uncertain as to Rafferty's exact whereabouts. "Over here," Rafferty said, directing Pruitt to the correct aisle.

There was enough light for Pruitt to see Rafferty's big pistol. "Say, what's this all about?" he asked. "I don't like people pulling guns on me."

"Just a precaution," Rafferty said, patting down Pruitt and pushing him a few feet into the aisle. "You wouldn't happen to be carryin' a pistol or knife, would you?"

"No. Why would I?"

Ignoring the question, Rafferty said, "All right, come along and we'll talk."

"Where are we going?"

"Out of range. If assassins are about, they've heard my voice, and I don't wish to make their work any easier than it has to be."

"We're all right here," Pruitt insisted. "Nobody followed me."

"Are you sure?"

"I wasn't born yesterday."

Rafferty gave Pruitt a long look. "By my standards, you were, Mr. Pruitt. Now, we either do this my way or we don't do it at all."

"Then I guess we don't do it," Pruitt said stubbornly.

Rafferty didn't like what he was hearing. "Why are you being so difficult, Mr. Pruitt? You indicated that you wanted to talk to me here, tonight. Well, here I am. Now let us talk."

Pruitt gestured down the aisle toward the center of the lumber stack and said, "How do I know you ain't going to shoot me if we go back there?"

Rafferty said nothing, but it was clear to him that Pruitt wasn't making sense. If he was so afraid of Rafferty, why had he specified that they meet in such an isolated place in the dead of night? Why hadn't he insisted instead that they meet in a crowded saloon or restaurant? Everything was beginning to feel wrong, and Rafferty made a quick decision. He cocked his revolver, leveled it at Pruitt's forehead and said, "Maybe I will kill you after all, Mr. Pruitt. Now come with me and we will have our talk."

Pruitt stared at the barrel and then into Rafferty's eyes. He said, "No, you're not the sort who would shoot down a fellow in cold blood. I'm walking out of here, Mr. Rafferty, and you can't stop me." Then, ignoring the pistol aimed between his eyes, he shoved Rafferty backward and turned to run out of the aisle. Rafferty was caught flatfooted, and he was more than a little astonished, too. There weren't many men who would have taken the chance Pruitt just had, though he had made the right wager, for Rafferty was indeed not the sort who would shoot down an unarmed man.

But he would certainly try to catch him. With a curse, Rafferty went after Pruitt, but he took only a couple of steps before something — maybe a premonition, maybe instinct, or maybe a lifetime of good luck when it came to bullets headed his way — caused him to stop just before he emerged from the protection of the lumber stack. Pruitt's luck was not as good. The instant he was out in the open, there were two loud cracks and his body jerked back into Rafferty's arms.

Rafferty knew rifle fire when he heard it and he also knew the peculiar heavy weight of the dead. As a third bullet slammed with a *thwack* into one of the boards over his head, sending out a spray of splinters, Rafferty dragged Pruitt farther back into the aisle and felt for a pulse in his carotid artery. All Rafferty could feel was warm blood gushing over his hand. Pruitt was gone and Rafferty knew that he would be too if he didn't move fast.

Like the good soldier he had been, Rafferty instantly assessed his situation, looking for whatever small advantage might mean life instead of death. Although he could not say exactly why, he had a distinct sense that more than one shooter was waiting for him in the darkness. He left Pruitt's body where it lay and moved quickly back down the aisle into the interior of the lumberyard. The aisles were arranged in a grid, with intersections about every thirty feet. Rafferty figured that whoever had killed Pruitt would now look for a clean shot through the passageway. In that situation, Rafferty, even in the dim light, would be a sitting duck.

Staying low, he covered the length of the aisle as fast as he could and had just made it into the first cross aisle before a bullet hissed past him. He kept on running, zigzagging down and across the aisles until he was somewhere near the middle of the lumberyard. As he neared an intersection, he finally paused to catch his breath and consider his next move.

It didn't take Rafferty long to realize that geometry was not in his favor if, as he suspected, there were at least two shooters. Moreover, if the shooters were at all smart—and Rafferty had to assume they were— they would be stationed at opposite corners of the rectangular lumberyard, enabling each to have a clear field of fire down two sides. And since Rafferty was no small target, he calculated that he would be a dead man the instant he tried to leave the lumberyard, just as Pruitt had been.

With no other good choice, Rafferty decided to stay put and call on the help of Mr. Stevens. This was how Rafferty referred to the custom .44-caliber pocket rifle, manufactured by the Stevens Arms Company of Massachusetts, that he liked to carry in dangerous situations. More than once Mr. Stevens had helped him out of a tight spot, most recently in the lethal confrontation that had brought the rune stone adventure to its unlikely conclusion.[3]

Feeling trouble in his bones, Rafferty had brought the pocket rifle along to his meeting with Pruitt, carrying it in a special holder inside his long raincoat. With speed borne of years of practice, he assembled the weapon, screwing on the long barrel and attaching the special skeleton stock to the grip. Finally, he slid a bullet into the chamber. Although the weapon, with its 22-inch barrel, was hardly a long rifle, it offered far better accuracy than Rafferty's pistol. The Stevens did have one drawback—it held only a single round.

Rafferty had just enough time to adjust the stock to his shoulder before he saw, down at the far end of the aisle, the figure of a man. The light was so poor that Rafferty could make out little beyond the man's basic form and the long object — undoubtedly a rifle — in his hands. Then the man gave a shout and a moment later bullets began coming Rafferty's way.

In a gunfight, especially at some distance, Rafferty had long ago learned that what usually won the day was the ability, as he liked to put it, "to calmly look the bullet in the eye." When lead started flying, even experienced marksmen were prone to fire wildly in the excitement of the moment, and that was just what the man at the end of the aisle was doing now. Rafferty, who had gotten down on one knee, heard a bullet slam into the dirt beside him, followed by two others that splintered the wood overhead. Watching the muzzle flashes, Rafferty aimed just to their right and squeezed off the round from his Stevens. There was a muffled scream, then silence. The firing stopped.

Taking no time to admire his handiwork, Rafferty chambered another round, then ran down the aisle to the next intersection, where he turned again before coming to a stop. He was certain the assassin he had shot was either dead or incapacitated, since the .44-caliber slug fired from the Stevens would knock a man down almost regardless of where he was hit. Now the question was how many other shooters were left. Rafferty did some quick thinking and concluded that there must still be at least two. His reasoning was that if there had been only two shooters to start with, it would have been foolhardy for one of them to go down one side of the lumberyard looking for Rafferty and thereby compromise the field of fire that kept him boxed in.

This conclusion provided Rafferty with scarce comfort, since it meant that he was still trapped in the lumberyard, with an unknown number of sharpshooters waiting outside for him. Even with the help of Mr. Stevens, Rafferty knew that the next time one of the assassins got him in his sights, the bullet that seemed to have been looking for him his whole life might finally find its target.

He quickly determined that, outnumbered and outgunned as he was, darkness would be his best defense. From where he crouched he had a bead on one of the two arc lights illuminating the yard and he immediately shot it out. The other light, somewhere behind Rafferty, would be more difficult to hit, but he decided to take the risk. If he could knock it out as well, the darkness in the aisles would be almost complete, and his chances of survival would become much greater. Yet he also knew that the shooters would be aware of his plan and would react accordingly. They, too, would have to take risks, perhaps even coming down the aisles after Rafferty, hoping to find and kill him before he could get a clear shot at the remaining light.

All of these thoughts ran almost instantly through Rafferty's mind, with an effect that was as pungent and immediate as a whiff of strong coffee. He was past logic now, in the elemental realm of instinct, and he began to move with the decisive ease of a man who has run out of choices. Looking around, he knew at once what he had to do.

Rafferty was in one of the cross aisles, where the ends of two-by-eight-inch planks were exposed, and he noticed that some of the boards had been so carelessly stacked that they protruded out from the main body of the pile, creating a kind of rough ladder to the top. Rafferty took off his raincoat and jacket, reloaded the Stevens, slid it under his belt at the back, and then used the irregular boards to make his ascent. When he got near the top of the twenty-foot-high pile, his feet resting on a ledge only a few inches deep, Rafferty poked up his head—presenting, as he full well knew, an easy target if one of the shooters spotted him—and looked for the remaining light.

He spotted it a hundred yards away, a brilliant white star hanging in the night sky. Out of the corner of his eye, he also saw something moving off to his left. A man perhaps, atop one of the piles just as he was. Rafferty ignored the movement and focused on the light, reaching back to bring out the Stevens with his right hand as he used his left to steady himself on his precarious perch. He took careful aim, aware that the movement on his left had stopped, and fired. Then all went dark.

BOOK TWO

The Wound of Time

Chapter Eleven

⋇

"It Was Just a Cheap Attempt at Blackmail"

FROM THE JOURNALS OF DR. JOHN WATSON:

WED., OCT. 4, 1899, WALDORF-ASTORIA HOTEL, N.Y., 9:30 A.M.: Inevitable finally occurred early this A.M., when H & Astor had bitter parting of ways. . . . Astor came to our room to complain about H's "sloth" in handling case & before long H told the little popinjay what he thought of him, his cousin & the whole "lunatic Astor clan." Bravo for H! . . .

THURS., OCT. 5, 1899, UNION STATION, CHICAGO, 1:30 P.M.: Jotting down these words as we await train north to Mpls. H yet to explain sudden decision to visit SR, saying only he had "premonition of some great trouble." More likely explanation: movement antidote to boredom, which to H most intolerable — & miserable — of conditions. Still, unlike H to speak of "premonition" since all for him must usually be logic & deduction. But I too have had strange feeling about SR's case & am most anxious to see him again. . . . Asked if we should telegraph ahead to SR re visit but H said he preferred to "surprise our friend."

FRI., OCT. 6, 1899, CITY HOSPITAL, MPLS., 4 A.M.: Awful news upon arrival here shortly after 2 A.M. Went to SR's hotel & told he had been taken to hospital after being "shot" & was "thought to be dying." H, face gone pale, summoned hack & we rushed to hospital. There, to our relief, found GWT, SR's Negro friend & partner, who as might be expected was astonished to see us. Told us SR was alive, tho condition unknown. GWT trying for hour to see SR but police refused to let him into room. Said he feared SR "badly wounded."

H, in cold fury, found a police captain & introduced himself as "Lord Baker," English financier & friend of SR who was in Mpls. doing business with [James J.] Hill. H told captain in no uncertain terms what would happen unless we saw SR "immediately." Captain, flat-headed man with dull gray eyes & obnoxious manner, refused & I feared H might assault the man. But as there were half dozen policemen in lobby, all fully armed, frontal attack did not seem wise. GWT fortunately intervened & cautioned patience, saying he had already "been in touch with a higher power."

H: "What do you mean?"

GWT: "I telephoned Mr. Hill. He was deeply disturbed to hear what had happened & promised to 'shake the city of Minneapolis to its very foundations'—those were his exact words—to make sure Shad is being well cared for. He also said he will personally see to it that I am allowed into Shad's room. He sounded extremely angry."

W: "God pity any poor functionary who must face Mr. Hill's wrath."

H: "Very well, we will wait for Mr. Hill to exercise his influence. But we will not wait for long."

GWT now told us about night's events. Said he was supposed to "act as backup" for SR, who was meeting man in lumberyard in north Mpls. & feared "assassins." But Thomas arrived late because trolley derailed on way to Mpls., blocking track & causing long delay, & no hack to be found anywhere. By time GWT reached lumberyard, SR had already been taken away on stretcher. Two other men lay dead, both shot. One named Jack Pruitt—same man SR was to meet in lumberyard. Other dead man not identified. GWT came to hospital as quickly as possible, arriving 2 A.M. Attempting to see SR ever since. Tho composed as usual, GWT concluded by stating he "would not be responsible for what happened next" if any harm came to SR.

H: "I assure you, I shall not permit that."

As I write, H growing more impatient by moment & preparing to have another go at police, in which case situation could rapidly get out of hand. Only hope is Hill will use his power as advertised & part waters for us. In meantime, can only pray SR is all right. . . .

Rafferty awoke—his ears ringing and his skull feeling as though a two-by-four had been driven through it—in unfamiliar surroundings. He was lying on a high, narrow bed in a windowless room with a polished maple floor, a bright electric light hanging from the ceiling and bare white walls. The room had a scrubbed, antiseptic look, and Rafferty soon concluded that he must be in a hospital or convalescent home of some kind. He was not, however, alone, for a uniformed policeman sat by the door.

At first Rafferty could remember nothing of the events in the lumberyard, for the throbbing pain in his head seemed to have banished all memory. This was a frightening sensation, for despite his casual and unpretentious air, Rafferty was famous for his memory. A face seen only once, a snippet of conversation, a small object caught in the corner of his eye, an obscure fact from a book read long ago—all found their places in Rafferty's infallible system of mental filing.

Wash Thomas, who was inclined to think that forgetting was sometimes the best thing a man could do, liked to call Rafferty's phenomenal memory the "devil's own gift," and even Rafferty himself sometimes thought it was as much a curse as an asset. Rafferty's memory followed no system organized upon the lines of pure logic. It was more like the collection of some eccentric librarian who, ignoring Dewey and his orderly march of decimals, had arranged everything in a manner perfectly clear to himself but incomprehensible to the world at large.

Trying to account for his circumstances, Rafferty slowly began to muster fleeting glimpses of the events that had put him in the hospital. He vaguely recalled the sound and smell of gunfire and even thought for a moment that he had been shot, but when he reached up to touch the back of his head, where the throbbing came from, he felt only a big knot and nothing else. He realized that he could not have been shot, since a bullet in the back of the skull would surely have been fatal.

Rafferty now started tugging at his fugitive memories, trying to bring them back from wherever they had gone to. It took awhile, but his mind began to clear and then the memories started pouring back, like water rushing from a ruptured dam. The lumberyard. Pruitt falling dead in his arms. The man he had shot. And then what? He recalled climbing up the end of the lumber pile and taking aim at the second arc light, but after that his memory stopped altogether.

Thinking the copper at the door might be able to fill in the blanks, Rafferty struck up a conversation. He soon found out that he was in City Hospital, where he had been taken about an hour earlier — around 2 A.M. — after the police found him unconscious in the Shevlin-Carpenter lumberyard. The copper told him that two officers who were patrolling nearby as part of an effort to discourage a recent wave of late-night lumber thefts had heard gunfire and rushed to the yard. As they arrived, they saw a man running off into the night but were unable to catch him or even to get a good look at his face. Searching the perimeter of the yard with lanterns, the policemen came upon Jack Pruitt's body. More officers were called in, and they discovered another dead man, identity unknown. [1]

Rafferty, as it turned out, was the last to be found when a search of the entire yard was ordered. He was lying unconscious in one of the aisles with a large bump on the back of his head that appeared to have been caused by a fall, but there was very little blood and no sign of other serious injuries. His Stevens rifle — marred by a jagged bullet hole just above the trigger guard — was on the ground not far away.

Once he had chewed on this information, Rafferty quickly developed a theory as to how he had ended up in the hospital. Just as he shot out the second arc light, which was the last thing he remembered, the man he had seen on his left must have fired a round as well. The bullet, intended for Rafferty, had instead struck his rifle, knocking it out of his hands and causing him to tumble from his perch on the lumber pile. The fall left him unconscious, and Rafferty was willing to bet that had not the police arrived in such a timely fashion, there would at the moment be a large funeral in the works for him across the river.

Not long after entertaining these melancholy thoughts, Rafferty suddenly remembered something far more important — the incriminating photograph of Randolph Hadley. The original should be in his inside coat pocket. He reached for it, only to discover that he wasn't wearing his coat any more. Or his pants for that matter. All he had on was a long gown.

The police, he knew, would have searched through his clothes, so he could only assume that Hadley had been shown the photograph of his indiscretion. Rafferty expected the police, or perhaps Hadley himself, to come in at any moment and begin their interrogation. Instead, a tall man entered the room and said in a smooth, musical voice, "Ah, the famous Shadwell Rafferty. How nice to meet you at last."

⁂

Arthur Adams was known to Rafferty only by looks and reputation, but now, as Rafferty stared up at the famous politician, he had to admit that the man's looks, at least, were impressive. The mayor wore a blue pin-striped suit, a red silk vest, a crisp white shirt with gold cufflinks, and a fine felt bowler, which sat jauntily atop his large head. Altogether, he seemed to be a man without a care in the world, though Rafferty knew better.

Adams dismissed the policeman with a nod, pulled up a stool next to Rafferty's bed, sat down and said, "Well, Mr. Rafferty, I understand you've had an interesting night. It was a scene from the O.K. Corral at the lumberyard, or so the gendarmes inform me. The air thick with lead, men dropping like flies, chaos all around, et cetera, et cetera. I must say, you are about the most troublesome fellow I have ever met, sir. I can only conclude that it is because you are from St. Paul. My dear father always warned me about that city across the river. 'Too damned many Irishmen,' he said, and I see now what he meant."[2]

"Why, I am no trouble at all," Rafferty replied, "though I admit to bein' Irish. As for St. Paul, it is on the whole a safer place than Minneapolis, I think, since I don't recall bein' shot at recently on the other side of the river. Nor does corruption run quite so rampant there as it does"—here Rafferty paused to deliver a small grin—"in certain other places nearby."

"Well and carefully put, Mr. Rafferty," Adams said, offering a small smile of his own. "But 'corruption' is not a word I much care for. It always bespeaks something bad, don't you think, when in fact there is nothing evil about what goes on here. You see, all the good people of Minneapolis want from government are a few simple things. They want their streets watered and oiled in summer and plowed in winter. They want the streetlights to come on at night and to burn reliably. They want policemen to come when they're called and take care of troublemakers. They want a park or two where their children can play. And when times are hard, as they have been of late, they want to know there is someone they can go to for extra food or coal, or help with the rent. Oh yes, and did I mention that, on the whole, they would rather not pay any taxes?"

Rafferty nodded and said, "And in exchange for all these benefits all you ask in return is a little honest boodle. Am I right, Mr. Mayor?"

Adams shrugged and said, "Is that so bad?"

"I can live with it," said Rafferty, who had never thought highly of the stuffed-shirt, blue-nosed, antisaloon crowd, full of religion and righteousness, who in recent years had been striving to reform St. Paul, Minneapolis, and every other city in America. Still, there was a line to be drawn between a decent amount of graft and wholesale thievery, and Rafferty knew Adams had stepped over that boundary long ago.

Adams said, "You sound like a most reasonable fellow, Mr. Rafferty, which is good. What say we reason together."

"By all means."

"Splendid! Then let us begin with this," Adams said, producing the photograph of Randolph Hadley in the throes of lovemaking. "It depicts an unfortunate episode, for which Mr. Hadley has already apologized most profusely. He deeply regrets his improper behavior. Alas, the flesh is weak, as I'm sure you know from your own experience as a man of the world."

"'Tis true," Rafferty agreed, "though as far as I know my moments of weakness have never been immortalized by Eastman Kodak."

"Well, in any case, I am sure Mr. Hadley will be pleased to have the photograph back. Tell me where you got it, if you would be so kind."

Rafferty said, "'Twas in the possession of the late Michael O'Donnell before it happened to fall into my hands."

"How convenient. And what do you intend to do with the copies you've no doubt made already?"

"For the moment, I plan to do nothin' with them. And if they turn out to have no bearin' on Mr. O'Donnell's murder, then you have my word that I will burn them all."

"Very well," said Adams. "I will take you as a man of your word. Now, where did you obtain the picture?"

"'Tis immaterial. Your coppers and Hadley's men just didn't do as good a job of searchin' for it as they should have. And they were lookin' for it, weren't they, when they tore apart O'Donnell's house after his death?"

"That, to use your word, Mr. Rafferty, is 'immaterial.'"

"On the contrary, it's the most material issue of all," said Rafferty. "If you and Mr. Hadley knew of such a photograph, and perhaps others equally incriminatin' that were bein' used for the purpose of blackmail, why that would be a fine motive for murder, would it not, Mr. Mayor?"

Adams let out a sigh and said, "Mr. Hadley, you should know, wanted to visit you tonight, but I talked him out of it. He has a terrible temper, and I was afraid he might lose it in response to a statement just like the one you've made. You really must be more careful about making wild allegations.

"They didn't sound all that wild to me."

"Consider this then, Mr. Rafferty. If you really think that Michael O'Donnell's death was the product of some great official conspiracy—whether in response to attempted blackmail, labor organizing, or whatever—then why are you alive at this moment? Why didn't the police, who must be part of any conspiracy, kill you at the lumberyard? It would have been the easiest thing in the world to do, don't you think?"

Rafferty had to admit the mayor had a point. "All right then," he said, "let's assume for the sake of argument that you and the other authorities of this city are pure as the driven snow. What, then, was Mr. O'Donnell doin' with such a revealin' photograph?"

Adams said, "I cannot say for certain. However, I assume that he was indeed intending to use it for blackmail or some other nefarious purpose. For a man such as himself, it would have served as ammunition in his war against law and order. By discrediting Randolph Hadley, he no doubt hoped he could discredit the alliance as well."

Rafferty pondered this response and said, "By the way, who's the lovely lady Mr. Hadley is frolickin' with in the photograph?"

The mayor's face darkened and he said, "The woman's identity is of no consequence whatsoever."

"I cannot agree. What if the lady in question was the wife of some rich contributor to the Secret Alliance? That would be of far more consequence than if she was, say, a courtesan."

"The truth is, I do not even know the woman's name, nor do I care to know it. She was just a whore, Mr. Rafferty, a common whore. Like many men, Mr. Hadley visits a sporting house now and then. I suspect that even a paragon of virtue such as yourself has on occasion done the same thing. Mind you, I do not defend his behavior—he is a married man and should know better—but I do think that what he did is not the worst sin in the world either."

"Nor do I," said Rafferty, whose face betrayed nothing as he listened to the mayor. Unless Charles Wellington ran a whorehouse in his spare time, which Rafferty thought unlikely, then Adams was lying.

Rafferty said, "And just where was this sportin' house of which you speak, Mr. Mayor?"

"Is that really important?"

"Could be. From what I can tell by lookin' at the picture, it must be a very high-class establishment. The place almost looks like a rich man's apartment, but I could be wrong."

Adams's sharp eyes took in Rafferty with a look that suggested a volatile mix of bemusement and anger, and he said, "All right, Mr. Rafferty, you have made your point. It is obvious that you know the photograph was taken in Mr. Charles Wellington's apartment at Zier Row. Mr. Hadley used the place for assignations. This was most regrettable and improper behavior on his part, especially since Mr. Wellington knew nothing of it."

Rafferty now realized that he must have been followed to Zier Row, for how else could Adams have been so certain that Rafferty knew about the townhouse?

"Do you know how the photograph was taken or how Mr. O'Donnell got his hands on it?" Rafferty asked.

"No, but it has all the earmarks of a setup. Such things have been done elsewhere, I am told, by union agitators, anarchists, and that breed of men."

"And Mr. O'Donnell, I take it, was one of 'that breed' in your opinion?"

"Of course he was. He was an agitator and a troublemaker—one of all too many in this city."

"And yet not long before, as I understand it, he worked for you. How do you explain his abrupt change of heart?"

"If I could explain why men do what they do, Mr. Rafferty, then I imagine the world would beat a path to my door and bow down before my wisdom. But I make no such claim for myself. Mr. O'Donnell, from what little I know of him, seems to have been a very impressionable young man and therefore easily swayed by one political wind or another."

"And that is the best explanation you have?"

"Do you have a better one?"

"Not at the moment, but I'm workin' on it," Rafferty said.

"You do that, Mr. Rafferty, you do that. First, however, I would like to hear about your adventures in the lumberyard, since they may bear some relationship to the murder of Mr. O'Donnell, which is of course a blot upon the city. And please, don't stint on the details."

Rafferty was sinfully adept at impromptu prevarication, but in this instance he saw no reason to greatly shade the truth, so he gave a straightforward if sketchy account of his meeting with Jack Pruitt and its violent conclusion.

"Come, come, Mr. Rafferty, you owe me a better tale than that," Adams said. "You're alive solely because the excellent police of this city came to your rescue. Now it is your turn to help the police. I must know what Pruitt told you. The information could be crucial in helping us identify Mr. O'Donnell's real killer. Besides, it is in your best interest to tell the truth. Otherwise, there could be unpleasant consequences."

"And what might those be?"

An eerie Mona Lisa smile creased the mayor's face. He said, "Before I came to visit you, I had a chat with Mr. Childress, my chief of police. His initial analysis of the evidence at the lumberyard is, to put it bluntly, not in accord with the story you have just told me. There are certain inconsistencies, I fear."

"Name them," Rafferty demanded.

Adams shrugged and continued, "There is no point in getting into details at the moment. However, the situation is serious enough that it may be necessary to place you in custody until such time as a grand jury reviews the matter and considers an indictment. I would hate to see that happen, since the grand jury system here in Minneapolis can be abominably slow. Indeed, men have been known to linger behind bars for months until the proper panel is convened. It is even claimed that certain influential politicians control the process, though I myself have seen no evidence of it. Now then, Mr. Rafferty, do you suppose you could assist me by providing the information I seek?"

Rafferty had heard that Adams was a sweet piece of work, and now that he had seen the man in action, he was impressed. Never before had he been threatened in such a charming, yet unmistakably sinister way. Nor had he any doubt that the police, if they chose to, could cook the evidence at the lumberyard to make him look guilty of murder.

"I can't tell you what I don't know," Rafferty said, "and it will do you no good to threaten me with trumped-up charges. Imagine all the bad publicity that might bring about, especially if the gentlemen of the press somehow got their hands on one of the copies I made of Mr. Hadley's revealin' picture. 'Twould be quite a scandal, I'm sure."

Adams nodded and said, "I am beginnin' to think you missed your calling in life, Mr. Rafferty. You have the low, dishonest mind of a good lawyer."

"I will take that as a compliment," said Rafferty, "even though I've been tellin' you the truth. When I went to the lumberyard, I was merely hopin' to talk to Mr. Pruitt about Michael O'Donnell's union activities, but the assassins struck before I had a chance to ask any questions."

"And who were the assassins, do you suppose?"

"Could have been Hadley's men, or some of the Pinkertons who are nosin' around after me, or the coppers, or maybe some of O'Donnell's union friends. There seems to be no shortage of people who want to kill me."

"You are not in an enviable position, are you Mr. Rafferty? However, there is little doubt that the assassins were radicals—probably friends of Pruitt, who may have been killed by accident."

"What of the other dead man—the one I shot?" Rafferty asked.

"He was about forty years of age, carried no identification, and was dressed in ordinary workingman's clothes. The police tell me he carried a rifle of excellent quality—a .30-30-caliber Winchester that was found beside his body."

"Describe the man for me, if you would."

"As I understand it, he was short with dark curly hair, a scarred face, and—"

"There is no need to go on," Rafferty broke in. "I know the gentleman."

Adams raised a curious eyebrow. "Is that so? Tell me more."

"He was followin' me for a while, just as your agents are now, Mr. Mayor."

"I would know nothing about that," Adams replied, "but I am interested to learn more about this fellow you shot who you now claim had been following you. Did you happen to learn his name?"

"Earl Smith, or so I'm told. He worked at the Wellington Mills with Michael O'Donnell. Does the name ring a bell?"

"No, but I will pass on the information to the police. However, you can be certain this Smith was a radical of some kind."

"How do you know that?"

"Because all the evidence in the death of Michael O'Donnell points toward the involvement of radical elements—anarchists, socialists, syndicalists, whatever they call themselves. And there is the threat of more violence, especially with the president coming for a visit."

Rafferty was skeptical of the mayor's claim that radicals were behind O'Donnell's murder, though he couldn't deny the possibility. The trouble was that anarchism had become a convenient specter trotted out by the moneyed classes every time some group of poor workingmen tried to better their lot. The tragic events at Haymarket Square in 1886 had set the demon loose, and the monster had become so useful over the years that it now was invoked under all manner of specious circumstances. And Adams, Rafferty knew, would not hesitate to use the monster if it served his own corrupt ends.

Rafferty said, "So are you sayin', Mr. Mayor, that the revealin' photograph of Mr. Hadley is just a sideshow of some kind when it comes to this business?"

"Exactly. It was just a cheap attempt at blackmail on O'Donnell's part. He perhaps thought it could buy some relief from Mr. Hadley's effort to root out the anarchist element in this city. When that did not work, O'Donnell—who seems to have been a very slippery fellow—perhaps turned on his own people and threatened to expose them in exchange for money. The result was what happened on Tenth Street."

"And why was your old family home chosen as the site for the hangin'?"

"I imagine it was part of the scheme to implicate the alliance and my administration in the murder."

The man was smooth, very smooth, and Rafferty decided the time had come to ruffle his feathers. He said, "Well, I must say, Mr. Mayor, you have an explanation for everything. 'Tis most impressive. By the way, did you also enjoy the lady's pleasures at Zier Row?"

Adam's normally inscrutable features registered a hint of alarm, but only a hint. He slowly shook his head and said, "I fail to see what possible difference it could make if I had a bit of sport with some lady of the evening."

"Ah, I disagree. The way I see it, if an incriminatin' photograph of Mr. Hadley could be a motive for murder, then equally incriminatin' pictures of other prominent people could be an even bigger motive."

"You are being preposterous," the mayor said.

"Am I? If that's the case, what was your coach doin' at Zier Row last Monday night?"

"I have no idea what you're talking about, Mr. Rafferty," Adams said as he stood to leave, "but I have some advice for you, sir, and it is well worth heeding. You will regret it if you keep prying into this matter. You want to chew and chew until you find every bone in the yard, no matter how deep it's been buried. If you keep digging, sir, if you keep digging, you just might find you have dug your own grave."

"You are not the first man who has tried to dig a grave for me, Mr. Mayor," Rafferty replied, "but you will find I'm a hard man to bury."

"I have buried much bigger men than you," Adams said. "You would do well to remember that, sir." The mayor then stood up, tipped his hat in Rafferty's direction, and walked out of the room.

Shortly thereafter a police captain entered the room, and Rafferty expected he would receive a grilling—or worse. Instead, the captain said, "You have visitors, Mr. Rafferty. Also, I'm to tell you that you are free to go at any time."

The captain left, after which Rafferty experienced one of the great surprises of his life.

◌◌

"Well, if it isn't Mr. Earl Hayes himself," said James McParland, looking down at the naked figure on the examining table. "What do you have to say for yourself, Earl?"

Being dead, Earl Hayes had in fact nothing to say, though his mere presence in Minneapolis spoke volumes from McParland's point of view.

McParland and Randolph Hadley had come to the Hennepin County morgue on Friday afternoon to have a look at the man shot dead by Rafferty in the lumberyard. Except for the large hole in his chest, Hayes looked to be in fine physical condition, which McParland said was to be expected of a man of his "background and accomplishments."

"I first met Mr. Hayes a couple of years ago at the Bunker Hill Mine in Idaho," McParland said as he grabbed a handful of the dead man's curly black hair and lifted up his head to make a closer inspection of his features. "He was a ringleader of all the trouble up in the Coeur d'Alene region."

"He was with the Western Federation of Miners, I take it," said Hadley.

"Oh yes," said McParland, suddenly dropping Hayes's head, which hit the table with a loud thud, "he was a federation man all the way"—here McParland allowed himself a small smile—"and an unusually hard-headed one at that."

The federation was well known as one of the most radical and violent labor organizations in the nation, though some argued that its members had little choice given the legendary intransigence of the western mine owners. Only a few months earlier the federation had gone on a destructive spree after the owner of the Bunker Hill Mine refused to recognize the union. Hijacking a train, which became known as the Dynamite Express, hundreds of federation members traveled to Bunker Hill and blew up a large concentrator at the mine. Eventually, federal troops were called in to restore order.[3]

"Mr. Hayes was intimately involved with the federation," McParland continued. "It is even said he rode in the locomotive cab on the Dynamite Express last spring. Mr. Rafferty certainly did us a favor by eliminating him."

"It is the only favor he has done us," said Hadley.

"Perhaps, but we are going to need all the favors we can get in the next few days. Mr. Hayes, I'm afraid, is not the only prominent anarchist to arrive in Minneapolis lately. Have you ever heard of a woman named Mary McGinty?"

"No, what of her?"

"Well, it may or may not be her real name, but she is the terrorist believed to have been involved with the Lauer gang. As you know, Detective Wooldridge in Chicago has already sent out a warning that she, and perhaps another member of the gang, may be here in Minneapolis. Our Chicago office has now confirmed that she did indeed travel to Minneapolis at some point this year."

This was alarming news and Hadley said, "I do not like the sound of any of this, Mr. McParland, especially with the president coming in for a visit. If this McGinty woman is here, then she must be planning something."

"The trouble is, we don't know for sure that she's still here," McParland said. "You're right to be worried because if she really is in Minneapolis, I doubt that she's been spending her time baking cookies."

CHAPTER TWELVE

ঔৎ

"There's People in There That'll Kill You"

FRI., OCT 6, 1899, WEST HOTEL, MPLS., 6 A.M.: SR alive & well! What joy to write these words after long night of waiting & hoping. Hill our savior. To our surprise, great man himself stormed into hospital at 4:30 A.M., two lawyers at his side, judicial writ in hand, & look in one good eye such as would pulverize granite into dust. Amazed, of course, to see H & me but spent little time on pleasantries. Instead, he instructed police captain to "call his superiors on the nearest telephone." Captain, thoroughly cowed by Hill's imperial presence, did so & came back a changed man, very apologetic & cooperative. Were ushered into SR's room at once, expecting the worst & instead found him regaling police guard with story of how he once played poker with Wild Bill Hickok! (Note: Heard story before, probably not true). When he saw us, SR could hardly contain his joy & gave H, who looked embarrassed, a hug that nearly crushed life out of him.

Examined SR (who has shaved off his beard!) & found no injuries other than large bump on head & several bruises, tho he reported he had been "knocked out" after fall in lumberyard. After this, told us whole story of his night, ending with remarkable conversation with mayor of Mpls. at hospital. . . .

H. AFTER LISTENING TO SR'S TALE: "You are lucky to be alive, Mr. Rafferty."

SR: "I've always been lucky that way. Bullets don't seem to care for the taste of my flesh."

H, SMILING: "We are most appreciative for that dispensation from the Almighty."

. . . SR released from hospital just after 5 A.M. & we thanked Hill profusely. He left at once for St. Paul, as he was to leave shortly on trip to Northwest. Took SR by hack to West Hotel, where he had been staying in Mpls. Told SR to rest, while GWT, H, & I took turns guarding his room, in case more "assassins" were about. Am sitting now outside his room, marveling at events of last 48 hours & wondering what will come next. H, meanwhile, thinks we are in "for a great adventure."

FRI., OCT 6, 1899, RYAN HOTEL, ST. PAUL, NOON.: SR slept only three hours & then wished to return to saloon in St. Paul. GWT, H, & I accompanied him on trolley & arrived without incident at 9:45 A.M. All of us—along with old newspaper friend J[oseph] Pyle—soon held "summit" meeting at saloon, where we received enthusiastic greeting from "Young Sherlock."

H, always great lover of dogs, happy to see that his gift to SR had grown into "such a fine-looking English bulldog," to which SR replied, "Ah, but he barks with an American accent." Much laughter all around & I at once felt perfectly at home, as was always case in SR's presence.

Soon got down to business, however. H began by announcing intent to stay in Mpls. until case "brought to a conclusion," which much pleased SR. Took detailed notes of conversation that followed, as it was most interesting to listen as H & SR went thru case discussing possibilities.

SR provided overview of investigation to date & went on to take blame for much of what happened night of our arrival in Mpls.: "'Twas a botched job all the way round. I should have allowed more time for Wash to get to Mpls. If he'd been there, everything would have turned out differently. As it is, all I have to show for my night's work are two dead men, either of whom would have been an excellent source of information. Now they're silent for all eternity. 'Twas also foolish to carry along that picture of Mr. Hadley cavortin' in the buff. Now Hadley, the mayor, & their friends know I'm aware of what went on at Zier Row & it will be harder than ever to wring the truth from them."

GWT: "You were not at fault, Shad. I must take the blame. I should have been there."

H: "Both of you are being too hard on yourselves. Having seen you in action during the ice palace affair, Mr. Thomas, I have no doubt that if humanly possible you would have been on the scene to assist Mr. Rafferty. It was simply bad luck that you were held up by the streetcar accident. As for you, Mr. Rafferty, I think everyone here would agree that your performance last night was extraordinary given how carefully the ambush was set up. I am curious, however, as to how the assassins knew about your meeting with Mr. Pruitt."

SR: "As am I. One possibility is that I was tailed, tho I took precautions. 'Tis also possible someone I talked to earlier tipped off the assassins, either deliberately or accidentally."

H: "I concur, tho it seems to me there is a third possibility as well."

SR: "Ah, I see you've been thinkin' along the same strange lines as I have."

W: "And what might those 'strange lines' be?"

H: "Perhaps we will discuss that point later. In the meantime, let us move on to other aspects of the case. To begin with, Mr. Rafferty, I am interested in your conversation with the mayor at the hospital. I take it that you are not satisfied with the version of events the mayor provided, especially concerning the activities at Zier Row."

SR: "No, I'm not satisfied. The mayor, you must understand, is a regular pirate, a man who's been sailin' his whole life on a sea of lies. I suppose he's spotted the truth now & then on some distant shore, but

I doubt he's ever bothered to pay it a visit. Trouble is, I'm not sure what he's lyin' about in this business. Maybe there were more shenanigans than we know of at Zier Row, involvin' other prominent people. Maybe Mr. O'Donnell took a whole album of revealin' photographs. 'Tis curious all the way around, especially considerin' that the place of sin is owned by no less a figure than Charles Wellington."

H: "I am much intrigued by that fact. Tell me more about Mr. Wellington."

SR deferred to Pyle, who as newspaperman had followed Wellington's career closely. He now provided much valuable info re Wellington & disaster of 1878. . . . Went on to report Wellington reputed to be "richest man in Minnesota" except for [James J.] Hill.

PYLE: "I've heard he's worth $40 million, tho nobody knows for sure. Men like him don't make a habit of broadcasting their true wealth."

H: "I see. Tell me, what sort of man is Mr. Wellington? I should like to know about his character."

PYLE: "Well, for starters I can tell you that he's known to be a hard man, tho he's also very pious. He's a deacon at First Baptist Church & has given at least a hundred thousand dollars to an orphanage he founded, but when it comes to expanding his business empire, he's absolutely ruthless. There were once dozens of independent mills at the falls, but now only a handful survive. Mr. Wellington has gobbled up many of the small fish & the Pillsburys have taken most of the rest. His milling complex is not only the biggest at the falls, but it's also said to be the biggest & most sophisticated flour mill in the world. President McKinley is going to tour it when he comes to town." [1]

H: "Is Mr. Wellington still active in the business?"

PYLE: "As far as I know, he is, tho he became something of a recluse after his wife passed away some years back. She had a cancer of some kind & died an agonizing death. It took something out of the old man, from what I've been told, but he still attends to business. Lives at a big estate out on Lake Minnetonka & does his work from there."

H: "Do you know if he spends much time at his city townhouse?"

PYLE: "Couldn't tell you for sure, but I doubt it. Then again, if Shad is right & his place at Zier Row has been turned into a high-class brothel, maybe he spends lots of time there, even if he is getting up in years. He must be at least seventy-five by now."

H: "I see. And what is Mr. Wellington's relationship, if any, to the mayor of Mpls., Mr. Adams?"

PYLE: "I don't know. Do you, Shad?"

SR: "No, but I'd like to find out. I'd also like to know more about Mr. Wellington's ties to the Secret Alliance. Most of the big businessmen in Mpls. contribute money to the alliance, tho from what I understand, they generally won't admit to it in light of the organization's violent methods. 'Twould be interestin' to learn just how closely the alliance, the mayor & Mr. Wellington are connected & how much money circulates back & forth among them."

H: "I agree, Mr. Rafferty. It is also imperative that we find out more about what occurred at Zier Row & in particular identify the 'lady' of the house, if that is the right word to describe her. A firsthand inspection of the premises may be necessary."

SR: "You mean breakin' & enterin', I presume."

H: "Something like that. It also seems to me that at least four other avenues of inquiry demand our immediate attention. The first concerns the mysterious tale of the Tunnel Boys. What was Mr. O'Donnell doing in the tunnels beneath the Wellington Mills just before his murder & what was the 'something big,' as he told his sister, that was about to happen? Second, what does the Ratman know & how can we locate him? Third, what do we really know about Mr. O'Donnell & his family? Fourth, why did Mr. O'Donnell have in his possession two telegrams in codes similar to those used by the Pinkerton Detective Agency?"

GTW: "On your last point, Mr. Holmes, I can tell you that those telegrams were definitely in Pinkerton code. I just got off the phone with a fellow who used to be a telegrapher here & when I read him the telegrams, he said right away, 'Those are Pinkerton messages.'"

H: "Ah, capital work, Mr. Thomas! We therefore can state with confidence that Mr. O'Donnell had some connection with the Pinkertons. The nature of that relationship, however, remains a mystery. Now then, Mr. Rafferty, are there other issues you wish to address?"

SR: "Well, there are always the three questions you asked in one of your telegrams. I admit to bein' stumped about where Mr. O'Donnell's clothes went or even why it's important to know. On the other hand, I can see why you asked if Mr. O'Donnell was a criminal, since he certainly seemed to die a criminal's death & he probably was a blackmailer at the least. Fact is, I even had a startlement, as Wash likes to call it, in church after you posed the question about O'Donnell maybe bein' a criminal."

W: "Just what was this startlement?"

SR: "'Twas the idea that the whole case might have to be turned upside down—that maybe it wasn't the Secret Alliance that killed Mr. O'Donnell but his own union friends who might have committed the deed. It's an idea I'm still playin' with, tho I'm not ready to absolve the alliance of anything just yet. Now, before I forget, I want to go back to the third question you asked in that telegram, Mr. Holmes. You wanted to know when the night soil man, Mr. Shelton, was killed. Well, that's interestin' when you think about it. I'm assumin' he was murdered because he saw something on the night O'Donnell was hanged, but if he did, then why wasn't he silenced at once? Why did it take almost forty-eight hours before he had his unfortunate 'accident'? I can think of several possible explanations."

H: "As can I, Mr. Rafferty, which is why it would behoove us to find out who, if anyone, Mr. Shelton might have talked to during those forty-eight hours."

GWT: "I would be willing to make such inquiries. I know several of the cartmen in Mpls."

SR: "Do you now, Wash? And how did you come upon their acquaintance, if I may ask?"

GWT, GRINNING: "It so happens I have a lady friend in Minneapolis whose brother is a cartman."

SR, SLAPPING GWT ON BACK: "By God, Wash, have you already gone through all the eligible women in St. Paul & must now look for companionship across the river?"

GWT: "I am not the only one to look across the river in that regard, Shad."

Much bantering ensued—during which it was learned SR apparently has "lady friend" of his own in Mpls.—until H finally brought us back to topic at hand.

H: "I am sure your inquiries in Mpls. will prove invaluable, Mr. Thomas, & I look forward to your report. Now then, Mr. Rafferty, you were wondering why I asked about Mr. O'Donnell's clothes. I posed the question because I was curious whether the clothes might have been left in the old house where he died. It occurred to me that the house could have been set afire because the murderers feared it might contain fragments of clothes, personal items, stains, or other clues which might implicate them. This would be most likely, I believe, if the murder was in fact committed by the - alliance or the police, since burning down the house would have been just one more part of what you Americans like to call a cover-up."

SR: "'Twould also bolster the official argument that the murder was the work of anarchists, who are well known for burnin' & blowin' up things."

W: "Do not forget that they are also fond of murder, as several heads of state have learned in recent years."[2]

H: "We shall not forget that, Watson. Now, one more time, Mr. Rafferty: Are there any other matters in this case which you believe need to be dealt with immediately? You have far deeper knowledge of this business than I do, & I wish to be certain that you are satis-fied with my analysis of the situation."

SR: "You've done an admirable job, Mr. Holmes, & I have no com-plaints, tho it would also be nice to know who tried to kill me in the lumberyard."

PYLE: "My God, Shad, I forgot to tell you. Mr. Griggs, my Minneapo-lis reporter, telephoned this morning to report that the police have pos-itively identified the man you shot. His real name is Earl Hayes, tho he also goes by Earl Smith, but here's what's really interesting: This Hayes fellow is a known provocateur & a card-carrying member of the West-ern Federation of Miners. I do not have to tell you what that means."

SR: "No, you do not. It means trouble."

Pyle then provided details re federation & its shocking record of violence in Idaho & elsewhere. . . .

H: "It seems that at every turn your case grows more interesting, Mr. Rafferty."

SR: "True, & I'm beginning to wish it would stop doin' so."

H: "It is, I acknowledge, a complicated affair, but I have found that at the bottom of most complexities is some great simplicity in the form of an elemental human motive. In this case, however, we have yet to determine what that motive is, which is why we must pursue two broad avenues of inquiry. One leads toward the Secret Alliance & the most powerful men in Mpls. If these elements are indeed re-sponsible for cold-blooded murder committed under color of law, then I need not tell any of you how dangerous our work here will be. The other road leads in the opposite direction, toward the anarchist underworld inhabited by the likes of Earl Hayes. The motive for murder in this case is murkier. Revenge for some act of betrayal, as the rat trap suggests, would seem the most logical motive, but there are other possibilities—a falling out among confederates, for exam-ple—that cannot be ignored. Here, too, our work will be perilous, for as Dr. Watson has noted, the anarchists of today have no com-punction when it comes to committing murderous deeds."

SR: "You've stated the situation well, Mr. Holmes, & from this point on all of us must be very careful. There are assassins about, as we now know only too well, & they will be lookin' for other chances to do their bloody work."

. . . After more discussions, course of action agreed upon—"divide & conquer," as SR put it. H & I agreed to keep watch on Zier Row for few nights & look for opportunity to "do a little creative burgling," in H's words. Will also begin inquiries into O'Donnells & their history. H thinks answers to be found in Chicago & will contact our friend Wooldridge of police there. Meanwhile, SR will investigate tunnels & continue efforts to locate Ratman & will also try to speak to Wellington. SR & Thomas will also explore Pinkerton angle. Adjourned meeting before noon so our hosts could attend to customers.

As I write, H already planning "surveillance" at Zier Row tonight & is writing out telegram to Wooldridge in Chicago. The game is afoot. . . .

After the noon-hour crowd had cleared, Rafferty went up to his apartment to read the late edition of the *St. Paul Dispatch* and get a little rest before heading off to Minneapolis with Holmes and Watson. Wash Thomas was already on his way there to speak with his "lady friend" about her brother and the other cartmen of the city. Holmes, meanwhile, was wading through the complete file of newspaper clippings about O'Donnell's murder. Watson—a thoroughly sensible man in Rafferty's estimation—was taking a nap.

The late edition of the *Dispatch* offered a sizable account of the shootings in the lumberyard, but Rafferty discovered that his name was never mentioned in connection with the incident. Instead, the official version of events, no doubt carefully concocted by the mayor and his stooges at the police department, stated that Pruitt and "a man as yet unidentified" had gotten into an argument and "apparently killed each other." The article went on to state that "it is believed the two men were vying for the affection of a dancer at one of the downtown burlesque houses."

Rafferty had to hand it to the mayor—the man had a knack for making up a good story and the clout to make it stick. Still, the very fact that Rafferty's name had been scrupulously excised from the affair was highly suggestive. It meant that Adams, the police, and presumably Randolph Hadley were all fully committed now to sweeping the dirt of Michael O'Donnell's death as far under the rug as possible and hoping no one would notice. Someone else, Rafferty soon learned from the *Dispatch*, had other ideas.

Under a headline that simply said RALLY PLANNED, another story in the newspaper reported that

> A rally to protest the supposed role of the Citizens Alliance in the death of Michael O'Donnell, who was found murdered on September 28 at the old Adams house in Minneapolis, will be held Sunday at Loring Park. The rally is being organized by the dead man's sister, Miss Addie O'Donnell, who will also be the main speaker.
>
> The event, however, is not expected to attract a large crowd, as the better class of laboring men in the city, rather than listen to the usual rabble-rousing speeches, will no doubt choose to cheer on President McKinley and the returning men of the Thirteenth at Sunday's parade.
>
> Police Chief Childress, who is personally directing the investigation into Michael O'Donnell's death, said this morning that "there is not one trace of evidence to suggest that the Citizens Alliance had anything to do with the matter and it is unfortunate that such talk continues nonetheless."
>
> Although a placard bearing the alliance's name was found dangling from the dead man's neck, Chief Childress said this was clearly a "dodge designed to throw us off the scent." The police, he said, "continue to pursue many good leads and are confident that the real murderers will soon be brought to justice."
>
> As for the rally, the chief said the police "will not interfere so long as those in attendance conduct themselves in a lawful and civilized manner." However, he said any illegal behavior will be dealt with "quickly and firmly." He also said that the police "will be out in force to ensure that order is maintained and the public protected."

Rafferty was taken aback by the story. Addie O'Donnell had mentioned nothing to him about planning a rally on her late brother's behalf, and he wondered why. Perhaps she hadn't told him because she knew what he would say. The rally certainly didn't strike Rafferty as a good idea, for it would only roil waters that were already thick with mud. Yet Rafferty knew there was nothing he could do to stop Addie O'Donnell once she had made up her mind, no matter how wrongheaded she might be.

のひ

Well before Rafferty sat down to read his newspapers, Randolph Hadley was dealing with the first unpleasant repercussion from the incident in the lumberyard. The unpleasantness was provided by Charles Wellington, who rang up Hadley just before noon to demand information and answers.

"I need to know, Mr. Hadley, what is going on, and I need to know at once," Wellington said in his insistent, abrasive manner, which had all the confident force of wealth and power behind it.

"Good afternoon, Mr. Wellington," Hadley replied. "What exactly do you need to know?"

"The lumberyard, Mr. Hadley, tell me about the lumberyard. I am not foolish enough to believe what I read in the newspapers, which is why I have my own sources of information."

This was all too true, as Hadley knew from rueful experience. Although the milling king lived as a virtual recluse at his Minnetonka estate, he seemed to know everything that went on in Minneapolis. It was reputed that he had dozens of paid sources scattered throughout the city. Indeed, Hadley knew that at least one of these spies—identity unknown—worked within his own organization. Aware that he was confirming what the old man already knew, Hadley now gave a straightforward account of the previous night's events at the sawmill.

Wellington absorbed this information, then said, "How much does this Rafferty know?"

"As I've told you before, we can't be certain. He has at least one photograph and may have more. He certainly knows about Zier Row."

"Too bad he wasn't shot with those anarchists," Wellington said.

"I have been thinking the same thing."

"Who was his English friend who showed up at the hospital?"

Hadley, who was in his office in the Chamber of Commerce Building, removed a small file from his desk drawer and paged through it. It was a copy of a report filed by the police captain who had been at the hospital.

"All I know is that the man identified himself as Lord Baker and that he claimed to be a good friend of Rafferty's who just happened to be traveling through town. Quite a cheeky customer, according to the captain. There was a second Englishman at the hospital, but the captain didn't get his name."

"I hope you realize how odd all of this is, Mr. Hadley. Why would a common saloonkeeper like Rafferty have friends among the English nobility?"

"I don't know, sir."

"Well, make it a point to find out."

"Of course. Incidentally, I'm sure you know that James J. Hill also showed up at the hospital."

"Yes, he and this Rafferty are very close. A pity, because it means we must be careful. I will take on Mr. Hill if need be, but it would be much easier if that could be avoided. He is a large rock and not easily moved. Very well then, Mr. Hadley, what is your plan?"

Hadley sketched out what he intended to do next, trying to make it sound as if he had everything under control. "We will keep track of Mr. Rafferty's movements and act accordingly. We will continue to look for the photographs, though nothing has turned up thus far and we have, to be frank, no good leads as to their whereabouts. We are actively searching for the Ratman. As you suggested, he may have seen something. We are also watching Addie O'Donnell, who is a known troublemaker. Mr. McParland is looking into her background, again per your suggestion. If you have any other ideas, sir, I would be pleased to hear them."

There was a brief pause before Wellington said, "And what about Mary McGinty? Are you looking for her as well?"

The question surprised Hadley, who wondered why Wellington would be concerned about some shadowy Chicago terrorist. "I believe Mr. McParland has some information about the woman," Hadley said, "but beyond that—"

"Find her," the old man broke in, passion infiltrating the usual chill of his voice. "It must be your first priority. She is here, Mr. Hadley—I am absolutely convinced of it."

"What makes you so certain, sir, that she is in Minneapolis?"

"Let us just say that Miss McGinty has been in contact."

"What sort of contact?"

"That is my business, not yours, Mr. Hadley. She is here and she must be rooted out. Do you understand?"

"Of course," Hadley said, though in fact he was not at all sure how he would go about "rooting out" a phantom such as Mary McGinty. Even McParland and the vaunted Pinkertons had no good description of the woman, nor could they offer any specifics as to her whereabouts. Hadley debated whether to express his concerns to Wellington but decided against it. The old man had no tolerance for excuses of any kind. Hadley would just have to hope that McParland and his men could find a way to locate the mystery woman.

Wellington now said with a trace of disgust, "I trust you will deal with the other woman as well."

Hadley knew who the old man meant. "Yes, I will do what is necessary. Everything will be taken care of tonight."

"It had better be. I will call you tomorrow. In the meantime, I may have to speak with Mr. Rafferty myself."

The line then went dead. It was always that way with Wellington, Hadley thought—no hellos, no good-byes, just business. No wonder the old bastard was so rich.

ᵧᵩ

After Rafferty had finished the newspapers, he went back down to the saloon to chat with Thomas and a few of the regular customers. It was half past one, and he hoped to take it easy for a few hours in anticipation of the busy night ahead. Rafferty had just poured his second mug of coffee when a tall man dressed in resplendent livery came through the door and walked toward the bar.

"Belong to anybody you know?" Thomas asked, nodding in the direction of the coachman.

"Doesn't look familiar," Rafferty said.

When he reached the bar, the tall man gave a slight bow and said, "I have a message for you, Mr. Rafferty." He then handed over a small envelope.

Rafferty opened it and found a handwritten note inside that said, "I should like to see you today, at four o'clock, at Thornhill. My coachman has further instructions. Someone will be at the Wayzata station to pick you up. Please come alone." The note was signed, in bold strokes worthy of John Hancock himself, "Charles F. Wellington."

The coachman said, "There is a train leaving St. Paul at 2 P.M. that will reach Wayzata by 3:30. I am instructed to bring you to the depot here if that would be convenient."

Having just survived a well-planned ambush, Rafferty was suspicious. "How do I know you are who you say you are?" he asked the coachman.

The man calmly replied, "You may telephone Mr. Wellington and he will confirm everything that I have said. I assure you the invitation is genuine. I will give you the proper telephone number if you wish."

"Do that," Rafferty said, "and wait here."

Rafferty went back to his office and used the telephone there to have an operator connect him to the number he had been given. First, however, he asked if the number was indeed that of Charles Wellington. The operator assured him that it was.

"Wellington residence," came the response after the call was put through. The speaker had a clipped, almost British-sounding voice. "Who shall I say is calling?"

"Shadwell Rafferty."

"One moment please."

After a short wait an old man's voice came crackling over the line. "I see you are a cautious man, Mr. Rafferty. That is always a wise thing. Now, sir, will you do me the favor of paying a visit? We have much to talk about."

"'Twould be my pleasure," said Rafferty. "I will see you at four."

Rafferty hung up and went at once to Holmes's room to alert him to Wellington's invitation. Then he went back down to the saloon, where the coachman still stood by the bar.

"All right," Rafferty said, "let's go for a ride."

CHAPTER THIRTEEN

⌘

"Something Sinister Is Coming My Way"

FROM THE JOURNALS OF DR. JOHN WATSON:

FRI., OCT. 6, 1899, RYAN HOTEL, ST. PAUL, 4 P.M.: Am jotting down these words as H & I prepare to go to Mpls. for night of surveillance at Zier Row. H in grand mood—eager, bursting with ideas & prepared for whatever night may bring. He even spent time playing with SR's bulldog. Found this amusing, especially hearing name Sherlock called aloud so often. . . . I am tired but have learned thru years that it is price paid for privilege of participating in H's investigations. Would not trade it for any other experience in world.

SR gone off to interview Charles Wellington, milling magnate with apartment at Zier Row where photo taken. Seemed stroke of good fortune that Well[ington] would request meeting at crucial moment, but H likes to say "luck comes only to those who are prepared to receive it."

H told SR before leaving that timing of Well interview "could not be better" & wished we could go along. But agreed that as Well had requested to see SR alone, no point in upsetting him.

W: "What do you think Mr. Rafferty will learn from the great man?"

H: "I cannot say, but it will be something useful, I am sure. Mr. Rafferty, as you well know, is an excellent interviewer, in part because

his manner is so deceiving. He can be all charm, thereby putting his
subject at ease, & yet he does not miss the slightest nuance of the
conversation. He would have been a fine barrister, I think."

We are to leave here at 4:30 P.M. & will take streetcar to Mpls.,
as that is quickest means of transport. H imagines we will be followed but will not bother to "lose our shadows," in his words, until
we reach Mpls. H also confident our watch at Zier Row will bear
fruit & I must believe him, as he has remarkable sense of timing.
Same true of SR, & I have often wondered whether detection not
only skill but gift, like talent for music or art. Gift in this case ability
to somehow end up in right place at right time. Hope that will prove
true tonight. . . .

As he rode a Great Northern train through Minneapolis and out to
the lakeside village of Wayzata, Rafferty was grateful that Joseph Pyle
had been able to provide so much information about Charles Wellington. Although Rafferty had been familiar with the broad outlines of
Wellington's story, he had never really paid much attention to the details. Pyle, however, had brilliantly sketched the man's life, including his
triumphs and tragedies.

Like many of Minneapolis's founders, Wellington had come from
Maine, a shopkeeper's son intent on extracting his share of riches from
the bounty of the Northwest frontier. Starting as a lowly clerk for one of
the mills at St. Anthony Falls in 1860, Wellington gradually amassed a
fortune through a combination of hard work, high intelligence, shrewd
bargaining, a little judicious thievery, and a good bit of luck. His first
great triumph came in 1874, when he opened his first A Mill, a twelve-
hundred-barrel-a-day colossus reputed to be the largest and most tech-
nologically sophisticated flour mill on the continent. Not even the
Pillsburys could compete with it.

Then, four years later, on a warm May evening that no one alive then
in Minneapolis would ever forget, Wellington's world literally came
apart. One of his great mill's flinty French buhr stones, used to grind the
wheat, somehow touched off a spark, igniting flour dust in a nearby settling chamber. Moments later, the mill—seven stories high and built of
stone walls six feet thick at the bottom—blew itself to pieces. Hardly a
trace was found of the fourteen unfortunate men inside at the time. Four

workers in adjacent mills, which were heavily damaged or destroyed, also died in the explosion.

When rescuers arrived, they found a giant heap of smoking rubble, with not a single stone from the walls of the mill still in place. One huge stone, having been shot from the mill like a mortar shell, was found nearly a mile away in the front parlor of a certain Mrs. Livingston, who fortunately was in the kitchen cooking supper when the limestone projectile crashed through her roof and landed with disastrous results on her best parlor chair. Some debris even made its way to St. Paul, where windows were shattered along Summit Avenue. The blast itself was heard for a distance of more than twenty miles.[1]

It was after this disaster that Wellington moved out of his house on Tenth Street to the baronial splendor of Thornhill on the far green shores of Lake Minnetonka, fifteen miles west of Minneapolis. And even though he rebuilt the mill, Wellington was never quite the same man afterward, acquiring religion along with his money. One wag suggested that this sudden conversion was inevitable in a man who had already sent eighteen others to heaven. Wellington's newfound religious sentiment, however, had not altered his notorious antiunion views.

Rafferty could not remember ever meeting Wellington, or even seeing him in person, which was not surprising given the magnate's secretive ways. Following the disaster at the A Mill, Wellington dropped from the social whirl in Minneapolis. Some years later he lost his wife to cancer, causing him to retreat even further from everyday life, to the point where he conducted all of his business from home, using factotums to carry out his orders. So complete was Wellington's withdrawal that unbidden visitors were never welcome at his mansion. Instead, as Rafferty had discovered, one could only be *summoned* to Thornhill for an audience with its famously reclusive master.

Rafferty's train pulled into the small station at Wayzata, on the north shore of the lake, at 3:25 P.M., precisely on schedule. Once off the train, Rafferty walked through the depot's waiting room and out to the front drive to see if a coach had arrived for him. He noted that he was again being followed—this time by a stout man in a pea-colored coat—but saw no reason to make a scene. While waiting for the coach, Rafferty lit a cigar and then waved to his shadow, who quickly turned away as though he had not seen the gesture. At exactly 3:30 P.M. by his watch, the largest coach Rafferty had ever seen, pulled by several thousand dollars worth of gorgeous horse flesh, pulled into the drive and came to a stop in front of him.

"You would be Mr. Rafferty," said the driver, a sad-eyed man dressed in the same splendid livery worn by the messenger who had delivered the invitation. "Please step in, sir. We will be at Thornhill in ten minutes."

Rafferty climbed up into the coach and sat back to enjoy the ride on one of the hand-tooled leather seats. The sun was still out, though low, dark clouds were massing to the west, foretelling a change of weather. Off to the south the big lake shimmered in the buttery October sunshine. As an avid angler, Rafferty had gone after bass and pike more than once on the lake. Even so, he could hardly claim to know Minnetonka well, for it was a whole series of lakes connected by narrow channels, forming a tangle of water and land in which it was all too easy to become lost.[2]

Like the lake, Wellington's financial empire was said to resist easy mapping. As far back as the early 1880s, according to Pyle, he had branched off from flour and taken up numerous other profit-making ventures, all tied together in an intricate knot of interlocking holding companies so complex that not even the best antitrust lawyers in Washington could ever hope to sort them out.

The coach now swung around the northern side of Wayzata Bay and followed a winding road through forest and field, all ablaze with brilliant autumn colors. Rafferty occasionally caught glimpses through the trees of large houses hugging the shore of the lake. Once considered to be remote from Minneapolis, the lake had blossomed with development after being connected to the city by rail in 1867. Huge resort hotels soon sprang up, and in the 1880s tourists from around the nation came to Minnetonka to enjoy its cool summer breezes and ride the big steamers that cruised among the bays, points, and islands.

As the years went by, however, the lake's grand hotels — all-wooden structures built strictly for seasonal use — gradually lost their cachet and, one by one, were either razed or burned down. In the meantime, Minneapolis's moneyed class had begun to colonize the lake, putting up "summer" homes that, if not quite the equivalent of the famed "cottages" at Newport, were nonetheless impressive examples of Victorian architecture at its most charmingly excessive. Many of them truly were summer places only, but Thornhill had been a year-round residence from the day it was built, as befitting Wellington's desire for a home far from the bustle of the city.[3]

Situated at the end of a peninsula, the estate consisted of nearly fifty acres, most of them heavily wooded. The house itself remained entirely hidden from the road, as Rafferty discovered when the coach passed through a thick stand of hardwoods, made a sharp turn, and stopped in front of a small iron gate. Most of Minnetonka's gentry prided themselves on impressive gates, but that was not the case at Thornhill, where the gate, mounted to a pair of simple brick piers, bore no identification or insignia of any kind. A man standing by the gate quickly swung it open to admit the coach.

Only after the coach had negotiated two more tight curves did the house itself come into view. Set atop a long green hill that rolled up from the lake as smoothly as a carpet, the house was a white clapboard Colonial blown to monstrous size—Wellington's effort to achieve present happiness by purchasing an imaginary past. The coach pulled up beneath an enormous semicircular portico that looked as though it might have been lifted whole from an antebellum plantation. A servant rushed out at once to open the door for Rafferty.

"This way, sir," he said, taking Rafferty's hat. "Mr. Wellington is waiting in the library."

The servant led Rafferty into a grand entry hall with an elliptical staircase, through a pair of rococo-style parlors and finally into the library—a two-story-high room in the classical manner, lined with bookshelves on three sides, and illuminated by two tall windows facing the lake. In the middle of the room, resting on a heavy oak stand, was a huge block of rough stone that seemed completely out of place in such elegant surroundings. Not far from this peculiar artifact was the largest desk Rafferty had ever seen. Sitting behind it, engrossed in a thick tome, was Charles Frederick Wellington.

He looked up as Rafferty was announced and said, "Come over and sit down. Might as well enjoy God's gift of light."

Rafferty took a seat across from his host and was immediately struck by the fact that Wellington failed to convey the sense of physical prowess so common to titans of the business world. Dressed in a funereal black suit, he was short and skeletally thin, with an unusually large head, a prominent Adam's apple, and long bony fingers that somehow reminded Rafferty of tentacles. Wellington's gaunt features had a kind of monkish asceticism—a small mouth with pale thin lips, a slender nose, and sunken cheekbones. Only a few strands of gray hair survived on the smooth desert of his scalp. Wellington's gray eyes were sharp and probing, and under their unnerving gaze Rafferty felt as though he were in the presence of an elderly undertaker sizing up his potential as a corpse.

Wellington now said in a raspy voice, "I am not a popular man, Mr. Rafferty. Do you know why that is the case?"

Maybe it has something to do with your less than delightful personality, Rafferty thought, but replied instead, "I can't say that I do, sir."

"It's because of jealousy, Mr. Rafferty. Jealousy, pure and simple. You see I possess a rare gift. Do you know what that is?"

"I'm guessin' it's not modesty," said Rafferty, regretting his words as soon as he'd spoken them. It was foolish to bait the old man, but Rafferty couldn't help himself in the presence of such insufferable arrogance.

Wellington, however, seemed to take no offense. Fixing his undertaker's eye on Rafferty, he said, "You are right, Mr. Rafferty, it is not modesty, which is useful for maidens but of little value in the world of business. My gift—and perhaps my curse as well—is vision. Most men hardly see past tomorrow, and so they are surprised when one day the future overtakes them. I favor a much longer view. Let me show you something."

The old man opened the wide center drawer of his mammoth desk and took out a set of large maps. He slid one of the maps over to Rafferty and said, "Here is the St. Anthony Falls milling district as it appeared in 1874, the year I put up my A Mill. Note the other mills around it. There are well over a dozen, all in the hands of different owners."

"I see them," Rafferty said.

Wellington handed Rafferty a second map. "Here is the milling district as it stands today. As you can see, most of those old mills are still there, along with a few new ones. There is one significant difference. I now own most of these mills. Do you know how that happened?"

Rafferty studied the map for a moment, then said, "I'm guessin' you bought out the other millers, Mr. Wellington."

The old man shook his head and said, "No, sir, I *drove* them out of business—one by one. And how did I do that? By grinding better flour at lower cost than they could. By anticipating shifts in the market that they did not. By hiring away their best millwrights and engineers. And only then, when their businesses were in ruins, did I buy them—for a song, I might add. Now then, here is one more map. It shows the milling district as I envision it in the future."

Rafferty looked at the map and was surprised to see nothing but blank space in place of the Wellington milling complex.

The old man caught Rafferty's perplexity and chuckled in an eerie sort of way. He said, "That's right, Mr. Rafferty, everything will be gone one day. How do I know that? Because I have studied the forces that are at work in the milling industry, and I can see the inevitable decline that will occur in Minneapolis. That is why I have been busy buying up properties in Buffalo, New York. Buffalo is where the future of flour milling lies in this country."[4]

Rafferty sensed that he was hearing an old story, one that Wellington had told time and again to demonstrate his superiority to the rest of benighted humanity. "I won't dispute your word," Rafferty said, "though I'm wonderin' just what your point is, Mr. Wellington. I'm thinkin' you have not called me all the way out here just to give me a lecture on what a brilliant businessman you are and how I might apply these lessons to saloon keepin'."

For the first time Wellington showed irritation, his cold eye falling on Rafferty like a spray of ice water. He said, "My point, sir, is that I see the shape of events where others see only chaos. My point is that nothing will stop me from going about my business. My point is that when I want something, I get it. Do you understand me now, sir?"

"You could not be clearer in that respect," Rafferty said, "though I am still waitin' to hear what it is you expect to get from me."

"You shall find out soon enough. Now, let us turn to matters at hand. I understand you are investigating the death of that young man—what was his name, O'Donnell?—who was murdered at my old house. Now, I cannot say exactly why the young man was murdered, or who committed the crime, or even why my old house was destroyed. But I can tell you that I believe the murderers have a larger purpose and that, sir, is to kill me."

"What makes you think that?" Rafferty asked.

Instead of providing an immediate answer, Wellington slowly got up and walked over to the blue-gray block of stone—about two feet long and a foot wide and deep—that formed the room's unlikely centerpiece. The old man rubbed one hand softly over the stone, as though stroking a favorite pet. Rafferty found this gesture exceedingly strange.

"Tell me, Mr. Rafferty, what do you think about this unusual curio of mine?" Wellington asked.

Rafferty went over to take a better look at the stone and noticed as he walked around it that one side—the side facing away from him as he had entered the room—was charred to an almost complete black. He then said, "Looks like a piece of the local limestone, Mr. Wellington. Platteville is what I think they call it. 'Tis the stone that was used for many a buildin' here in the old days."

"Very good. And what about that charred side on the stone? What do you make of that?"

Rafferty studied the stone for a minute and said, "'Twould appear it was in a fire at some point. A very big fire by the look of it."

"Oh, it was," said Wellington. "Any idea where it might have come from?"

Rafferty knew he was being tested. He said, "'Tis from the old A Mill, I imagine, the one that exploded."

"Yes," Wellington said, "that one. A piece of the past, you might call it."

"'Tis not a piece of history I would think you'd want to be reminded of," Rafferty observed.

"Ah, there is where you are wrong, Mr. Rafferty. From my point of view this stone is a monument to growth and change, and an emblem of success. The fact is, I am thankful for what happened in May of 1878. It was the greatest failure of my life, but failure is sometimes the best thing for a man. When the mill exploded, I was forced to rethink, and the knowledge I thereby acquired enabled me to build new, far better mills that remain to this day the finest in the world."

"Your failure cost quite a few lives, as I recall," Rafferty pointed out.

"Eighteen," Wellington said, "and several other men were maimed, quite horribly, for life. I brooded over that fact for a long time, but I have gotten over it. I could not even tell you the names of the dead men now. Am I callous? Perhaps, but the reality is that I can do nothing about the accident any more. Nothing. I can only accept that what happened was part of God's plan."

Rafferty had found that when people spoke of "God's plan" they were usually referring to someone else's misfortune, thereby confirming their own lofty status before the Almighty. Rafferty saw no reason to share this piece of wisdom with the old man, so he moved on. "That is most fascinatin', sir, but I'm still wonderin' why you believe that whoever killed Mr. O'Donnell—and a poor cartman named Joe Shelton, I might add—is really after you."

Wellington rubbed his hand along the rough face of the stone again and said, "I think it to be so because, as I have said, I am a man who sees the shape of things when other men do not. Something sinister is coming my way, Mr. Rafferty, coming closer every day. I can feel it, like a wind rattling in my bones."

The old man's unsettling words sent a chill down Rafferty's spine. He certainly had not expected to hear the captain of industry sounding like one of those crazy spiritualists who pretended to summon up the spirits of the dead.

Rafferty asked, "Do you have any idea what this sinister thing may be?"

"It is related to the forces of anarchism now abroad in this land," the old man said, going back to his desk and sitting down. Rafferty did likewise.

"What makes you say that?" Rafferty inquired.

"As I said, it is a thing I know in my bones. There is someone, Mr.

Rafferty, who wishes to do me great harm. I believe this same person murdered Mr. O'Donnell. Unfortunately, the local police are, in my judgment, a group of incompetent fools, and I am convinced they will not find the guilty party. That is where you enter the picture, Mr. Rafferty."

Wellington removed an envelope from one of the desk drawers and slid it over to Rafferty. "Open it, if you would."

Rafferty did so, and found the envelope stuffed with one-hundred-dollar bills. "What's this for?" he asked.

Wellington rose from his chair and walked over to the windows, from which he could see his splendid lawn rolling down to the lake. "It is a simple matter," he said. "I wish to hire you to identify O'Donnell's murderer, who, I am certain, intends to kill me next. The envelope contains five thousand dollars. I propose to pay you an additional five thousand dollars if your investigation meets with success. There is, of course, one condition."

"Ah, I imagined there might be. Cash money has a way of attractin' conditions like a magnet in a junkyard."

Wellington said, "You are quite the character, aren't you, Mr. Rafferty? You have a quick answer for everything, it seems, but I suggest you think before you say anything more. There is a great deal of money to be made here, Mr. Rafferty, and you are in a position to make it if you so choose."

"I'm listenin'," Rafferty said.

"Good. The condition has to do with Mr. Randolph Hadley. I understand that you have become aware of certain unsavory activities that occurred at my townhouse in Zier Row. Is that correct?"

"It is. You are very well informed, Mr. Wellington. I see you have been talkin' with Mayor Adams."

Wellington's pale cheeks flushed with anger. "I do not truck with that man," he said. "He is nothing but a common thief and a violator of God's laws."

Rafferty was surprised by the vehemence of these comments. "Some of your fellow business leaders don't appear to share your sentiments," he noted. "From what I've heard, the mayor has plenty of support among the moneyed men of Minneapolis."

"Anyone who supports that man will regret it in the end, I can assure you. As the Bible says of the devil, 'When he speaketh a lie, he speaketh of his own: for he is liar, and the father of it.'"[5]

Although Rafferty disliked Bible quoters, he had to admit that in this instance the words hit their mark. Arthur Adams was a champion liar all right, though Rafferty wondered why Wellington despised the mayor with such venomous intensity, given that mendacity was an ordinary feature of political life.

"'Tis obvious you hate the mayor with a powerful passion," Rafferty said. "I'm curious why."

"And you shall stay curious," Wellington replied, "as it is none of your business. Mr. Hadley, on the other hand, is a friend, and I am sorry to hear that he has committed a most indiscreet act. In a certain way, I may be to blame."

Wellington's admission seemed entirely out of character. "Why do you say that?" Rafferty asked.

"I say it because Mr. Hadley would never have been at my house had I done my Christian duty."

"I take it you're sayin' you should have done more to stop what was goin' on at Zier Row?"

"Precisely. You see, I have suspected for some time that Mr. Hadley was using my townhouse as a place for assignations."

"What made you suspicious?"

"That is immaterial. Suffice it to say that I am not without resources when it comes to such matters."

"I see. But if you believed Mr. Hadley was doin' something improper at your house, why didn't you put a stop to it?"

"A very good question, sir. The answer, I'm afraid, is that I acted on sentiment instead of good business sense. I like Mr. Hadley, who in my estimation is a real leader among men and who has done me a number of favors over the years. I thus gave him the benefit of the doubt when he denied the reports I had been hearing. Now it appears he will have to pay a price for his foolishness unless, perhaps, you and I can come to an arrangement."

"Ah, I see now. You want me to turn over the picture as part of my 'investigation'?"

"Yes, it would be a helpful thing to do, don't you think? Naturally, I would take good care of it."

"I'm sure you would."

"Well then, what do you say, Mr. Rafferty?"

Though Rafferty was "comfortable," as he liked to put it, he was also the kind of man who generally spent what he made and did not bother himself with the dull business of laying up a nest egg. He had no immediate family—the vagaries of fate had seen to that—and he saw no reason why he should leave the world any wealthier than he had entered it. Ten thousand dollars was an impressive sum, enough to clear away the last of the encumbrances on his saloon and provide plenty of extra spending money as well.

Trouble was, Rafferty did not like being bribed, and Wellington's offer of payment for an "investigation" reeked with the sweet, unhealthy odor of hush money. The old man was used to buying things and now he wanted to buy Rafferty's silence, just as he would any other commodity.

Wellington drummed his bony fingers on the desk top and said, "Well, sir? What will it be?"

Rafferty said, "Your offer is most generous, Mr. Wellington, and most surprisin', since I'm hardly known to you."

"On the contrary, I know you quite well, for I have made it my business to look into your record. It is clear that you have already made far more progress than the police in uncovering the truth of what is happening here."

"I appreciate your kind words, but I still can't help wonderin' why you'd want to hire a fellow like me to track down a bunch of murderin' anarchists. The Pinkertons or one of the other detective agencies could put a hundred operatives in the field if need be. I'm assumin' money is no object."

Wellington shifted slightly in his chair and let the merest hint of a smile form on his mouth. "Money is always an object, Mr. Rafferty. When it ceases being so, I will be finished. You are right, however. I could, if I wished, give the Pinkertons free rein, but I have good reasons for not doing so."

"Do you now? I'd be curious to know what they are."

"I'm sure you would. Perhaps some day I will tell you. Now then, Mr. Rafferty, let me have your answer. Do you wish to work for me or not?"

"'Tis a mighty fine offer, Mr. Wellington, but I think I'll pass. Truth is, ten thousand dollars would buy a year of my time, and I'm not sure I want to be bought for that long."

"Very well," said Wellington, who immediately rang a button on his desk to summon a servant. "But I must tell you, Mr. Rafferty, that you are making a foolish mistake. Good day, sir."

As Rafferty was led back through the house, he found himself thinking that he had missed something during the interview. There was, he sensed, a vital connection to be made if only he could see it. Once outside, Rafferty saw that clouds had now rolled in over the lake, and the scent of rain was in the wind.

CHAPTER FOURTEEN

⬥⬥

"I Think He Might Be Living in There"

FROM THE JOURNALS OF DR. JOHN WATSON:

SAT., OCT. 7, 1899, WEST HOTEL, MPLS., 2 A.M.: Have taken three draughts of strong tea in order not to succumb to sleep & forget any details of memorable events of this night. Wish I had stamina of H, who shows no sign of weariness despite strenuous activities. H now conferring with SR & expect report shortly. What a pair they make! So similar in energy & conviction & much like wild boys, always plotting some grand adventure together. Or perhaps more like one of H's beloved chemical reactions in which two different but related substances combine to produce dramatic & startling effects. . . .

As to the night's events, all began calmly enough. Left Ryan Hotel in St. Paul at 4:30 P.M. wearing dirty old raincoats salvaged from "lost & found" at SR's saloon. H said coats "part of our disguise" but offered no further explanations. Arrived Mpls. business district 5:30 P.M. & went at once into large department store where we eluded man who had followed us on streetcar.

Our destination Well[ington]'s apartment at Zier Row, to which SR had provided directions. Reached row house at dusk after vigorous walk. Zier Row large red brick building extending around corner: four stories high, steep French-style roofs, towers, much ornament, & leaded glass. Walked past apartment belonging to Well but did not stop, as H wished to avoid attracting attention. H noted apartment building across street with basement entry beneath steps.

H, GLANCING TOWARD ENTRY: "That will be our observation post tonight, Watson. Let us hope we are not disappointed."

W: "What if we are?"

H: "Then we shall come back tomorrow night & the night after that if necessary. If Mr. Rafferty is correct, & I believe he is, Zier Row occupies a crucial intersection in this affair. It is the one place linking O'Donnell directly to Randolph Hadley, as well as indirectly to Mr. Wellington. Of course, it appears Mayor Adams is also familiar with the apartment & may use it for assignations of his own. It is a house with secrets, Watson, & I intend to find them out."

We continued around block & inspected alley behind Zier Row from other end. Saw that row house L-shaped with rear entrances to apartments opening on courtyard. After H satisfied we knew "lay of the land," walked to small restaurant some blocks away recommended by SR. Ate quick supper & waited for complete darkness.

Returned to Zier Row before 7 P.M., passing only handful of pedestrians in neighborhood, as night had turned chilly with light rain & fog, tho nothing like London variety. Lights shone out thru several shaded windows in Well's apartment. H much pleased to see this, noting "lady of the house must be home." Took position under steps across street & began wait, having no idea what to expect. Vantage point allowed us to see front of row house & down alley behind in event someone came or went by back door.

W: "Is there any visitor in particular we should be looking for?"

H: "No. Anyone — man or woman — who enters or leaves that apartment must be considered suspect. If anyone does leave, Watson, you must follow, as discreetly as possible. I will stay to watch for further developments."

W: "What if someone enters?"

H: "Then we shall find out, by one means or another, who that person is."

Surprised to see H had brought along bottle of cheap wine & asked why, as he generally did not consume ardent spirits when on hunt so as to keep mind perfectly clear.

H: "Have no fear, Watson. I have not turned into a toper. The wine—a most unpalatable muscatel—is merely a precaution in the event a policeman or some other curious soul discovers us huddling here in the darkness. We will then pass ourselves off as two 'gentlemen of the street' sharing a bottle. The old raincoats will give us the proper appearance for men of such a kind."

Waited hours under steps & I grew very cold. Brought to mind last night of ice palace adventure when icy fog enshrouded St. Paul & we waited for arrival of killer. . . .

At 9:30 P.M. brief excitement when wagon stopped on street near apartment. H thought driver might be someone in disguise but not so. Driver tied down part of load that had shifted & moved on.

Wait continued past 10, 11, & midnight. H silent & alert as always & promised we would "stay all night" if need be. My teeth began to chatter & I wished H had brought along brandy instead of wine. Hardly any pedestrians after 11, tho did see policeman pass by on other side of street. Did not see us, however, & was soon out of sight.

Action at last at 12:15 A.M.! Large carriage with liveried driver pulled to stop across from us. Man got out & bounded up steps to Well's apartment. Could not see face in dim light but man tall & slender, wearing top hat & caped raincoat. Pitched forward as he walked, suggesting great eagerness & purpose. Man rang doorbell & was admitted at once to apartment, tho could not make out person who opened door. Carriage then left.

H: "Judging from Mr. Rafferty's description, that is Mr. Randolph Hadley who has just gone into the apartment. Perhaps he intends to spend another evening with the woman inside. If so, we have a very long night ahead of us, Watson."

W: "But what will we learn merely by standing here in the cold?"

H: "Discipline, for one thing, but you are correct, Watson. There is little to be learned from our present vantage point. That is why I propose to pay a visit to the lady of the house once Mr. Hadley leaves. She will hardly be in a position at that point to deny the affair & I am inclined to think she will have much to tell us if pressed to do so. Once we have gotten the truth out of her, we will then be in a position to deal with Mr. Hadley."

Steeled myself now for miserable night, as I supposed Hadley would not emerge until after daybreak.

Another surprise at 12:45 A.M. All lights in apartment extinguished & moments later carriage approached from east, on 9th St. Soon saw that carriage an open phaeton—two-seated variety but much smaller than large coach in which Hadley arrived. Impossible to get good look at driver, who wore wide-brimmed hat & long coat of type favored by hacks. Carriage turned into alley behind row house.

H: "Come along, Watson. I wish to get a better look at that carriage & its occupant."

Followed H across street toward alley, entrance to which very dark as no street lamps nearby. Stopped at end of row house & peered around corner into alley. Faint light visible from lamp in rear courtyard, sufficient to reveal dim outlines of phaeton, which had stopped about 100 feet in from street.

H put finger to lips & motioned me to come with him. We crept along next to row house, staying in its shadow so as not to be seen. Had taken only few steps, however, when two shadowy figures— one tall & thin & possibly Hadley himself, the other much smaller & possibly a woman—emerged from courtyard & climbed into phaeton. Driver set in motion & carriage soon at 8th St. end of alley. From there it turned west toward business district.

H raced down alley, I following behind. By time I reached 8th, carriage already out of sight & H looking very unhappy.

W: "Did you see who was in the carriage?"

H: "No, but the larger of the two figures was by no means dissimilar to Mr. Hadley. The smaller one, I am almost certain, was a woman."

W: "But why—"

H: "An excellent question, Watson. Why would Mr. Hadley arrive at the front door in one carriage & leave via the back door in another, & with a woman at that? It does not on the face of it make any sense, unless—"

W: "He thought he was being watched & wished to escape with his female friend."

H: "Ah, my dear Watson, you are becoming too clever for your own good, for that is indeed one possibility. There is also another, which is that the man we saw leaving was not Mr. Hadley."

W: "Then who? The mayor perhaps?"

H: "I doubt it. He has a stockier build, from what I understand. He also has his own coach, according to Mr. Rafferty."

W: "Who else would it be? You don't think it was Mr. Wellington himself?"

H: "No. Mr. Wellington is at least 75 years old. Men of that age do not as a rule move as quickly as the figure whose outlines we saw in the alley. It was almost certainly a younger man."

W: "What about the woman? She must have been the mistress of the house."

H: "So it would appear. There is only one way to be certain & that is to pay a visit to the apartment."

W: "Even though Mr. Hadley may still be there & it's one o'clock in the morning?"

H: "Mr. Hadley has already had at least one visitor at this late hour, so I see no reason why he should object to two more, if he is in fact still inside."

Walked back down alley toward courtyard, where single electric lamp provided feeble illumination. Thought H would continue to front of building to ring doorbell, but he went instead to inspect back door of Well's apartment. Door wide open. . . .

Rafferty got off the train at Minneapolis Union Depot at quarter past five and walked toward the flour mills clustered around St. Anthony Falls, a half mile to the east. His plan was to find out more about the tunnels in which Michael O'Donnell had apparently spent some of his last hours. And since the Ratman was known to be a habitue of the area, Rafferty hoped he might get lucky and meet up with the elusive street character somewhere in the depths. As far as Rafferty could tell, he was not being followed anymore, but he kept a sharp eye out as always.

Charles Wellington's complex, built up over many years, dominated the great row of flour mills that stretched for two blocks along the west side of the falls. There were easily a dozen buildings in the complex. Foremost was the seven-story A Mill, which like its ill-fated predecessor, was constructed of massive limestone blocks. A motley collection of other structures—warehouses, grain elevators, a small office building, and a wheelhouse, among others—completed the sprawling complex.[1]

As Rafferty approached from Washington Avenue, what he couldn't see was the Mississippi itself or the famous waterfall that had spawned Wellington's industrial kingdom and the booming city around it. Just a half century earlier the Falls of St. Anthony had been one of the continent's great natural spectacles—the only place where the Mississippi River ran wild on its two-thousand-mile course from northern Minnesota to the Gulf of Mexico. At the falls the river plunged sixteen feet over a broad limestone shelf before twisting and foaming down another fifty feet through a narrow gorge. Although hardly a match for Niagara, the falls was so powerful that in the 1840s its roar could sometimes be heard ten miles down river, in the nascent city of St. Paul. The Sioux called the falls *Minirara*, or curling water, but this beautiful name was rejected in 1680 by Father Louis Hennepin, probably the first European to see the cataract. Hennepin, as famous for his lies as his explorations, named the falls after his patron saint.

There was nothing religious about what happened thereafter. Perfectly situated between vast pineries to the north and prairies ideal for wheat growing to the south and west, St. Anthony Falls was one of the most coveted waterpower sites on the continent. In the 1850s Wellington and his fellow Yankees began the task of harnessing it. They did their work so well that by 1899 the cataract as the Sioux and Hennepin had seen it was gone, transformed into one of the most intensely developed industrial sites on earth.[2]

Wellington's mills and the others stood shoulder to shoulder along a power canal paralleling the falls, long since hidden beneath a protective wooden apron. The mills gulped in water from the canal and sent it plunging down thirty feet or more through penstocks to large turbines, which in turn powered an array of shafts, belts, pulleys, and other mechanical contrivances. Once the falling water had done its work, it was sent back to the river through a maze of brick-lined tailrace tunnels carved out of soft sandstone.[3]

The whole system was a masterpiece of hydraulic engineering, and it had helped make Charles Wellington and a few other millers rich beyond their dreams by supplying power that was both cheap and, except in times of extreme drought, reliable. Even so, there were constant disputes over the water—in their greed the millers could never get enough of it—and cheating of all kinds was said to be rampant. Nor did anyone seem to care that the price for this glorious progress was the destruction of the historic falls and the creation of a riparian wasteland choked with industrial debris.

Rafferty wasn't very familiar with the milling district and as he neared the Wellington complex, he realized that reaching the river itself would require some doing. The mills reared up behind a steel moat of railroad tracks, so that the river itself seemed entirely blocked off. After a couple of false starts, Rafferty looped around the south side of the mills and followed Eighth Avenue South toward the river. He crossed a second set of tracks and then a third, which ran on a platform above the canal along First Street. Mills loomed over both sides of the platform, forming a dark, narrow, intimidating canyon nearly three blocks long.

The air, Rafferty noticed, had begun to acquire an unpleasant malty aroma and was powdered with bits of grain blown from passing railcars. Crows and other birds had long since discovered this accidental feast, forming food chains along the rails and ignoring the trains that regularly passed a few feet away. Over the rumbling of the trains, Rafferty could hear the steady hum of machinery inside the mills as well as the venting of large exhaust fans designed to clear away potentially explosive flour dust. But he still couldn't hear, or even see, the river itself.

Dodging trains, Rafferty walked toward an iron trestle carrying yet more railroad tracks toward the last mill in the line, which was identified

by a large sign as the Palisade. Off to his left, waste water from a mill—
which one, Rafferty couldn't begin to tell—hurried in an open tailrace
toward the river. Surprisingly, the area appeared bereft of people, except for an occasional trainman, and no one challenged Rafferty as he
made his way through the tangle of bents, beams, and piers that supported the trestle. Once past this last obstacle, he reached a high bank
from which he could at last see the river. The view was not inspiring. His
friend Jim Hill's stone-arch bridge, which curved gracefully to the
north, was about the only pleasing object in view. Otherwise, the falls
area reminded Rafferty of a battered and forlorn old mining district—
only in this case, instead of ruining a mountain for its gold, men had
ruined a river for its power.[4]

Rafferty soon realized that he was not actually standing on the banks
of the river itself. Instead, he had by accident stumbled upon exactly
what he was looking for—the main tailrace channel. Tunnels serving in-
dividual mills were visible along one side of the channel, pouring out
spent water from turbines. The tunnels hardly looked inviting, even to
someone desperately in need of shelter, and Rafferty might have written
off the whole legend of the Tunnel Boys then and there had he not spotted two boys down by the channel, idly tossing stones.

"How'd you fine lads like to make a little money?" Rafferty shouted
down.

The boys, dressed in dirty clothes and probably not much older than
fourteen, turned around and stared up at Rafferty. Both were wiry and
tough looking—street urchins without a doubt. "What do we have to
do?" one of them asked suspiciously.

"Come up here and I'll tell you."

The boys scrambled up the steep embankment, using rocks and
bricks for handholds, but stopped warily a few feet in front of Rafferty.
They obviously were no fools.

"Do you lads come down to the tailrace often?" he asked.

"Let's see some money," the taller and, by the looks of it, older of the
two boys said. "And we're no queers, so keep your distance."

"Nor am I," said Rafferty, fishing out a pair of silver dollars from one
of his pockets and tossing them at the boys. "Now then, there's more of
these for the two of you if you can answer my questions. All right?"

"Sure," said the older boy, "but don't try nothing."

"Are there people down in the tunnels?"

The older boy, who apparently planned on doing all the talking, laughed and said, "Lots of 'em. Tramps mostly. But for sure you don't want to go in at night."

"Why not?"

"There's people in there that'll kill you, that's why, mister. Especially in the Wellington tunnels."

"Have you been in those tunnels lately?"

"I'm not crazy," the boy said, looking at Rafferty as if he were. "Nobody goes in there if they know what's good for them."

Then the younger boy piped up, "Except for the lady. She goes in there all the time."

This was an intriguing piece of information. Rafferty could think of only one woman off hand who might have gone into the tunnels, and he described her in detail to the younger boy.

The reply was profoundly disappointing: "She could be the one, but I only seen her a couple of times from the back as she was going in the tunnel. She wasn't fat or nothing, that's for sure."

"When was the last time you saw her?"

The boy thought for a moment and said, "A couple of weeks ago, maybe, just before dark. Me and Louie"—he nodded in the direction of the older boy—"hang around down here a lot."

"I gather that. Was the woman usually alone when you saw her or was she with someone?"

The older boy spoke up. "I seen her once with a guy. We figure they were doing you know what in there," he added, making an unmistakable gesture with his pelvis.

"Somehow I doubt that," said Rafferty. "Can you describe the man you saw her with?"

"He was short and had a real ugly face," said Louie. "Full of holes. He looked bad."

"You're right there, son. He was a bad man," said Rafferty, struck by how many times he seemed to be running across the shadow of Earl Hayes. "Have you seen him or anybody else down here lately?"

"Naw, but we've been busy," said Louie. "Besides, like I told you, it ain't healthy to get too close to the people who hang around here."

"Do any of these people have names?" Rafferty asked.

"I wouldn't know," said Louie.

George, the younger boy, now came to the rescue again. "Come on, Louie, what about Sid? Everybody knows him. He's crazy. Likes to eat rats, he does. Ain't that right, Louie?"

"Aw, shut up, George. You talk too much. Besides, Sid don't eat rats, he just catches 'em."

"Ah, this is most interestin', lads," Rafferty said. "As it so happens, the Ratman is an old acquaintance of mine. I'd greatly enjoy talkin' to him again one of these days. Exactly when and where did you last see him?"

Louie gave Rafferty a shrewd glance. "It'll cost you," he said, obviously sensing an opportunity to add to his net worth.

"I'm willin' to pay if the information is good," said Rafferty. "Now tell me about the Ratman and be quick about it, or neither of you will see another penny. Is that understood, lads?"

"All right," Louie said, adding, "say, are you some kind of detective?"

"Could be. All right, let's hear about Sid."

The boys reported that they had last seen the Ratman late in the afternoon two days earlier. He had been standing at the entrance to one of the Wellington tunnels. When he saw them, the boys said, the Ratman scurried back inside. The boys called out his name but he didn't respond, as he usually did.

"It was funny because the Ratman always likes to talk," Louie said, "but he acted like he was afraid of us."

"And you haven't seen him since?"

"No."

"But I think he's living in there," Louie said, gesturing toward the tunnels.

George nodded in agreement. "Lots of rats for him to eat."

"What makes you think he's living in the tunnel?" Rafferty asked.

"Because he's around here all the time. Besides, the way I've heard it, he knows the tunnels better than anybody. There's miles of 'em, you know."

"So I've heard. Now then, lads, I want you to show me the tunnel where you saw the Ratman two days ago."

"Are you going to arrest him?" Louie asked.

"No," said Rafferty, "but I may just save his life."

Despite the help of his girlfriend's brother, Wash Thomas did not have an easy time finding a cartman who had been a friend of the late Joe Shelton. Although Shelton was a familiar figure, he also had a reputation as a solitary and secretive man who kept his distance from people—a trait that was perhaps inevitable given his odiferous line of work. It took Thomas all afternoon to track down a cartman with useful information. The man's name was James Johnson, and he happened to be black—a stroke of good luck, as it turned out.

Race had seldom if ever been an advantage in Thomas's life, and though he was well known in St. Paul, he still had to cope almost daily with slights large and small, not to mention ugly comments and even overt acts of hostility—all because he was black. He had forgotten none of these incidents—and never would—but he had also managed to live his life as he wished and had not allowed resentment to poison his heart. Nor had he ever been afraid to stand up for himself, or for other black people, and he often appeared before the city council and even the state legislature on civil rights issues.

Having Rafferty as a friend and partner had made Thomas's life easier, to be sure, and he knew that he would always have at least one powerful ally in any situation where prejudice did its hateful work. Yet what Thomas liked most about Rafferty was that he was wise enough to accept the fact that there were things he could never know when it came to understanding what it was like to live as a black man in a white man's world.

James Johnson knew all about this reality, of course, and probably would not have given Thomas any useful information had he been one of those white men. As it was, Johnson—a rather dour, broad-faced man of fifty or so, with a barrel chest, short stout legs, and a deliberate way of speaking—was hardly a font of information. Thomas had found him, after many inquiries, on the city's North Side, in a rundown tenement well known to be a "Negro building."[5]

Thomas knew from long experience that what a poor man wanted, as much as anything else, was an opportunity now and then to enjoy the good things in life, just as rich men did every day. To that end, Thomas had brought along a fifth of the saloon's best Kentucky bourbon, which Johnson was now working on with evident pleasure. The alcohol was also loosening his tongue.

Thomas said, "You mentioned, Mr. Johnson, that Joe Shelton was not a man who kept close friends. Still, he must have known a good many people simply from making his rounds throughout the city."

Johnson nodded and said, "Oh, he knew plenty of folks all right. It was just that Joe didn't truck with them much, that's all. He was kind of high and mighty that way."

Thomas found it hard to imagine how a man who made his living by collecting human waste could be considered high and mighty, but he did not dispute the point.

"Course, what you've got to know about old Joe is that he had money," Johnson said. "Richest s——t collector in town, he was."

"Is that a fact? How did he come by it?"

Johnson emitted a chuckle and poured another shot of bourbon. "Won himself a lawsuit, that's how. Got some fancy lawyer to represent him and before they were done, why old Joe had a nice little pile."

"What sort of lawsuit?"

"I don't know about such things. I think it had to do with him and his city license. Joe was always complaining about how the city cheated him on this or that. It's true, but in this town everybody gets cheated, the way I see it. Anyway, Joe went right up to the mayor's office one day and made a fuss. Got tossed out by the coppers, from what I heard. After that, he found a lawyer."

"Do you know the lawyer's name?"

"No. Joe told me once but I forget."

"When did Joe win his lawsuit?"

Johnson scratched the back of his head as a stimulus to thought, and finally said, "I'm thinking it was last year sometime."

Thomas continued probing but could get nothing else of value from the cartman. He thanked Johnson for his help and stood up to leave. Johnson pushed the bottle of bourbon across the table and said, "Don't forget this."

"Keep it," Thomas said with a smile. "You've earned it."

It was nearly four o'clock by the time Thomas left Johnson's apartment and walked to the nearest streetcar stop. He figured he'd have just enough time to make it downtown to the Hennepin County courthouse before it closed for the day. When he got to the courthouse—housed in the towering new municipal building on Fourth Street—Thomas went to the clerk of court's office and inspected the large book listing all civil filings for 1898. He soon found case number 648, *Joseph Shelton vs. City of Minneapolis*, and asked to see the file. The clerk, a prissy little man with a monocle, gave him the usual sort of stare, as though amazed to discover that a black man might actually be able to read and comprehend something as complicated as a lawsuit.

When the file finally arrived, Thomas thumbed through the three-page complaint, which contained standard legal boilerplate. At the end of the complaint, however, Thomas found a familiar name—one that Rafferty and Holmes were sure to find most interesting.

Not long after Thomas left the courthouse, Arthur Adams came to a decision. He had left city hall early and gone home, intending to change clothes and then enjoy a Friday night out on the town. His plans abruptly changed when he found out what the day's mail had brought. Now, as he sat in his library gazing out at the panorama of downtown Minneapolis, he was already on his third glass of Scotch. Normally he limited himself to two, but after receiving the photograph, he knew that considerably more alcohol would be needed to get through the evening. He also knew that the time had come to act.

The photograph—which was disgustingly clear—had arrived in a large manila envelope. Attached to the picture was a brief note, addressed in blocky printed letters to HIS DISHONOR, THE MAYOR. All the note said was WON'T THE PEOPLE OF MPLS. BE INTERESTED WHEN THEY SEE THIS?

Oh, yes, Adams thought, they will be interested and then they will be ready to run me out of town on a rail. But Adams would not allow that to happen, for he had planned well. His only concern was timing. President McKinley was due in just two days, and Adams wanted above all else to stand in triumph with the nation's leader, even if scandal lay waiting like an executioner in the wings.

The one problem Adams could foresee was Randolph Hadley. Although the leader of the alliance had himself been caught cavorting at Zier Row, his tolerance for more exotic forms of sexuality was extremely limited. No, Adams thought, Hadley would neither forgive nor forget, and he would make trouble if he could because he was, in his own way, a righteous man. Unlike the rich businessmen who funded the alliance, Hadley had never succumbed to bribery or other forms of chicanery. He was not in the business of subduing the laboring classes because of money but because he thought it the proper thing to do.

Men of principle, Adams knew, were always the worst kind to deal with, and the ones least likely to act out of rational self-interest. Clearly, something would have to be done about Hadley, and soon, or all could be lost.

Chapter Fifteen

✧

"Get Off Me, You Brute"

From the journals of Dr. John Watson:

Sat., Oct. 7, 1899, West Hotel, Mpls., 2:30 a.m.: Am taking more tea to combat growing weariness. H & Rafferty still meeting. Have just talked with GWT, who reported he has most interesting news. . . .

As for events at Zier Row, must conclude with account of extraordinary discoveries in house. H as surprised as I to find back door open, for in chill night air closing any outside door would be matter of course. Someone obviously had left in great haste. But why such hurry? As we stood by door in fog & dim light, had foreboding that something sinister awaited inside. H must have felt same, for he asked if I had my pistol, tho he knew I always carried it if danger anticipated.

W: "It is in my pocket."

H: "Good. Be prepared to use it."

Followed H, who had brought along small lantern, into first room — kitchen, as we soon found out. Shades drawn & room pitch black except for weak glow from lantern. Paused to listen for sound elsewhere in apartment. Heard nothing except ticking of clock in adjacent room. H found electric light & turned it on.

W: "Do you think it wise to switch on a light?"

H: "In this situation, Watson, it is anybody's guess as to what is wise, but I do know that we need more light. Now then, would you be so kind as to announce our presence?"

W: "You mean call out?"

H: "Exactly. If anyone is still here, I do not wish to surprise him. Instead, we will present ourselves as passersby who happened to see the back door open & worried that a burglary had occurred."

W: "I doubt we would be believed."

H: "I have found, Watson, that in circumstances such as these it is better to offer a poor lie than none at all. Now, put that booming basso of yours to use."

Called out three times at top of lungs, asking if anyone at home or in need of help. No response.

H: "It would appear we have the house to ourselves."

W: "Either that, or someone is waiting in ambush."

H: "In which case, Watson, I am sure your legendary skill with the pistol will save us."

As I stood watch at door to next room, H made brief inspection of kitchen. Found nothing unusual, though H did note ashtray on table filled with cigarette stubs. H picked up stub & examined it closely.

H: "These are Mogul cigarettes—an Egyptian brand & quite expensive. Rather harsh as well. As a rule, only a rather well-to-do man would smoke them, and certainly not a woman of any class."[1]

W: "Perhaps they are Mr. Hadley's."

H: "Perhaps, but I would point out to you, Watson, that there are eight stubs in the ashtray, & by the smell of them, they were smoked very recently. As Mr. Hadley apparently was in this house for only a few minutes tonight, it would be logical to conclude that someone else was here in the kitchen smoking them before Mr. Hadley arrived."

H put one stub in coat pocket & we then went from kitchen through butler's pantry into dining room outfitted with massive table, high-backed chairs, & heavy oak sideboard. Quickly went through sideboard drawers & found nothing. Continued thru arched doorway into front parlor—large, well-furnished room, fireplace beneath marble mantle, stained-glass window by front door. Near door, open staircase with finely turned newel post & spiral balusters leading up to second floor. H noted drapes covering window were slightly open, suggesting woman might have stood there watching for Hadley's arrival. If so, had she seen us? Posed question to H.

H: "Our hiding place beneath the steps is certainly not visible from this window. However, it is possible that someone standing here could have seen us arrive & then grown suspicious. That would account, I suppose, for Mr. Hadley & the woman going out the back door. Yet it would not necessarily account for their leaving the door wide open, nor would it explain the switch of carriages. Indeed, if Mr. Hadley thought he was being watched from out front, it would have made more sense for the carriage to come into the alley from Eighth Street, where we would not have spotted it as quickly."

W: "So you conclude we were not seen?"

H: "I will conclude nothing, Watson, until I know more."

Next we examined parlor. Noted nothing out of ordinary & went up to second floor. Paused at top of steps to listen again for sounds, but apartment incredibly quiet. H led way with lantern. Found large room—another parlor of some kind—facing out toward street. This room sparsely furnished & looked as if seldom used. Bathroom & bedroom to rear, also showing no evidence of recent use.

Climbed stairs to third floor in dead silence, not a single tread squeaking beneath feet. H noted he had seen light in at least one window on this floor before Hadley's arrival. Inspected rear portion of floor first & found pair of small sleeping chambers. Assumed these were guest bedrooms, as servants, if any, would be consigned to quarters in attic.

Adjusting flame on lantern, which had begun to flicker, H turned toward front room — almost certainly boudoir where Hadley had inadvertently posed for photograph. Door to room shut & H now called out in event, as he put it, "that someone inside is sleeping or is otherwise engaged." No answer to his calls.

H now listened one last time, detected nothing, pushed open door & stepped inside bedroom just as lantern flickered again & went out. Heard loud crash as H tripped over something in dark & tumbled to floor.

W: "Are you all right, Holmes?"

H: "Yes, I am fine. But I fear someone else has been hurt, or worse. Can you strike a match, Watson?"

I did so at once & was appalled by sight which greeted my eyes. Two bodies lay on floor within inches of each other. One that of naked woman, other was fully clothed man.

H got back to feet & managed to relight lantern, so that full scope of tragedy now revealed itself. Woman lay on back, legs spread, horrible X-shaped slash marks across breasts & privates. Lavender scarf hung loosely from neck beneath ligature marks that gave evidence of strangulation. Man, dressed in elegantly tailored blue suit, also lay on back, arms sprawled, gray eyes open & already beginning to flatten from loss of fluid, head tilted to one side. Clotting blood oozed from large bullet hole in right temple. Next to him on floor was heavy, short-barreled revolver — .44 caliber by looks of it. Odor of death & gunpowder hung in air.

Bent down to examine bodies. Both almost certainly dead but checked carotid pulse & respiration. No signs of life. Man had long face, fine features, heavily lidded eyes, short graying hair. Perhaps 55 years old. Skin waxy, lips & nails turning blue, body still warm. Probably dead no more than half hour. Woman — possibly in late 20s or early 30s, long auburn hair, full figured — also warm to touch, tho less so than man. Some evidence of lividity but no signs of rigor mortis. Little blood from slash wounds, suggesting made after death.

H: "It would appear Randolph Hadley has enjoyed his last assignation, for the dead man fits his description in every particular. The woman, I should not be surprised to learn, is the same one who appeared with him in the candid photograph. The world is supposed to believe, I presume, that Mr. Hadley first killed her & then committed suicide. It has all been carefully staged."

W: "But what of the terrible wounds on the woman's body, Holmes? What is their purpose?"

H: "I cannot be certain. They may be designed to suggest that Mr. Hadley acted in the throes of some great passion, a spurned lover who left his mark, as it were. Yet I wonder. It is just as possible that the wounds reflect the murderer's genuine anger & hatred. I find it significant, for instance, that like Michael O'Donnell, the woman was left naked & exposed, perhaps as a final humiliation."

Desk lamp on vanity nearby & H turned it on — risky, he admitted — but wanted more light to inspect crime scene. Began with survey of room, which was large & handsomely appointed. Four-poster bed, unmade & with pillows piled by headboard, against one wall opposite windows. Small tables to either side. Woman's silk robe on floor next to bed, along with undergarments. Vanity with mirror nearby, also highboy & two chairs. Oriental rug covering much of hardwood floor.

H walked around room in usual methodical way — looked at carpet, examined woman's clothing, opened drawers of highboy & vanity. Found nothing except more articles of clothing & usual cosmetics. H stopped, however, near door where we had entered & got down on one knee with magnifying glass to inspect floorboards & wainscoting.

H: "There are traces of blood here, Watson, though an attempt has been made to clean up. Judging by the length of the streaking, I should think a good bit of blood was spilled. I have also noted small grooves in the carpet not unlike those which would have been created by a pair of heels being dragged along."

W: "Ah, so you think Mr. Hadley may have been shot just as he entered the room & was then placed next to the woman's body."

H: "I can see that I shall put nothing past you today, Watson. Yes, it is almost certain that Mr. Hadley was not shot where his body lies. Presumably, the police will notice this fact when they investigate."

W: "Speaking of the police, do you intend to notify them?"

H: "I do not think that would be wise. The bodies will be discovered soon enough. Mr. Hadley is a man with many obligations &, I believe, a family. I do not doubt his coachman or someone else will come looking for him in the morning, if not before. In any event, he — and the woman — are beyond our help."

Getting back to feet, H went to window, opened drapes slightly & peered out across 9th St. toward apartment building where we had waited under steps.

H: "There can be no doubt, Watson, that this is the room where the photograph was taken. The cornice across the street is unmistakable. The next question, therefore, is how the photograph could have been made without Mr. Hadley's knowledge."

Answer soon revealed itself. Wall behind bed wainscoted in oak panels, as was entire room, to height of about 5 feet. Heavy crown molding atop wainscoting. H noticed at once that small piece of molding behind bed was gone, neatly cut out with saw. Door to right of bed opened into large closet. H went in & seconds later I saw his lantern shining through hole behind bed.

H, COMING BACK INTO ROOM: "Well, it is now apparent how the picture was taken. There is plenty of room at the back of that closet to set up a large camera. Perhaps Michael O'Donnell himself hid there & took the photographs. Still, it would have been a tricky business."

W: "Because of the light, or lack of it?"

H: "No, I should think that in daylight, with the curtains open, this room would be very bright. Certainly bright enough to take a decent —

or in this case, indecent—picture. The problem would be how to do so without Mr. Hadley becoming aware of the activity. There would have to have been a signal of some kind, after which the photographer could have opened the peephole & quickly snapped a picture while Mr. Hadley was distracted. All of this would have required exquisite timing & undoubtedly the cooperation of the woman involved."

W: "To provide the signal, you mean?"

H: "Yes. Moreover, the woman's cooperation would have been necessary to ensure that Mr. Hadley was in the right position to be captured by the camera. She would also have had to say something, or make some noise, in order to mask the click of the shutter. Moreover, the very fact that the photograph was made in daylight suggests that the woman was an accomplice to the blackmail scheme. Normally, people engaged in illicit amorous encounters would prefer a darkened room, wouldn't you agree, Watson?"

W: "Having no experience in such matters, I will defer to your judgment, Holmes."

H: "You are too modest, my dear Watson. In any event, it was a clever trap that Mr. O'Donnell—or whoever took the pictures—set here. One might call it a new variation on the panel house, in which a man's reputation, as opposed to his money, is stolen. I am also inclined to think that our hidden photographer did not go to such great trouble solely to obtain a picture of Mr. Hadley. There are more photographs, I am certain of it."[2]

W: "Of other prominent men, I assume."

H: "Yes. Unfortunately, we do not know who those men might be— tho intelligent guesses are possible—nor do we know where the photographs themselves are to be found."

W: "Perhaps the police have already found them."

H: "That is possible. Yet from what Mr. Rafferty told us of his conversation with the mayor, I suspect the pictures are still unaccounted for."

H now returned to bodies. Noted evidence of powder burns on Hadley's temple, indicating shot came at close range. Also noted ligature mark on woman's neck consistent with scarf being used for strangulation. Inspected revolver & verified one round fired.

Going down again on hands & knees & taking care to avoid blood pooling by Hadley's head, H now carefully examined corpse. Unbuttoned Hadley's coat & found holster, empty, under left arm. Then went through coat, shirt, & pants pockets. Found penknife, loose change, handkerchief, engraved watch, & wallet of fine Moroccan leather. Wallet contained about $50 in currency along with several business cards, mostly Hadley's own.

H went through cards — including one from barber in West Hotel, another from tailor, & third from downtown haberdasher.

H: "Mr. Hadley was a man who took his looks very seriously, it would appear. The worms, I imagine, will be less fastidious. Aha, what have we here?"

W: "Have you found something?"

H, TURNING A BUSINESS CARD OVER IN HIS HAND & STUDYING IT CLOSELY: "Indeed I have. Take a look at this, Watson."

Card H handed me printed in embossed typeface & said simply JAMES McPARLAND, BARCLAY BLOCK, DENVER, listing telephone number below. Name sounded vaguely familiar to me, but H knew it at once.

H: "James McParland! It has been a while since I have heard that name. Mr. McParland, Watson, is the famed Pinkerton detective who infiltrated the Molly Maguires in the Pennsylvania coalfields back in the 1870s. At last report, he was head of one of the agency's divisions. I find it most suggestive that his business card should turn up in Mr. Hadley's wallet. Perhaps they were friends."

W: "Or perhaps they were working together on some matter."

H: "An intriguing thought Watson. By the way, have you looked at the other side of the card?"

Turned over card & discovered series of notes scrawled in crabbed handwriting. Notes said, "Mary McGinty. Left Chicago. Description? In Mpls? Check with Well."

W: "Do you know what this means?"

H: "No, but it is likely that 'Well' refers to Charles Wellington. As for Mary McGinty, the name is unfamiliar to me, but I find it most interesting that she apparently has connections to Chicago, where Mr. O'Donnell & his sister also came from. Perhaps our friend Wooldridge will know of this McGinty woman. Whoever she is, it would appear she has some relationship with Mr. Wellington. It would also appear she is a person of considerable importance. Otherwise, how could she have attracted the attention of Randolph Hadley, James McParland & Charles Wellington at the same time?"

H took out watch & noted it was 1:15 A.M. Had been in apartment only half hour but seemed much longer. H now returned all items, including Hadley's wallet & business cards, to their proper pockets.

H: "There is no more to be done here, Watson, short of searching the entire house & that would be too time-consuming. Still, I would like to know who the dead woman is. In my experience, a woman almost always carries a handbag, but I found none in this room. Nor did I see a bag or purse anywhere else in the house."

W: "The police will be able to identify her, I should think."

H: "Yes, but I do not like relying upon the police for information. It is a sign of failed detective work. But I see no other choice at the moment. All right, Watson, let us be on our way. I am anxious to talk with Mr. Rafferty to see what he has learned."

Went out as we had come in, thru back door, which we left open as found. Walked down alley to 8th & then through quiet streets to West Hotel, H silent, while I could not help but wonder who had so brutally murdered two people in what was supposed to be chamber of love. . . .

ⅅᵞᵖ

A mile or so from Zier Row, in living quarters that offered no hint of elegance, Sid the Ratman sat by a small fire feeding on pieces of waste wood he had retrieved from the dark, roiling waters of the Mississippi. A fire was always welcome in the dank chill of the tunnels, though it was dangerous too, for the smoke could easily become suffocating in such a confined space. It might also attract visitors and that was not desirable from the Ratman's point of view.

For the past few days he had been holed up in the maze of tailrace tunnels beneath the mills at St. Anthony Falls. He had plenty of food — he had several caches hidden in the tunnels — and drinking water was readily available from the springs that seeped through the brick-lined walls. He had company too, for there were rats everywhere, lurking like small devils in the darkness. Already the Ratman had killed sixteen of the noxious creatures and then burned their carcasses until only bits of bone remained.

The Ratman had gone to ground because he was afraid for his life. Although not entirely rational, he was far from stupid. Having lived on the streets for years, he had well-honed instincts for survival and could feel trouble in the air the way others might sense rising humidity before a storm. And there was plenty of trouble going around at the moment. The police and other bad people were looking for him, and he had nearly fallen into their clutches twice in recent days.

The first time, he had been minding his own business outside Clausen's Saloon on Second Street when a big copper came by and gave him the evil eye. The Ratman understood what that look meant and disappeared into a maze of back alleys before the copper could catch him. Then, the next night, deep within the tunnels, he had heard the coppers banging around, calling out his name, but they had gotten lost soon enough and never came close to his hiding place. Somebody else was in the tunnels too — the Ratman had heard distant voices several times — but he was certain they would never find him either.

The Ratman felt safe because he knew the tunnels better than anyone else. There were maps of the tunnels — most of which were tailraces, though a few sewers were mixed in — but the maps were all wildly inaccurate. That was because in the old days, none of the mill owners had bothered to report their tunneling work to the city or anybody else. They just dug where they pleased. And if one tunnel encountered a problem (as had happened years back when tunnelers broke into an old cave with a fallen roof), the mill owners abandoned it and dug another one because the sandstone was so easy to work. Over the years, the Ratman had explored the whole crazy system, which was full of dead ends, hidden passageways, debris-filled caves, old wheel pits, and abandoned subbasements from long destroyed mills. It was his world and he knew its dark passageways by heart.

Still, the Ratman was thankful for his ally, who had first warned him that "bad people" besides the police were looking for him. It had something to do, he knew, with the poor young man he had found hanging at the old house on Tenth Street. Perhaps the rats did not like that he had set a trap to protect the body and were now seeking their revenge. His ally had suggested a different reason—that something the Ratman had seen or heard might expose the Secret Alliance and its murderous act. The Ratman remembered the scene of the hanging in perfect detail, down to the very words spoken by the three people, but he had no particular interest in their meaning. Even so, he had told his ally everything.

The ally had wanted him to leave Minneapolis for a while, but where would the Ratman go? No, he would be safe in the tunnels, free to fight the rat armies on his own terms and beyond the reach of ignorant men who did not understand the simple perfection of his life.

"It was right there," said Louie, pointing down from an embankment overlooking one of the tailraces from the Wellington A Mill. "That's where we saw the Ratman."

Shadwell Rafferty peered down the embankment, which ended in a low stone wall that formed one side of the tailrace. A few feet from the wall a shallow stream of water raced past, pouring out from a tunnel bored into bedrock beneath the huge mill. Farther away, a second tunnel issued from the mill, sending more water out to the river.

It was, Rafferty thought, a cold and gloomy spot, permanently shaded by the long Minneapolis Eastern Railroad trestle that ran between the mills and the main tailrace channel. A train soon rumbled along overhead, sending down a cascade of hot cinders and causing the trestle to creak ominously.

Feeling a chill, Rafferty buttoned the top of his raincoat and asked Louie, "Was the Ratman actually down there by the water?"

"He was standing right by the east tunnel—the one that's closest to us," the boy said. "Most times, of course, nobody could stand there on account of the water comes out like Niagara. But the river is awful low this year."

"Sure is," chipped in George. "You could probably go all the way back in those tunnels right now. Not that you'd want to, though."

Rafferty consulted his watch and saw that it was half past five, giving him less than an hour of daylight. His first thought had been to go into the tunnels himself in search of the Ratman, and he had even brought along a small lantern that he kept in one of the pockets in his raincoat. But he realized now that with night coming on, and with the layout of the tunnels a complete mystery to him, it would be foolhardy to go exploring for the Ratman. Instead, he decided to wait near the tunnels until darkness fell, hoping that the Ratman, a famously nocturnal creature, might emerge from his den.

"All right, lads, you've earned your money," Rafferty said, giving Louie and George two more silver dollars apiece. "Now, I don't wish to see either of you again today. Understood?"

"Sure," said Louie, staring happily at the coins in his palm, "but if you ever need the goods on anybody else, just come around and we'll help you out, mister. We know everything down here."

"Everything," George echoed.

"I'm sure you do," Rafferty said, then watched as the boys scrambled back up the embankment and out of sight.

Rafferty made his way down toward the tailrace, dropped over the three-foot-high wall, and walked back along the gravelly edge of the stream toward the tunnel entrance. The opening was about ten feet high and in the form of a brick-lined parabolic arch. Rafferty stepped a few feet inside and instantly felt a damp chill that cut to the bone. No wonder the Ratman was known for always wearing heavy winter clothes — he would have had to in order to survive in the tunnels.

"Well, I guess there is no avoidin' sentry duty," Rafferty said to himself as he came back outside. He found a spot along the wall off to one side of the entrance where he could sit and still be in a position to surprise anyone emerging from the tunnel. Of course, if the Ratman happened to be coming the other way — that is, back into the tunnels — well, it would then be a footrace and Rafferty didn't much care for his chances against an agile, wily opponent who knew every inch of the ground.

He took up his position on the wall, determined to wait at least two hours before calling it a night. Before long, drizzle began to fall, and

Rafferty wondered whether Holmes and Watson were having any success with their mission at Zier Row. Rafferty wanted a cigar—if for nothing else than the illusion of warmth it would provide—but decided it would be too risky, since the Ratman probably had an acute sense of smell.

By half past six, Rafferty was already miserable, the drizzle having turned to light rain that had somehow seeped inside his shoes, leaving him with wet and very cold feet. But he had told himself he would stay for another hour, and he had always made it a habit of living up to his own promises.

A few minutes before seven, his feet now feeling as though they had been marinated in ice water, Rafferty thought he heard the faint sound of whistling. He stepped down from his perch on the wall and gripped the revolver in his coat pocket. He listened intently, trying to ignore the soft patter of raindrops around him, but he could hear no more whistling. Perhaps his imagination had been playing tricks on him, or perhaps his hearing—always exceptionally acute, as was Holmes's— had in fact caught the first sounds of someone approaching.

Rafferty crept toward the tunnel entrance, stopping just off to one side, his back flat against the surrounding brick wall. Had the whistling come from within the tunnel? If so, Rafferty figured he would soon hear echoing footsteps, and he began to prepare himself for a possible confrontation. Rafferty didn't think the Ratman would present much of a danger, but then again, who was to say it was the Ratman approaching, if indeed anyone was?

But as Rafferty waited tensely by the tunnel, he heard no footsteps. Nor was there any more whistling. He was about to chalk it up to a false alarm when a figure suddenly emerged from the tunnel and passed him in the darkness, as quietly as a bat slicing through the night sky.

"Hold it!" Rafferty shouted, lunging at the fast-moving figure. By sheer luck, Rafferty caught a belt of some kind and dragged the figure to the ground.

He then heard a familiar voice, "Get off me, you brute, or I will shoot you down." Immediately after this alarming statement, he felt the barrel of a revolver nuzzle his cheek.

"Ah, Miss O'Donnell, fancy meetin' you here," said Rafferty. "I'm just hopin' you don't have an accident with that big pistol of yours, as the consequences would be extremely painful to me."

Chapter Sixteen

⤫

"His Exact Words, Sir, Exact Words!"

FROM THE JOURNALS OF DR. JOHN WATSON:

S AT., OCT. 7, 1899, WEST HOTEL, MPLS., 6 A.M.: Intriguing news on several fronts! Am convinced end of this tangled affair in sight, but do not know exactly where we will find it. . . .

H & SR emerged from strategy meeting at 3:15 A.M. & 4 of us—GWT also present—met in H's room. All had stories to tell & discussion lively despite lateness of hour. H enjoying himself more than in months, pacing from one end of room to other, smoking pipe & firing off questions like salvos from ship of line. SR by contrast relaxed in chair, sipping whisky from tall glass & chewing on cigar, taking everything in. GWT perhaps calmest of all—he is impressive man & could be outstanding detective in own right if not for implacable color barrier in America. He began with report on inquiries re dead cartman, Shelton.

Told of locating friend of cartman. . . . Then learned Shelton had won lawsuit against Mayor Adams & city of Mpls. Upon checking filings, GWT discovered lawyer for Shelton was J. Winston Phelps, well known for representing radicals & also acquainted with Michael O'Donnell.

GWT: "It may just be a coincidence, of course, that the cartman knew Mr. Phelps, but I judge it to be an interesting coincidence."

SR: "As do I, Wash. Trouble is, the connection proves nothing."

H: "True, yet I should like to know more about Mr. Phelps. Does he have a particular way of walking, for instance? Would he stand out in a crowd?"

Odd questions, I thought, tho SR understood immediately.

SR: "Ah, I see what you're gettin' at, Mr. Holmes. I've met the man only once but I assure you that he presents a most distinctive appearance. For one thing, he likes very colorful clothes —"

H, LOOKING AT SR'S ORANGE, RED & GREEN PLAID SUIT: "A fondness which I would venture to say you share, Mr. Rafferty, tho I am sure your taste is more exquisite in every respect."

SR, GRINNING: "Ah now, Mr. Holmes, you had best watch what you say. I don't wish to be accused of havin' exquisite taste, as it would ruin my reputation as a saloonkeeper, but I will tell you that my clothes are drab compared to the outfit Mr. Phelps had on the night we met. 'Twas pink beyond all hope of redemption. He definitely stands out in a crowd."

H: "I see. I imagine you plan to have another talk with him."

SR: "Today, if possible. I will trot out Mr. Shelton's name & see what sort of response I get."

. . . . H now turned to subject of grisly discovery at Zier Row. Tho H had already briefed SR, lengthy discussion ensued. Final decisions made re how to proceed with investigation in light of new murders. Also agreed that would let police deal with identifying woman as, said H, "We already have more business than we can handle." H added he believes "a good many of the answers to our most pressing questions may be found in Chicago."

GWT: "When do you expect to hear from Detective Wooldridge?"

H: "I cannot be certain, but I hope we will have word from him by later today. I asked for a great deal of information & I anticipate it will take some time to reply. I have already sent him a second message regarding Mary McGinty. If anyone has answers for us, it will be indefatigable Mr. Wooldridge. There is definitely a Chicago connection to what is happening here. O'Donnell, his sister, & the mysterious McGinty woman are all from Chicago, as I believe is Mrs. Burke, the saloonkeeper."

SR: "True, tho I would point out she's been in Mpls. for nearly twenty years."

H: "I see. What about Mr. O'Donnell's widow? Is she perchance from Chicago as well?"

SR: "I don't know, but I'll find out. I'm guessin' she will be— everybody else we've run across seems to be from there, even Mc-Parland."

W: "But his offices are in Denver, I believe."

SR: "That's his headquarters, but I understand from talkin' to some Pinkertons I know in St. Paul that McParland spends plenty of time in Chicago. The locals hate havin' him so close, since he's famous for poppin' in unannounced & firin' people for the slightest infraction. They'd just as soon he'd stay in Denver, which is a lot farther away, or so they tell me after a few beers. I must hand it to Wash, by the way. He informed me just a few days ago that some Pinkertons were askin' questions about me, even tho they didn't identify themselves as such. Of course, neither of us thought someone like McParland might be involved."

H: "You will be interested to know that Mr. McParland is at this very moment in Minneapolis."

SR CAUGHT UNAWARES, FOR **H** OBVIOUSLY HAD NOT REVEALED THIS INFORMATION EARLIER: "Is he now, Mr. Holmes? Well, you're up to your old tricks, I see, pullin' large rabbits out of small hats & leavin' us all to wonder how it was done."

H, SMILING: "There was no magic, I assure you—just the usual process of reasoning. You see, since Mr. Hadley had Mr. McParland's business card in his possession, I thought it likely that the two men might have met recently, perhaps even here in Mpls. I then proceeded on the assumption that a man of Mr. McParland's stature, if he was indeed here, would stay at the best hotel in the city, which is where we are at the moment. Therefore, Mr. Rafferty, I resorted to your time-honored method of obtaining information — bribery — & for $5 received the full story from a bellboy not half an hour ago. Mr. McParland & two bodyguards are in room 812 & have been at the hotel since the day after Michael O'Donnell's murder. Quite a coincidence, I should say."

SR, GIVING A LOW WHISTLE: "Ah, it certainly is, tho not a happy one. From what I've heard, Mr. McParland is the slipperiest snake in the Pinkerton nest. If he's involved in this business, then we've got even more trouble on our hands than we thought."

H: "True, Mr. Rafferty, yet I must admit I relish the opportunity to meet the man. His undercover work in the case of the Molly Maguires was most extraordinary. Indeed, Watson has even spoken of what a marvelous tale could be spun out of Mr. McParland's adventures."

W: "Holmes is right, tho I doubt I will ever get around to writing it."[1]

SR: "Ah, I'm sure you will one day, Doctor. In the meantime, the question is how best to approach this McParland fellow. From what I've heard, he's very suspicious about meetin' with people he doesn't know."

H: "I am sure we can find a way. Now then, Mr. Rafferty, I believe it is your turn to report, for you have had the busiest day of all, between your interview with Mr. Wellington & your adventures in the tunnels."

On subject of Well[ington], all agreed his attempt to bribe SR distasteful but hardly surprising.

SR: "'Tis clear Mr. Wellington knows far more about the goings on at Zier Row than he admitted. I'm also of the opinion that his effort to obtain the incriminatin' picture of Mr. Hadley was motivated by more than just his friendship for the man. There was self-interest involved."

W: "Are you suggesting, Mr. Rafferty, what I think you are?"

SR: "Yes, I'm indeed suggestin' that Mr. Wellington wished to buy me off because he's worried that I may have unflatterin' pictures of him as well. I think he put that wad of cash in my hand to see if I was ready to deal."

W: "But the man is 75 years old. Surely at his age — "

SR: "He should know better. I agree. However, 'tis my experience that sometimes the older the rooster, the friskier he is because he knows he doesn't have much time left to play in the henhouse. I can't prove a thing, of course, but I'll be interested to see how Mr. Wellington reacts to the news of two stiffs bein' found in his apartment — one of them his good friend, Randolph Hadley. The newspapers will have a field day & the old man will almost be forced to issue a statement of some kind."

H: "Speaking of the newspapers, I think it would be wise to pass on a tip to our good friend, Mr. Pyle, just in case the police try to cover up the events at Zier Row. Now, Mr. Rafferty, let us hear about the rest of your conversation with Mr. Wellington as well as your discoveries in the tunnels. I am sure Dr. Watson will want to hear every word, as he no doubt intends to write up this matter for one of those sensational magazines to which he contributes with such enthusiasm."

Thus urged on by H's usual hyperbole, SR took floor & talked without letup for 30 minutes, mostly about his encounter with Addie O'Donnell & Sid the Ratman. . . .

When Addie O'Donnell heard Rafferty's voice, she put down her pistol and said, "My apologies, Mr. Rafferty. I did not expect to find you here."
"The surprise was mutual," said Rafferty, getting up to his knees just in time to sense a shadow coming up behind him.

"Don't!" Addie O'Donnell shouted. "He's a friend!"

"Oh, that is different, yes, very different," said Sid the Ratman, lowering the baseball bat with which he had been preparing to bash out Rafferty's brains. "And I know the voice, sir, know it well. You are the fellow troubled by rats in the cornice. Or was it your friend at the Bellingham Apartments by Zier Row?"

Well, thought Rafferty, there's nothing wrong with the Ratman's memory. "Yes, it was my friend who had the rat problem," Rafferty said, getting to his feet, "and since we've all stopped tryin' to kill one another, perhaps we can sit down and talk."

"All right," said Addie O'Donnell, "but we should go back inside. Sid is more comfortable there."

After lighting a long candle he carried in one of his coat pockets, the Ratman led the way. They followed a path that ran along one wall of the tunnel several feet above the stream of waste water rushing down from the mill. When they had gone perhaps a hundred feet into the depths, Rafferty began to hear a pulsing roar, which he soon realized must be a turbine turning somewhere up ahead in the darkness.

But before they reached the turbine, a narrow tunnel came in from the left, and they followed it until it opened into yet a third uphill tunnel that had the smell of an old sewer, which in fact it was. Only after several more turns did they reach the Ratman's temporary home, a small niche in the sandstone where he kept blankets, tins of food, and other necessities.

"Sid sleeps in a different part of the tunnels every night," Addie O'Donnell said as they all sat down on the blankets around the flickering candle, which did little to illuminate and nothing to warm the dank, foul chamber that the Ratman called home. The Ratman opened some canned beef from his stash and began eating, while Addie O'Donnell turned to Rafferty and said, "I suppose you are wondering what I am doing here tonight."

"The thought has crossed my mind."

"Well, I am doing exactly what you are, Mr. Rafferty. I am investigating my brother's death. And Sid, I have learned, has much information about how my brother died."

"I see, and how did you come to connect the Ratman—Sid, that is— to your brother's murder."

"The same way you did, I am sure," she said. "When I saw in the newspapers that a rat trap had been left by my brother's body, I thought at first, as everyone did, that it was meant to suggest he was some sort of traitor. Then a new thought occurred to me. What if Sid, who I knew always carried traps with him, had by some chance come across Michael's body and left a trap behind to protect him? So I went looking for Sid. I found him here tonight and he told me all about putting down the trap. He told me many other interesting things as well. We were just leaving when we ran into you."

"Leaving for where, if I may ask?"

"I intend to take Sid to my apartment to get him some warm food and perhaps a bath. I am not sure he is safe in these tunnels anymore. The police have been looking for him."

"They may not be the only ones," Rafferty noted. "Be that as it may, I'm curious, Miss O'Donnell, how you knew where to find Sid when no one else could? Are the two of you friends?"

"Yes, we are," she said, squeezing the Ratman's hand. "Sid is a fine and sweet gentleman who has simply had a hard time in life." She went on to explain that she had first run across the Ratman in the summer as he delivered one of his curbside lectures. Over the next few months she had talked with him frequently on the downtown streets and gradually won his trust by bringing him food and what little money she could spare.

"I knew he was living here in the tunnels," she said, "so I came down earlier. I simply called out his name until he appeared."

"I see," said Rafferty, not sure if he believed her story. "Well, Miss O'Donnell, you have done some fine detective work. Would you mind if I had a little talk with Sid? I would like to hear firsthand what he saw on the night of your brother's death."

"Go right ahead," she said, "but let him explain things in his own way." She then turned to the Ratman. "Sid, I want you to answer Mr. Rafferty's questions, just as you answered mine. Can you do that?"

The Ratman, who was removing the last of the beef with a rusty old fork, looked up and said, "The poor young man. Rats would have gotten him, I'm sure. Dirty, secretive creatures, they are."

Rafferty could see he would have to be very careful about how he phrased his questions, given the Ratman's tendency to harp on the subject that preoccupied his life.

"Ah, you are right about those rats, Sid. They are devils all right. Do you suppose the men who strung up the poor young fellow knew that? They should have, since there were two of them."

"Three," said the Ratman. "Jack and Earl and the other one."

Two familiar names, Rafferty thought. Jack was probably Jack Pruitt, though Rafferty couldn't be sure. As for Earl, Rafferty was willing to bet a fine bottle of Irish whisky that it must have been Earl Hayes. The famous dynamite artist and labor agitator, it seemed, had helped kill Michael O'Donnell. But with both Pruitt and Hayes now dead themselves, the mystery of why they had killed O'Donnell remained as elusive as ever. Rafferty therefore focused on the other man at the scene.

"The third fellow, I take it, didn't use a name?"

"Sergeant."

"That was his name? Sergeant?"

Addie O'Donnell broke in. "No, but the man apparently had a very deep voice that reminded Sid of one of his sergeants in the great war."

"You were in the war, Sid?" Rafferty asked.

"Second Minnesota," he replied, stiffening slightly as though ready to deliver a crisp salute. "Mill Springs, Corinth, Perryville, Chickamauga, Chattanooga, Atlanta, Sherman to the sea. Saw them all, I did, and blood spilled like water. Uncle Billy Sherman! Now there was a man, sir, who knew how to deal with rats."[2]

"I'm sure he did," Rafferty said, "but gettin' back to what happened on Tenth Street, could you describe any of the men you saw?"

The Ratman shook his head. "Hiding," he said by way of explanation.

As Rafferty continued his questioning, he learned, with an occasional assist from Addie O'Donnell, that the Ratman had actually seen very little of the hanging and that in any event, the killers were all wearing hoods. But he had heard—and remembered—a great deal. Though the Ratman was clearly demented, he was also, Rafferty began to understand, a close observer of the world and an acute listener, which was perhaps not surprising in view of how much time he spent in dark places.

Slowly Rafferty teased out the entire conversation the Ratman had overheard as the three men went about hanging a dead man.

"They thought it was funny about Mr. Wellington," the Ratman said at one point.

This was the first mention of the milling magnate, and Rafferty's ears perked up. "Did they now, Sid? And what was so funny about him?"

"He was a monument and that was funny."

"You mean, Mr. Wellington?" Rafferty asked.

"No, the poor young man."

Rafferty gave Addie O'Donnell a questioning look, but she could offer no help. "This is the first I've heard of it," she whispered.

"So the dead man, Mr. O'Donnell, he was a monument. Is that what the sergeant said?" Rafferty asked the Ratman.

"Why, who else would have said it? I told you, it was the sergeant. He said they were making a monument to Wellington. His exact words, sir, exact words! Now, it must have been funny because they all laughed. I did not see the humor in it," the Ratman added solemnly.

Although Rafferty wasn't sure how to interpret the remark about O'Donnell being a "monument to Wellington," he thought it sounded odd, especially since the murderers seemed to find it amusing. Rafferty wanted to press the Ratman on the point, but thought it would be futile, so he moved on to other questions about the night of the hanging. The Ratman, however, had little else to offer.

Rafferty now broached the topic of the tunnels themselves. Michael O'Donnell, according to his sister, had believed something sinister was going on in them. The Ratman, as their most knowledgeable denizen, should certainly know if this was true.

"You've got a nice little place here, Sid," Rafferty now said. "Peaceful and all your own. I understand there have been some strange things happening down here lately—people coming and going at all hours, some of them maybe even looking for you. Is that true?"

"They'll never find me," the Ratman said. "I know all the secret places. Not even the rats know the places I know."

"So I guess you haven't seen too many of the people looking for you. How about a woman, Sid? Did you ever see a woman down here?"

"Miss Addie," he said.

"Any other woman? A woman with a man perhaps?"

"No."

"You're sure about that?"

"Miss Addie," the Ratman repeated.

"But you've seen men in the tunnels, haven't you?"

"I hear things," the Ratman said.

"What sorts of things?"

The Ratman shrugged and pointed down the tunnel. "Voices back there."

"What were the voices saying?"

"Couldn't tell. Far away. Probably the rats. Some of them can talk, you know. I hear them, laying their dirty little plans in the darkness."

Rafferty tried posing more questions, but the Ratman had stopped listening and would soon speak of nothing except the creatures that haunted his life.

Addie O'Donnell said, "I doubt you will learn any more tonight, Mr.

Rafferty. Sid needs to rest. I'll take him to my place. He'll be all right there."

"I'm not sure that's such a good idea. The police may be watching you, Miss O'Donnell."

"Oh, but they are watching me — I know that for a fact. They are not very good at it, however, and we will have no difficulty returning to my apartment unobserved."

"Well, I'll go along just to be safe, if you don't mind."

"Suit yourself," she said, standing up and dusting off the denim jeans she was wearing beneath her long jacket. Rafferty had never seen a woman in jeans before, but then again, Addie O'Donnell was not just any woman.

With the Ratman again serving as guide, they started back toward the entrance to the tunnel. Out of curiosity Rafferty asked Addie O'Donnell what she had concluded from the Ratman's account of her brother's hanging.

"Is it not obvious?" she said. "Charles Wellington and his Secret Alliance were behind it, just as I've always suspected."

"Ah, I'm not so certain."

"Really, and what causes you to have doubts."

Rafferty now wondered whether he should tell her what he knew about Earl Hayes and his connection to the most extreme sort of labor radicals. There was also the matter of the Pinkertons — and the possibility Michael O'Donnell had somehow been tied in with them. And, of course, there was the ugly business at Zier Row, which strongly suggested that Michael O'Donnell had been involved in a particularly vile form of blackmail. How much did Addie O'Donnell really know about her brother's unsavory activities and connections? Rafferty couldn't be sure, and he decided it would be best not to tip his hand.

"I have good reasons for my doubts," Rafferty finally said.

"And they are?"

"I would rather not say at the moment."

"You still do not trust me, I see," she said, anger flaring in her voice. "Very well, if that is how it is to be, then expect no more favors from me."

Once outside the tunnel and into the chilly night air, they walked back under the railroad trestle and then out toward Washington Avenue. Addie O'Donnell lived not far from the milling district in a large tenement known as Noah's Ark. They reached the rear of the three-story tenement, which occupied half a block off Washington, without encountering any sign of trouble.

"We are fine now," Addie O'Donnell said. "Good night, Mr. Rafferty. I will be in touch."

"When?"

"Soon."

"Before Sunday's big rally? I'm curious why you didn't mention your plans to me."

"I did not see that it concerned you."

"Ah, now that's peculiar when you think about it," Rafferty said, feeling a rising sense of anger and frustration. "Why do you think a rally having to do with the death of a man whose murder I'm investigatin' would *not* interest me? And why would you go off lookin' for the Ratman and *not* mention your plans to me? What else, I'm wonderin', have you *not* told me about?"

"Oh, and you have been so forthcoming with me," she said sarcastically. "You're just like all the men I've ever known. What you do is your business and heaven forbid that a woman dare ask any questions. Well, Mr. Rafferty, I do ask questions, and when I do *not* get satisfactory answers, as I have *not* always had from you, then I make it a point to find out those answers on my own. And that is all I shall say on the subject. Good night, Mr. Rafferty!"

With that parting remark, she put an arm around the Ratman and the two of them—as unlikely a pair as Rafferty had ever seen—walked off down a narrow alley leading toward Noah's Ark.

"Well," Rafferty mumbled to himself as he lit a cigar, "I handled that beautifully."

Rafferty caught a streetcar on Washington and took the short ride up to Hennepin. The West was just a few blocks south, at Fifth, but on a whim Rafferty turned in the opposite direction, toward city hall and the river. He was cold, wet, and tired, but he always seemed to do his best thinking on foot, and he wanted to walk, even though drizzle continued to fall, before returning to the hotel. Besides, he figured Holmes and Watson would be returning very late from Zier Row, so there was no reason to rush.

He sauntered past the old City Hall Building, where Arthur Adams ran his empire of thievery, and then into Bridge Square—once the commercial heart of the city but now evolving into a harsh, liquor-soaked skid row. Ramshackle stone and brick buildings lined the square, which

was actually in the shape of a long triangle formed by the acute intersection of Hennepin and Nicollet Avenues near the river. Union Station,
many of its trains arriving via James J. Hill's great stone-arched bridge,
stood just past the end of the square, on the west shore of the Mississippi, and hackmen were doing a brisk business ferrying newly arrived
passengers to the West and other downtown hotels.

Many of the buildings around the square, including city hall itself,
were adorned with large strips of red, white, and blue bunting in anticipation of the president's visit on Sunday. Rafferty had been so caught up
in the O'Donnell case that he had paid scant attention to all the excited
newspaper stories heralding the big event.

When he reached the end of the square, Rafferty turned around and
headed back south on Nicollet. Here he found even more elaborate
preparations for McKinley's visit. Both sides of the street had been lined
with mock marble victory columns surmounted by shields and American flags. Evergreens strung on invisible wires connected the columns,
and from almost every store window large pictures of the president
stared out upon the triumphant scene.

Rafferty considered himself a patriot, but he was not at all inspired by
the nation's little adventure in the Philippines. He had seen the "glory"
of war firsthand, and he understood its appeal to young men anxious to
test themselves, as he had been so long ago on the haunted fields of Virginia. The Philippines campaign had been nothing like the bloodbath of
the Civil War, and for all he knew the young men returning with the
Thirteenth Minnesota were still full of vinegar after their excursion
against native peoples halfway around the world.

Still, Rafferty wondered what these men might think had they seen
the First Minnesota return, in 1863, from the war in the East. The First
had left a thousand men strong and returned with barely a third of that
number, having sown every battlefield from Bull Run to Gettysburg
with its dead, among them, at the very last, Rafferty's own brother,
killed at an obscure Virginia crossroads known as Bristoe Station. Well,
thought Rafferty as he stopped to look at one of the overblown photographs of McKinley, hail to the chief and pray he does not find a bigger
war in which to sacrifice young lives.[3]

Rafferty then turned off Nicollet and walked back toward the hotel,
his mind turning from thoughts of a distant war to the battle at hand. He
was beginning at last to see the extent of the battlefield, to appreciate the
sheer scope and complexity of it, and to know at last who the real enemies were. This was a great relief because for more than a week now,

Rafferty had been fighting in a kind of fog, never sure where the enemy lay. Now with Holmes and Watson on the scene, he felt greatly reassured.

As Rafferty thought back to his two previous cases with Holmes, he realized that the great detective's most sublime virtue was his unwavering belief in the triumph of reason. Rafferty himself was less sanguine in this regard — he thought there were dark mysteries in the world that reason could never penetrate — but he envied Holmes's reassuring certainty. Holmes's scintillating intelligence, enormous energy, and unbending will were all vital to the magic he worked, but it was his supreme air of confidence that Rafferty admired above all. Rafferty possessed much the same sort of confidence, but his was tempered by what he liked to call the Celtic curse — a sense that life would always strike a tragic note in the end.

Rafferty did not dwell long on such thoughts, however, for like Holmes he was addicted to the hunt and could be ruthlessly single-minded when the circumstances demanded. And now, as he stepped into the West's spacious lobby, Rafferty felt more strongly than ever that he would soon know the terrible truth behind Michael O'Donnell's murder. What he couldn't know was how dangerous the final road to that truth would be.

CHAPTER SEVENTEEN

⟨⟩

"It Will Be Haymarket All Over Again"

FROM THE JOURNALS OF DR. JOHN WATSON:

SAT., OCT. 7, 1899, WEST HOTEL, MPLS., 6 A.M.: . . . Many questions after SR finished account of meeting in tunnel with A[ddie] O'Donnell & Ratman.

W: "Your encounter with Miss O'Donnell was an amazing coincidence, Mr. Rafferty. Are you convinced that she was telling you the truth about how she came to be in the tunnels?"

SR: "I'm convinced of nothing when it comes to that woman, Doctor. I do not know if she's a great saint or a great sinner, or perhaps even both. I admit I can't read her as I can most people."

W: "So she may have been lying."

SR: " 'Twould not surprise me in the least."

W: "What of the Ratman? Was he telling the truth?"

SR: "Oh, I have no doubt he was, accordin' to his own lights. Trouble is, he is lookin' at the truth from a different vantage point than the rest of us, so I don't know if he sees what you & I see. But I was struck by what he heard & I would take that information to the bank without fear or hesitation."

H: "The remarks he overheard referring to Mr. O'Donnell as a 'monument to Wellington' are particularly intriguing. They suggest that Mr. Wellington is even more closely tied to this affair than at first suspected. Moreover, as Mr. Rafferty has already informed us, the milling baron states that he is convinced he will be the next target of the killers. If this is true — & Mr. Wellington's veracity is very much in question — we do not yet know why he would be marked for death, unless he is simply a victim selected at random by anarchist fanatics."

W: "Do you think that is the case, Holmes?"

H: "No. I am convinced there is some specific grievance motivating all that has happened here."

SR: "I'd be willin' to bet that Mr. Wellington knows what the grievance is but, for reasons of his own, chooses not to reveal it."

W: "Why would he be so reluctant?"

SR: "Ah, Doctor, I wish I knew."

More desultory discussion now ensued & as all except H were weary from the night's exertions, our meeting was finally adjourned, leaving me to write these notes before urge to sleep becomes overwhelming.

8 P.M.: Yet another day of frenetic activity, beginning when I was awakened at 9 A.M. by H. Have not had time to set down one word until now. Reason: H has gone to bed! First sleep, I believe, in three days, tho he will be up & about soon, so must write quickly.

Will begin with report from [Police Detective Clifton] Wool[dridge] in Chicago, as it contained significant news. He did not reply to H's telegrams with one of own but instead telephoned late morning. H took call & spent half hour talking with Wool, a most striking & loquacious character, tho given to exaggeration in usual American manner.

After H rang off, gave me detailed account of conversation. Chief revelation from Wool concerned Mary McGinty, name found on business card in Randolph Hadley's wallet. McGinty woman, H & I surprised to learn, now believed to be one of Lauer gang—terrorists who tried to dynamite Chicago water tower & who Wool had mentioned, tho not by name, in letter sent to us in N.Y. She now thought to be in Mpls., possibly with other surviving member of gang—a man—tho all information re whereabouts, activities, appearance, etc., "extremely sketchy," Wool said.

One curious fact: No good description of McGinty exists, as she often in disguise & very "shadowy & elusive figure," according to Wool. Not even certain as to age. He also reported some believe McGinty a "Pinkerton spy" & therefore no terrorist at all. Supposedly, woman by that name was "planted" by Pinkertons into gang, informed on them, & "escaped" to spy on other anarchists. H said Wool skeptical of this theory, tho quoted him as saying "with the Pinkertons & their love of secrecy for its own sake, you can never be sure of anything."

As to H's other questions—mostly involving O'Donnell clan—Wool less able to help. Noted there were 100s if not 1000s of O'Donnells in Chicago & would need more info to provide background on Michael, Addie, etc. Oddly, he did know of Majesty Burke, SR's friend. Said her father was engineer for Chicago, Burlington & Quincy Railroad who became opponent of 1877 strike. Eventually forced to leave Chicago when life threatened by fellow workers. Later wrote antiunion pamphlet widely circulated by business interests of city. . . .

H also brought up subject of McP[arland] to Wool, who said the Pinkerton man had reputation for great cunning.

W: "Did Mr. Wooldridge know why Mr. McParland had come to Mpls.?"

H: "No, but he thought it possible that Mr. McParland was looking for Mary McGinty."

W: "Do you believe that to be the case, Holmes?"

H: "I believe only in the truth of the evidence, Watson, & at the moment I have none regarding Mr. McParland's intentions. However, we will try to speak to him later tonight."

W: "Here at the hotel?"

H: "No. Mr. Rafferty & I have already talked over the telephone this morning (note: SR went to St. Paul in A.M. with GWT to check in at saloon) & concluded it would be best to approach him in a public setting, where witnesses are present. Mr. McParland, as we know, is a suspicious man & has with him two bodyguards, one of whom is known to be extremely proficient with pistols—a gunslinger, in American parlance. The great Pinkerton man is also a gambler &, I am informed, will be playing poker tonight not far from here. We will approach him in the gambling hall &, I hope, catch him off guard."

. . . Final editions of afternoon papers arrived at 3 P.M. with strange & unexpected news, tho nothing re corpses at Zier Row. News concerned Phelps. Article in *Mpls. Journal* most complete, reporting "mysterious disappearance of the prominent & controversial lawyer." Story stated Phelps last seen at office 5 P.M. yesterday after reminding secretary to prepare papers for court hearings next morning. Never made it to hearings & failed to contact office, after which secretary—a certain "Mrs. Tyson"—became alarmed & called Phelps's home. Learned from servant there Phelps left about 8 P.M. previous night, saying he was going to show downtown, but never returned. Secretary said Phelps "famous for punctuality" & "unprecedented" for him to miss court hearings. She then called police to report him missing, tho no evidence of foul play.

SR & Thomas back by this time. H found story of Phelp's disappearance "ominous," as did SR, who decided to visit Phelps's office (only 3 blocks from hotel) to see what he could find out from secretary.

H, meanwhile, seemed content to loll about room. Told me he wished to "spend the afternoon digesting the great mass of possibilities which this case presents." Otherwise not talkative, tho stated again he believes "some shadow from the past" hangs over entire affair. I mentioned this observation to SR, who said he was "of a similar mind," but went on to note that "in a case as dark & murky as this one, a shadow can be a hard thing to find."

. . . Just as SR about to leave for Phelps's office, another surprise! Majesty Burke, saloonkeeper & SR's friend, & J[acqueline] O'Donnell, widow of deceased, appeared at hotel to discuss "urgent matters" with SR. SR asked if we would like to meet women & of course H agreed. Went down to lobby; found them waiting in chairs by fireplace. SR introduced us as "visiting English friends" with "some experience in the workings of Scotland Yard," which certainly true, as Insp. Lestrade would attest to.[1]

Mrs. Burke quite beautiful—tall, full figured, striking hazel eyes, thick brown hair, deep contralto voice. J O'Donnell much younger, slim & dark, short brown hair, intense eyes, & sadness lingering in her manner like faint aroma of perfume.

After introductions, Mrs. Burke explained she & J O'Donnell had just received "disturbing information" & stopped by hotel "on chance Mr. Rafferty might be in."

SR: "I'm happy we are able to be at your service. Now then, what is this disturbin' news you speak of?"

MRS. BURKE: "It concerns Addie. As you know, she has organized a rally tomorrow at Loring Park to protest the supposed role played by the Secret Alliance in Michael's death. It is expected that perhaps 1000s of union men will be there, tho with the president coming no one can be sure if she will really draw a crowd. Even so, the police & the alliance men will be out in force & ready for trouble. Well, I fear that is exactly what will happen because Jacqueline & I believe that someone intends to throw a bomb at the height of the rally. It will be Haymarket all over again."

Effect of these dire remarks was, as might be imagined, electric.

H: "How did you come by this extraordinary information, madam?"

MRS. BURKE: "I'm sorry, but I cannot say, nor can Jacqueline. We are sworn to secrecy. But I believe the information to be absolutely true."

SR: "Who will be tossin' this bomb, Maj? Did your informant tell you that?"

MRS. BURKE: "No, but there are said to be radicals coming in from out of town — Chicago, Denver, even New York — with the intention of creating chaos. We have been told one of these desperate men may be carrying a bomb."

SR: "Does Addie know about this?"

J O'DONNELL: "I cannot say what she knows. But to be honest with you, Mr. Rafferty, I would be very surprised if she *doesn't* know what may happen tomorrow. Addie is not an easy person to fool."

H: "Are you saying, therefore, that Miss O'Donnell is part of the plot?"

J O'DONNELL: "Oh no, not at all. I do not wish to accuse Addie of anything. She is one of the most remarkable women I have ever met. It is just that, well, that —"

MRS. BURKE: "What Jacqueline is trying to say is that Addie is very headstrong & continues to believe her brother was murdered either by the alliance or with its connivance. Given these feelings, we fear that her passion for what she believes to be justice may overcome her good judgment."

SR: "Who else is aware of the bomb threat?"

MRS. BURKE: "You are the only people we have told."

H: "Do you intend to go next to the police?"

J O'DONNELL: "We would rather not — at least not yet. The police would only use such a threat as an excuse to wage all-out war on the working people of this city. Michael did not die to see such a thing happen."

SR: "Well then, what would you have us do if the police are not to be involved?"

MRS. BURKE: "You are the one person we know we can trust, Shad, & since you have vouched for these English gentlemen, then we must trust them as well. We would like you to talk with Addie & see if you can convince her to call off the rally. It would be the best thing for everyone. If the rally does take place, there is almost certain to be violence & even the president himself might be at risk."

W: "The Secret Service, I should think, would cancel the president's appearance if it believed the situation here to be dangerous."

SR: "Don't count on that. Bill McKinley is an old warhorse & tho I care little for his politics, I would never question his bravery. Nothing will be canceled unless he agrees to it, & I'm bettin' that he won't be put off by the mere possibility of labor unrest in Mpls. Still, the Secret Service should certainly be notified about the threat of a bombin' tomorrow."

H: "I agree. As it so happens, I am acquainted with a certain prominent official in the Secret Service & could alert him to the situation here without provoking the police into an overly vigorous response."

J O'DONNELL, LOOKING AT HER COMPANION & THEN AT SR & H: "I guess that would be all right. I just do not want to get Addie in trouble."

SR: "Don't you worry, Mrs. O'Donnell. I will find Addie yet today & have a talk with her. Everything will be all right, I promise, but it would be mighty helpful if you or Maj could at least give us some better idea as to where you learned about the possible bomb threat."

J O'DONNELL: "I am truly sorry, Mr. Rafferty, but a solemn promise was made & I intend to keep it. I am sure Maj feels the same way."

Mrs. Burke nodded her assent & with that the two women prepared to leave, tho I knew H wished to question them at greater length, especially re Chicago background. SR, however, more interested in pursuing Phelps's whereabouts, & since women unlikely to talk without SR present, H finally gave in. SR then left for Phelps's office, promising he would be back in time for supper. . . .

✍

It was quarter to four by the time Rafferty reached Phelps's office in Temple Court, a late 1880s office building whose six floors were well stocked with lawyers both reputable and otherwise. Mrs. Tyson, the secretary mentioned in the *Journal*'s story, turned out to be a small, gray-haired woman in a white blouse and dark brown skirt. She sat at a desk in the reception room of the office and looked up as Rafferty entered. She had a pinched face, a slender nose that supported a pair of reading glasses, and dark inquisitorial eyes.[2]

"May I help you?" she asked, removing her glasses to get a better look at Rafferty.

"You would be Mrs. Tyson, would you not?" Rafferty said in the most official-sounding voice he could muster—the resonant basso of authority.

"Yes. What can I do for you?"

Rafferty knew he couldn't simply waltz in and ask to rifle through Phelps's office, so he decided on an old dodge he had used many times. Pulling out a fake badge, he flashed it past the secretary and said, "I'm Inspector Holmes, with the local authorities. I need to take a look at Mr. Phelps's office to make sure we haven't overlooked anythin' in our efforts to locate him. If you will show me the way—"

To Rafferty's surprise, the woman said, "I'm afraid I didn't see your identification—Inspector Holmes, was it?"

"Yes, Holmes," he said, showing her the badge again.

She put her glasses back on and studied the badge, as though examining a rare jewel for flaws, and said, "Why, I believe you got this at Woolworth's. My grandson has one just like it. You'll have to do much better than that, I'm afraid."

"You're mistaken, madam," Rafferty said, hoping to bluff his way through.

"I know a fake when I see one," she replied with a sharp look suggesting that the badge wasn't the only phony she had in mind.

Rafferty saw he had been beaten. It was time for another approach—abject apology.

"Well, I guess you've caught me," he admitted. "Do you know how many men I've managed to fool with that toy badge?"

"Men, in my experience, are always easy to fool," said Mrs. Tyson, who obviously was not so easy to deceive herself. "Now, what is it you want, whoever you are?"

"The name is Shadwell Rafferty," he said, "and—"

"Of course you are!" she interposed, her tight mouth crinkling into a smile. "I thought you looked familiar. We met once, long ago. I'm Adele Tyson. My late husband, Elmer, was a lawyer for many years in St. Paul before moving here to Minneapolis. I'm sure you must remember him."

Rafferty did indeed, though he didn't mention to Mrs. Tyson that her deceased husband, in addition to being a fine lawyer, was a well-known gambler with a taste for red-headed harlots.

"I didn't know he had passed on. You have my condolences," Rafferty said.

"I have survived nicely, thank you, though I suppose half the whores in the Twin Cities mourned the loss of a good customer," she said casually, delivering yet another surprise. "Well, Mr. Rafferty, why are you so interested in looking at Mr. Phelps's office?"

"I imagine you want the truth," Rafferty said.

"If I can get it."

Rafferty then explained, in a very general way, the nature of his investigation, along with his belief that Phelps may have had "some connection to the unfortunate event on Tenth Street and related criminal matters."

Mrs. Tyson now offered up a third surprise. She said, "You think Mr. Phelps is dead, don't you?"

Here Rafferty could be completely truthful for a change. "I have no idea, ma'am. All I know is what I read in the newspapers, which report that he has gone missin'. Do you believe him to be dead?"

"I fear for the worst," she said. "This job was Mr. Phelps's life, though he'd never admit to such a thing. Both of the hearings he had scheduled this morning involved important cases. He would never have missed them unless something terrible had happened. I would not be surprised to learn that he has been murdered. He knew a great many dangerous people, or so he liked to tell me."

"Did anything seem out of the ordinary when you last saw him yesterday?"

"Not really. As I told the newspapers, he simply reminded me to have some papers ready for his court appearances this morning. I will say he did seem a bit distracted by something after that long phone call."

"What call was that, if I may ask?"

"Late in the afternoon, around half past three. It was from a woman. Quite young by the sound of her."

"I take it you didn't recognize the voice."

"No, and I'll also answer your next question—I didn't listen in on the conversation. But Mr. Phelps was on the phone for close to an hour. He usually doesn't talk that long, so it must have been important."

"Do you happen to know of any young women who might be clients or friends of his?"

"I do not. Mr. Phelps, as I'm sure you know, was not attracted to women, young or otherwise."

"What about a young woman by the name of Addie O'Donnell? Was she an acquaintance?"

"Not to my knowledge, though it seems to me I have heard the name. Wasn't she Michael O'Donnell's sister?"

"Still is," said Rafferty. "I was hoping Mr. Phelps might have talked to her recently."

"If he did, I wasn't aware of it," Mrs. Tyson said decisively.

"I see. Now, with your indulgence, there is one other person I'm interested in. As I understand it, Mr. Phelps once represented a poor cartman named Joe Shelton. Is that correct?"

Mrs. Tyson smiled and said, "Indeed it is. Mr. Phelps always liked to call Joe his most fragrant, as opposed to flagrant, client."

"So the two men knew each other well?"

"Certainly. In fact, Mr. Phelps told me he would see Joe on the street quite often. Mr. Phelps won a lawsuit against the city on Joe's behalf, and Joe was very grateful. I remember Mr. Phelps joking once that he wished he had lost the suit, just so he could keep Joe from approaching him. Why do you ask about him? Do you think Mr. Phelps was somehow linked to Joe's recent death?"

"Ah, Mrs. Tyson, I see you have the detective's turn of mind. But there is really very little I know at the moment, which is why—"

"You wish to rummage through Mr. Phelps's office."

"You're not one for mincin' words, are you, madam," Rafferty said. "Yes, I would like to poke around a bit."

"Well then, go have your look," she replied, rising from her chair and unlocking the door to Phelps's office. "Take as long as you like. I'd trust you sooner than the crooked police. But don't walk away with anything, if you please, and most certainly don't tell anyone that I let you in."

"You have my word on both counts," Rafferty said, "and my thanks."

Once inside Phelps's office, Rafferty again found himself in the position of searching for something that he wouldn't know the value of until he found it. But he believed Phelps must somehow be connected to Michael O'Donnell's murder and the tangle of events that had followed.

Rafferty began to search in Phelps's desk, where he found nothing out of the ordinary in the drawers or compartments. Atop the desk was a large glass ashtray—a souvenir of the 1886 Industrial Exposition—and there were several cigarette butts inside. He copped one, knowing Holmes would want to look at it. Rafferty then moved on to a nearby filing cabinet, the only one in the office. There were three drawers, all stuffed with a wild miscellany of items—letters, bills, pamphlets, newspaper clippings, even an envelope with some faded family photographs. The envelopes and folders did not appear to be filed in any order, so Rafferty simply started with the top drawer and worked his way down, going through every scrap of paper.

After half an hour of tedious work, he reached the bottom drawer, which turned out to be the worst of the lot. Here folders and envelopes were stuffed together so tightly that it required brute force to pull anything out. Still, Rafferty plowed through it all, sitting on the floor to avoid getting up and down constantly.

His work proved fruitless until he reached a large manila envelope near the back of the drawer. The envelope was marked "Miscellaneous"—hardly a promising title—but what Rafferty found inside was intriguing. It was a well-thumbed copy of *Revolutionary War Science,* the infamous how-to manual written by anarchist Johann Most in 1885. Rafferty had heard of the book, said to be much favored by bomb throwers, but he had never seen a copy before. He paged through it and quickly saw that it was very much as advertised—the sort of book that anyone with mayhem in mind would find indispensable. Rafferty called in Mrs. Tyson and asked if she knew why Phelps might have kept such an inflammatory volume hidden in the deepest recess of his file cabinet.[3]

"Mr. Phelps had many"—here she paused for the right word—"*unusual* friends," she said. "He may have gotten it from one of them. I can tell you that it's not an exhibit for a lawsuit. If so, it would have been marked."

Rafferty said, "You're a dear woman, Mrs. Tyson, and I cannot thank you enough. By the way, did Mr. Phelps smoke cigarettes?"

"Occasionally."

"Do you happen to know which brand he favored?"

"I never paid attention. As far as I'm concerned, they're all equally bad."

"'Tis hard to argue with that, madam. Again, my thanks, and if Mr. Phelps should happen to show up—"

"I'll tell him to contact you. But I have a terrible feeling that he isn't going to show up. Something has happened to him, I know it."

"Well, Mrs. Tyson, let us hope that in this instance you're wrong."

"You will find that I am usually right," she replied matter-of-factly, and Rafferty didn't doubt it for a minute.

As Rafferty walked back to the West Hotel, James McParland sat in his top-floor suite, brooding over brandy and cigars and trying to see his way out of deepening trouble. Only hours before he had received word of Randolph Hadley's death, and the news hit hard. Hadley was a bit of a prig, McParland thought, but he was at least an honest man, with a soldier's discipline and devotion to duty. The same could not be said for Mayor Adams and his scheming minions. Indeed, McParland rued the day he had been sucked into the deep sinkhole of waste and corruption that passed for government in the city of Minneapolis. Of course, it was the idiots in the Chicago office who were to blame.

Unfortunately, when big money talked, the men at Pinkerton head-quarters listened, with great enthusiasm, no matter how foolish or dangerous the idea, for the simple reason that lengthy undercover cases meant big fees for the agency. Still, it might all have worked out, even after the great act of treachery became all too apparent. The Chicago office had failed to move quickly enough, however, and had paid the price.

As McParland saw it, he now faced a series of distinct but interrelated problems, beginning with Hadley's shocking death. McParland did not believe for a minute that Hadley had committed suicide over an affair of the heart, as the newspapers were sure to suggest. No, he had been murdered. Finding the murderer, however, would not be easy and could prove perilous—in more than just the sense of physical danger.

There was also the problem of the contraband information left in the wake of the undercover activities in Minneapolis. If this information became public, it could forever besmirch the reputation of McParland's beloved Pinkertons, and he would do everything in his power to keep that from happening. Of course, the information would also bring about the ruin of certain leading citizens of Minneapolis, though McParland hardly cared about that.

The meddling Irishman—Rafferty—was another problem. The man was no fool, and he seemed to be closing in on the truth. Worse, he had recently acquired the help of some Englishman who claimed to be a lord and who obviously had money and connections. Hadley had wanted to "take Rafferty out of the game," as he put it, but to McParland that option seemed less attractive with every passing moment. Rafferty simply had too many friends in high places, and even an "accidental death," no matter how carefully arranged, would arouse intense suspicion. No, Rafferty would have to be neutralized in some other way, although Mc-Parland wasn't sure what it might be.

As if McParland didn't have enough to worry about, there was also the matter of Mary McGinty. With William McKinley due in Minneapolis tomorrow, the thought of a shadowy terrorist on the loose was not comforting. McParland had already alerted the Secret Service, although there was in truth little he could tell them. Absent some specific and concrete threat, however, McParland knew there was no chance the president would agree to cancel his visit.

At six o'clock McParland's ruminations were interrupted by the arrival of William Borden. McParland had ordered the Minneapolis agent-in-charge to appear for another dressing down over the shamefully inept performance of his men in trying to tail Rafferty. They had lost him again today in Minneapolis, leaving McParland in the dark, which was not where he liked to be.

"You were warned about the price of failure," McParland said when Borden, his eyes downcast and his shoulders slumped, stood before him. "Even so, you managed to lose Mr. Rafferty again. I eagerly await your explanation."

Borden saw no point in offering excuses, so he told the truth, "Rafferty is simply too clever for us. I doubt anyone could follow him for long without being spotted."

McParland replied to this admission of failure with a withering attack in which he pointed out all of Borden's shortcomings in painful detail. He then said coldly, "Your last paycheck will come in the mail, Mr. Borden. That will be all."

Borden had known what was coming and left without a word. He took the elevator down to the hotel lobby and then walked out onto Hennepin Avenue. Normally, he would have caught a streetcar to his apartment but he decided to walk, despite the deep chill in the air.

He felt angry and ashamed, like a dog that had just been kicked for no good reason. McParland, the old bastard, had been right about one thing, however. It was time for Borden to leave the Pinkertons. He didn't need any more abuse, and there were other, more honorable, ways for a man to earn his living. Still, Borden would leave with one small satisfaction, for he was in possession of a piece of information that McParland, if he hadn't been such a complete son of a bitch, might have found very useful.

Earlier in the afternoon Borden had belatedly read in the newspapers that one of the men killed in the gunfight at the lumberyard was Earl Hayes, alias Earl Smith, late of the Western Federation of Miners. As it so happened, before McParland's arrival in Minneapolis, Borden had been investigating a certain Earl Smith in connection with a major theft at the Soudan Mine in northeastern Minnesota. The investigation had even tracked the stolen goods to Minneapolis, where they were delivered to someone named "A. Lauer," whom the local Pinkertons had never been able to identify.

Now Borden was certain that Smith had in fact been Earl Hayes, the feared labor terrorist. This put a whole new light—and a very dangerous one—on the situation. Borden had intended to tell McParland about Hayes's apparent involvement in the theft at the mine, but McParland had been so busy telling Borden what a complete and hopeless idiot he was that the chance never came up. Well then, thought Borden as he got out a cigar and lit it, to hell with McParland and to hell with the Pinkertons. Let them worry about finding the fifty pounds of dynamite Earl Hayes had stolen from the Soudan Mine.

Chapter Eighteen

&

"He May Have Been Murdered for Doing His Duty"

FROM THE JOURNALS OF DR. JOHN WATSON:

SAT., OCT. 7, 1899, WEST HOTEL, MPLS., 8 P.M.: . . . SR back for supper & with curious news re anarchist book found in Phelps's office. . . . H familiar with Johann Most & said his followers "among the most dangerous men of our time." Deeply worried by this development & said he fears "more than ever" violence at labor rally tomorrow as well as threat to president. SR in agreement & after usual discussion made final plans for night. H & I will sound out McP[arland] at gambling hall, using "big bluff," as SR called it. . . . Meanwhile SR & Thomas will attempt to track down A[ddie] O'Donnell. Will all meet back at hotel at midnight.

Supper at hotel dining room — prime rib & "walleyed pike," SR's favorite — but apprehension in air, much as I felt before battles in Afghanistan. H hardly touched food & even SR uncharacteristically quiet. SR & Thomas left 7:30 P.M. & am now waiting for H to awaken so we can confront McP. . . .[1]

SUN., OCT. 1, 1899, WEST HOTEL, MPLS., 4 A.M.: Am setting down these words in anticipation of day of danger & high excitement, for now clear calamity may occur unless we intervene. H & I have spent last few hours with SR & GWT, exchanging info & plotting strategy for what H believes will be "decisive day."

Exceptional developments on two fronts Sat. night, beginning with our visit to gambling hall & talk with McP. H & I left hotel at 10:30 P.M. &, per instructions from bellboy who provided info re McP, walked up Hennepin Ave. toward gambling parlor owned by man named Danny Brown. Vaudeville houses, theaters, saloons, restaurants, etc. — all brightly lit with electric lamps — lined avenue & many people about despite cold.

SR had told us avenue also home to illegitimate "night trade" in basement gambling dens, tippling houses, brothels, & other business catering to vice. All under watchful eye of police, who — to quote SR — "enforce the law only in the sense that loan collectors of the leg-breakin' variety enforce good credit."

Soon reached destination — small, dingy saloon known as Tooze's, beneath which said to be gambling hall. Saloon occupied corner of soot-stained brick building & hardly looked like first-class establishment. Near saloon's entrance, flight of stone steps descended to basement. Walked down to door, painted red & illuminated by naked light bulb, but with no identifying sign. H knocked. Door opened slightly & head of very large bald man appeared. He asked in unpleasant way what we wanted.[2]

H, DISPLAYING $10 GOLD PIECE IN PALM: "I have been told gentlemen such as ourselves might find entertainment here. I hope we have the right address."

Bald man eyed gold piece, then us. After brief consideration took money & motioned us inside, where surprise awaited. Danny Brown's gambling parlor quite elegant — walls paneled in English oak, red plush carpeting, cut-glass chandeliers, etc. Furnishings formed backdrop for variety of gaming tables much like those found in continental casinos. Noted sounds common to all places of gambling — spinning balls, rattling slots, cards sliding across felt tables — mixed with steady hum of anxious & expectant voices.

Stopped at teller's cage by door, bought chips, then surveyed room. At least 100 men in place, along with dealers, bartenders, tellers, & handful of provocatively dressed women who, H remarked, "are probably not here for an evening of whist." Walked toward center of room, trying to blend with crowd, & soon noticed table in far corner where seven men & dealer playing cards. Went in that direction but stopped at roulette wheel near card game.

H: "The short, stocky man with spectacles at the card table is Mr. McParland, judging by the bellboy's description."

W: "He looks rather ordinary."

H: "I imagine that is one of the great reasons for his success as an undercover agent—he does not stand out in a crowd. Now, Watson, you know the plan. I shall wait for an opportunity to join the poker game. When I do, be on the alert. The man sitting at McParland's left—the one in the buckskin suit who resembles an American cowboy—is undoubtedly a bodyguard. I imagine there is another one not far away."

W: "Very well, Holmes. In the meantime—"

H: "Let us look inconspicuous. Roulette is not a game of any great interest to me, but perhaps we can enrich ourselves while waiting."

Half dozen players gathered around roulette wheel, & H with doff of hat joined game, as did I. H's pile of chips soon grew while mine dwindled steadily. Glimpsed now & then at men seated around poker table. Noted "cowboy" next to McP not playing cards, suggesting H right in thinking him a bodyguard.

McP occasionally said word or two to cowboy but otherwise quiet. Judged him to be about 55, plump jowly face, bushy gray mustache, thinning gray hair above large forehead & alert blue eyes behind gold-rimmed spectacles. Wore tweed suit over bright red vest accented with small diamond stickpin, & in overall appearance might have passed for traveling soap salesman.

Played roulette for half hour, then saw poker player stand up & leave, complaining of being "wiped out." H placed one more bet, then went to poker table. I stayed by roulette wheel, watching & listening.

H, STANDING BY TABLE: "I see a gentleman has left the game. Is there room for a new hand?"

Dealer—dapper little man in swallowtail coat—said there was after cautioning H that "this is a high-stakes game." Chips $50, as was minimum ante. Rich for my blood but not for H.

H, TAKING VACANT SEAT ACROSS FROM McP: "Well, I have always said there is no point in a man playing poker unless he is serious about it. What are we playing, gentlemen? Stud? Draw? Or is it perhaps something more exotic?"

Tho H not temperamentally inclined to games of chance, which he found irrational, he had long been intrigued by poker. Once described game to me "as a test of both wills & mathematics, & therefore of considerable interest."

Dealer said game was five-card stud.

H, PUTTING HANDS ON TABLE (FOR REASONS I SOON UNDERSTOOD): "That is an excellent game. I am sure Mr. McParland would agree."

Statement drew no sign of alarm from McP, but cowboy's eyes narrowed & right hand disappeared under table.

McP, IN TENOR VOICE WITH TRACE OF BROGUE: "I fear you are mistaken, sir. The name is Smith. Thomas Smith, of Chicago."

H: "Really? And who is your companion, the gentleman who has just gone for the pistol at his belt? Would he be Mr. Jones, by chance?"

McP, EVENLY: "He might be. But you have me at a disadvantage, sir, as I do not know your name."

H: "My name is not important at the moment. However, I am in possession of some information that will be of interest to you."

Now saw large man with stevedore's build & blunt head resembling business end of hammer come up to table & stand behind H. Assumed him to be other bodyguard.

McP, ADDRESSING H STERNLY: "I am here to play poker, sir, & I trust you intend to do the same. If not, I suggest you move along—quickly."

H: "You are forgetting, Mr. McParland, about the information I have for you. I know you will want to see it."

Now time for H to play "big bluff" he & SR had planned.

H, TURNING TO DEALER: "Would you be kind enough to remove the piece of paper from my inside coat pocket? I would do it myself, but I do not wish Mr. McParland's bodyguards to become overly excited."

Dealer looked at McP, who nodded, then took folded sheet from H's pocket & handed it to McP. He unfolded it & read slowly, showing no expression. Refolded paper & put in pocket.

McP: "Gentlemen, please excuse me. There is a matter I must attend to. Why don't you join me in the manager's office, Mr. Whoever You Are."

H, NODDING IN MY DIRECTION: "I have an associate who will join us. He is unarmed, as am I, & knows all that I know."

McP: "All right, he can come along, but I strongly advise you not to make any trouble."

Moments later found ourselves seated by mahogany desk in office of Brown, owner of establishment. McP sat behind desk. Large bodyguard stood behind us, while cowboy—silver-plated revolver resting in lap—occupied chair to one side, no doubt to watch our hands. Brown himself nowhere to be seen, but McP obviously familiar with office, for he opened panel behind desk to reveal well-stocked bar.

McP: "Care for a drink, gentlemen?"

H: "Not at the moment."

McP, STARING AT H: "Good for you. I have no use for men who drink in a tight situation, and make no mistake, that is what you are in. Now then, sir, what is the meaning of this threatening note you have handed me?"

H: "I should think its meaning is quite clear, & it is not a threat. It is merely a statement of the situation in which you find yourself."

McP, TURNING TO COWBOY: "Listen to this note, Charlie. It says, 'Unless you wish to see your name in every newspaper in the Twin

Cities in connection with the murder of Michael O'Donnell, you will talk to me now.' I would call that a threat, wouldn't you?"[3]

CHARLIE, GLARING AT H: "Sure sounds like it. Maybe I should just take care of this fella right now."

McP, ADDRESSING H: "Perhaps, sir, we should go back to the beginning. Just who in blazes are you?"

H: "I imagine you have heard of me, Mr. McParland. I am Sherlock Holmes & my friend is Dr. John Watson."

McP: "Is that a fact? Sherlock Holmes and Dr. Watson in the flesh! Why, I'll be damned. Imagine meeting two such famous Englishmen right here in Mpls. Well then, let me introduce you to my assistant" — McP motioned toward cowboy — "Prince Albert."

CHARLIE, GRINNING: "Nice to meet you gents."

H: "Enjoy your moment of amusement, Mr. McParland, & then consider this: During your adventures with the Molly Maguires, you infiltrated a ring of criminals led by a giant named Pat Dormer, who ran the Sheridan House tavern. One day you came across a notebook written in a peculiar cipher, made a copy, & passed it on to your superior, Allan Pinkerton. Later you met with Mr. Pinkerton & learned that the code had been deciphered by a certain English detective, then building a reputation for himself, by the name of Sherlock Holmes. The code used a primitive system of transpositions based on every third letter, but the information itself comprised nothing more sinister than Mr. Dormer's account of various romantic trysts with married women in the vicinity. As the notebook thus proved to be of little value, it was never made public at any of the trials by which so many Molly Maguires were sent to the gallows. To this day, only you, members of the immediate Pinkerton family, & Sherlock Holmes himself know about the coded notebook. Am I correct in all the particulars, Mr. McParland?"[4]

Effect of speech on McP remarkable. Amusement gave way to disbelief & then utter astonishment.

McP, NODDING: "You are absolutely correct in every detail. I am honored to make your acquaintance, Mr. Holmes. You as well, Dr. Watson, & please pardon my earlier comments. It is just that I could scarcely believe the great Sherlock Holmes would come all the way to Mpls. on an insignificant matter such as the O'Donnell case."

Tone of last remark seemed provocative, indicating McP not one to be overwhelmed by H's reputation.

H: "Murder is never insignificant, Mr. McParland, nor is the truth. Dr. Watson & I are here to assist our friend, Mr. Shadwell Rafferty, in his investigation into the death of Michael O'Donnell."

McP: "Why do you think I could help you?"

H: "For the simple reason that Mr. O'Donnell was a Pinkerton agent."

This news to me, for H had only hinted at possibility earlier.

McP: "I fear you have been misinformed, Mr. Holmes."

H, COLDLY: "You would be ill-advised to lie to me, Mr. McParland. It would be a pity if your justly celebrated career were to end in a scandal tarnishing not only you but the entire Pinkerton Agency. However, there is an alternative."

McP: "In my experience, Mr. Holmes, there is always an alternative. What might it be?"

H: "The truth. Tell me exactly why Mr. O'Donnell was sent to Mpls. & what he did while he was here & I will do everything in my power to ensure that neither you nor the Pinkertons are dragged any further into this affair. Otherwise, I cannot promise anything except very unflattering publicity."

McP, AFTER MOMENT'S THOUGHT: "Very well, I will take the chance, Mr. Holmes, & tell you the whole story. I must trust that you are a man of your word & will keep strictly confidential what I'm about to reveal."

H: "Have no concerns in that regard."

McP now told us that earlier in year, Pinkerton's Chicago office received word from reliable source that Mary McGinty possibly in Mpls. Reports vague, but Chicago office decided to send Michael O'Donnell up to infiltrate radical elements with the hope of finding her. Shortly before murder O'Donnell reported he had obtained solid lead & was close to identifying McGinty woman, but must have been found out & murdered by gang.

Once McP done, H peppered him with questions re O'Donnell's background, details of activities in Mpls., name of other gang members, etc., but received only vague answers. Finally, he tried new tack.

H: "What can you tell me about Addie O'Donnell? Was she indeed the dead man's sister, or is she a Pinkerton provocateur as well?"

McP, IRRITATION EVIDENT IN VOICE: "She is his sister in so far as I know. She certainly is not a Pinkerton operative."

H: "What of Mr. O'Donnell's wife? Is it usual for agents to wed while undercover?"

McP: "Of course not. We were not told of it. The wedding was strictly in violation of agency policy."

H: "I see. What other company policies did Mr. O'Donnell violate?"

McP: "As you well know by now, he apparently was blackmailing Randolph Hadley."

H: "Were other leading citizens caught by Mr. O'Donnell's camera?"

McP: "Even if I knew, I couldn't in good conscience tell you. But I don't know & frankly I don't care."

H: "I am touched by your display of scruples, Mr. McParland. Tell me, what did the Pinkerton Agency do once it learned of Mr. O'Donnell's unauthorized activities?"

McP: "Naturally, we made plans to pull him out of Mpls, but the radicals got to him before we could & removed him by other means, as it were."

H: "Most convenient for you, wasn't it? Of course, there is another possibility, which is that the Pinkertons did away with their own operative to tidy up what had become a very messy situation."

McP, ANGRILY: "We are not murderers, Mr. Holmes, & you would do well to remember that. Now, I've told you all that I know about Michael O'Donnell. I trust you will uphold your end of our agreement. Revealing my presence in Mpls. to the newspapers could have dire consequences. It is quite possible Mary McGinty is still here, & if she is, the president himself could be in danger when he visits tomorrow. You must understand that."

H: "I understand perfectly. I also understand that you have not met your end of the bargain because I have yet to hear the full truth. I must hear it now, or I will have no choice but to alert the press about the role of the Pinkerton Agency here. It will not, I assure you, make for pleasant reading."

Battle of wills between two warriors had now reached zenith, but I saw that H held upper hand. H knew McP must be supremely calculating man & astute judge of people—otherwise would not have survived years undercover with Molly Maguires. As such, he would weigh choices carefully & conclude best chance lay in telling truth. Am sure H also counted on McP's loyalty to Pinkertons & desire to spare agency disgrace.

McP now leaned back in chair & gazed up at ceiling, then smiled at H.

McP: "You cannot fault a man for trying, Mr. Holmes, now can you?"

H: "No, I cannot."

McP: "So it's the whole story that you want, is it? Very well, you shall have it, but I will hold you to your promise. None of this is to become public."

H: "I understand. I have no wish to embarrass you or the Pinkertons."

McP: "All right, then, the truth is that Michael O'Donnell was origi-nally sent here to investigate Mayor Adams. Our agency was hired to do so by Charles Wellington, who is a longtime client of the agency. He is also personally acquainted with both William & Robert Pinkerton. It was not, in other words, the kind of job the Chicago agent-in-charge felt he could turn down. Had I been on the scene, you may be assured the decision would have been different."

H: "I do not doubt it. Now, why exactly did Mr. Wellington wish to have the mayor investigated? Did it have to do with the graft & cor-ruption rampant here, or was there another reason, perhaps center-ing on illicit activities at Zier Row?"

McP: "It all had to do, Mr. Holmes, with the mayor's unusual predilec-tions in sexual matters. He is queer, you see. Likes to circulate stories about bedding down women left & right, but the fact is he's queer as they come. Mr. Wellington finally learned what was going on at his apartment — which, of course, the mayor & his friends had been using for their own immoral purposes for years — and he hit the roof. It was clear to our agents that he didn't care a jot about the mayor being one of the biggest crooks in the Northwest. But being a queer — well, that was another thing entirely, and he wanted the truth so he could run Adams out of town. Michael O'Donnell was hired to get the evidence."

H: "What made the Chicago office select him for such a sensitive job?"

McP: "He was a skilled undercover operative. He had worked a couple of jobs in the Colorado mines & done signal service there. Most importantly, he was unknown in Minneapolis, never having been to the city before."

H: "Once he arrived, Mr. O'Donnell started out, as I understand it, by obtaining a job in the mayor's political organization as an assis-tant ward heeler."

McP: "That's right. Then he moved on to other types of undercover work."

H: "Such as his photography at Zier Row?"

McP: "Yes. He sent back reports to Chicago about his plans for taking secret photographs at the apartment. However, he never told the Chicago office exactly who he photographed, nor did the agency ever see any of the pictures. It would appear that when he set up shop at Zier Row, he stumbled onto a blackmailer's gold mine. As you know, he managed to get compromising pictures of Mr. Hadley, & it's likely there were plenty of others. Unfortunately, O'Donnell saw a chance to make a lot of money in a hurry & he took it."

H: "How did you find out about his extracurricular activities?"

McP: "From Mr. Hadley. He showed us a blackmail letter demanding five thousand dollars for one of the more revealing photographs. Of course, it took us only a fraction of a second to figure out who the blackmailer must be."

H: "I see. Did Hadley know it was a rogue Pinkerton man who had taken the pictures?"

McP: "Ah, now you see our delicate little problem, Mr. Holmes."

H: "Yes, it must have been a 'delicate' problem indeed for the Pinkerton agency. One of your own had embarked upon a blackmail scheme, & it would have been most embarrassing to have to acknowledge that fact to a client of Mr. Wellington's stature. What did you intend to do about your predicament?"

McP: "As I said before, our intention was to get O'Donnell out of Mpls. at the first opportunity. After that, we hoped we could convince him, by one means or another, to turn over the pictures he'd taken."

H: "I imagine you were prepared to resort to very strong means indeed."

McP: "The strongest possible. I, for one, would like to have gotten my hands on that rotten little turncoat, but then the situation changed overnight."

H: "What happened?"

McP: "Mr. Wellington had a change of heart, or so it seemed. He called our Chicago office & instructed the agent-in-charge to drop the investigation of the mayor."

H: "Did he say why?"

McP: "He said it was because something more important had come up."

H: "Did he say what it was?"

McP: "Only in a vague way. He said he had begun to fear that 'an angel of vengeance' was on his trail & that we must find this mysterious person, who was somehow tied to one of the local labor unions. That, at least, was the official reason for Mr. Wellington's decision to close out our investigation of the mayor."

H: "Do you believe the official story, Mr. McParland?"

McP: "It could be true. Then again, a person with a suspicious cast of mind might entertain other possibilities."

H: "Such as blackmail, perhaps?"

McP: "Yes. It's possible, for example, that the mayor turned the tables on Mr. Wellington. Arthur Adams is as slippery as they come, & who's to say he didn't find some dirt on the old man & threaten to expose it? Of course, it's just as possible that O'Donnell was blackmailing Mr. Wellington. Maybe the old man got caught with his pants down. That could explain why Mr. Wellington insisted on keeping O'Donnell in Mpls. to investigate the supposed threat against him. It would have made much more sense to have brought in another undercover agent for that purpose. Mr. Wellington, however, would not hear of it."

H: "An intriguing thought, Mr. McParland. Incidentally, did Mr. Wellington know Michael O'Donnell was Pinkerton's undercover agent?"

McP: "No, we didn't tell him, as is standard procedure, but he might have found out anyway. There is nothing like money to flush a secret out of hiding."

H: "I would not dispute that. Why didn't you simply pull Mr. O'Donnell out of Mpls. at that point? I would think the agency could have concocted any number of excuses to explain his sudden removal."

McP: "That particular option was not deemed possible at that time. I can say no more."

Not sure what to make of McP's evasive statement, but suggested to me O'Donnell had found way to threaten own employers. H now moved on to other questions.

H: "I am still curious about Addie O'Donnell. Did anyone in the Pinkerton Agency know before sending Michael O'Donnell to Mpls. that she was working as a labor organizer here?"

McP, GRIMACING: "That was a surprise. So was his marriage, as I've told you. However, I know very little about the two women, other than that Addie O'Donnell is quite a firebrand. Of course, in a way this turned out to be convenient. As her brother, Michael had no problem infiltrating the ranks of labor when that became his assignment."

H: "By the way, do you know for a fact that Michael was Addie's brother?"

McP: "What are you suggesting?"

H: "Nothing. I am merely curious. Did you ever check their birth records, for instance?"

McP: "No, but perhaps I should have."

H: "Perhaps. In any event, the hour is growing late & I will not trouble you much longer, Mr. McParland. However, I am still left with the question of who actually murdered Michael O'Donnell, not to mention the cartman, & now, as you must be aware, Randolph Hadley & his lover."

McP: "There should be no confusion on that score, Mr. Holmes. It is all the work of anarchists, as your friend Rafferty's shootout in the lumberyard demonstrated. Earl Hayes was one of the most feared dynamite terrorists west of the Mississippi, & the fact that he was in Mpls. & may even have linked up with Mary McGinty is a matter of great concern."

H: "So I have been told. However, there are those who say Mary McGinty is a mirage cleverly set out by the Pinkertons to lure in radicals & anarchists."

McP, CHEEKS REDDENING WITH INDIGNATION: "That is a calumny, advanced by enemies of our agency. Rafferty's encounter with Earl Hayes should be enough to convince you that Mary McGinty & her fellow radicals are no figments of the imagination. I will admit that I'm not sure if she remains in Mpls at the moment, for she has a 242way of dropping from sight as soon as her pursuers close in, but surely it must be clear to you from Mr. Hadley's assassination that murderers are at loose in this city. What other explanation could there be? I assure you that the radical threat is very real. Even Michael O'Donnell believed so & he paid for that knowledge with his life."

H: "How do you know that?"

McP: "In his last report to our Chicago office, he stated that he had begun to infiltrate a dangerous radical group. He even identified a man we now know to have been Earl Hayes as a likely member. O'Donnell also believed he was closing in on Mary McGinty. I trust, Mr. Holmes, that you see the supreme irony in this. Michael O'Donnell was a liar, a cheat, a blackmailer, a disgrace to the Pinkertons in almost every way, & yet we think that in the end, he may have been murdered for doing his duty."

H: "Yet you would not deny, would you, that others—the mayor & Mr. Wellington, for example—also had good reasons to wish Mr. O'Donnell dead?"

McP: "I would not deny it, but I think it very unlikely that either of those men played a role in O'Donnell's death. As you are the great detective, Mr. Holmes, I'm sure it will all become clear to you in time."

McParland stood up, signaling end to interview. He then reminded H again of promise to maintain confidentiality.

H, RISING TO SHAKE MCPARLAND'S HAND: "You have nothing to fear."

McP: "I have much to fear, Mr. Holmes, for there are many aggrieved men who would like to see me dead. But I have always had a certain knack for survival. I hope the same will be said of you & Dr. Watson when this affair is over. Good day, sir, & tell your friend Rafferty I should like to have a drink with him some day. He is quite the character."

McP & bodyguards left. H & I did likewise, emerging from the club near midnight & walking quickly back to hotel.

H: "Well, Watson, what did you think of the famous Pinkerton man?"

W: "I must admit, Holmes, that I do not know whether to believe a word of what he told us."

H: "Nor do I, tho I am inclined to think his tale was sufficiently fantastic to be the truth."

Reached West just before midnight & found SR & GWT waiting with startling news of their own. . . .

Earlier that evening Rafferty and Thomas began their search for Addie O'Donnell in the obvious place—at her apartment in the sprawling tenement known as Noah's Ark. Its real name was Beard's Block, and it was the largest building of its kind in the city, with over eighty apartments housing a hodgepodge of recent immigrants, mainly Norwegians, Swedes, and Irish.[5]

Rafferty wasn't sure which apartment belonged to Addie O'Donnell, so he and Thomas went to the office, where a consumptive clerk with a blotched red face stated that he was "prevented by regulations" from revealing the apartment numbers of tenants to "strangers." These regulations were summarily waived after Rafferty greased the clerk's palm with a silver dollar. The clerk then directed them to apartment 312.

The apartment, like all others on the third floor, could only be reached by an open wooden staircase in the rear of the U-shaped tenement, which wrapped around a large courtyard. Rotting sheds and heaps of trash filled the courtyard, illuminated by a single arc lamp. Although it wasn't yet eight o'clock, the tenement seemed surprisingly quiet. Saturday night, Rafferty thought. Everyone must be out on the town.

Rafferty, with Thomas right behind, was huffing by the time they had climbed the steps up to apartment 312, and he paused to catch his breath on the narrow landing in front of the door. He could see no lights through the window. Nor was there any sign of life from adjoining apartments. Once he had his breath back, Rafferty rapped firmly on the door. No answer. Two more knocks yielded the same result.

"Well, Wash, I guess we might as well take a peek inside," Rafferty whispered. Using a small light, he examined the door lock, an 1880s-vintage Yale model of no particular distinction. It would be sinfully easy to pick. Selecting a suitable instrument from the small kit he had brought along, Rafferty inserted it into the lock, did a little maneuvering, heard a satisfying click, and pushed open the door.

Rafferty found a lamp and turned it on, revealing a small parlor, sparsely furnished but neatly kept. All the furniture—an upholstered settee, a side chair, a desk, and a large oak bookcase stocked with weighty tomes—had the well-worn look of hand-me-downs, as did the frayed carpet on the floor. A pair of floral prints, along with a large family photograph, hung on the rough plaster walls.

The picture had been taken, according to a gilded inscription in one corner, in the studio of a Chicago photographer. It showed an attractive but weary-looking woman standing next to a luxuriously bearded, heavyset man who sat on a straight-backed chair and stared at the camera with a stark, intimidating gaze. Two children, a girl and boy, stood on the other side of the patriarch dressed in their best Sunday clothes. One look at the girl, who appeared to be about ten, left no doubt as to her identity. Even at that age, there was in Addie O'Donnell's eyes something of her father's fierce resolve. The boy, a year or two younger than his sister, must have been Michael. His face was harder to read, but he seemed aloof, hiding himself from the camera's probing lens.

Rafferty had just such a photograph of his own family, before an epidemic swept away his parents and he and his brother were sent to live with a distinguished family of Boston Brahmins. Every so often he would take out the picture, which he could not bear to have hanging on the wall, and look at it, to study the faces of the dead and to marvel at his own unlikely survival.

A quick search of the parlor yielded nothing of note, so Rafferty moved on to what he presumed to be the bedroom, while Thomas kept watch out the parlor window. Rafferty found a gas jet by the bedroom door and turned it on. He was not prepared for what he saw. Whereas the parlor had been perfectly neat, the bedroom was in disarray—shards of glass from a toppled lamp littered the floor, clothes were strewn around an open wardrobe, two chairs lay overturned, needles and spools of thread spilled out of an etui atop an old Singer sewing machine. Only the bed, tidily made, seemed to be in normal condition. But what gave Rafferty pause was something else, for the chaos of the room was dappled with dark strains, on both the floor and walls, that could only be blood.

"You'd better have a look at this, Wash," Rafferty said.

Thomas came in, saw the evidence of carnage, and whistled softly. "Looks like something got slaughtered in here," he said.

"'Tis not a pretty picture," Rafferty agreed. "The question is, who does all this blood belong to? Miss O'Donnell herself? The Ratman, who was supposed to be stayin' with her? Or could it be someone else's?"

"No way of telling," Thomas said.

"Well, Wash, since we're here, we'd best have a good look around. Did you see any signs of life outside?"

"Quiet as a morgue," came the reply.

Rafferty soon made another discovery. On the floor by the wardrobe he found a piece of rope about three feet long, with handles at either end. It was a garrote, of a kind he had seen only once before, in the hands of a certain strong-arm robber who used the rope to subdue or even strangle his victims. The garrote gave Rafferty an idea about what might have happened in the room. Why it happened, however, remained a mystery.

While Rafferty continued to search the bedroom, Thomas examined a small adjoining bathroom. He found bloodstains in the sink and on the floor. Someone had obviously washed up after what must have been a brutal struggle. Rafferty came in for a look and shook his head. "Amazin' how much blood there is," he said. "Yet 'twould appear that both parties somehow survived the battle. Either that, or a body was dragged out of the apartment."

"Addie O'Donnell's?" Thomas asked.

"I hope not, Wash, I truly hope not. I didn't find a suitcase in the bedroom, nor were there many clothes. 'Tis therefore possible she left on her own power, but if she did, she must have gone in a great hurry. Otherwise, I doubt she would have left behind that family photograph in the parlor. Now, let's finish up. The longer we stay, the better the chance we'll get ourselves in trouble."

The only other room in the apartment was a kitchen just big enough for a stove, an icebox, a sink, a cabinet with drawers, and a small table. There were clothes hooks by the door and beneath them Rafferty found a large lambskin glove. Although Rafferty had big hands, the glove fit perfectly, leaving no doubt it belonged to a man. The Ratman perhaps? But Rafferty couldn't imagine Sid, who was small in stature, having such large hands.

Next, Rafferty went through the cabinet drawers, and struck gold not once but three times—"'twas the mother lode of this entire case," he later told Holmes. His first find was a handwritten note with a telephone number beneath it that read, "Hennepin Clerk of Court, marriage license." Was Miss O'Donnell planning to marry? If so, who was the groom? Rafferty decided either he or Thomas would have to pay a visit to the clerk of court's office to find out.

Rafferty's second find was equally tantalizing. At the bottom of the drawer, folded inside a manila envelope, was a plan that appeared to show part of a large structure. The plan depicted columns and beams, various objects that looked to be machinery of some kind, and an array of belts, shafts, and pulleys. Tiny handwritten notes were scattered about the drawing next to larger Xs. One said, "5 here." Another said, "10 here—up high." Yet another said, "Start here—15 ft. per/min."

Rafferty knew an engineering drawing when he saw it, but he wasn't certain what this one showed. The scrawled notes were a complete mystery. Rafferty folded up the drawing and put it in his coat pocket. He had a friend in St. Paul who might be able to explain the drawing, and Rafferty decided to send it across the river for inspection in the morning.

The final discovery, in the same drawer, was a booklet extolling the virtues of Lakewood Cemetery, the favorite burial ground for Minneapolis's elite. Rafferty idly thumbed through the booklet and found a drawing someone had circled in bold red ink. The drawing, and a brief text beneath it, described a monument to the eighteen workers killed in the 1878 explosion of the Wellington A Mill. The pamphlet stated that the monument had been erected at Lakewood some years after the disaster by Wellington and other milling magnates. Rafferty now recalled something the Ratman had told him, and he began to see, for the first time, the haunting shadow of a deadly connection to the past.

Chapter Nineteen

⊗⊕

"She Will Be There"

FROM THE JOURNALS OF DR. JOHN WATSON:

SUN., OCT. 8, 1899, WEST HOTEL, MPLS., 4 A.M.: . . . Sat down with SR & GWT at once & H gave full account of interview with McP[arland], after which SR told of startling discovery at A[ddie] O'Donnell's apartment. . . .

Even H uncertain what to make of situation but thought clues pointed to some "desperate act which must soon be consummated, in all likelihood in connection with President McKinley's visit." President due in city late A.M. to ride at head of parade, visit Wellington Mills, & deliver speech at Exposition Hall.[1]

H: "There are numerous points of vulnerability, & of course there is also the giant rally planned by Miss O'Donnell."

SR: "Assumin' she is not at the moment collectin' debris at the bottom of the Mississippi."

H: "Yes, assuming that. What is certain is that we need more information & need it quickly. The possibilities in this affair are so numerous that our only hope is to narrow them down with the little time available to us."

SR: "Well, I'm thinkin' there are at least two things we must do come daybreak. One is to get into the clerk of court's office, even tho it's Sunday, & check the records there to see if we can find out why Addie O'Donnell was so interested in marriage licenses. Mr. Pyle, who has plenty of contacts, can probably help us. The other thing we must do is pay a visit to Lakewood Cemetery. I don't mind admittin' that I'm haunted by the fact that the men who hung Mr. O'Donnell spoke of their actions as being a monument to Charles Wellington. You have said more than once, Mr. Holmes, that the answers we are seekin' probably lie deep in the past. Maybe the monument at the cemetery will provide those answers."

H: "I have been thinking much the same thing, Mr. Rafferty, but I believe Dr. Watson & I should be the ones to trek out to the cemetery in the morning. You & Mr. Thomas would then be free to examine marriage licenses, after which you could be on the watch for any trouble at the rally, which I believe is scheduled for 10 A.M. — the same hour as the president's arrival. If Watson & I leave on an early streetcar, we could be back from the cemetery by the time the rally starts in Loring Park. We could even plan to meet you there."

SR: "I've no objections to that. As it is, I'd like to stick around the hotel for a while in the mornin' to hear from Mr. Reed. He's the engineer in St. Paul who's goin' to look at the drawing I found in the apartment. I'll find a willing lad & send it over with him by streetcar first thing in the mornin'. Mr. Reed will get back to me quickly, you can be sure."

H: "Then we have done our work for the night. Now we must wait to see what the morning brings."

8:30 A.M.: Telephone call from Pyle just minutes ago. Asked if we had heard labor rally cancelled. News to us. H, who took call, told by Pyle rally called off because A O'Donnell "could not be found anywhere." Pyle then asked if we knew her whereabouts.

W: "What did you tell him?"

H: "The truth, which is that we do not know where Miss O'Donnell is. However, the fact that she has disappeared on the eve of a rally she herself had planned must be regarded as sinister in the extreme."

SR & H both in somber mood as we went down for breakfast. . . .

11 P.M.: A day like none other I have known, & I scarcely believe anything I write will do justice to adventures we encountered or great tragedy which came so close to occurring. Day started out pleasantly, however, for after sharing breakfast with SR & Thomas, H & I caught streetcar in front of hotel at 9:30 A.M. for ride to Lakewood Cemetery. Crowds already building downtown for presidential parade, to start at 11 A.M., and streetcar slowed by heavy traffic. H impatient as always & looked as if he might bolt from seat & sprint to cemetery rather than endure snail's pace of ride.

Bought morning newspapers to read along way & all had story of Hadley's death, described as "shocking" & "a great tragedy" but depicted as suicide following murder of woman. Many lascivious details offered. *Tribune* described Zier Row as "love nest," while *Times* called it "illicit trysting spot." Curiously, no mention apartment belonged to Well[ington] ("money trumps ink," H remarked sardonically), nor was dead woman identified, tho much made of her "naked & voluptuous form." Pyle's *Globe* had most details, but even his reporters could not tease out woman's name, which H said "must surely be known to the police."

Cemetery located on South Side of city between two large lakes & said by SR to be quite beautiful. Found in city guide that Lakewood established in 1870s by prominent men of city & designed upon "garden" concept then coming into favor. Grounds occupied highest point in Mpls & incorporated 250 acres of woods, ponds, & hills, much of which as yet undeveloped.[2]

Finally arrived 10:30 A.M. at streetcar stop at cemetery's western edge, near large lake. Cemetery presented gloomy scene under shrouded sky, & steady drizzle seemed to wash away any traces of brilliant autumn colors seen only day before. Had no map of cemetery (booklet found by SR did not include one) & so had to explore for milling monument. Followed winding road past large funerary monuments — Egyptian obelisks, classic temples, Gothic chapels, etc. — of size & grandeur befitting cemetery's wealthy clientele.

After walking some time, saw what appeared to be administration building — squat stone structure that looked like monument in own right—& went inside to ask for directions. Clerk informed us we had somehow gone past milling monument, which was just north of streetcar stop. Then doubled back & finally saw tall obelisk of gray granite commemorating tragic explosion.

Obelisk rose to height of 30 feet from pedestal & had been erected in 1885 by Mpls. Millers' Assn., according to inscription carved on one side. Wondered why it had taken 7 years to commemorate worst disaster in city's history & also surprised to see inscription made no mention of Well's mill. Instead, it simply stated monument had been built IN MEMORY OF THOSE WHO LOST THEIR LIVES IN THE GREAT MILL EXPLOSION, MAY 2, 1878. Below, carved in larger letters, was epitaph of sorts LABOR WIDE AS EARTH HATH ITS SUMMIT IN HEAVEN. Above these inscriptions was carving of bevel gear like those found in mills, but with single tooth missing.[3]

We stepped around to east side of monument & found names of 9 dead workers inscribed on pedestal. None in any way familiar. Then circled around to west side of obelisk, facing lake, to look at names of other 9 victims. Let my eye go down list of dead: OLE P. SCHIE, CLARK WILBUR, JOHN E. ROSENIUS, PETER HOGBERG, JACOB V. RHODES, CHARLES KIMBALL . . . Then H & I saw it—name we knew only too well! For moment my heart seemed to stop, stilled by awful premonition of disaster, while H's face turned pale & ghostly as death itself. . . .

"I understand you had a chat last night with Mr. Rafferty's English friend," said Arthur Adams, leaning back in his chair and propping up his feet on the massive mahogany desk in his city hall office.

"Yes, he found me at Danny Brown's place," said James McParland.

Though it would be only an hour before Adams joined the welcoming committee at Union Depot for President McKinley, the mayor seemed to be in no particular hurry.

He was a cool one, McParland had to admit, and damned smart. McParland knew he had to be careful even though he despised the man.

"Did you catch the fellow's name, by the way?" Adams asked.

McParland figured Adams would never believe the truth. He said, "The gentleman never gave his name, but I gather he's had some experience as a detective."

"I see. Strange that you wouldn't press him on the point, Mr. McParland, but then there are many strange things happening these days. I find it strange, for example, that you didn't tell me right away about your conversation with this English fellow. Have you forgotten you're working for me now?"

"I haven't forgotten," McParland said, though it was in fact something he would very much have liked to exorcise from his mind. Even more, he would have liked to watch his two bodyguards—who stood behind him at the table—beat the mayor to a bloody pulp. Too bad the mayor had him over a barrel.

For his part, Adams did not trust McParland in the least. It had been Hadley, a good man but in the end a fool, who had insisted on bringing in McParland to clean out the stables. Before then, everything—including the abortive investigation of the mayor himself, ordered by that lunatic puritan Charles Wellington—had been handled out of the agency's Chicago office. But the Pinkerton men there had proved no match for him, Adams recalled with satisfaction, for they and their spy O'Donnell had picked the wrong man to blackmail. Minneapolis was full of embarrassing skeletons—you could practically hear them rattling every time a wind blew up—and Adams had spent much of his life locating them. Even the august Charles Wellington had certain embarrassing kinks in his character, not to mention a less than spotless past, and it had not taken long to persuade him to take his moral crusade elsewhere.

Adams had McParland in the palm of his hand as well, and the Pinkerton man knew it. The dirty business of Michael O'Donnell would be a profound embarrassment to the Pinkertons if it were leaked to the press, as Adams had threatened to do some weeks earlier, anticipating Holmes in this respect. Of course, McParland had made the usual counter threat.

"What would the world think, Your Honor, if it knew you were queer?" he had asked when Adams had first suggested he might have to tell all about Michael O'Donnell's unwholesome blackmail scheme.

"The world would be shocked," Adams had replied, "and my career would be ruined." Then he had delivered the knockout punch: "But you must understand, Mr. McParland, that I have always believed I will be ruined in the end, and so I do not worry about the inevitable. That is what makes me different from other men. If ruination comes tomorrow, so be it. Just remember that when I go to hell, as I surely must, I will have a tremendous amount of company."

Adams could still remember the incredulous look on McParland's face upon hearing those words. McParland was a poker player and, naturally, he was trying to figure out whether Adams was bluffing. He finally decided that he wasn't, and that was how Adams had acquired the services of the Pinkerton agency. But he knew he hadn't acquired Mc-Parland's loyalty, which was why he was curious about the conversation at Danny Brown's.

"What did the Englishman want?" Adams asked.

"Information, what else?" McParland replied.

"And did you provide him with any?"

"No," McParland lied. "He got nothing from me."

"I see," said Adams. "Well then, Mr. McParland, I guess that all is well, isn't it? Have a nice day. Perhaps we will talk again soon."

"Not if I can help it," McParland said.

After McParland and his bodyguards left, Adams went over to the window and looked out over the city he ruled. He knew now that he had very little time left, especially in view of the fact that Sherlock Holmes— of all people—had now become involved in the O'Donnell affair. The mayor, of course, had learned of Holmes's arrival almost immediately— it paid to have good contacts in New York.

Adams suspected McParland had told the famed detective every-thing, probably in exchange for a promise that the Pinkertons would be kept out of the scandal at Zier Row. This meant the mayor had only one option left. Before he took that step, however, Adams intended to spend a day with the president of the United States and no one—not even Sherlock Holmes—was going to deny him that honor.

When President William McKinley stepped off his train that morn-ing, Minneapolis was ready for him. Smoothed over, cleaned up, and dressed in its finest raiment, the city was as meticulously prepared as a young swain courting the girl of his dreams. The streets, dung-laced dirt and mud most of the year, had been oiled and wet down, though special care had been taken to route the president along those few thorough-fares paved with asphalt. Garbage had been picked up a day early, and alleys visible from the parade route had been cleaned of their detritus— in some instances for the first time in living memory.

The last-minute cancellation of the rally planned at Loring Park had also brightened the public mood, for it now seemed no protest would mar the president's visit. Nevertheless, the police, ever in fear of anar-chist mayhem, had made a preemptive strike in the wee hours of the morning by rounding up anyone suspected of "disloyalty." By the time

the roundup was over, a hundred or so socialists, anarchists, syndicalists, and others thought likely to possess radical ideas had been carted
off to jail for the day on a variety of specious charges.

Even so, security around the president remained tight, given the un-
settled nature of the times. The Secret Service had been alerted, by Mc-
Parland and later by Holmes himself, to the possible presence of Mary
McGinty in Minneapolis. But agents knew the president would not cancel his plans on the basis of such vague information and so had not even
broached the idea. Still, extra police had been ordered in from St. Paul
to line the parade route, where McKinley, who would be in an open carriage, was thought to be most vulnerable.

Unaware of these security concerns, property owners along the route
had decorated their buildings with flags, bunting, banners, drapery, gar-
lands, swags, presidential pictures, patriotic paintings, and anything else
that seemed appropriate for so august an occasion. One department store
mounted a giant American eagle, complete with movable wings, on its
rooftop. Another store settled for a mammoth heroic painting of the
Thirteenth Regiment vanquishing the Philippine insurrectionists, who—
in keeping with the jingoistic spirit of the age—were depicted as blood-
thirsty monkeys. The *Journal* reported that a wealthy Park Avenue
homeowner, as stout a McKinley man as the republic could muster, had
even taken the extraordinary step of repainting his entire house in red,
white, and blue in the hope of pleasing the presidential eye.

Although the city had hosted the 1892 Republican National Conven-
tion and had been visited by previous presidents, including Ulysses S.
Grant and Grover Cleveland, McKinley's visit was understood to be different from any that had come before. For one thing, McKinley himself
was a far cry from the dumpy, crowd-shy Grant or the equally uninspir-
ing Cleveland. McKinley, it was widely agreed, looked presidential. He
was tall, handsome, silver haired, and stately, with a firm chin and broad
forehead that bespoke leadership. He was also popular, at least among
the people who counted, for his war with Spain had given the eager nation a chance to flex its military muscle with a maximum of bravado and
a minimum of casualties.

McKinley's day was to be full. After a welcoming ceremony at Union
Station, he was to go to the start of the parade at Twenty-sixth Street
and Park Avenue on the city's South Side. Once the parade reached
downtown, the president would leave his carriage and mount a reviewing stand, where he would watch the returning veterans from the
Philippines as they marched past. This would be followed by a visit to

the A Mill, arranged some weeks earlier by Charles Wellington himself. A longtime supporter of the president, Wellington planned to personally guide McKinley through the gigantic mill. From there the president would go on to the culminating banquet at Exposition Hall.

By half past ten, as Holmes and Watson were arriving at the cemetery, crowds along the parade route had already swelled into the tens of thousands. Although the police had anticipated huge crowds, the weltering mass of humanity turned out to be far beyond anyone's expectations. October 8, 1899, everyone agreed, was going to be a memorable day in the history of Minneapolis.

⸱⸱⸱

Rafferty and Thomas had to fight their way through the crowds and did not reach the courthouse until well after nine o'clock. Joseph Pyle had come through for them, locating a clerk who was willing — for a payment of twenty dollars in gold — to open up the clerk of court's office for unauthorized inspection of the records. The clerk, a nervous young man with thick eyeglasses, hovered over Rafferty and Thomas while they examined every marriage license recorded in Hennepin County up to that point in 1899. There turned out to be hundreds of names. Licenses were entered chronologically and, in a separate register, alphabetically by the groom's last name, with the bride's name following.

Rafferty plowed through one register and Thomas the other. It was tedious work, for they were not certain what name to look under, fearing an alias might have been used. When either found a name that seemed interesting, they would then have to seek out additional information, such as home addresses and names of parents provided on application forms filed elsewhere. After an hour and a half of work — a far longer time than Rafferty had anticipated — he and Thomas finally managed to clear the last name. They had found nothing.

"'Tis a vast blank," Rafferty said. "If Addie O'Donnell got married this year, the county of Hennepin doesn't know about it."

"Maybe it wasn't this year," Thomas noted. "Or maybe she was just planning to get a license."

"'Tis possible," Rafferty acknowledged, slamming the register shut out of frustration. "Still, I thought —"

What happened next was a moment Rafferty would always remember, for he suddenly had one of the great startlements of his life. It came so completely out of the blue that he would later tell Wash Thomas that "it was like the revelations of the saints, only without the complicatin' presence of the divine."

Rafferty's moment of illumination centered on an incongruity so obvious and elemental that he could scarcely believe he had missed it. Someone had told him a story that made no sense on the face of it, but only now had he realized that it was false in every respect. Yet Rafferty hardly had time to berate himself for his own stupidity before a second insight came rushing into his mind. This time what he saw was the missing object of his dreams. Ever since his interview with Charles Wellington, Rafferty had sensed that there was a connection—a link between things—that would point him to the truth. Try as he might, he had been unable to see the link, which seemed to hover like a mirage at the far horizon of his mind's eye. No more. The mirage had now given way to an unmistakable vision.

"I must talk to Charlie Reed," he now told Thomas.

Reed was a prominent structural engineer in St. Paul. Rafferty had known him for years and was confident he could decipher the drawing from Addie O'Donnell's apartment.[4]

Rafferty found a telephone in the courthouse lobby, put in his nickel, and gave the operator Reed's number. "Did you get the drawin', Charlie?" he asked when they were connected.

"I did."

"Well, what's the verdict?"

"The drawing shows part of a mill, Shad. The way everything is set up, I'd say it's one of the big flour mills at St. Anthony Falls. It's definitely a water-powered mill. You can see on the drawing where the main shaft comes up from the turbine. The drawings also show a large industrial steam engine."

"What part of the mill are we talkin' about?"

"The basement, or maybe even a subbasement," Reed said.

"What about the Xs on the drawing and the notes next to them?"

"Sorry, but I have no idea what those are. They're certainly not standard representations for an engineering drawing. Same for those numbers scrawled by the Xs. At first I thought they might be some sort of floor-load calculations, but they're too small for that. It's a mystery to me."

"Thanks, Charlie," Rafferty said and hung up, feeling a sense of dread, as though he had just taken in a sudden breath of icy air.

๑๗๒

Rafferty knew now where the final scene would be played and what he had to do. So did Wash Thomas, with whom Rafferty had shared his moment of insight.

"I guess we must go to the mill," Thomas said. "She will be there."

"I'm afraid so. I only wish Mr. Holmes was with us, but we can't delay."

"We could always notify the police or even the Secret Service."

"And would either believe the outlandish tale we'd be forced to lay before them? Or that a certain Mr. Sherlock Holmes of London has joined us in the investigation? No, 'twould be a poor chance, Wash, and besides we don't have time for arguin' with the coppers or anyone else. If anything is to be done, we will have to do it ourselves — or Bill McKinley is a dead man."

The courthouse was only a few blocks from the milling district, but with the entire city gathering to the west along Nicollet Avenue to watch the parade, not a cab was to be found, so Rafferty and Thomas had to walk. Rafferty now remembered an item they would need, so they detoured over to Washington Avenue, where they found a hardware store, which, like almost all businesses in the city, was closed on Sundays.

"We'll just have to open the store up," Rafferty said, kicking in the front door with such force that it tore away from its hinges.

Rafferty surveyed the damage and said, "The Ratman is right. They don't build the way they used to. All right, Wash, let's grab a couple of lanterns. We're going to need them."

Once they had two lanterns filled with kerosene, they continued down Washington for several blocks before turning toward the mighty row of mills that in just twenty-five years had transformed Minneapolis from a lonely dot on the prairie into the world's flour-milling giant. Rafferty knew the milling district reasonably well after his earlier visit, and he led Thomas around to the river side of the Wellington complex. They walked under the railroad trestle until they reached the mouths of the two tailrace tunnels issuing from the A Mill.

Thomas stared down into the dark maw of the tunnels and said, "Looks like the gates of hell. You first, Shad."

With a grin Rafferty ignited his lantern and plunged into the darkness, Thomas right behind. They entered the same tunnel in which Rafferty had stumbled across Addie O'Donnell and the Ratman, but with no Ratman to serve as guide, Rafferty decided his best bet would be to follow the race straight back to the turbine, directly under the mill. From there they'd have to reconnoiter, and pray they could find Mary

McGinty before she sent them, and the president of the United States, to oblivion in many small pieces.

William McKinley, riding in an open carriage with Mayor Arthur Adams, led off the great parade exactly on schedule at eleven o'clock. The drive down Park Avenue was slow, and it was half past twelve before the procession reached downtown, where McKinley—joined by Adams and other dignitaries—took his place on the reviewing stand. By this time, all of downtown was in gridlock, with crowds so thick around the presidential viewing stand on Nicollet Avenue that McKinley was able to reach it only after a phalanx of police had cleared the way.[5]

As the afternoon wore on and the drizzle magically gave way to splendid October sunlight, the crowd continued to multiply, as though cultured in a vast petri dish. From his place on the viewing stand, McKinley could see nothing but an excited mass of humanity all the way down Nicollet to the river. Adams was exultant as he surveyed the scene, for he had once again proved he could "deliver" Minneapolis for McKinley. Charles Wellington, seated behind the president and doing his best to avoid any contact with the "pervert," as he thought of Adams, was less excited, for he hated crowds. But a chance to show the president his A Mill was an opportunity that would probably not come again, and so Wellington had consented to make a rare public appearance.

Once the soldiers of the Thirteenth had passed, brass bands sounding and the multitudes roaring their approval, McKinley and his group slipped away from the reviewing stand and into a small shop where the secret Service had established a secure area. The President, already weary from the day's tumultuous events, seemed grateful for the quiet and, even more, for a chance to relieve himself.

When the president emerged from the shop's bathroom, the head of his Secret Service detail—a senior agent named Matthew Patterson—approached him and said, "I must advise you to change your schedule, Mr. President. The crowds are far larger than any of us expected. In order to get to the banquet on time, I think it would be best to skip your visit to the mill. I'm sure Mr. Wellington would be happy to give you the grand tour another time."

"Nonsense," protested Wellington, who had perked up at the mention of his name. His eyes cutting into Patterson like knives, he said, "No one will mind if the president is a few minutes late for the banquet. I have made costly preparations for his visit and I see no reason —"

"Nor do I," McKinley broke in. "Charles here has kindly offered to show me his famous mill and I intend to take him up on that offer. As he said, people will understand if we don't get to the banquet exactly on schedule."

"In my judgment, Mr. President, we really —" Patterson began.

McKinley cut him off. "I have made up my mind, Matthew. I will hear no more discussion on the matter."

Chapter Twenty

"Do You Remember Louis Lingg?"

FROM THE JOURNALS OF DR. JOHN WATSON:

Sun., Oct. 8, 1899, West Hotel, Mpls., 11 p.m.: . . . Name we read, letters neatly incised in cool gray stone, was PETER McGINTY.

Bouquet of fresh flowers rested at base of monument & H spotted envelope among petals. Inside found note, penned in choppy, anxious hand. It read, "Father, you shall have justice at last. Love, Mary."

"Fool!" H said to himself. "I should have known. Come, Watson, we have not one second to spare."

Followed H at full sprint to administration building, where H went behind counter & took phone from startled clerk. Young man rose to object but silenced by H's steely glare.

H, INTO PHONE: "Operator, this is an emergency. I must speak to police headquarters at once." Long pause. "You cannot be serious! Surely, there must be some way to reach the police."

Another pause, after which H slammed down phone & came back around counter.

W: "What is wrong?"

H: "I am told that the telephone lines into police headquarters are completely overwhelmed, apparently because of problems relating to the huge crowd that has gathered for the parade. No calls are going through at the moment & the operator is not sure when any will."

W: "We must go to the mill! We still have time if Mary McGinty is there."

H: "She is there, Watson. I am certain of it."

We returned to streetcar stop & caught trolley back toward downtown. All went smoothly until car reached Loring Park, near downtown, where labor rally had been scheduled. Car came to stop in heavy traffic. [1]

H, TO CONDUCTOR: "Is there some problem up ahead?"

Conductor said there was "huge backup" because of crowds gathered for parade & "we could be stuck for hours."

H: "It is hopeless, Watson. We must find another way."

Left streetcar & saw traffic already jamming up behind us. Not far back noted handsome landau with liveried driver & bewhiskered gentleman in back.

H, GESTURING TOWARD LANDAU: "We shall take that one."

Understood at once. Ran back to carriage & H told driver to get down, as we needed to use vehicle. Driver looked incredulous but instantly complied after I took out Colt revolver & cocked it. Felt like common street criminal but saw no alternative. Then went up & took reins. Rider—who wore vicuna coat & had smug look of man well satisfied with station in life—uncooperative & demanded to know "meaning" of our action.

H, OPENING CARRIAGE DOOR: "I am sorry, but we have a dire emergency. We require your carriage immediately."

MAN: "Who in blazes do you think you are?"

He responded by reaching in, grabbing man by coat collar & tossing him from carriage.

MAN: "Why this is highway robbery!"

H, JUMPING UP TO JOIN ME: "Yes, I believe it is. Move, Watson, move!"

As traffic on Hennepin Ave. impossible, I turned carriage into park & cut across, tearing up grass & scattering birds. Went around edge of small pond & thru park until we reached street leading toward downtown. Tho neither H nor I had been to milling district, H, as per habit, had pored over maps before arrival in Mpls. & seemed to know city as well as native. Crossed parade route on 10th St.—where "all the trouble started," H noted—& nearly ran down members of crowd waiting for president, not to mention several policemen. Thought police might give chase but apparently preoccupied with crowds, so no one pursued us.

Continued down 6th Ave. S., passing Washington Ave. where SR & GWT had gone to Noah's Ark to look for Addie O'Donnell. With H shouting directions, crossed railroad tracks & headed toward mills which rose up before us in somber masses of brick & stone, solid as old Scottish castles. Crowd already gathering along 2nd St. in anticipation of president's visit to mill but paid little attention to us as we drove past.

H: "There is the trestle, Watson, of which Mr. Rafferty has spoken. The entrance to the A Mill's tailraces will be somewhere beneath it."

Brought team to halt & would have gone off on foot at once had H not possessed usual presence of mind.

H: "We shall need light, Watson. The dash lamp should serve nicely for that purpose."

Removed lantern from carriage & followed H beneath trestle running between mills & large race paralleling river. Little activity on this side of mills & so quiet could easily hear murmur of falls upstream from Hill's bridge. Kept to edge of main race, which was wide & shallow, waters tumbling like mountain brook. Smaller races, flowing between stone walls from tunnels beneath mills, emptied into main race at regular intervals. Soon realized we did not know which of smaller races issued from A Mill. H, however, had committed plan of mill district to memory & stopped when he saw sign for CONSOLIDATED ELEVATOR on large structure.

H: "The A Mill's tunnels should be directly below unless I am mistaken."

In my experience, H seldom mistaken & was not in this case. Descended steep embankment to main race, peered around heavy stone abutment & saw mouths of two tunnels. A MILL in faint lettering carved into each keystone.

H: "Mr. Rafferty said he found Miss O'Donnell & the Ratman in the east tunnel. That is where we shall go first."

Very little water coming out of tunnel, suggesting mill not operating at moment, & tho worried what would happen if we encountered sudden burst of water, I followed H into yawning mouth. Fears quickly allayed, for elevated path ran along one side of tunnel & obvious it was designed for access even in high water. Tunnel reeked of sewage & damp grain—altogether unpleasant. No doubt home to many rats, tho saw none. Bats, however, much in evidence & encountered entire colony hanging in dark abundance from ceiling of small side chamber.

Had gone perhaps 50 yards & made one turn, so that tunnel mouth no longer visible, when H, whose hearing always exceptional, put finger to lips.

H, WHISPERING: "Do you hear it, Watson?"

W: "No. What is it?"

H: "Footsteps, & they are coming our way."

H quickly doused lantern & we crept back into side chamber occupied by bats, finding no way to avoid layer of guano on floor. Took out revolver & listened intently. Then saw flickering light from lantern on opposite wall & shadow of figure holding it. Just as figure passed, H leaped out & pinned man's arms while I put pistol to his head & cocked it.

H: "Do not try anything, sir, or you will regret it. Now — "

Reply startled us: "Is that you, Mr. Holmes?"

W: "Mr. Thomas! How did you — "

GWT: "There is no time to explain, but you must know that they have Shad & I fear they are going to kill him."

H: "Who has Mr. Rafferty?"

GWT: "It must be Mary McGinty & her ally — but I didn't see them. It all happened too quickly. I was going out to look for help or find another way into the mill, but now that you're here — "

H: "Say no more. No harm shall come to Mr. Rafferty if we can help it. Now, show us where he is."

Followed GWT deeper into tunnel, taking another turn before reaching tall brick-lined chamber with huge iron pipe — penstock, GWT informed us — in middle. Penstock, easily 6 feet in diameter, came down through hole in ceiling, then made 90-degree turn to discharge water into race. Turbine inside obviously not turning, as no noise or water gushing from pipe.[2]

GWT, POINTING TO RUSTED IRON DOOR IN CORNER OF CHAMBER: "That's where Shad figured he could get up into the mill."

Door was shut but unlocked & heavy padlock — which looked as if blasted open by gunfire — lay on floor.

GWT: "We took one look at the lock & figured somebody wanted to get through that door in the worst way. That's when we found the ladder on the other side. Be careful in there. I almost got shot."

Door opened into chimneylike chamber 20 feet high & just wide enough for man to stand in. Trapdoor visible at top. Wooden ladder attached to one wall but went up only halfway before breaking off.

GWT: "When we got here, that ladder went all the way to the top. Shad insisted on going up first & wouldn't hear otherwise. So I stood down here with my pistol, trying to cover him while he went up with his lantern. But Shad's not exactly a slender fellow & I couldn't even see the trapdoor once he started up the ladder. I told him he'd be a sitting duck if anybody above was watching that trapdoor. Didn't stop him, of course."

H: "I am not surprised to hear that. Then what happened?"

GWT: "Well, I watched as Shad climbed the ladder. I couldn't see much except Shad's behind, but when he got to the trapdoor he pushed it open, looked around a bit, & then climbed up through it. I waited, figuring he'd tell me what he found, but when I didn't hear anything for a while I started to worry, so I yelled up & asked if he was all right."

W: "Did you get a response?"

GWT: "You might say so. Somebody fired a shot down from the trapdoor—just to get my attention, I guess—& then Shad appeared again, only he didn't say anything. He had a long crowbar in his hand & pried away the upper part of the ladder. I knew then that somebody must have a gun to his back. Then he looked down at me & shouted, 'Get away now, Wash, or we're both dead men.' After that the trapdoor snapped shut & I just sat there for a while trying to figure out what to do. Truth is, I'm still not sure."

H: "We must find another way to reach the room above us."

W: "I see no choice but to do as Mr. Thomas did. We must go back & find another way into the mill."

GTW, LOOKING AT WATCH: "That won't be easy. The president could be arriving any minute & there will be tight security once he does."

H: "Then we shall simply have to make our way through. We—"

Now received one of great shocks of life, for voice suddenly came out of darkness behind us.

VOICE: "There's another way, don't you know, another way, gents, if it's the big Irishman you're looking for."

Strange little man with long beard, dressed in tattered wool coat, stocking cap, & mittens emerged from gloom, carrying candle. Noted rat trap dangling from chain around neck.

H: "Ah, how nice of you to join us, sir. I assume I have the pleasure of addressing Sid the Ratman?"

RATMAN: "Well, who else would I be? Who else could take you thru these tunnels & find that Irishman? Who else but the Ratman could do that?"

H: "No one, I am sure."

RATMAN: "No one! No one! You are right there, sir, right as rain. Nice fellow, that Irishman. Knows what terrible things the rats are doing. Too bad she got him. Too bad."

H: "You mean the woman you've seen down here."

RATMAN: "Of course that's what I mean. She is working with the rats. I am sure of it now, sure of it. Come along, then, come along. I'll show you the way. But watch for the rats! They are always plotting, always planning, & they will attack if they can, the little devils!"

H: "We will be most careful, sir, & we will by all means follow your lead."

Thus H, GWT, & I found ourselves far underground, in middle of great industrial complex, being led by madman in hopes of stopping mad woman planning to assassinate president of U.S.! All seemed so beyond bounds of reason that I began to feel as if I had blundered into some bizarre dream from which at any moment I might snap awake into normal light of day, but dream only grew stranger, for Ratman now led us into passageway so narrow we were barely able to squeeze thru. Passage also lower than tunnel we had left & all of us except Ratman had to duck as we walked.

H: "What sort of tunnel is this, Sid?"

RATMAN: "Tailrace for the old Pettit Mill, built 1875, burned down May 2, 1878. Went up with the Wellington A, it did, in the great disaster. 18 men blown to bits. A sad day for Mpls! Oh, a sad, sad day!"

To my great surprise, Ratman now recited names of all 18 victims—names I recognized from monument at cemetery.

H: "I see your reputation as a historian is as advertised, sir. What else can you tell us about the explosion at the A Mill? Do you know much about Mr. Peter McGinty, one of the men who died?"

RATMAN: "'Peter McGinty, aged 36, born in County Cork, Ireland, arrived in Mpls. 1866 from New York State after service in Civil War. Only recently in employ of Wellington Mills at time of death. Widower. Left behind 9-year-old daughter.' All in the *Tribune*, May 4, 1878, page 2. You can look it up. Oh, & watch your step here, watch it. The rats have been about their dirty work & the ceiling is falling in. Very dangerous."

Ratman did not exaggerate, for we now entered area where series of cave-ins had reduced tunnel to little more than long crack in rock. Had sudden fear: What if Ratman leading us away from SR & only *thought* he knew how to reach him? Whispered this possibility to H, who replied that "when only one hope exists, there is no choice but to cling to it."

After perhaps 50 yards, tunnel narrowed even more & had to walk sideways, bend over, crawl, or go thru contortions to get over & around debris obstructing passage. Also seemed to be walking uphill, tho not certain. Sandstone walls closing in so tightly felt I could hardly breathe. Began to sweat profusely despite damp chill & knew would be eternally grateful for sun & sky once clear of these awful confines. Of course H went forward with usual iron resolve while GWT, largest of us all, had mighty struggle to negotiate most constricted passages but refused to be stopped by any obstacle. Ratman, with elfin build, had easiest time of all.

H: "How much farther?"

RATMAN: "Not far, not far. Just follow me & put your trust in the Ratman."

Deliverance! After making sharp turn, passageway widened into broad corridor lined with bricks. Lanterns soon revealed, however, that corridor ended abruptly in boarded-up doorway.

RATMAN, POINTING TOWARD DOORWAY: "The Irishman will be in there, with the woman & her army of rats. She has been training them for the day when they will be let loose upon the city. I am sure of it. Oh, the Ratman knows, he does. He knows."

H: "What is on the other side of that door, Sid?"

RATMAN: "Engine room. Auxiliary Corliss steam engine, coal powered, 1,000 horsepower. 'The New Wellington Mills,' *Tribune*, Aug. 5, 1880, page 4. You can look it up."[3]

Went with H & GWT to examine doorway, which was arched opening cut thru sandstone. Heavy wooden planks nailed across it. Tiny slits of lights visible between planks but could not see through into room beyond.

H: "Well, it seems we have encountered another obstacle."

GWT: "Not to my way of thinking. I say we take a run at those planks & knock right thru them. Whoever is in there will get the surprise of their lives when we come crashing in."

W: "Or we will be the ones surprised when the planks refuse to break. In that case, anyone inside will be alerted to our presence."

GWT: "Oh, the planks will break. You can count on that."

H: "You are absolutely certain of that, Mr. Thomas?"

GWT: "I am."

H: "Then I see no reason to wait. Mr. Thomas. We will follow you."

We now directed Ratman to stand clear as we stepped back about 10 feet so we could take run at doorway before putting shoulders to it. On count of 3, GWT put his formidable mass in motion & went at door with H & me on his wings, like flying wedge. Hit planks with all our strength & they gave way with tremendous crash & shower of splinters.

Force of impact sent us tumbling to ground. Scrambled back on all fours & saw to my surprise that we had cover, for after crashing through planks had run head-on into, & upended, large tool chest standing against inside of doorway. Got bearings & saw we were in long, high, & narrow room, perhaps 20 by 50 feet, with row of thick timber pillars running down middle. Occupying center of room, sunk into floor, was huge steam engine with spoked iron flywheel so large it nearly reached ceiling. Big wheel & engine motionless, as was huge power shaft overhead, indicating mill shut down. Electric lights strung above, but engine room grew dim toward other end, where grated iron door visible in corner. No sign of SR, however.

Took in these features in instant, but something else about room far more extraordinary, for it had become home to what seemed like nest of gigantic snakes. These actually fuses connected to bundles of dynamite sticks placed around base or top of pillars. Idea, clearly, was to blast away pillars so entire mill would collapse on itself, killing anyone inside. Coiling maze of fuses connecting dynamite bundles led by various shunts & branches to single ignition point no more than 10 feet in front of us. If anyone now sought to light fuse, we would have clear shot at them.

H, WHISPERING TO GWT & ME: "We have met with a stroke of luck. Observe how many bundles are linked to the fusing. Miss McGinty is obviously well aware that it will require a great deal of dynamite to bring down this mill. Detonating just one or two bundles of dynamite will not serve her purpose. It is all or nothing, & the main fuse is now under our control. Unfortunately, she has Mr. Rafferty & I fear she will try to use him as a bargaining chip."

GWT: "We can't let that happen. She will kill him if we don't stop her."

H: "I understand, but we must not act rashly. She must realize now that the game is lost. We must try to talk to her."

GWT: "She won't give in, Mr. Holmes. We must go after Shad."

H: "I see no harm in trying to talk first."

We finally agreed on that course & H called out to her.

H: "Miss McGinty, it is time to give yourself up. Your plan cannot succeed, for the fuses are now under our control & you will be unable to light them."

No response.

H: "We know you are here & that you have Mr. Rafferty. The police will arrive at any moment"—how convincingly H can lie!—"& further resistance will be futile. Please, come out now & you will not be harmed."

Then heard woman's voice, coming from behind grated door in far corner, "You must leave now or your friend will die! Do not think I am bluffing."
M[ary] M[cGinty] had spoken!

GWT, SHOUTING BACK: "Shad! Shad! Can you hear me?"

H, GENTLY CUPPING HAND OVER GWT'S MOUTH & CALLING OUT: "We cannot consider leaving unless we hear from Mr. Rafferty. Otherwise, how do we know that he is not already dead?"

W: "Holmes, you do not think—"

H: "I pray that Mr. Rafferty is alive, Watson, but we must have proof."

Long pause & then, to our relief, heard SR's voice: "I'm all right but do not let her—"

GWT, VERY AGITATED: "Shad! What happened? Shad, are you hurt?"

MM: "You have now heard with your own ears that Mr. Rafferty is alive, but he will not be for long unless you leave. You have 30 seconds to go or I will shoot him down. This will be your last warning."

W: "I say we rush her. It is our only hope."

GWT: "I agree."

H, CALM AS ALWAYS IN MIDST OF CRISIS: "We cannot leave, for to do so would allow Miss McGinty to detonate the dynamite. Yet I do not like Mr. Rafferty's chances if we rush forward without a plan. There must be a better way."

W: "What is your plan then?"

H: "That is the trouble, Watson. I do not have one."

Upon hearing these words, GWT took matters into own hands, leaping out from behind tool chest with wild yell & dashing toward end of room where SR being held. He had almost reached Corliss engine, halfway across room, when shots rang out & he fell to floor, clutching right leg. At same instant, power shaft overhead began to turn, rattling & shaking room as it gained momentum.

H: "My God, the president is here! We have no time."

Now came one of H's great moments, in which his quickness of mind & courage demonstrated to utmost.

H, STARING AT BUNDLE OF DYNAMITE AT BASE OF COLUMN PERHAPS 6 FEET AWAY FROM WHERE GWT HAD FALLEN: "Quick, Watson, give me your pocket knife."

Did so without question or delay.

H: "Now, we shall do precisely as you have suggested & rush Miss McGinty. But first I intend to create a diversion. When you hear me shout, you must at all cost keep your head down. Do you understand?"

W: "Of course. But what do you —"

H: "I intend to detonate some dynamite."

W: "Good God, isn't that terribly dangerous?"

H: "I am trusting that none of us will be hurt and that Mr. Rafferty will be protected behind the door. But if I am wrong . . ."

He did not complete thought. Instead, he rose to feet & ran toward GWT. H reached closest pillar, from base of which dynamite sticks angled up like stalks of deadly plant. H used knife to slice away stick of dynamite & short section of fuse. I expected to hear gunfire momentarily, but either MM did not see H or was preoccupied. H then ran to GWT & dragged him behind engine, which now became shield between them & MM.

Without pausing, H struck match & lit fuse, holding dynamite stick until last second before throwing it into darkness on far side of engine.

H, AT TOP OF VOICE: "Fire in the hole!"

Ducked down behind tool chest & then came tremendous boom. Room went nearly dark—all lights except one shattered by blast. I ran forward at once through dust & debris, not knowing who, or what, I would find. . . .

Shadwell Rafferty had stared down the barrel of a pistol more than once in his life, but this time he thought it might be the last unless an awful lot of good fortune came his way. Looking into Mary McGinty's feverish eyes and watching how expertly she handled her big Colt revolver, he could see that she would not hesitate to take him along on a trip to eternity.

That trip, he knew, was likely to be explosively fast, for he had gotten a good look at the fusing and bundles of dynamite in the engine room. The dynamite explained the mysterious numbers on the drawing Rafferty had found in Addie O'Donnell's apartment. They were instructions, presumably penciled in by Earl Hayes, showing how many pounds of dynamite were to be placed around key structural columns in the mill. Rafferty also figured that the second set of numbers on the drawing referred to the burn rate of the fuses—about fifteen feet a minute. That would be about right, he knew, for "quick match," which is what the fuses looked to be.[4]

As his mind processed this lethal information, Rafferty found that while he was no more enthused about the idea of dying than anyone else, he felt no great fear. For all his easy bonhomie, Rafferty had always possessed a fatalistic streak, and he knew there were no happy endings in life. He even found a certain dark amusement in his situation, for who could have foreseen that the fates would finally catch up to him in the basement of a flour mill? Still, he was a soldier, and if he could find a way to do it, he intended to go down fighting.

Rafferty had been given little time to consider his means of defense, however, for Mary McGinty had put a pistol to his head and disarmed him within seconds after he'd climbed up through the trap door. Then, after ordering him to warn off Thomas and destroy the ladder, she'd marched him at once into an almost pitch-black chamber at the far end of the engine room. The chamber was secured by a heavy iron door with a small grated opening that admitted just enough light for Rafferty to see Mary McGinty's face.

"We'll wait here," she now said, expertly binding Rafferty's hands behind his back while she kept her pistol firmly lodged at the back of his head. Rafferty had found over the years that women and pistols were a volatile combination, and he thought it unwise to resist. Besides, he knew Mary McGinty had killed before and would readily do so again. All Rafferty had now was the power of words, and he tried to use them as they waited in the dim light—for what, he wasn't certain.

"You don't have to do this, Mary," he said. "Think of the innocent people who will die if you set off that dynamite. Walk away now, just walk away, and I'll promise you a fair head start before I call in the coppers. There has been enough killin' and more blood is not the answer."

"Blood is the only answer I have," she said quietly, "and the only one the oligarchs of this nation understand, even if their blood must be mixed with the blood of the innocent. I am sorry if innocent men must die but the fact is, they die every day. My father was innocent and it earned him nothing except instant oblivion. As for walking away, it is too late—far too late—for that."

She had now confirmed what Rafferty had suspected after his epiphany in the clerk of court's office (and what Holmes and Watson had just learned at the cemetery). Rafferty said, "I can only imagine how terrible your father's death must have been, but—"

"You know nothing," she said fiercely. "Nothing. Do you have any idea what it is like to lose every single trace of someone you love? My father was not merely murdered by the criminality of Wellington and his kind, he was obliterated. When the mill blew up, father disappeared off the face of the earth. Men dug at the ruins for days, but they found not one piece of father for me to bury and mourn. Not a shred of clothing, a bone, nor even a shard of glass from his pocket watch was left behind. He had been made to vanish forever, all because of the greed of one man. And now that man shall pay at last for his infamy, as will that lickspittle McKinley."

Rafferty could see there would be no dissuading her from her deadly plans. She was afire with the kind of fervor that only the saints and the mad can sustain, and death would hold no fear for her. That left Rafferty with no choice but to stop her, or die in the attempt.

As he tried to improvise some strategy that had even a ghost of a chance of working, he kept on talking. "What are we waiting for, if I may ask?"

"Movement," she said. "When the mill comes to life, then it will be time."

Rafferty had to think for a moment before he understood what she meant. Then it came to him: When the power shaft in the engine room began to turn, it would be a signal that the President was in the mill, receiving his demonstration from Charles Wellington. It would also be a signal for Mary McGinty to unleash the act of destruction that was her lifelong obsession.

"I hope you know you can't possibly get away with this," Rafferty said, though he didn't really believe it.

"Getting away," she replied ominously, "is the least of my concerns."

Rafferty was considering what he should say next when he heard a loud crash from the other side of the engine room. He didn't know it, but Holmes, Watson, and Thomas had arrived.

Several floors above, William McKinley was having a much more pleasant afternoon. He and his party, which included Wellington and Adams, were touring a large room where the mill's array of porcelain rollers ground tons of wheat every day. Only a handful of workers—dressed in starched white uniforms and standing crisply at attention—were required to man the machinery.

"It is quite an operation you have here, Charles," remarked the president. "I must tell you I had expected to see something rather different."

Charles Wellington had heard the same comment from other distinguished guests who had visited over the years. Like the president, most visitors expected to see some variation of a traditional grist mill, complete with creaking wooden shafts and pairs of circling stones grinding the hard wheat. But that was ancient history. Wellington's mill was, by contrast, a marvel of automation, a giant processing center where the grain moved along conveyors, through hoppers and chutes, and then into a dizzying array of machines in which it was ground, sifted, purified, and graded. In all, there were 19 grinds and 180 separations before the flour was finally packed in bags for shipment to a hungry world.

"Visitors to my mill are always surprised by the size and efficiency of it," Wellington proudly told the president. "They expect to see grain everywhere and numerous workers at their tasks, but in fact the modern mill is almost entirely mechanical in nature, and has only limited need of human labor. Indeed, Mr. President, I should imagine that the day will come when we will need no men at all to run a mill like this. The machines will be perfected to the point that everything will run on its own."

McKinley, ever the politician, stepped forward to shake the hand of the nearest worker, then said, "Well, Charles, I am happy to see that you still have a few men in your employ."

"As am I," put in Adams, who stood next to the president. "No political party could stay in power long if machines took all the jobs of working men. Machines can't vote."

"A pity," Wellington said, directing a baleful glance at the mayor. Then he turned to McKinley and said, "Now, Mr. President, I should like to show you how this great factory of mine works. I think you will be surprised yet again when you see it in actual operation."

"By all means, Charles, let us see your masterpiece," responded McKinley with a smile.

Wellington nodded to one of the men in white, who then went over to a large lever along the far wall. Using both hands, he threw the lever, and the dormant machinery sprang into operation with a deep and satisfying rumble.

✍

When Rafferty heard Holmes's voice and then Thomas's, he took hope. Yet he also realized that by trying to save his skin, they would be putting their own lives, and possibly the president's as well, in jeopardy. Their first priority must be to stop Mary McGinty from detonating the dynamite. Rafferty tried to shout out words to that effect, but she silenced him with a vicious blow to the forehead from the butt of her heavy pistol. The blow sent him toppling over on his side, where he lay momentarily dazed, blood pouring out from the jagged wound on his brow.

What happened next was a blur, but Rafferty remembered hearing a gunshot, very close to him, and then the noise of the shaft overhead as it began to rotate. Fighting to regain his senses, he got back up to a sitting position and violently shook his head, trying to get the blood out of his eyes. He saw Mary McGinty crouched by the door and then heard someone—was it Holmes?—shout, "Fire in the hole!"

Rafferty had worked in the Nevada silver mines, where blasting was an everyday occurrence, and he knew what dynamite could do. He rolled back over on his side, hoping to shield himself from further injury. The blast came a moment later with an earsplitting boom. Debris moving at supersonic speed pounded at the heavy iron door but couldn't penetrate it. Dust vacuumed from the dirt floor had no such problem, however. It poured through the door's grated opening and created a choking cloud.

When the dust finally began to settle, Rafferty—his ears ringing and his clothes covered with dirt—rolled over and got up to his knees, his hands still bound behind his back. He shook his head again to clear his eyes and was astonished to see in what little light remained that Mary McGinty was gone.

"She's escaping," he bellowed at the top of his lungs and, still on his knees, pushed open the door with one shoulder. The explosion had shattered most of the electric bulbs in the engine room, which was now bathed in an eerie brown twilight that reminded Rafferty of a faded photograph. Struggling to his feet, Rafferty saw two figures approaching through the last swirls of dust. One of them was tall and gaunt and moved like a shadow. Holmes! Watson, pistol in hand, was at his side. But where was Wash? Surely, he would be with them. Then he saw a familiar black face emerging from behind the Corliss engine.

"She winged me, Shad, but I'm all right," Thomas said.

Rafferty was about to greet them all when he noticed two other figures at the opposite end of the room. They were rolling on the ground and appeared to be in mortal combat. With their ears still ringing from the explosion, neither Holmes nor Watson had heard the commotion.

Rafferty could think of nothing to do but yell at the top of his lungs, "Behind you!"

Holmes spun around and, without a word, raced back toward the two figures. Watson followed, with Rafferty forming the rear. As they approached, Rafferty saw that one of the figures was Mary McGinty and the other was the Ratman. They were wrestling over her pistol. But how had she gotten to the other end of the room so quickly?

There could be only one explanation, Rafferty thought, and it suggested remarkable presence of mind on her part. Amid the dust and noise of the explosion, she must have made a desperate and, from the point of view of Holmes and Watson, entirely unexpected decision. Instead of staying behind the iron door after the blast and defending herself there, she ran immediately for the fuse, passing right by Holmes and Watson in the darkness, dust, and confusion. Her bold maneuver might have paid off had it not been for something that she could not possibly have expected.

As Rafferty was later to learn, when she reached the end of the fuse and bent down to light it, the Ratman emerged from his hiding place in the tunnel and knocked her down from behind. Now, as Holmes and Watson rushed up to help, Rafferty saw that the Ratman was getting the worst of the fight. Mary McGinty had managed to shake free of the old man, pushing him away with her legs so that she could sit up. As she did so, she conveniently found her pistol, which had been knocked to the floor in the initial struggle. Rafferty watched as she brought up the pistol and took dead aim at the old man.

She never got the shot off. Coming up at full gallop, Watson fired first with his trusty Colt. His aim was true and the bullet struck Mary McGinty in the shoulder, spinning her around and knocking her to the ground as the pistol flew out of her hand. The Ratman then got to his feet and quickly backed away.

"It's over, Miss McGinty," Rafferty shouted as he drew up beside Holmes and Watson. "You must give yourself up."

She was wearing a long black raincoat, corduroy trousers, and the kind of heavy boots preferred by laboring men. Yet even in this masculine garb, Rafferty was struck by her slim, feminine features. In different clothes, with her hair let down, she might easily have passed for a rich young woman of the upper class, except for her eyes, which burned with the unquenchable fire of true belief.

Despite her wound, she got back up to her feet, all the while staring at her three pursuers with a look that seemed to combine profound hatred with overwhelming sadness. It was a look Rafferty would carry in his memory, like an old wound, for the rest of his life.

Ignoring the weapon trained on her, she backed up a few steps and then darted into the tunnel by which Holmes, Watson, and the Ratman had entered the engine room. She didn't know it, but she had gone into a trap. Vibration from the blast had loosened rocks in the tunnel's ceiling and sent them tumbling down so that they completely blocked the passage only a few feet from the entrance.

Seeing she had no way out, Mary McGinty turned around and stared again at the three men who had ruined her life's work. Her face was pale, her eyes still afire. She said nothing, nor did Holmes or Watson, who sensed that just as Rafferty had begun the case, so he must now be the one to end it.

After Watson had finally untied his hands, Rafferty slowly advanced toward her. Caught with no escape, she almost seemed like a small, vulnerable child, and even though he knew she would have killed him, Rafferty found himself wanting to save her from the loss and terror of her life. Speaking softly, he said, "Please, Mary, you must give yourself up. Your father, I'm sure, would ask that of you if he were here."

She looked at Rafferty and then asked in a calm voice, "Do you remember Louis Lingg?"

Rafferty did not understand the question at first. "I'm afraid —"

She interrupted him. "Mr. Lingg was one of the men unjustly convicted of the Haymarket bombing. He was sentenced to death, only they never hung him."

Something terrible now jogged in Rafferty's memory. Louis Lingg, he began to recall, was the man who had committed suicide in an especially grotesque way in his cell. He had taken a stick of dynamite, or perhaps it was a mercury fulminate blasting cap, and then . . .[5]

Before Rafferty could complete the thought, the stick of dynamite was already in her hand. It must have been in one of her coat pockets.

"Let this be a light unto a better world where there is justice for all mankind," she said, igniting the short fuse with a match and holding the deadly stick before her face, much as a worshipper might display a votive candle.

"Look out," Rafferty shouted, and dove for cover. Holmes and Watson did likewise. An instant later the explosion boomed in the tunnel, sending out a shower of rock and sand. Then Rafferty — feeling sick at heart — went into the tunnel and looked at the broken remains of Mary McGinty, the Chicago terrorist.

Several stories above, amid the clattering of machinery in the world's greatest flour mill, the two explosions had been heard but felt only as a mild shaking.

The look of alarm on Charles Wellington's normally passive face drew the president's attention.

"Is something wrong, Charles?" he asked.

"No, not a thing," Wellington lied. "It is possible we have had an equipment problem somewhere in the mill."

"Well, let's hope we all aren't blown sky high," Arthur Adams said, relishing an opportunity to embarrass Wellington. "One destroyed mill is enough for any man—or any city, for that matter."

"Yes, I'd forgotten about that," McKinley said. "You had to completely rebuild after that terrible explosion. When was that again?"

"Long ago," said Charles Wellington. "Long ago."

CHAPTER TWENTY-ONE

⹂

"Do Not Confuse It with an Apology"

FROM THE JOURNALS OF DR. JOHN WATSON:

S UN., OCT. 8, 1899, WEST HOTEL, MPLS., 11 P.M.: . . . After terrible scene of suicide, had decision to make re authorities. Knew H did not wish to linger in Mpls. & explain activities, tho McP[arland] could always reveal our presence if he chose to. Yet H did not wish to leave SR without support should authorities make trouble. SR, however, immediately put H at ease.

SR: "You & Dr. Watson should be leavin' pronto. The explosions will bring down the coppers for sure & unless you want to get caught up in this tangle & have the papers breathin' down your necks, goin' out that tunnel right now would be the best thing you could do."

H: "Are you certain you & Mr. Thomas will be all right?"

SR: "I've yet to meet the copper I couldn't handle & as for Wash, his hide is so tough I'm surprised the bullet didn't bounce right off."

I had by this time examined Thomas & while his "hide" no thicker than that of any other man, wound to his thigh was clean shot that had missed bone & artery. Had stanched flow of blood & thought he would make quick recovery.

H: "Then we shall follow your advice, Mr. Rafferty, & look for you at the hotel this evening. But I promise that if the police try to detain you or press any charges, I will not allow it."

SR: "Fair enough. Now get goin' before it's too late. Wash & I & the Ratman"—who showed no ill effects of his battle with Mary McGinty—"will take care of matters."

Returned to tunnels & had no trouble reaching daylight. . . .

SR & Thomas back at West at 9:30 P.M. Cause for celebration! Went to hotel bar where SR, who normally would not drink before midnight, made exception & ordered whisky for all. GTW reported doctors at hospital concurred wound not serious, so bandaged & disinfected it & sent him on way.

Now followed lengthy discussion of case in all particulars, tho SR first told us what had happened at mill after H & I left. . . .

"My hat is off to you, Mr. Rafferty," said Arthur Adams, who like many others that evening was happy to be alive. "But how on earth did you know who the McGinty woman was and what she intended to do?"

The mayor was not the only man interested in Rafferty's reply. Also on hand in a waiting room at City Hospital were James McParland, two Secret Service agents, a half dozen policemen, and a stenographer. President McKinley, meanwhile, had already been whisked out of the city, for fear that another attempt might be made on his life.

Rafferty had been busy answering questions since the moment when a dozen police and Secret Service men, alarmed by the explosions, had burst into the engine room—only seconds after Holmes and Watson left. At first the coppers had been in no mood to hear Rafferty's story, what with fifty pounds of dynamite lying about, but then the mayor intervened. Adams vouched for Rafferty as "a trustworthy man" and allowed him to explain briefly what had happened. Pronouncing himself satisfied, the mayor had then permitted Rafferty to accompany Thomas to the hospital.

Rafferty had a good idea why the mayor had been so solicitous, and he returned the favor in his official statement, omitting many salient details, such as Michael O'Donnell's secret employment by the Pinkertons. The extent of O'Donnell's candid photography at Zier Row was also glossed over. All of this disagreeable business, as Rafferty saw it, was a matter for Adams, the Pinkertons, and Wellington to deal with, however they saw fit.

Fudging the truth had not been difficult for Rafferty, since there was so much of it he didn't know anyway. Rafferty had never encountered a case that ended with the satisfying perfection of a first-class mystery yarn, and the O'Donnell affair was no exception. In the real world, the story was never complete and doubts always lingered like an inscrutable aroma.

Fortunately, the mayor's query regarding Mary McGinty was one that Rafferty could answer, and he provided a complete—and more or less truthful—account of how his suspicions had been aroused in the clerk of court's office. He also described several other clues that had led to the ultimate unmasking of Mary McGinty. Then he ignited a cigar and asked, "Any other questions, gents?"

There were: questions about the deaths of Michael O'Donnell, the cartman, and Randolph Hadley; about the old tunnel leading into the engine room and how Rafferty had discovered it (the Ratman received full credit); and even about the two mysterious Englishmen who had so suddenly appeared in Minneapolis and aided Rafferty with his investigation ("they are merely old friends," Rafferty continued to insist, "who have some experience in criminal investigation.") Rafferty handled the grilling with his usual mixture of aplomb and selective honesty. It was eight o'clock by the time he completed his statement.

Then it was the turn of the press, and Rafferty answered still more questions. After an hour or so, he begged off, promising he would be available the next day for interviews (the first and most detailed of which would be with Joseph Pyle's *Globe*).

James McParland, who had said little during the interrogation, caught up with Rafferty after the impromptu press conference. He said, "You have my gratitude and that of the Pinkertons, Mr. Rafferty. You have left us out of this business, just as your friend Mr. Holmes promised. In turn, I promise you that I will not reveal the identity of the 'two Englishmen,' as you call them."

"Thank you," said Rafferty, "but I'm thinkin' this business is far from over. There's a mighty stink in the air here and people won't hold their noses forever."

"Perhaps you're right," McParland admitted. "Then again, I once heard a man say that money is the loveliest of all perfumes. Apply it liberally, and even the worst stench begins to smell like roses. And the mayor, I'm told, is quite a fancier of roses."

"He will need a very large garden in this case," Rafferty said.

"Perhaps so. By the way, we've found out where the dynamite came from. Mr. Hayes went to work at the Soudan Mine up on the Iron Range last spring. It's an underground mine and they do a lot of blasting. He left in July at about the time fifty pounds of dynamite disappeared."

"Wasn't the theft reported?"

"Of course. Our operative in Duluth investigated at once and even traced the dynamite to Minneapolis, but somehow or other, we lost track of it."

"Fancy that," said Rafferty.

"I do not fancy it one bit," McParland said, thinking of that little son of a bitch Borden. "There will be consequences, you may be certain. Well, Mr. Rafferty, I guess this is where we part ways. I hope we meet again under more pleasing circumstances. Take care of yourself."

"You, too," said Rafferty.

When Rafferty and Thomas arrived back at the West, they spent the next two hours going over the case with Holmes and Watson. But even with Holmes's powerful intellect shining a searchlight into every dark corner of the affair, many questions remained, and Rafferty wasn't sure when, if ever, they would be answered.

⁂

The following morning Thomas said his farewell to Holmes and Watson and returned to St. Paul. Rafferty intended to do the same, but first he accompanied his friends to Union Depot. There, after delivering the inevitable crushing bear hugs, he said his good-byes as well, feeling a deep sense of loss and wondering when he would see them again.

Rafferty had hardly gotten back to St. Paul, however, before there were additional developments. That afternoon a youngster playing at Noah's Ark opened one of the old storage sheds in the building's courtyard. Inside, the boy found the body of J. Winston Phelps. The cause of death was no mystery, for a scissors blade protruded from the lawyer's back.

The day also brought another revelation—the identity of the woman found dead with Randolph Hadley. Her name was Rita Devaney, and she was described memorably by one of the afternoon newspaper as "a sinuous chanteuse from New Jersey doing business of late in Minneapolis." Exactly how she had become involved with Michael O'Donnell and his blackmail scheme was never determined, though Rafferty suspected she had also been his lover. This would explain, he thought, the brutal slash marks on her body, for Mary McGinty was not a woman to cross, in love or war.

The most intriguing news of all arrived in the mail the following Monday. It was a copy of a typewritten letter written by Mary McGinty the day before her death. Copies were also sent, by an unknown party, to the offices of every daily newspaper in the Twin Cities. Rafferty's copy, however, was the only one that contained a personal postscript. The letter, which Rafferty and Thomas read that afternoon at the saloon, went as follows:

To Whom It May Concern:

I am now dead and so beyond the care, or reprobation, of the world. Nonetheless, I wish to address, posthumously, certain questions and doubts which may linger in connection with recent events in the city of Minneapolis. I offer this letter by way of an explanation. Do not confuse it with an apology.

I was born Mary McGinty in the city of Minneapolis in the year 1869. When I was but two years old, my mother died of the influenza, and my father was left to raise me alone, with only the help of an elderly aunt. My father, Peter McGinty, was at that time employed as a bagger in the Cataract Mill at St. Anthony Falls. In 1874, however, he went to work, on the promise of better pay, in a similar capacity at the new A Mill then only recently opened by Charles Wellington, the great capitalist and murderer of men.

My first memory of father, who was a strong yet gentle man, is of him coming home after a work day, his overalls white with flour dust and his shoulders slunk down in weariness like those of an old draft horse. The flour bags then, as now, weighed 100 lbs., and it was father's job to lift them from the filling machines and stack them onto wooden pallets for delivery to waiting boxcars. This work left him, after many years, with a very bad back, but he would never complain of it, as jobs were scarce.

On my 9th birthday, May 2nd of 1878, a day that will forever be a black mark upon Minneapolis, I remember father saying that he had decided to leave his job at the A Mill, which he believed to be unsafe on account of the flour dust that had been allowed to build up in it. There had been a series of small fires and explosions at the mill immediately prior to this time and father was very worried. Mr. Wellington, he said, was "too cheap" to install proper dust-collecting equipment, as all that mattered to him was squeezing every last penny out of his business. Still, my father went to the mill that evening in order to work a second shift by way of a favor for another man whose wife had fallen sick. Such generosity was typical of my father and much commented upon by all who knew him.

We lived in a tenement less than a mile from the mill, near Seven Corners, and soon after my father left that evening, we heard the great explosion, which sounded like the summoning of Armageddon. My aunt rushed to the window and looked out, and then tears began to stream down her cheeks. "Oh, your dear papa," she cried, for she must have realized at once that there could be no hope of his survival.

The explosion left no trace of my father or most of the other men who died. They had been evaporated into oblivion, and if there is a more horrible kind of death, I do not know of it. As for Charles Wellington, he sent my aunt a check for $100 but did not even bother to offer his condolences. It was clear my father meant nothing to him.

My aunt's heart was broken by this tragedy and within six months she had gone to her grave. As I had no other relatives in the city, I was eventually sent to the orphanage not far from Lakewood Cemetery, which had been established by that most "kind" and "generous" of men, Charles Wellington. I will not bother with a recitation of the cruelties large and small inflicted on me at that inhuman institution. Suffice it to say that at the age of 16 I escaped, never to return.

After a time, I found my way to Chicago and went to the offices of *The Alarm*, a newspaper that I had chanced to read and that seemed to me fearless in its attack upon the capitalist classes, for which I had already formed a most profound hatred. I asked for work at *The Alarm*, found a mentor who shared my passion, and so began a new life.[1]

Once I decided to devote myself to the cause of social justice, I acted without fear or pity to achieve the greater good. There is much of which I could write, including my role in the Haymarket affair and the Lauer case, but I see no reason to resurrect such matters now. Let the history books speak to them. These experiences, however, were all in the form of a prelude, for the great goal of my life was to return to Minneapolis and oversee the destruction of Charles Frederick Wellington.[2]

Then one day I chanced to meet Mr. Earl Hayes, a man of great courage and ingenuity who was especially skilled in the art of destruction by dynamite. Mr. Hayes agreed to assist me in a plan I had carefully devised over a period of many months. He also told me he knew how to obtain as much dynamite as would be necessary for the job at hand.

By the Fourth of July—"Independence Day" in the land of the unfree—he had managed to acquire 50 pounds of Mr. Nobel's invaluable substance. The dynamite then found its way to Minneapolis, as did Mr. Hayes himself, who soon thereafter hired on as a packer at the A Mill—the very same position held by my father before he and 17 other men were murdered by avarice. I had also reached Minneapolis by this time and taken a job at the North Star Woolen Mill.

Late in July fate once again intervened, in the form of another chance encounter—this time with Michael O'Donnell. Our meeting occurred at a labor picnic where he had given a fiery speech on behalf of the cause. I was much impressed with his oration, and with the bold look in his eyes, and I thought he might prove a useful man. In due time I took him as lover and pretended to be his wife. Naturally, I did not reveal to him my secret plans, though I intended to do so once I became convinced of his trustworthiness.

Michael, however, soon confided in me a secret of his own. He said he "had the goods" on several leading men of the city, including Randolph Hadley, Mayor Adams, and even Charles Wellington himself! At first he would not reveal exactly what he knew, but it did not take me long to learn the truth, which was that he had been taking photographs of a most revealing nature at an apartment building called Zier Row. I also learned that he intended to use these incriminating pictures for purposes of blackmail. If you have received this letter, then you will also receive duplicates of these photographs. I urge you to distribute them widely, as they show how the "great men" of Minneapolis have made a mockery of the morality they supposedly prize above all else.

Unfortunately, it turned out that Michael was not the man I hoped he would be. Indeed, I discovered that he was in fact a notorious Pinkerton operative whose insidious work had sent at least one miner to the gallows in Colorado. I made this discovery in September, not long before Mr. Hayes and I learned of McKinley's impending visit and his plan to tour the Wellington Mills. Imagine the joy I felt upon receipt of this news, for I saw an opportunity to strike a magnificent blow against Charles Wellington, his fellow oligarchs, and their puppet—McKinley.

The problem now became what to do about Michael. The Traitor, as I shall henceforth call him, had by this time gone to work in the Wellington Mills, where he began to develop suspicions about Mr. Hayes. How this happened I am not certain, though it is possible Mr. Hayes, who was inclined to drink to excess, made a careless slip of the tongue. I put Mr. Hayes on alert, and he soon reported back to me that the Traitor had been seen one night entering the A Mill's tailrace tunnels.

This was the final straw. The tunnels were crucial to our plan, as it was through them that we were able to bring dynamite into the mill and store it for use on the glorious day when Wellington, McKinley, and other enemies of the people would be destroyed. After we had moved all of the dynamite into the mill, the time came to deal with the Traitor.

Here, however, a stroke of good fortune intervened. Before we could act, others stepped in to do the necessary work. Although crude efforts have been made to lay the blame for his death on "radicals" or even on that army of reactionaries known as the Secret Alliance, it should be obvious to one and all that his murder was the work of the Pinkertons, and no one else. He had become a liability with his double-dealing and blackmailing, and so had to be eliminated. Ask Mr. James McParland, the king of deception himself, to state the truth for once in his worthless life and you will know who killed the Traitor, though I have no compunction in stating that I would have executed him myself had the chance arisen. I suppose some will think it cold for me to celebrate the death of a man whose bed I once shared, but as he was a liar and an enemy of the people, he got in the end exactly what he deserved. Death to the Traitor and to all traitors of the cause!

Unfortunately, after the Traitor's death, Mr. Hayes was killed. This was a great blow to me, but a soldier must always accept the possibility of death on the field of battle. Mr. Hayes shall not be forgotten when the roll call of the heroes of labor is sounded!

With Mr. Hayes gone, I faced the prospect of finishing my work alone. At the same time, I realized that there was one more task to be accomplished before McKinley's arrival. I therefore went to Zier Row one night intending to shoot Randolph Hadley while he was enjoying an evening of carnal recreation. Instead, I discovered that he had already ended his miserable existence and that of the whore who served him. What pleasure I took from the sight of this enemy of the people lying in his own polluted blood!

I am aware that many will consider my acts at the A Mill to be monstrous, but how do they compare to the acts of murder and rapine committed every day by the rulers of a society that is far more monstrous than any single person could ever be? War is being waged upon the masses of this nation by their capitalist masters, and as I saw it, I could either submit to a lifetime of oppression or fight for the rights of the people. I chose to fight. After all, what is life about if it is not about taking sides?

I will conclude by saying that aside from Mr. Hayes and myself, no one else was involved in the plan to dynamite the mill, and should any other person be held accountable, a great injustice will have been done. As I hold no hope of, or belief in, an afterworld, I wish for the citizens of Minneapolis and the nation to know that I was motivated in everything I did by a desire to make the only world we have—the world of the living—a better and a fairer one, so that every man, woman, and child may enjoy in full measure the splendors of the earth. And I am certain that one day such a world will be ours.

Yours in the cause of justice,

Mary McGinty

The handwritten postscript below read:

Mr. Rafferty: In that you struck me as a man of unusual capacity and some awareness of the great issues of our time, I think it only right to answer a few questions for you and you alone.

I imagine you are wondering about Mr. Pruitt. His death, I assure you, was no accident. As you may have surmised, it was he who told us of your plan to meet him in the lumberyard. Unfortunately, Mr. Pruitt had begun to waver in his dedication, which is why the first bullet was reserved for him, lest he expose everything. I must also tell you that you fought magnificently that night. Even so, I would certainly have killed you in the end had not the police arrived.

One other thing: You told me when we talked at the convent how time would soften the pain of old wounds. I have not found that to be so. My father's death was a wound to the heart that not even time could heal. Therefore, I saw my salvation—and my cure, as it were—in Charles Wellington's demise, and I can only hope that he will join me soon among the silent ranks of the dead. Only then shall my heart be whole again.

"'Tis quite a letter, Wash," Rafferty said after he had read it aloud. "Of course, it would have been better if she'd told the truth. 'Twas not the Pinkertons, but Mary McGinty and her gang who murdered Michael O'Donnell. And, of course, Randolph Hadley did not kill himself or his lady friend—that too was Miss McGinty's work. Nor am I convinced her meetin' with Earl Hayes was purely a matter of chance, as she claims. I'm thinkin' she may have met him earlier as part of the Lauer gang, since Detective Wooldridge in Chicago was under the impression that a woman *and* a man were on the run. It's also worth notin' that she fails to mention the murder of Mr. Shelton, the night soil man, and I'm pretty sure I know why."

"I'm listening," Thomas said.

"The way I see it, Wash, Miss McGinty was tryin' to protect J. Winston Phelps, who was the third member of the conspiracy. In fact, I'd guess he was at the lumberyard along with Earl Hayes and Mary herself. And I'm certain he was at Zier Row, smokin' those Mogul cigarettes, on the night Hadley and his Miss Devaney were murdered. Holmes confirmed that the cigarette I took from Phelps's office was the same brand. Considerin' all this, there can't be much doubt that Phelps was the tall man Holmes and Dr. Watson saw leave the apartment with the woman we now know to have been Mary McGinty.

"As for Joe Shelton, I'm guessing he saw Phelps—who was a hard fellow to miss if you knew him at all—as he was leavin' the scene of O'Donnell's murder. When Phelps found out, probably because Shelton tried to extort money from him, he arranged for the cartman to have a fatal 'accident.'"

"Looks like you've got everything figured out, Shad," Thomas said.

"Not quite. There's still one big piece of the puzzle missin', but I think it'll turn up soon. In the meantime, there's a phone call I need to make to Chicago."

"Who are you calling?"

"Let's just say I'm in need of a little publishin' history," Rafferty said, "and I think I know who can provide it."

Rafferty's missing piece turned up a week later when police traced a certain female fugitive to a rooming house on the North Side of Chicago. Within hours she was on a train back to Minneapolis in the custody of two marshals. After pulling a few strings with Pyle's help, Rafferty was able to arrange an interview a day later at the Hennepin County jail, where the woman was being held on charges of conspiracy to commit murder (in the case of the president) and second-degree murder (in Phelps's death).

Rafferty found her in surprisingly good spirits, despite her Spartan accommodations. She wore a dark pleated skirt, a maroon waistcoat, and a white blouse. Her large hazel eyes registered only mild surprise when Rafferty walked into a small interview room and sat down across from her.

"'Tis good to see you again," he said. "I trust your train ride from Chicago was not too unpleasant."

"I have had better," she replied and then, as usual, got directly to the point: "May I ask why you have come to see me, Mr. Rafferty?"

"Why, I've come to get you out of here, for I know you didn't murder Mr. Phelps, as the newspapers are suggestin.'"

"How do you know that?" she asked quietly.

"Because I broke into your apartment not long after you struggled with Mr. Phelps and saw the evidence firsthand. 'Tis quite apparent you acted in self-defense. Now, I'd like you to tell me all about it."

Tears now glistened in Addie O'Donnell's eyes—something Rafferty suspected did not happen often. "Please excuse the tears," she said, "but you must realize how comforting it is to have an ally at this moment."

"I understand," Rafferty said. "When you are ready, please tell me everything that happened, beginnin' with how you helped Mary McGinty escape from the authorities in Chicago."

Her eyes opened wide in surprise. "How did you—" she began.

"'Twas not difficult," Rafferty interposed. "In her final letter, Mary McGinty spoke of a 'mentor' she'd had in Chicago at *The Alarm*, an anarchist newspaper there. You were that mentor, as I discovered a few days ago by talkin' to a police detective I know in Chicago who remembered that you had once worked for the paper. Now then, please tell me everything."

Over the next hour, Addie O'Donnell recounted how she had indeed helped the sixteen-year-old Mary McGinty upon her arrival in Chicago in 1885. Barely twenty herself, Addie had been struck by the young girl's passion, energy, and intelligence, and she had introduced her to Chicago's radical underworld. But the bombing at Haymarket Square a year later changed her life.

"I was appalled by the violence," Addie O'Donnell said, "and determined from that point forward to disassociate myself from the anarchist movement. But Mary plunged into it, for she was burning with hatred for the monopolist class."

The two women went their separate ways—and were not to meet again until March of 1899 when Mary McGinty came back to her old mentor for help. "Of course, I had heard rumors of her alleged involvement in the water tower bomb plot," Addie O'Donnell said, "but she insisted she had had nothing to do with it. Besides, she seemed a changed person. Her manner was soft-spoken and she claimed to have become deeply religious. She also told me that she was through with anarchism and wanted to begin a new life elsewhere. I was already making plans to move to Minneapolis in April to help organize workers at the woolen mill, and Mary said she would like to go with me."

"And you believed what she had told you about being a changed person?"

"Yes, though I have since come to wonder if she knew before she came to see me that I was going to Minneapolis. I suspect she did. I was probably just someone she used—a legitimate cover, so to speak."

After arriving in Minneapolis, Mary McGinty—who had by then changed her name to Jacqueline Parker—led a quiet life at first. Then came Addie O'Donnell's chance meeting with her brother—"it happened just as I told you before," she insisted to Rafferty. This was soon followed by his momentous encounter with Mary McGinty and their sham marriage.

"And just when did you start gettin' suspicious of your supposed sister-in-law?" Rafferty asked. "For that is what happened, is it not?"

"It is," she admitted, "but I would be interested first to hear how you reached the conclusion that Jacqueline O'Donnell was in fact Mary McGinty."

"Well now, you actually provided the breakthrough, Miss O'Donnell," Rafferty said. "'Twas that little note I found in your apartment about marriage licenses that got me goin'. I wondered what to make of the note. Did it refer to your own marriage perhaps? Or were you merely intendin' to marry? Then again, I thought the note might refer to someone else's marriage—maybe one that you wanted to check on. But when Mr. Thomas and I went through all the 1899 marriage licenses in Hennepin County, we made a surprisin' discovery, and it didn't concern you. What we found, of course, was that your brother hadn't been married in 1899—not to Jacqueline or anybody else. In other words, Jacqueline was livin' a lie along with her supposed husband.

"That's when I had what my friend Mr. Thomas calls a startlement. You see, Jacqueline had told me she and Michael got hitched by a justice of the peace. Yet this same woman presented herself as a devout Catholic. She'd even gone to live in a convent after Michael's murder. If she'd been a real Catholic, of course, she would've insisted upon a church marriage—the only kind the church recognizes. Nor would she have been willin' to live in sin with a man. So you see, I'd caught her in a big fat lie. And as I was ponderin' this conundrum, lo and behold a picture suddenly slipped into my mind.

"I remembered something I'd seen in her room in the convent when I interviewed her. There was a bookcase, and on it were two bookends made of burned dark gray limestone. 'Twas the very same kind of stone—from the old A Mill—that I later saw in Mr. Wellington's library. From that point on it wasn't hard to put two and two together. I figured Jacqueline O'Donnell must be Mary McGinty, and that she might well be the daughter of one of the men killed in the explosion of 1878. Some friends of mine"—Rafferty saw no reason to mention Holmes and Watson—"then went to Lakewood Cemetery and found Peter McGinty's name on the monument there. Of course, the cemetery pamphlet I found in your apartment suggested you were also aware of Mary McGinty's past."

"I was," Addie O'Donnell admitted. "I knew Mary's father had died in the explosion. I even went out with her to the cemetery once. That is when I got the pamphlet. But please believe me when I tell you I had no idea she intended to blow up the mill and kill the president."

"I believe you. Mary McGinty fooled a great many people, as it turns out. In fact, she was tellin' fibs right up to the last day of her life — thus that 'bomb plot' she hatched for the rally you were plannin' to hold. 'Twas a brilliant stroke, her idea bein', I suppose, to divert police attention away from the president's visit to the mill. She even got Maj Burke to join her when she came to report the bomb threat to me. Poor Maj was taken in like everyone else and thought the threat was real. Of course, what Mary McGinty didn't anticipate is that by tryin' to kill you, she also killed the rally. I'm sure her plan was to publicize your murder, blame it on the alliance, and so ensure a huge turnout for the demonstration."

"I still find it hard to believe, Mr. Rafferty, that she could be so cold-hearted and deceitful."

"Yet you did come to believe she was not what she claimed to be," Rafferty noted. "Tell me, what aroused your suspicions?"

Addie O'Donnell smiled and said, "I guess you could say, Mr. Rafferty, that you also provided me with a clue, though inadvertently. You see, my first real sense that something was wrong came the evening after I talked to you at Immaculate Conception. Afterward, I went back to Michael's house, thinking I might have overlooked something there. Just as I arrived, I saw Mary coming out the front door with a man."

"Was he by chance a shifty-looking fellow with a pock-marked face?"

"Why yes. Do you know him?"

"I did. His name was Earl Hayes and he was one of Miss McGinty's fellow conspirators. I shot him dead later that very same night at the lumberyard. For all I know, he and Miss McGinty may even have been plannin' that nasty little episode when you ran into them. Did you talk to her outside the house?"

"Yes, but she seemed very uncomfortable. She told me that the man was an old friend of Michael's who had stopped by to offer his condolences. I can't say exactly why, but I didn't believe her. The man — she said his name was Mr. Smith — looked like a street tough to me, and I started to wonder if Mary had gone back to her anarchist roots. So I decided to do some detective work."

"I see. Is that how you came across the plan of the mill I found in your kitchen drawer?"

"Yes. I confess that I used a pretext to search her room one day when she was gone from the convent. I found the drawing in a suitcase under her bed. It seemed a strange thing, so I took it."

Rafferty nodded and said, "Now, let me ask you this. How is it that you didn't know whether Mary and your brother were actually married? Wouldn't you have gone to a wedding had there been one?"

"They claimed they had eloped and been married by a judge one weekend when I was gone. They had a whirlwind courtship, so I wasn't really surprised. But I can see now that I should have asked more questions."

"Ah, I see. What did you do after you learned—as I presume you did by checking the courts records—that they were not in fact man and wife?"

"Well, I went over to see Mary and confronted her. I told her to her face that I knew she had been up to something and that I intended to find out. I was also beginning to suspect that she had been involved in Michael's murder."

"Why?"

"She said some very nasty things about Michael that night, about his having an affair with a 'well-known strumpet,' or words to that effect. When I asked her if she was involved with the local anarchists, she just laughed and told me the idea was ridiculous. She also told me to mind my own business. I had never heard her talk that way before, and I knew something was not right."

Rafferty said, "You are quite the detective, Miss O'Donnell, but why didn't you come to me with this information? And why did you plan a big rally to protest the Secret Alliance's supposed role in Michael's death when you suspected others were actually behind his murder?"

"I saw an opportunity, Mr. Rafferty, to arouse the laboring people of this city and I believed I should take it. Besides, I still thought it possible that the Secret Alliance had murdered Michael. As for why I didn't reveal my plans to you, the truth is that Michael was my brother and I felt that if anyone should uncover those guilty of his murder, it should be me. But remember that I did give you the newspaper article about the Tunnel Boys."

"So that I could find out for you whether the information was significant, I imagine."

"I will not deny it, but it was not my intent to exploit you in any way."

Rafferty wasn't so certain about that, but he let the matter drop. "In any event, your stubborn desire to play solo detective nearly got you killed."

"I know. I take it Mr. Phelps was part of the dynamite scheme with Mary."

Rafferty nodded and said, "Oh yes, he was in it up to his eyeballs. The great defender of the downtrodden at some point crossed over into the anarchist camp. How he hooked up with Mary McGinty we may never know, but I suspect the dynamite plot was not the first crime he'd ever been involved in. And, of course, there can be no doubt that he directly participated in your brother's murder."

"What makes you so certain?"

Rafferty now explained to her his theory regarding Joe Shelton.

"That is not much evidence upon which to build a case against Mr. Phelps," she noted.

"Maybe, but I'm bettin' a search of Mr. Phelps's house and other property will turn up some incriminatin' items. Besides, I've got other evidence. I found a dynamitin' manual at his office. There's also the matter of how I first came to be followed—by Earl Hayes—on the night I visited Mr. Phelps's apartment. Mr. Phelps was one of the few people then who knew I was investigatin' Mr. O'Donnell's death. 'Tis logical to think that he was the person who tipped off Miss McGinty and her associates to my activities. Finally, there's evidence that he spent a long time on the telephone with a woman—undoubtedly Mary—just before he went out to kill you."

"But why was he sent to murder me? I had no real proof that he or Mary had committed any crimes."

"True, but I suspect Miss McGinty had figured out—probably by talking with the nuns—that you must have stolen the mill plan from her suitcase. You were a threat, Miss O'Donnell, and Mary McGinty had a direct way of dealin' with people such as yourself, even if you had once been a friend. She wanted you out of the way, and with Mr. Phelps's help she very nearly succeeded."

Addie O'Donnell nodded and said, "You do not have to tell me that. When I entered my apartment that night, all I remember is a rope suddenly being pulled around my throat. I struggled and managed to grab scissors from my sewing case. I swung wildly, there was a spray of blood, and then Mr. Phelps fell to the floor. I thought he was dead, but I guess he was not."

"No, after you left, he must have crawled out of the apartment, down the steps, and into that old shed, probably thinkin' he could rest and get out of the wind. Instead, he died there. 'Twas the garrote, by the way, that led me to conclude you were the intended victim. Still, after fendin' off Mr. Phelps, you decided to leave town instead of reportin' what happened to the police. Why?"

"Surely, you must know the answer. I am a labor organizer—a socialist and anarchist as far as the powerful men of this city are concerned. Do you suppose they would have listened for a moment to my claim of self-defense? No, I was certain they would find a way to railroad me to prison, or the gallows, if they could manage it. For all I know, they still may do it, Mr. Rafferty."

Rafferty reached over the table and took her hand in his. He said, "No, Miss O'Donnell, that will not happen. You have my word. This awful business is over. No one is goin' to be railroaded. Enough blood has been shed and I will allow no further injustice to be done. 'Tis time to let the dead lie in peace and let the livin'—you included—go on with their lives."

Addie O'Donnell looked into Rafferty's wide blue eyes, which had seen so much of the world, and said, "Do you know that you are just about the most remarkable person I have ever met, Mr. Rafferty?"

"Well," said Rafferty with a grin, "I guess I do all right."

EPILOGUE

✑

"Rest Quietly"

FROM THE JOURNALS OF DR. JOHN WATSON:

FRI., NOV. 10, 1899, 221B BAKER ST., LONDON, 3 P.M.: Another letter today from SR, full of more news re O'Donnell case. Biggest development: discovery & arrest of A[ddie] O'Donnell, who H & SR had always believed was alive. . . .

After reading letter aloud, H—who now engrossed in curious affair of mute lodger at Colville Place—immediately wrote & posted reply, as follows:[1]

My Dear Rafferty:
I am hardly surprised that your ideas regarding what happened at Miss O'Donnell's apartment—including the late Mr. Phelps's attempt at murder—have now been confirmed by the lady herself. However, I was surprised to learn that she is now being held in jail, & I am in agreement with you that while her conduct in the entire affair was not above reproach, it was not criminal. The courts, I trust, will agree.

As for your conduct, I must say again that it was simply superb throughout the investigation. Your instincts were unerring & your courage, as always, an inspiration. Indeed, I am unconvinced in retrospect that you & your estimable partner, Mr. Thomas, required the small amount of assistance which Watson

& I were able to render. Combined with the revelations in Mary McGinty's final letter (I must thank you again for sending a copy), the information provided by Miss O'Donnell would seem to answer the last significant questions hanging over the case, which I regard as your most brilliant investigation to date.

I was also intrigued to learn of the "clean sweep," as you described it, that has already begun in Mpls. No great city can survive for long the absolute corruption of its government, & I am confident that the enlightened citizens of Mpls will indeed "throw the rascals out," beginning with Mayor Adams.

As for Watson & myself, we have recently become involved in a most sinister & absorbing case, the details of which I am not yet at liberty to discuss. Unfortunately, it does not appear from your letter that a case of comparable interest is now engaging your unique talents. Given the dearth of criminal activity in St. Paul, perhaps you will now come to London—as you have promised to do on more than one occasion. You would of course always be welcome at our modest flats & I am certain that somewhere in the vast expanse of London we could find a criminal matter that would command your attention & interest.

In the meantime, Watson & I shall look forward to your next correspondence & pray that we will find you then to be in good health & once again "on the hunt."

With warmest regards,
Sherlock Holmes

Rafferty proved to be right about the fate of Addie O'Donnell. In late November, a Hennepin County grand jury declined to indict her in J. Winston Phelps's death, which was ruled justifiable homicide by reason of self-defense. The same jury also absolved her of any role in the plot to assassinate President McKinley and destroy the A Mill. Although her own dramatic testimony influenced both decisions, the discovery of incriminating items in a basement storage room at LaVeta Terrace, where J. Winston Phelps had lived, proved to be even more exculpatory.

When the door to the room was broken open, investigators found dynamite, fuses, mercury fulminate detonators, a Remington rifle (which Rafferty, who had always believed there were three shooters aiming for him in the lumberyard, took as final proof of his theory), a sawed-off shotgun, three pistols, and, most surprisingly, a new-model Colt machine gun, complete with crates of ammunition. How Phelps had obtained the gun, and how he had managed to hide it away in the closet without it being seen, would forever remain mysteries.

This event was soon to be overshadowed by the revelations in Mary McGinty's letter, especially as they related to the improprieties at Zier Row. Ever mindful of who buttered their bread, the local newspapers were initially reluctant to dignify such sordid goings-on and published only expurgated versions of the letter. This exercise in good taste—or, as Rafferty would have called it, a cover-up—didn't last for long. On October 22, the upstart *Daily News* of St. Paul published the entire letter, and soon every paper in the Twin Cities was wallowing gleefully in the scandal.

The press had been forced into honesty for the simple reason that the show-all photographs had by this time become common currency in Minneapolis, courtesy of Mary McGinty. Had she been so unwise as to send the photographs from Zier Row only to the newspapers, or to a selected few civic and political leaders, the whole business might conceivably have been hushed up. Stranger things had happened in Minneapolis.

But she had not taken any chances. Instead, she had flooded the city with titillating images, sending out copies of the photographs to union leaders, churchmen, women's groups, and even libraries. In a matter of days, or so it seemed, most of Minneapolis was either being regaled or revolted by the sight of such luminaries as Arthur Adams, Randolph Hadley, and Charles Wellington caught frolicking in the buff. Five other prominent men—an attorney, the owner of a large wholesale hardware firm, and three members of the city council—had also been captured on film, while dozens of others lived in mortal fear that they might be unwittingly disrobed in public.

Among those caught by the camera, none was subjected to as much vilification as Mayor Adams. While the other offenders had been photographed in the embrace of a woman (usually Rita Devaney), Adams's bed partner was obviously a man, described in the *Daily News* as a "handsome young Adonis." That single revelation, as it turned out, was sufficient to fulfill Adams's self-prophecy that he would one day be ruined.

As the new century approached, what came to be known as the "Zier Row Scandal" prompted a long overdue municipal housecleaning in Minneapolis. Though some cynics believed that Michael O'Donnell's photographs would in the end prove to be little more than a lascivious side show, they in fact gave impetus to a reform element that had been building in Minneapolis for several years. Spurred by public demand, a special grand jury was soon impaneled, and under the leadership of a vigorous foreman began to sweep away the whole tawdry web of municipal corruption in which the city was entangled.

By the spring of 1900 the first indictments were handed down, and among those later sent off to state prison were the chief of police and ten of his officers, five city department heads, three members of the city council, several building contractors, and an assortment of gamblers, including Danny Brown. Minneapolis's days as an open city were over.

Mayor Adams, however, was not among the miscreants sent to prison. Only hours before a squad of special investigators came knocking at his door, Adams vanished, along with what was later determined to be nearly $1 million in ill-gotten cash. Neither the mayor nor the money was ever seen in Minneapolis again. There were periodic reports that he had been sighted in Mexico, Brazil, or Bolivia, and others that he was enjoying life on a Mediterranean island, though these were never confirmed.

Rafferty was not especially upset by the mayor's escape. "'Tis a terrible thing to confess, but I always liked the fellow," Rafferty remarked to Wash Thomas one evening. "Mayor Adams was an honest public official in his own way, for he never pretended he was in it for anything other than the boodle. 'Twould appear now he's got enough to last him a lifetime."

Others who played a role in the strange case of Michael O'Donnell and Mary McGinty came to varying fates in the early years of the new century.

Sid the Ratman continued to wander the downtown streets, but never completed his "big book of buildings," which was later found to consist largely of indecipherable notes. The Ratman died, apparently of a stroke, in September 1901 in an alley behind the Globe Building, where he presumably had gone to visit the scene of his son's death. Scores of Minneapolitans contributed toward a grand funeral, and the Ratman was sent off to the next world in style at a service attended by hundreds at the Church of the Immaculate Conception. Rafferty (with a contribution from Holmes) helped pay for a grave site at Lakewood Cemetery. The inscription on the tombstone read THOMAS GOODALE (SID THE RATMAN), SOLDIER, HISTORIAN OF THE CITY, ENEMY OF RATS.

Oddly, William McKinley, whose life the Ratman had helped to save at the A Mill, died only a few days later, on September 14, 1901, a week after being shot by an anarchist in Buffalo, New York, like Minneapolis, a city famous for its flour mills.

Charles Wellington was by this time already gone. The profound embarrassment caused by the scandal at Zier Row made him even more reclusive, and thereafter he lived the life of a shut-in at his Lake Minnetonka estate. In December of 1900 he contracted a cold, which soon turned into pneumonia, and he died the day after Christmas. Expressions of sympathy poured in from distinguished members of the business community, but attendance at his funeral was sparse. He was buried beneath a massive tombstone at Lakewood Cemetery within eyeshot of the monument to the men killed in the 1878 explosion. He left behind no heirs, and his entire estate—estimated at $40 million—went to charity, including a sizable bequest to the orphanage where Mary McGinty had lived after her father's death.

James McParland lost his battle to keep a lid on the story of Michael O'Donnell's work as a Pinkerton operative. Mary McGinty's letter gave away much of the secret. Then, several months later, the full story emerged, with a wealth of embarrassing detail, in the *Minneapolis Tribune*. Rumor had it that Arthur Adams himself had leaked the story to the newspaper the day before he disappeared. McParland, however, suffered no damage from these revelations and went on to further adventures with the Pinkertons. In 1905 he became a key player in one of the most celebrated cases of the era—the assassination of former Idaho governor Frank Steunenberg, who was killed by a dynamite bomb placed at the front gate of his house in Caldwell, Idaho. McParland was instrumental in bringing leaders of the Western Federation of Miners to trial for the crime, but all were ultimately acquitted.[2]

Addie O'Donnell moved back to Chicago not long after she was cleared of all charges in Phelps's death. She continued her union organizing efforts there and, in 1902, married a fellow organizer. Later, Rafferty heard, she went on to New York City and became active with the American Federation of Labor.

As for Rafferty himself, the year 1899 ended on a quiet note, though it was remarked upon with considerable interest in St. Paul that he was frequently seen escorting Majesty Burke to plays, concerts, and other events. There were even whispers of marriage, which Rafferty took great pains to deny. Then, in the summer of 1900, came a case that was to thrust him onto the front pages of every newspaper in America when he was called upon to penetrate the Chicago underworld to rescue a hostage whose name was known in every corner of the globe. In this adventure, as in others that followed, Wash Thomas continued to serve as Rafferty's partner and confidant.

In the days after Mary McGinty's death, Rafferty found that she had come to occupy a special place in the territory of his dreams. He saw her sometimes as a child running to the window of her apartment as the great mill, and her father with it, disappeared in billows of dust and smoke. Other times he saw her outside the lumberyard, deadeyed, aiming a bullet at his heart. Mostly he saw her down in the old tunnel, at once trapped and fearless, holding the dynamite in her hand as carefully as a sacred relic.

He finally decided that he would have to exorcise her spirit, and so not long after the new century arrived, he boarded a streetcar on a bitterly cold winter afternoon and rode all the way out to Lakewood Cemetery. Mary McGinty was buried there, by a certain irony, in a potter's grave, unmarked and unmourned. Under naked trees and a thick mantle of snow, the cemetery was cold, empty, and quiet—like death itself, Rafferty thought—and no bad thing in the end. He knew he would never find her grave in the deep snow, and so he made his way to the tall gray obelisk adorned with a broken mill gear. He placed a small bouquet of flowers, already dying in the cold, at the base. He read again the names of the men whose lives had been blasted away on that terrible day in 1878, and he bowed his head to say a brief prayer, wondering as always if his small words could penetrate the immense silence of the heavens. He thought of the young woman who was the final victim of the great disaster and hoped that she had found at last a peaceful heart.

"Rest quietly," he said, and walked off through the hard white snow.

Notes

To the reader: These end notes are intended to provide additional background information about people, places, and events depicted in this book. However, they are not essential to the story and may safely be skipped by those inclined to do so.

Prologue

1. "French flats" was a term for what today would simply be called an apartment building. Because they featured so many living units in close proximity, such buildings were considered vaguely immoral by proper Victorians, although they eventually got over it. The old Minneapolis Public Library was a beautiful Romanesque-style sandstone building that opened in 1889. It was demolished in 1961 after the completion of a larger, but much less attractive, new library a few blocks away.

2. The Wellington-Adams house shows up in numerous real estate atlases of Minneapolis from the nineteenth century. It was on the northwest corner of the intersection of Tenth Street and First Avenue South (now Marquette Avenue). Unfortunately, I have been unable to find any photographs of the house or its grounds, but there are good descriptions of the property in Minneapolis newspapers of the time.

3. The Second Minnesota Infantry Regiment, organized in July 1861, saw action at many of the major Civil War battles in the Western Theater—perhaps most notably in Chickamauga, Georgia, in September 1863, where it sustained heavy casualties as part of General George Thomas's dogged defense of Snodgrass Hill, an action that saved the Union Army from disaster. Later that year, the regiment took part in the famed charge up Missionary Ridge near Chattanooga. The regiment concluded its war service by marching with General William Sherman through Georgia and the Carolinas in 1864–65. For more about the regiment, see Kenneth

Carley, *Minnesota in the Civil War* (Minneapolis: Ross & Haines, 1961; rev. ed., St. Paul: Minnesota Historical Society Press, 2000).

Chapter One: "They Strung Up Michael"

1. The journals of Dr. John Watson, in sixteen volumes, may be found in their original form at the British Museum in London. However, a duplicate set is available at the University of Minnesota's celebrated Sherlock Holmes Collection in Minneapolis, and it was there that I consulted the journals. Watson's account therein of the case involving the Secret Alliance is well known among Sherlockian scholars, but it has never been widely publicized because the investigation was in fact initiated by Shadwell Rafferty. In order to tell the full story here, I decided to construct a conjectural account of Rafferty's activities (based upon a handful of personal letters and other documents left behind at his death in 1928) and combine it with the pertinent sections of Watson's journal. The result is a narrative of the case from two distinct but interrelated viewpoints. A few notes on style: I have used ellipses (. . . .) to indicate where I have edited journal entries to avoid repetition. Otherwise, I have tried to present journal entries exactly as Watson wrote them. To this end I have retained, whenever possible, Watson's characteristic abbreviations. These include initials or shortened forms for frequently used names, such as H (Holmes), W (Watson) and SR (Shadwell Rafferty); the ampersand (&) in place of the word "and"; and certain simplified spellings (for example, "thru" and "tho"). In places where I felt it necessary to explain an abbreviation to the reader, I have inserted the additional information in brackets.

2. The *Campania* was launched in 1893 by the Cunard Line and was considered among the finest liners of its time. Holmes and Watson had taken the same ship to New York twice before, most recently in the spring of 1899 at the beginning of the adventure later recorded as *Sherlock Holmes and the Rune Stone Mystery*, ed. Larry Millett (New York: Viking, 1999.) John J. Astor IV was a great-grandson to the legendary John Jacob Astor (1763–1848), founder of a fur trade and real estate empire. The Waldorf-Astoria was actually two separate hotels—the Waldorf, built in 1893 by William Waldorf Astor, and the Astoria, built next door in 1897 by John J. Astor IV. The two men were cousins and had a long-running feud, in which Holmes obviously became entangled. Despite their feud, the cousins operated the two hotels, considered the grandest in New York, as one unit. Designed by Henry J. Hardenberg (also responsible for the famed Plaza Hotel and the Dakota Apartments in New York), the Waldorf-Astoria was located on Fifth Avenue between Thirty-third and Thirty-fourth streets. The hotel was razed in 1929 to make way for the Empire State Building. A new Waldorf-Astoria, which still stands, opened in 1931 on Park Avenue at Fiftieth Street.

3. The Battle of Manila Bay, in the Philippines, occurred on May 1, 1898, and was the decisive naval action of the Spanish-American War, which had begun less than a month earlier. During the seven-hour battle, Commodore George Dewey's Asiatic Squadron of four cruisers (including his flagship, the *Olympia*) and two gunboats encountered ten Spanish warships in Manila Bay and destroyed, damaged, or captured all of them. Almost four hundred Spanish sailors were killed in the fighting, while Dewey's squadron suffered only eight casualties and no damage to its ships. The war with the Spanish was over within months, but American forces occupying the Philippines later became embroiled in fighting with insurgents on the

islands. The "naval parade" Watson refers to was held on September 29, 1899, in New York Harbor and included more than 250 vessels, led by warships from Dewey's squadron.

4. Watson does not state the exact amount of Holmes's fee anywhere in his journal. But if the fee offered by Astor was indeed the largest of Holmes's career, it would have exceeded fifty-thousand dollars—the amount Holmes was paid by James J. Hill for his work in the 1894 case published as *Sherlock Holmes and the Red Demon*, ed. Larry Millett (New York: Viking, 1996.) In that instance, however, Holmes donated the entire fee to fire relief efforts in the town of Hinkley, Minnesota, where the affair of the Red Demon had taken place.

5. Lake Osakis is located in west central Minnesota not far from the city of Alexandria, which served as the setting for the *Rune Stone Mystery*. The lake was long one of Rafferty's favorite fishing spots and remains today a popular resort destination.

6. Rafferty received Sherlock as a gift from Holmes in February 1896 at the conclusion of the case published as *Sherlock Holmes and the Ice Palace Murders*, ed. Larry Millett (New York: Viking, 1998).

7. The Ryan Hotel, at Sixth and Robert Streets in downtown St. Paul, was built at a cost of $1 million in 1885 by Dennis Ryan, who had made his fortune in the Nevada silver fields. Rafferty, who had himself been a miner in Nevada, may well have known Ryan even before he came to St. Paul. City directories indicate that Rafferty opened his saloon at the hotel in 1888 and that it remained in operation there until 1920. The hotel was demolished in 1962 and no traces of the saloon are known to have survived.

8. The Thirteenth Minnesota Regiment was one of the three National Guard units from Minnesota that volunteered for service in the Spanish-American War. The regiment, with about sixty officers and thirteen hundred men, arrived in the Philippines in August 1898 and was placed under the division command of Brigadier General Arthur MacArthur, whose son Douglas was to become a much more famous general during World War II. The Thirteenth saw combat at the Battle of Manila on August 13, after which the Spanish surrendered. But Filipino insurgents soon ignited a guerrilla war that lasted three years and ultimately involved one hundred thousand American troops, including the Thirteenth. The regiment was finally ordered home in August 1899, having lost only seven men in combat but another thirty-four to disease. For more information on the regiment, see Virginia Brainard Kunz, *Muskets to Missiles: A Military History of Minnesota* (St. Paul: Minnesota Statehood Centennial Commission, 1958), 120–29.

9. During the Civil War, William McKinley (1843–1901) was a member of the Twenty-third Ohio Regiment, commanded by another president to be, Colonel Rutherford B. Hayes. At the Battle of Antietam, in Maryland, fought on September 17, 1862, McKinley's regiment (he was then a sergeant) was part of the Union Army's Ninth Corps, which saw heavy action on the southern part of the battlefield. The First Minnesota Regiment, in which Rafferty served, was part of the Second Corps and did its fighting on the northern side of the Union lines. It therefore seems unlikely that the two men would have met, but given the chaotic nature of the battle—the bloodiest single day of the war, with a total of twenty-three thousand casualties for both sides—anything is possible.

10. The only known lynching in Minneapolis occurred on April 28, 1882, when a man named Frank McManus, who was accused of raping a four-year-old

girl, was pulled from his jail cell by a mob of sixty men and strung up from an oak tree in front of Central High School. The high school at that time was located at the corner of Eleventh Street and Fourth Avenue South, just four blocks from the scene of Michael O'Donnell's hanging seventeen years later. An account of McManus's lynching may be found in the St. Paul and Minneapolis *Pioneer Press*, April 28, 1882, p. 6.

11.   The Soudan mine, on the Vermilion Range in northeastern Minnesota, opened in 1882 as an open-pit mine. The first iron ore ever shipped from Minnesota came from the Soudan, which was converted to an underground operation in 1892. Over the next seventy years, the mine — which eventually reached twenty-four hundred feet into the earth — produced more than fifteen million tons of iron ore. The mine became a state park in the 1960s and visitors can now descend into its depths. In recent years the mine has also become the site of a sophisticated laboratory used by physicists exploring questions relating to the amount of matter in the universe.

Chapter Two: "Do You Know Who This Man Is?"

1.   Delmonico's, renowned for its inventive cuisine and excellent service, was for many years the most famous of all New York City restaurants. Opened in 1827 by Giovanni and Pietro Delmonico, the restaurant occupied several locations before moving to Fifth Avenue and Twenty-sixth Street in 1876. It was there that Holmes, Watson, and Astor dined on lobster thermidor, one of many culinary creations — baked Alaska is another — attributed to the restaurant's chefs.

2.   The first sawmill in what is now Minneapolis was built by the U.S. government in 1821 at St. Anthony Falls and provided wood for construction of Fort Snelling, a few miles downstream. The first privately owned sawmill went up at the falls in 1848 and many others soon followed. As flour milling came to dominate the area round the falls in the 1860s, many sawmills moved upriver to the city's North Side, where they used steam for power. By the 1890s Minneapolis's mills led the nation in lumber production, churning out more than half a billion board feet in the peak year of 1899. It was not a long-lived business, however, and production began to fall off drastically after 1905 as the northern pineries were depleted. The city's last sawmill closed in 1921, exactly a century after the first mill was built at the falls.

3.   The old Minneapolis City Hall, where Adams maintained his office, was built in 1873 at the intersection of Hennepin and Nicollet Avenues. The building was small, crudely designed, and so poorly ventilated that workers inside were on occasion overcome by sewer gas. It was torn down in 1912 and replaced by a handsome park, which in turn was destroyed by urban renewal in the 1960s. The Hennepin-Nicollet intersection formed a long, narrow triangle that was called Bridge Square because it led directly on one end to the Hennepin Avenue bridge across the Mississippi River. The steel arch bridge mentioned here was actually the third span on the site — the other two being suspension bridges, the earliest of which (dating from 1855) was the first permanent span built anywhere across the Mississippi. A modern suspension span replaced the steel arch bridge in 1990. For more information, see Larry Millett, *Lost Twin Cities* (St. Paul: Minnesota Historical Society Press), 70–73, 90–91.

4.   For a complete account of the First Minnesota Regiment, see Richard Moe, *The Last Full Measure: The Life and Death of the First Minnesota Volunteers* (New York: Henry Holt, 1993).

5.   Pyle at this time was also well known to Holmes and Watson. He first met them in 1894 when he was sent to London by James J. Hill to seek out Holmes's services in the *Red Demon* case.

Chapter Three: "I Want a Man Who Thirsts for Justice"

1.   James J. Hill (1838–1916) was the founder of the Great Northern Railway and one of the leading business tycoons of the era. He became acquainted with Holmes and Watson in 1894 after hiring them to investigate the affair of the *Red Demon*, which concerned threats to his railroad interests. Two years later, in the *Ice Palace Murders*, Hill's St. Paul mansion (which still stands and is now a museum) became Holmes and Watson's base of operations. Hill held Holmes in the highest regard—the feeling was mutual—and presumably maintained regular contact with him in subsequent years.

2.   The 1890 census war was one of the most comical incidents in the long and sometimes fierce rivalry between the supposedly "twin" cities. Both cities resorted to skullduggery of one sort or another to pad their census counts. At one point, an armed deputy U.S. marshal from St. Paul arrested census workers in Minneapolis and confiscated their tally sheets. This prompted an immortal headline in the *Minneapolis Journal:* "The Mask of Hypocrisy Torn from the Malignant Face of St. Paul." Eventually delegations from both cities went to Washington to cry foul, and a new census was ordered. It showed Minneapolis had outpadded St. Paul, adding eighteen thousand illegal names to its total, while St. Paul managed only half that number. See Virginia Brainard Kunz, *St. Paul: Saga of an American City* (Woodland Hills, Calif.: Windsor Publications, 1977), 52–54.

3.   Hells' Half Acre (or in other cases, full acre) was a popular Victorian term for any poor and supposedly crime-ridden area. In the case of the district so described in Minneapolis, there is little evidence to suggest it was any better or worse than other run-down sections of the city.

4.   There was sharp division at this time between skilled and unskilled workers in the flour mills. Packers and nailers were essentially laborers who did the heavy work of loading, securing, and moving the barrels or, later, bags in which flour was shipped. Other unskilled laborers were classified as sweepers, oilers, or roustabouts. More-skilled and better-paid workers, known as millwrights, built and maintained the complicated milling machinery.

5.   There are a number of good accounts of the life and career of James Mc-Parland, who was indeed one of the most celebrated detectives of his day. See, for example, James G. Horan, *The Pinkertons: The Detective Dynasty That Made History* (New York: Crown, 1968). A much deeper, richer portrait can be found in J. Anthony Lucas, *Big Trouble: A Murder in a Small Western Town Sets Off a Struggle for the Soul of America* (New York: Simon & Schuster, 1997).

6.   The Palmer House hotel was built by Chicago businessman Potter Palmer (1826–1902) in 1870 and was considered for many years to be the city's outstanding hotel. Holmes and Watson stayed there in January 1896 while investigating a "delicate matter" involving Palmer's family. See *Ice Palace Murders*, 2–5.

7.   The strike in 1894 by workers at George Pullman's "model" industrial village on Chicago's far south side was the bloodiest in the city's history, with at least thirty-four men killed during several months of strife. The strike was eventually broken by a combination of federal troops and legal action. However, a commission

appointed by President Grover Cleveland later issued a scathing report that condemned Pullman for refusing to bargain and for grossly overcharging his workers for village services. For more on the strike, see Donald L. Miller, *City of the Century: The Epic of Chicago and the Making of America* (New York: Simon & Schuster, 1996), 542–47.

8. Robert Pinkerton and his brother, William, took over the Pinkerton Agency in 1869 after their father and the agency's founder, Allan Pinkerton (1819–84), suffered a debilitating stroke. Robert Pinkerton died in 1907; William, in 1923.

9. There are numerous references to Sid the Ratman (Thomas Goodale) in Twin Cities newspapers from the 1890s and in reminiscences from that period. For example, see Henry L. Griffith, "Minneapolis: The New Sawdust Town" in *Downtown: A History of Downtown Minneapolis and Saint Paul in the Words of the People Who Lived It*, ed. David Anderson (Minneapolis: Nodin Press, 2000), 78.

Chapter Four: "God Cuts Many Paths"

1. Grant's Tomb, where Ulysses S. Grant and his wife, Julia Dent Grant, are buried, is a 150-foot-tall granite structure located along the Hudson River at Riverside Drive and West 122nd Street in Manhattan. At the time of the naval parade, the tomb—among the largest mausoleums in the western hemisphere—was quite new, having been dedicated on April 27, 1897, by President William McKinley.

2. Clifton Wooldridge was one of the most famous detectives in the history of the Chicago Police Department. In addition to his tireless work tracking down criminals in the Windy City, Wooldridge was a skilled self-promoter who authored a breathless memoir entitled *Hands Up! In the World of Crime; or 12 Years a Detective* (Chicago: C.C. Thompson Co., 1906). More on his colorful career can also be found in Herbert Asbury, *Gem of the Prairie* (New York: Alfred A. Knopf, 1940; DeKalb, Ill.: Northern Illinois University Press, 1986), 106–29. The "other Holmes" mentioned by Watson was Henry H. Holmes, also known as Herman W. Mudgett. He was a brutal serial killer who preyed on women in Chicago in the 1890s and maintained a large house equipped with gruesome devices of torture. Wooldridge gave Holmes and Watson a tour of the house in 1896. For more on Henry Holmes, see Asbury, *Gem*, 177–96.

3. Wilson Hargreave was first mentioned by Watson in "The Adventure of the Dancing Men," a case dating from the summer of 1898 but first published in 1903. In the story, Holmes sends a cable to "my friend, Wilson Hargreave, of the New York Police Bureau [it was actually the New York Police Department], who has more than once made use of my knowledge of London crime." Hargreave sent back a helpful reply. There is no further mention of Hargreave in later stories, although he does turn up now and then in Watson's journal.

4. I have been unable to find published references to Adolph and Willie Lauer, despite Watson's statement that their case received "much press coverage," nor was I able to locate any stories in the Chicago newspapers or elsewhere about a plot to bomb the water tower in 1898. I can only surmise from this discrepancy that Watson—and later Rafferty, in his scattered memoirs—for some reason changed the real names of the terrorists and the exact circumstances of their crime.

5. The three large department stores mentioned here are long gone. What was eventually to become the most famous Nicollet Avenue department store—Day-

ton's (later Marshall Field's) — did not open in its present building at Seventh Street and Nicollet Avenue until 1902.

6.   The Church of the Immaculate Conception, which opened in 1873, was for a time the largest Catholic church in Minneapolis, but it was ultimately doomed by its location in the midst of a growing commercial district. Construction on a new and much larger church, the Basilica of St. Mary, began in 1907 at a site farther from the downtown core. The basilica opened for worship in 1914, and Immaculate Conception was torn down eight years later. See Peg Guilfoyle, *The Basilica of Saint Mary: Voices from a Landmark* (Minneapolis: Basilica of St. Mary, 2000), 9–13.

7.   The North Star Woolen Mill was founded in 1864. Although boosters dreamed that Minneapolis would one day become "the Lowell of the West," with numerous textile mills, this never happened. Instead, flour mills came to dominate the area around St. Anthony Falls, and by 1899 the North Star was the only textile mill left. It was a successful operation, however, and for many years manufactured all the woolen blankets used in Pullman sleeping cars. By 1925 the North Star had proclaimed itself to be the "principal woolen blanket mill in the United States" and was rebuilt that year using modern concrete-frame construction. The mill, however, shut down in the 1940s and never reopened. In 2000 the mill building was converted into loft-style apartments as part of Minneapolis's ongoing riverfront revival. See James Berman, ed., *Saint Anthony Falls Rediscovered* (Minneapolis: Minneapolis Riverfront Development Coordination Board, 1980), 49–50.

8.   The Kodak box camera, invented by George Eastman and first marketed in 1888, greatly simplified photography (it was the first camera to use roll film rather than glass plates), and quickly became a common household item. Just such a camera played an important role in the *Rune Stone Mystery*.

Chapter Five: "Spite, You See, Can Be a Form of Idealism"

1.   Madison Square, where the parade for Commodore Dewey concluded on September 30, 1899, is at the intersection of Broadway and Fifth Avenue in lower Manhattan. The area around the square had once been an elegant residential neighborhood where such luminaries as Theodore Roosevelt and Edith Wharton were born. By the turn of the century, however, it was rapidly evolving into a commercial district. Architect Stanford White's famous Madison Square Garden (1890, demolished 1968), located at the north end of the square, was its dominant building.

2.   The Comstock Lode, a great vein of silver, was discovered in 1859 along the flanks of Mount Davidson in western Nevada. The lode — named after one of its discoverers, Henry T. P. Comstock — created the boomtown of Virginia City and was one of the richest silver deposits in American history. It yielded up to thirty-eight thousand dollars worth of silver per ton of ore at a time when one hundred dollars a ton was thought to be quite good. The boom continued for about twenty years, spurred by a second big find in 1872, although mining continued well into the twentieth century. All told, the lode is said to have produced about $350 million worth of silver. It apparently could not buy happiness for Comstock himself, who died a suicide in Montana. For a good brief history of the Comstock Lode, see Mary Ellen and Al Glass, *Touring Nevada: A Historic and Scenic Guide* (Reno, Nev.: University of Nevada Press, 1983), 6–11.

3.   The New York draft riot, during July 13–16, 1863, was among the most vi-

olent civil disturbances in American history. It began as a protest against the National Conscription Act, which set up a lottery to draft men into the Union Army to replace heavy battlefield losses. Among other things, the act allowed rich men to buy their way out of service by paying three hundred dollars for a bonus that could be used to recruit a substitute. The lottery began on July 11 but met with violent protest, especially from the Irish working class. By July 13 full-scale rebellion had broken out in the city as gangs of men roamed the streets, burning, looting, and killing. The wealthy, Republicans, and blacks became popular targets, and at one point a mob even attacked the city's Colored Orphan Asylum, though all 237 children managed to escape. Fortunately for Thomas, the attack on Crooks Restaurant was repulsed; had it succeeded, he almost certainly would have been killed or seriously injured. All told, at least 119 deaths were confirmed during the riot, which was finally suppressed by 6,000 Union troops hurried to the city from Gettysburg, where the Army of the Potomac had just won a great victory. Among the troops sent to New York was Rafferty's First Minnesota Regiment. However, the regiment didn't arrive until August 23, well after the rioting. For a succinct account of the riot and its aftermath, see Edwin G. Burrows and Mike Wallace, *Gotham: A History of New York City to 1898* (New York: Oxford University Press, 1999), 887–99.

4. LaVeta Terrace, built in 1887 at Nicollet Avenue and Seventeenth Street, was one of the most lavish row houses in Minneapolis, with eleven three-story units, some having as many as thirteen rooms. For a time, it had no trouble attracting well-to-do residents such as J. Winston Phelps. But like almost all Victorian-era row houses in the Twin Cities, LaVeta Terrace lost its cachet after the turn of the century and was later subdivided into smaller apartments. The building was demolished in 1932. For pictures of the building and a brief history, see Millett, *Lost Twin Cities*, 194–95.

5. Lowry Hill, a glacial ridge just southwest of downtown Minneapolis, became home for some of the city's wealthiest citizens as early as the 1870s and remains so to this day. Originally known as the Devil's Backbone, the steep hill was later named after Thomas Lowry, developer of the Twin Cities streetcar system, who built a home on the hill in 1874.

6. The Pioneer Press Building (today known as the Pioneer Building) is still standing at the corner of Fourth and Robert Streets in St. Paul, though it was long ago vacated by the newspaper. The building's designer was Solon Beman, a Chicago architect whose other works include the industrial town of Pullman, scene of the bitter 1894 strike mentioned earlier.

Chapter Six: "We've Met"

1. Archbishop John Ireland (1838–1918) did indeed build a new St. Paul Cathedral, which opened in 1915 on a prominent hill overlooking the city and is one of the largest church buildings in the United States. The old cathedral that Rafferty frequented was at Sixth and St. Peter Streets. It was demolished shortly after the new church opened.

2. The West Hotel, at Fifth Street and Hennepin Avenue, opened in 1884. It was built by Charles W. West, a millionaire who migrated from Cincinnati to Minneapolis in 1875. The seven-story hotel, designed in a jaunty Queen Anne style, offered 407 rooms (140 of which came with private baths, then considered quite a luxury). The hotel's dominant feature was a skylit lobby alleged to be the largest of

its kind in the country—a dubious claim at best. By 1899, when Rafferty stayed there, the hotel was no longer in the West family, and it was soon to be eclipsed by newer, larger hotels built elsewhere in Minneapolis. The West was torn down in 1940. See Millett, *Lost Twin Cities*, 166–67, and Loring M. Staples, *The West Hotel Story, 1884–1940: Memories of Past Splendor* (Minneapolis: Carlson Printing Co., 1979).

3.   North Commons is the largest park on Minneapolis's North Side and was in 1899 a favorite gathering place for workmen and their families.

4.   The railroad strike of 1877 in Chicago left anywhere from twenty-five to fifty people dead and was one of the bloodiest events in the city's history. It came about after the Baltimore & Ohio Railroad announced a 10 percent wage cut in response to the depression then gripping the nation. Other railroads followed suit, and labor clashes soon occurred in many cities. The worst was in Chicago, the country's rail center, where something approaching open class warfare broke out. Federal troops were ultimately called in to quell the disorder. See Paul Avrich, *The Haymarket Tragedy* (Princeton, N.J.: Princeton University Press, 1984), 26–35. Cyrus McCormick (1809–84) invented his famous reaping machine in 1831 and in 1847 opened a factory on Chicago's West Side that eventually became one of the city's largest industrial operations, as well as the scene of frequent labor unrest.

5.   William Marcy Tweed (1823–1878) was arguably the greatest thief in American history and a brilliant politician who ruled over an unparalleled empire of corruption in New York City until his downfall in the early 1870s. For all the fascinating details see Oliver E. Allen, *The Tiger: The Rise and Fall of Tammany Hall* (Reading, Mass.: Addison-Wesley, 1993).

6.   The Boston Block, at Third Street and Hennepin Avenue, was built as a five-story office building in 1881 and then expanded to seven stories after a spectacular fire in April 1886. By 1899 it was already considered a less than first-class building, in good part because of its location in the so-called Gateway area, which was rapidly devolving into the city's skid row. The Boston Block was razed in 1942.

Chapter Seven: "Go Back to St. Paul"

1.   Grimpen Mire was the impenetrable bog that played an essential role in one of Holmes and Watson's greatest adventures, *The Hound of the Baskervilles*. Although the case had occurred ten years earlier, in 1889, Watson's riveting account was not published as a novel until 1902.

2.   The Shevlin-Carpenter was one of the largest sawmills along the Mississippi River north of downtown Minneapolis. The first mill on the site, at the foot of Fourth Avenue North, was built in 1868. Under various owners, the milling complex grew and became known as the North Star Mill, which by the 1880s was producing 110,000 feet of lumber a day. After a fire in 1886 the mill was rebuilt, and in 1893—again under new ownership—it was renamed the Shevlin-Carpenter. It shut down in 1906 and was dismantled a year later. See Scott F. Anfinson, *Archaeological Potentials of the West Side of the Central Minneapolis Waterfront* (St. Paul: Minnesota Historical Society, 1984), 65–67.

3.   The Twenty-seventh Indiana Regiment was one of four regiments from that state that served in the Army of the Potomac and saw action at many battles. Two enlisted men from this regiment stumbled into one of the great finds of the Civil War when they discovered a copy of Confederate General Robert E. Lee's battle

plan (contained in a document known as Special Order No. 191) in Frederick, Maryland, on September 13, 1862. The plan was brought at once to General George McClellan, commander of the Army of the Potomac, but he proved unable to exploit this precious information when he engaged the Confederates four days later at the Battle of Antietam.

4.   The new Minneapolis City Hall-Hennepin County Courthouse mentioned here was under construction from 1889 to 1906. Modeled after H. H. Richardson's famed Allegheny County Courthouse in Pittsburgh, the massive granite building featured a 345-foot-high tower that was until the 1930s the tallest structure in Minneapolis. The building still serves as Minneapolis City Hall (the county moved to a new building across the street in the 1970s) and is regarded as an outstanding example of the Richardsonian Romanesque style. See Paul Clifford Larson, *Municipal Monument: A Centennial History of the Municipal Building Serving Minneapolis and Hennepin County, Minnesota* (Minneapolis: Municipal Building Commission, 1991).

5.   The Molly Maguires were a secret society formed in the 1860s by Irish Americans working in the anthracite coalfields around Scranton, Pennsylvania. They have been the subject of much historical debate and tend to be depicted either as labor stalwarts attempting to fight oppressive working conditions or as terrorists who ruled by intimidation and murder. What is certain is that due largely to James McParland's undercover work for the Pinkertons, the organization was crushed by 1877, when after a series of trials nineteen Molly Maguires went to the gallows. See Horan, *The Pinkertons*, 204–37. The Western Federation of Miners was a labor union formed in 1893 in the Rocky Mountain mining regions. It was known for its militancy and became involved in a number of violent strikes. The federation affiliated with the radical Industrial Workers of the World (IWW) in 1905, but its power and membership declined prior to World War I. In 1916 the federation changed its name to the Union of Mine, Mill and Smelter Workers. There is a great deal of information about the federation and its early leadership in Lucas, *Big Trouble*.

Chapter Eight: "I Met a Man Much Troubled by Rats"

1.   The Minneapolis Globe Building was built in 1889, two years after completion of the newspaper's St. Paul building, where Joseph Pyle worked. I have been unable to find any accounts of the accident involving the Ratman's son, but it must have occurred in either 1888 or 1889. Both Globe buildings were the work of E. Townsend Mix, an architect who in 1890 went on to design one of Minneapolis's greatest works of architecture—the Northwestern Guaranty Loan Building. The Guaranty Loan (later Metropolitan) Building was twelve stories tall and included a spectacular iron-and-glass atrium. The building was senselessly demolished in 1961–62. By this time the Minneapolis Globe Building was also gone, torn down in 1958 to make way for a new public library. See Millett, *Lost Twin Cities*, 200–01, 222–25.

2.   Publications with offices on Newspaper Row in 1899 included the *Minneapolis Journal*, the *Minneapolis Times*, and the *Minneapolis Tribune*. Today, only the *Tribune*, stripped of its Minneapolis name and known simply as the *Star Tribune*, remains.

3.   Zier Row was built in 1889 to the designs of architect William Dennis. Like LaVeta Terrace, Zier Row initially attracted a well-heeled clientele to its spacious

four-story apartments. The building was subdivided by 1910 and gradually de-
volved into a none-too-grand apartment hotel said to contain 140 units. It was demolished in 1967.

Chapter Nine: "Rafferty Won't Be a Threat"

1. Jefferson Hope was a Californian whose tragic tale of lost love, murder, and
revenge forms the core of *A Study in Scarlet*, the tale (first published as a novel in
1888) that introduced the character of Sherlock Holmes to the world.

2. The Erie rat trap was one of half a dozen or so rodent traps advertised in
Sears, Roebuck & Co. catalogs of the era. An 1897 catalog claimed that the trap
could "always be depended on to catch rats. . . . It kills them instantly without
drawing blood, or otherwise scenting the trap." This marvel of modern technology
sold for twelve cents.

3. There was indeed a restaurant on the top floor of the Guaranty Loan Building, but the historical record is unclear as to who was operating it in 1899. I have
therefore supplied the name "Leonardo's" as a bit of poetic license. It is known that
the restaurant was operated for a number of years by a black man named Jasper
Gibbs. The restaurant included a rooftop garden said to be a favorite of lovers on
warm summer nights.

4. Although Rafferty's surviving correspondence includes quotations from the
Minneapolis Tribune article about the Tunnel Boys, I have been unable to find the
story, which presumably appeared sometime in 1898.

Chapter Ten: "Come Alone"

1. Codes were extensively used during the heyday of the telegraph. Most were
commercial codes—the first appeared in 1845—designed to help businesses keep
sensitive information out of the hands of their competitors. Many companies, including the Pinkerton Detective Agency, developed private codes that were used
for virtually all telegraph messages. For more on this topic, see Tom Standage, *The
Victorian Internet: The Remarkable Story of the Telegraph and the Nineteenth Century's On-
line Pioneers* (New York: Walker and Company, 1998), 105–26.

2. Rafferty, by all evidence, was a great collector of weaponry and is known to
have had a private vault in the basement of the Ryan Hotel where he kept his prized
guns. The .44 caliber Smith & Wesson he carried in this instance was probably the
company's First Model Revolver, introduced in 1881. This was a six-cylinder
weapon with barrels available in lengths ranging from four to six and a half inches.
Such legendary western figures as Belle Starr and Texas gunfighter John Wesley
Hardin are said to have carried this revolver.

3. The Stevens Arms Company of Chicopee Falls, Massachusetts, manufactured several popular "pocket rifles." Rafferty's appears to have been a custom version of the company's "New Model Pocket Rifle No. 40," first made in about 1896.

Chapter Eleven: "It Was Just a Cheap Attempt at Blackmail"

1. Minneapolis City Hospital was preparing to move into a new building at
Sixth Street and Seventh Avenue South at the time Holmes and Watson came to see
Rafferty. The hospital was renamed General Hospital in about 1920 and is today

known as the Hennepin County Medical Center. It is at the same location as it was in 1899, but the buildings from that era were all demolished in the 1970s.

2.   It's hardly surprising that Mayor Adams mentioned the gunfight at the O.K. Corral, since this was already a legendary piece of Americana by 1899. The gun battle—pitting Wyatt Earp, his brothers, and John Henry (Doc) Holliday against Ike and Billy Clanton and the McLaury brothers—is also the most analyzed shoot-out in the history of the American West. For a detailed look at this famous and controversial encounter, which occurred in Tombstone, Arizona, on October 25, 1881, see Paula Mitchell Marks, *And Die in the West: The Story of the O.K. Corral Gunfight* (New York: William Morrow, 1989).

3.   The Dynamite Express was the name given by the press to a Northern Pacific freight train hijacked on April 29, 1899, near the town of Wallace in the Coeur d'Alene region of northern Idaho. The hijackers were members of the Western Federation of Miners—about 250 in all—who had gone on strike. The miners, many wearing masks and carrying Winchester rifles, took the train to another mining town, Kellogg, where they obtained sixty boxes of dynamite. Later that day, the miners used these explosives to demolish a large concentrator and several other structures at the nearby Bunker Hill Mine. Federal troops, under the ultimate authority of President William McKinley, were soon brought in to restore order. See Lucas, *Big Trouble*, 111–15.

Chapter Twelve: "There's People in There That'll Kill You"

1.   John S. Pillsbury and his nephew, Charles A. Pillsbury, established the Pillsbury Company in 1874 and in 1881 built their gigantic A Mill on the East Side of St. Anthony Falls, almost directly across the river from Wellington's second A Mill, completed a year earlier. The Pillsbury A Mill, with a capacity of four thousand barrels of flour a day, was the largest in the world when it opened. The mill building—a National Historic Landmark—still stands today, although it no longer produces flour. There is a good description of the mill in Lucile M. Kane, *The Waterfall That Built Minneapolis* (St. Paul: Minnesota Historical Society Press, 1966; rev. ed., 1987), 104.

2.   The list of political assassinations in the 1890s included President Sadi Carnot of France, stabbed to death in Lyon, France, in June 1894; Premier Antonio Canovas del Castillo of Spain, shot dead in August 1897 in the Basque mountains; and Empress Elizabeth of Austria, stabbed through the heart in June 1898 at a lake resort in Switzerland. Italian anarchists committed all three crimes.

Chapter Thirteen: "Something Sinister Is Coming My Way"

1.   Buhr (or burr) stones were large, round grooved stones—often cut from special French quartz—that were used in tandem to grind flour in traditional grist mills. Such stones were still employed in the A Mill in 1878 when it exploded as a result of a spark that ignited a buildup of flour dust. Technological changes soon ended the use of millstones, which by the early 1880s had been replaced in many Minneapolis mills by porcelain or steel rollers. These rollers could grind flour with more precision and less heat than millstones. After the 1878 disaster flour mills also installed elaborate systems to collect potentially explosive dust. There are many accounts of the explosion at the A Mill, which attracted national publicity and re-

mains to this day the worst industrial accident in the history of the Twin Cities. For a contemporaneous description of the disaster from the *Minneapolis Tribune*, see Anderson, ed., *Downtown*, 59–60.

2. All told, Lake Minnetonka has at least twenty distinct bays, and while it is not a huge lake by Minnesota standards, its highly irregular shape gives it more than a hundred miles of shoreline.

3. The shores of Lake Minnetonka retain some of the most coveted real estate in Minnesota, and large houses—more than a few of which qualify as mansions—are spread all around the lake. There's an excellent history of the lake's residential development in Paul Clifford Larson, *A Place at the Lake* (Afton, Minn.: Afton Historical Society Press, 1998), 26–69.

4. Wellington's prediction regarding the future of flour milling in Minneapolis was accurate. In 1930—because of changes in railroad freight rates, the opening of the Panama Canal, and other factors—Buffalo, New York, did indeed become the nation's largest flour-milling city, a position Minneapolis had held for fifty years. Today all the flour mills on the west side of St. Anthony Falls have long since closed, although a number of the old mill buildings have been converted into apartments, hotels, and offices. James J. Hill's stone-arch railroad bridge, opened in 1883 and now a National Historic Landmark, has also been reclaimed and today serves as a bicycle and pedestrian pathway across the river. Plans are in the works for a large mill-ruins park that will highlight the history of the area, which may well have been the largest direct-drive, water-powered industrial complex in human history.

5. The passage quoted by Wellington is from the King James version of the Bible, John, 8:44. The entire verse reads: "Ye are of *your* father the devil, and the lusts of your father ye will do. He was a murderer from the beginning, and abode not in the truth, because there is no truth in him. When he speaketh a lie, he speaketh of his own: for he is a liar, and the father of it."

Chapter Fourteen: "I Think He Might Be Living in There"

1. The Wellington milling complex at its height consisted of about a dozen buildings, including four separate mill buildings, grain elevators, warehouses, a powerhouse, and a sack house (where flour was bagged). Railroad tracks ran on either side of the mills and, in some places, directly through them. Total capacity of the complex was said to be 6,000 barrels (or about 1,200,000 pounds) of flour a day. The A Mill alone could produce 3,000 barrels (or 588,000 pounds of flour) daily. The best overall account of the milling district remains Kane, *Waterfall*. For a brief look at the district's history, see Millett, *Lost Twin Cities*, 78–79.

2. By a certain irony, St. Anthony Falls, which turned Minneapolis into a major city, was actually formed—more than ten thousand years ago—near what is today downtown St. Paul. There the huge Glacial River Warren (of which the Minnesota River is the remnant) cut into an old valley and formed an enormous waterfall that originally was higher and wider than Niagara. As the falls receded upstream over thousands of years, they became much smaller, and were only about sixteen to twenty feet high by the time Father Louis Hennepin saw them in 1680 (they were then about a mile downstream from their present location). Even so, the falls, as all the early European settlers of the region recognized, were a magnificent water-power site, and their exploitation was quickly and ruthlessly accomplished. The nation's first hydroelectric station was built at the falls in 1882 and some elec-

tricity is still generated there today, but the age of flour milling is over, the last mill on the west bank having shut down in 1965.

3.   The original, three-hundred-foot-long, fourteen-foot-deep power canal by the falls was built in 1857 and was modeled on similar canals built in New England mill towns such as Holyoke, Massachusetts. The canal was extended another six hundred feet in 1865 and also deepened by four feet. A railroad trestle was built over the canal in 1878 and from that point on it was largely hidden from view. Today the canal has been filled in, though it is possible that sections of it could one day be reopened as part of the planned park in the area.

4.   The Palisade Mill, built in 1872 and demolished in 1940, was the last mill at the end of the power canal. It therefore had the greatest drop, or "head," of water — about fifty feet — of all the mills at St. Anthony Falls. This was important because power is determined both by the volume and height of falling water. In fact, Minneapolis, like other milling centers, had its own official measuring unit, known as a Minneapolis millpower, which was defined as the amount of power generated by thirty cubic feet of water falling twenty-two feet per second — or the equivalent of about seventy-five horsepower. Water was allotted to mills on the basis of this measurement. For more on the Palisade Mill, see Anfinson, *Archaeological Potentials*, 122. There is discussion of the "Minneapolis millpower" in Kane, *Waterfall*, 55.

5.   De facto racial segregation was the order of the day in Minneapolis, as it was in other northern cities, at the turn of the century. As a result, most of the city's fifteen hundred or so black residents in 1899 lived within certain well-defined neighborhoods (although blacks could be found in every ward of the city by then). See David Vassar Taylor, "The Blacks," in *They Chose Minnesota: A Survey of the State's Ethnic Groups*, ed. June Drenning Holmquist (St. Paul: Minnesota Historical Society Press, 1981), 73–91.

Chapter Fifteen: "Get Off Me, You Brute"

1.   Holmes was famous for his expertise when it came to tobacco, and so he would have had no trouble identifying the cork-tipped, Egyptian-made Mogul cigarette, which was popular at the time. In the "Boscombe Valley Mystery," from 1889, Holmes even mentioned writing a "little monograph on the ashes of 140 different varieties of pipe, cigar, and cigarette tobacco."

2.   The "panel" house was a type of brothel with rooms especially designed to accommodate thievery. The rooms had a hidden panel through which a man's wallet or other valuables could be taken from his pants while he was not in a position to be wearing them.

Chapter Sixteen: "His Exact Words, Sir, Exact Words!"

1.   Watson, of course, did "get around" to writing an account of McParland's adventures among the Molly Maguires in *The Valley of Fear*, which appeared in the *Strand Magazine* in 1914 and was published the next year as a novel. The second part of *The Valley of Fear* tells of a Pinkerton agent named Birdy Edwards (James McParland) and his battle against the Scowrers (Molly Maguires). Many of the novel's details were based on Allan Pinkerton's 1877 book, *The Molly Maguires and the Detectives*.

2.   The Ratman's account of the Second Minnesota Regiment's battles is accu-

rate and in proper chronological order. The regiment saw its heaviest fighting at Chickamauga, when out of 384 men in action, 45 were killed, 103 wounded, and another 14 captured.

3. The Battle of Bristoe Station, fought near the Virginia railroad stop of that name on October 14, 1863, was a smashing Union victory. The First Minnesota Regiment alone captured 322 Confederates during the fight, which turned out terribly for the men in gray when General A. P. Hill badly mistook the size of the Union force he attacked. Rafferty's brother was among only about 50 Union troops killed during the battle, in which the Confederates suffered 1,900 casualties. See Shelby Foote, *The Civil War: A Narrative: Fredericksburg to Meridan* (New York: Random House, 1963), 792–94.

Chapter Seventeen: "It Will Be Haymarket All Over Again"

1. Inspector G. (his first name is unknown) Lestrade of Scotland Yard was the official police presence in over a dozen of Holmes's adventures, including the very first—*A Study in Scarlet*. He is generally depicted by Watson as a dogged but uninspired investigator.

2. As its name indicates, Temple Court, at the corner of Washington and Hennepin avenues, was an office building that catered to Minneapolis's lawyers. The eight-story building, which opened in 1886, is believed to have been the first in the city to feature a skylit court (or atrium) at its center. Later renamed the Gateway Building, it was demolished in 1953.

3. Johann Most was one of the most intriguing characters in the anarchist movement of the late nineteenth century. Born in Germany in 1846, he had a hatred of authority almost from the cradle and ventured at an early age into radical politics. By 1878 he was on the run from his native land and soon turned up in London, where Karl Marx had also found a safe haven years earlier. While in London, Most started an influential revolutionary journal called *Freiheit* (Freedom). In 1882, Most left London for the United States, where he was to spend the remainder of his life. In 1885 he published the seventy-four-page booklet that was to make him infamous: *Revolutionary War Science, A Little Handbook of Instruction in the Use and Preparation of Nitroglycerine, Dynamite, Gun-Cotton, Fulminating Mercury, Bombs, Fuses, Poisons, etc.* Not surprisingly, the inflammatory pamphlet did not endear Most to the authorities or to the bourgeoisie, whom he usually referred to as a "reptile brood." Despite his open advocacy of violence, Most appears to have done all of his fighting with words, and he was never directly linked to any acts of terrorism. He died—of natural causes—in 1906. See Avrich, *Haymarket*, 61–67, 163–64.

Chapter Eighteen: "He May Have Been Murdered for Doing His Duty"

1. The one battle Watson is known to have been involved in during his military service was at Maiwand, in Afghanistan, on July 27, 1880. He was at that time an assistant surgeon attached to the Royal Berkshire Regiment. He was struck by a bullet from a type of musket known as a Jezail. In *A Study in Scarlet*, Watson wrote that he had been wounded in the shoulder, but in a later novel, *The Sign of Four*, he reported being struck in the leg. In either case, he made a full recovery.

2. "Tooze's" saloon, as Watson calls it, was operated by a man named Z. Z.

Rogers. His establishment became known simply as Two-Z's, which Watson then spelled as "Tooze's." Curiously, records indicate that the saloon was at Third Avenue South and Third Street, whereas Watson appears to locate it about eight blocks away, near Seventh Street and Hennepin Avenue. Moreover, the saloon as described in reminiscences from the period was far more elaborate than depicted by Watson. See Henry Broderick, "Memories of Early Minneapolis," in Anderson, ed., *Downtown*, 86–87.

3. McParland's bodyguard Charlie was almost certainly Charles Angelo Siringo, a Texan who began working as a detective out of the Pinkerton Agency's Denver office in the mid 1880s. William Pinkerton described Siringo, sometimes called the cowboy detective, as "tough as a pine knot." He had to be, since he survived any number of close calls during his long and colorful career, which often pitted him against the Western Federation of Miners. Siringo turned to writing in his old age and produced at least four books, including two memoirs and a 1913 volume with the intriguing title *Two Evil Isms: Pinkertonism and Anarchism*. For more on Siringo, see Lucas, *Big Trouble*.

4. Pat Dormer was the first Molly Maguire to befriend McParland, who entered the coalfields of eastern Pennsylvania in October 1873 posing as a drifter named James McKenna. At Dormer's saloon in the town of Pottsville, McParland won Dormer's trust by, among other things, dancing a jig, singing an old Irish ballad in a beautiful tenor voice, exposing a card sharp, defeating him in a fist fight and then shaking the man's hand and offering to buy him a drink. All of this, apparently, was just another day's work for the resourceful and fearless Pinkerton agent. See Horan, *Pinkertons*, 210–11.

5. Beard's Block, at Washington and Twelfth avenues south, was probably the largest tenement ever built in the Twin Cities, where housing of such a kind was never very common. The building was constructed in 1881 by Henry H. Beard, a wealthy Minneapolis real estate developer. It was intended to provide what today would be called low-income housing units — about eighty in all — primarily designed for working families. Beard's Block was demolished in 1931. See Millett, *Lost Twin Cities*, 154–55.

Chapter Nineteen: "She Will Be There"

1. Exposition Hall, officially known as the Industrial Exposition Building, was constructed on the east side of St. Anthony Falls in 1886 to house an industrial fair planned for that year. Financed through donations from businessmen and a public stock sale, the huge building was erected in just three months at a cost of $250,000. In 1892 its large central hall was modified to serve as the site of the Republican National Convention, at which Benjamin Harrison was nominated for president. In 1903 the building was purchased for use as a warehouse by Marion Savage, operator of a large stock-food company but best known to history as the owner of the legendary pacer, Dan Patch. The building was torn down in 1940, although its 260-foot tower survived until 1946. See Millett, *Lost Twin Cities*, 178–79.

2. Lakewood Cemetery, which remains one of Minneapolis's most beautiful places, was founded in 1871 by some of the city's leading businessmen. It was designed as a "garden" cemetery—a type introduced in this country in 1831 at Mount Auburn Cemetery in Cambridge, Massachusetts. The idea behind the garden cemetery was to offer a green and inviting alternative to the crowded old urban burial

grounds typical of the time. Many of Minneapolis's wealthiest and most prominent citizens are buried at Lakewood, which is also the final resting place of Minneapolis Mayor, U.S. Senator, and later U.S. Vice President Hubert H. Humphrey. See Susan Mundale, ed., *Haven in the Heart of the City: The History of Lakewood Cemetery* (Minneapolis: Lakewood Cemetery, 1992).

3. The milling monument, still in excellent condition, is located at the northwest corner of the cemetery, near Calhoun Boulevard and West Thirty-sixth Street.

4. Charles A. Reed, a native of New York, moved to St. Paul in the 1880s and developed a flourishing practice as a structural engineer. In 1891 he went into partnership with architect Allen H. Stem. The firm became especially known for its work on large railroad stations. Its most notable commission in this regard was Grand Central Terminal (1903–1913) in New York City. Reed and Stem won a limited competition for the project and developed the terminal's ingenious plan. Other architects, however, were largely responsible for the design of the terminal building.

5. The reviewing stand, according to newspaper accounts of the parade, was at Tenth Street and Nicollet Avenue, which would have put it just a block from the ruined remains of the Wellington-Adams house.

Chapter Twenty: "Do You Remember Louis Lingg?"

1. Loring Park opened in 1883 and was known then as Central Park. It was renamed seven years later in honor of Charles Loring, an early president of the Minneapolis Park Board. The park's pond, around which Holmes and Watson raced in their hijacked carriage, remains its most appealing feature. For a photograph of the park in the 1890s and a brief description of its history, see Larry Millett, *Twin Cities Then and Now* (St. Paul: Minnesota Historical Society Press, 1996), 64–65.

2. The A Mill had two turbines, each of which generated about 1,200 horsepower and typically ran at 60 revolutions per minute.

3. Corliss steam engines were named after their inventor, George H. Corliss (1817–88), and were built at his foundry in Providence, Rhode Island. They were the workhorses of the nineteenth century, with a unique valve gear that made them particularly efficient. The engines were widely used in mills and other industrial operations requiring a large, reliable source of power. Corliss is perhaps best remembered for the giant steam engine—forty-five feet high and generating 1,400 horsepower—that he exhibited at the 1876 Centennial Exposition in Philadelphia.

4. "Quick match," developed in France in the 1850s but not widely used in the United States for another thirty years, was a type of fuse made by soaking strands of cotton in a solution of potassium nitrate and then coating them with a layer of gunpowder. Rafferty's estimate of the burn rate—about fifteen feet per minute—is accurate, though it could be affected by such factors as temperature and humidity. Quick match was often placed in a waterproof wrapping, in which case it would burn much more rapidly. See G. I. Brown, *The Big Bang: A History of Explosives* (Phoenix Mill, England: Sutton Publishing, 1998), 178–79.

5. Louis Lingg (1864–87) was born in Germany and emigrated to the United States in 1885. He went at once to Chicago, where he became involved with that city's anarchist underground. An admitted bomb maker, he was one of eight men tried and convicted of murder after a bomb was tossed during a protest meeting at Haymarket Square in Chicago on May 4, 1886. The bombing left eight policemen dead and touched off a wild scene in which police fired into the crowd, killing an

unknown number of civilians. On November 10, 1887, the day before he was to be executed, Lingg placed an explosive cartridge in his mouth (the device had been smuggled into his jail cell by a friend) and lit it. The explosion tore out his tongue and much of his face but, amazingly, he remained alive—in agony—for six and a half hours before he died. See Avrich, *Haymarket*, 372–75.

Chapter Twenty-one: "Do Not Confuse It with an Apology"

1. *The Alarm* was an anarchist newspaper edited by Albert R. Parsons, which was published in Chicago beginning in 1884. On November 11, 1887, Parsons was one of four men executed in connection with the Haymarket bombing. His newspaper folded two years later.

2. It would be intriguing to know what role, if any, Mary McGinty played in the Haymarket affair. Her sex certainly would not have prevented her from working in anarchist circles, since the movement attracted its share of women, including Albert Parson's wife, Lucy. And, of course, one of the most famous anarchists of the time was Emma Goldman.

Epilogue: "Rest Quietly"

1. I have found no other reference to the affair of the "mute lodger at Colville Place," which appears to have been one of many cases Watson never committed to paper. The only "Colville Place" in London is a small alley in the Bloomsbury section of the city, not far from Bedford Square and the British Museum.

2. For a brilliant account of the Steunenberg case, see Lucas, *Big Trouble*.

Author's Note

Although this book is fictional, it is based—in varying degrees—on historic fact. Its cast of characters, for example, includes a number of real people, led by James McParland, who was indeed a famous Pinkerton agent (as was his bodyguard Charles Siringo). James J. Hill, Joseph Pyle, Clifton Wooldridge, and Sid the Ratman were also borrowed from the pages of history. In the Ratman's case, however, I was forced to fill in a great many blanks, since he receives only scant mention in the available historic record.

Another prominent character—Arthur Adams—is modeled on a real person. My inspiration for the slippery politician was Albert A. (Doc) Ames, a six-time mayor of Minneapolis who was spectacularly corrupt even by the loose standards of the Gilded Age. First elected mayor in 1876, he was in and out of office over the next fourteen years, finally winning his last mayoral race in 1900.

It was during his last term that Ames brought municipal thievery to new, and still unequaled, heights in Minneapolis. In other words, the open city described in this book didn't quite exist in 1899, but it was just around the corner. The situation soon became so rank that muckraker Lincoln Steffens devoted the second of his series of investigative articles on American cities to Minneapolis. "The Shame of Minneapolis," published in *McClure's Magazine* in January 1903, detailed the whole unsavory mess, although by that time Ames had already fled the city, and most of his cronies were either in jail or under indictment by a crusading grand jury.

My depiction of the Secret Alliance is also based, loosely, on historic fact. An antiunion organization known as the Citizens Alliance of Minneapolis was a powerful presence in the city for many years, but it was not actually founded until 1903. The organization's history has been documented in William Millikan, *A Union Against Unions: The Minneapolis Citizens Alliance and Its Fight Against Organized Labor, 1903–1947* (St. Paul: Minnesota Historical Society Press, 2001).

Almost all the buildings and places depicted in this book are genuine. The one notable exception is the Wellington-Adams House (though old mansions much like it could indeed be found on Tenth Street in 1899). Unfortunately, the West Hotel, Zier Row, LaVeta Terrace, Temple Court, the Globe Building, the Northwestern Guaranty Loan (Metropolitan) Building, Beard's Block, and numerous other monuments of nineteenth-century Minneapolis are long gone.

I also took pains to accurately depict the West Side milling district (except, perhaps, for some artistic license in my depiction of the tailrace tunnels). Readers should be aware, however, that Charles Wellington is an entirely fictional character. The huge A Mill where the book concludes was in fact called the Washburn A Mill and was built in 1880 by Cadwallader Washburn (1818–82), a pioneer Minneapolis businessman who later became governor of Wisconsin. The milling company Washburn founded eventually evolved into the Washburn-Crosby Company and then into General Mills, Inc., which is still headquartered in Minneapolis.

Washburn's first A Mill did indeed blow itself to pieces in May of 1878, killing eighteen men, although a worker named Peter McGinty was not among the victims. The monument in Lakewood Cemetery is also very real, and it remains a haunting reminder of the great explosion. The second A Mill from 1880 is now a ruin (long vacant, it was damaged by two fires, the first and most devastating of which occurred in 1991). However, the remaining walls of the old mill, which is a National Historic Landmark, will be incorporated into the park being planned for the area.

One other central element of this book is also constructed on a solid foundation of fact. President William McKinley really did visit Minneapolis in October of 1899 to deliver a speech and lead a parade in honor of the returning Thirteenth Minnesota Infantry Regiment. For various reasons relating to the structure of my narrative, however, I moved the date of McKinley's visit a few days forward. He was actually in Minneapolis on October 12, 1899, and the tumultuous scene that greeted him was very much as I have described it. There was, of course, no attempt on his life in Minneapolis, though his days were nonetheless numbered. One of many lengthy newspaper accounts of McKinley's visit can be found in the *St. Paul Pioneer Press*, October 13, 1899, p. 1.

Larry Millett is the author of six Sherlock Holmes mysteries. He is an architectural historian whose books include *Lost Twin Cities*, *AIA Guide to the Twin Cities*, and *Once There Were Castles: Lost Mansions and Estates of the Twin Cities* (Minnesota, 2011). As a reporter for the *St. Paul Pioneer Press*, he covered many beats and had the honor of writing clues for the newspaper's legendary Winter Carnival Medallion Hunt, which annually attracts thousands of treasure seekers. He lives in St. Paul.